# No Other Place

*Other Five Star Titles*
*by Irene Bennett Brown:*


Blue Horizons
Long Road Turning
The Plainswoman

# No Other Place

Women of Paragon Springs Series #3

## Irene Bennett Brown

Five Star • Waterville, Maine

Copyright © 2002 by Irene Bennett Brown
Women of Paragon Springs Series Book 3

Five Star First Edition Romance Series.

Published in 2002 in conjunction with Multimedia Product Development Inc.

Set in 11 pt. Plantin by Myrna S. Raven.

Printed in the United States on permanent paper.

**Library of Congress Cataloging-in-Publication Data**

Brown, Irene Bennett.
   No other place / Irene Bennett Brown.
      p. cm. — (Women of Paragon Springs : 3.)
   ISBN 0-7862-2816-4 (hc : alk. paper)
   1. Women pioneers—Fiction.   2. Kansas—Fiction.
I. Title.
PS3552.R68559 N6 2001
   813'.54—dc21                                    2001040391

# FOR

Rourke, Debbie, Carson, Chase, Chad;
Corey, Joyce, Cassie, Alex; Melia, Rich,
Briana, Serenity; Shana, Tony, Haden, McKenna and
Cole. With thanks for being the best family ever!

# Chapter One

Tonight at the mercantile would be the most important meeting of their lives for Paragon Springs' dozen or so residents and their many friends from around the valley. Holding her bonnet brim down against the blustery March wind, her rolled drawing tight under one arm and skirts whipping, Aurelia Thorne Symington struggled toward the sprawling soddy that was Paragon Springs' general store.

"Be with you as soon as I put up the team," her husband, Owen, called above the sound of the wind, adding, "Don't let this wind blow you away, sweetheart."

He chuckled affectionately and Aurelia smiled back over her shoulder. "Won't."

"I'm going to find Rachel," her young daughter, Zibby, shouted and scooted ahead.

Aurelia's thoughts were both anxious and hopeful as she pushed against the wind. She and other folks, who had arrived near-destitute in that country ten years before, had prospered reasonably well on their individual farms by raising and selling cattle and grain and cutting stone, but their hoped for town hadn't developed the way any of them had expected. Here it was 1883. Something had to be done.

The huddled buildings of the Paragon Springs road ranch—outfitting store, post office, and blacksmith shop—continued to draw travelers off the Western Trail, the Dodge to Ogalalla road. And scattered upper valley settlers continued to come to Paragon Springs to trade, as did those from the sandhills southward. Her friend, Emmaline Lee, continued to put out the weekly *Echo*, antidote to settlers' loneli-

7

ness on their widespread homesteads, and fulfilling their taste for news from "outside." She taught their children from a handful of books. Meg Gibbs' stone quarry and freighting business carried on; Meg's husband, Hamilton, had no shortage of legal cases, although most of them arose in Dodge City or elsewhere in the county.

But Paragon Springs could no longer stand still as a simple, dusty stopping place. The restless community's needs, and those of surrounding farm families, grew daily, unfulfilled. The time had come to build, to grow, to become a real town with accompanying benefits. Or, for its people to give up and move elsewhere.

She would never leave, Aurelia thought as she hurtled into the store and shoved the door closed against the wind. She smiled at Meg and Lucy Ann Walsh chatting together in a crowded corner. The three of them had started out ten years ago in a single soddy, later establishing the road ranch to serve travelers. Now they needed and wanted a town. With every breath in her body—Aurelia struggled against feelings of natural reticence—she would argue aplenty for it tonight.

She remembered when Hodgeman County was legally formed a few years back with Paragon Springs in the center. Seven miles to the southwest was the hamlet of Flagg, named for the farmer who built the town on his farm. The dusty streets of Flagg were hardly plowed off when, under pressure from a group of unscrupulous profiteers, farmer Flagg sold out to them and left the country.

Although from the start Flagg was little more than a "rowdy saloon, hitching post, and clothesline," the profiteers saw that the town was nevertheless named temporary county seat by the official voices from Topeka.

Oh, how it galled her! A blind man could have seen that centrally located Paragon Springs ought to have been the

seat. County affairs through Flagg had been conducted irreg-
ularly, if at all. County officers were scattered about the
country on their individual farms and had to be tracked down
for any kind of county business. Taxes were often forgotten
to be collected or were collected and dissolved in drink and
gambling by the County Treasurer. The probate judge kept a
number of signed marriage license blanks at the Flagg saloon.
The barkeep was authorized to fill in the blanks if a couple applied!

Paragon Springs as county seat was so much more desirable, but first it had to be formed into a real town so that a win
could be obtained by legal vote all over the county.

The mercantile, normally a roomy eighteen by twenty-
four feet, couldn't have held another soul, Aurelia saw with
satisfaction. At least twenty to twenty-five people had turned
out. Two or three hundred more folks were at home around
the county anxiously awaiting the result of tonight's meeting.
Chattering farmers and their wives were seated on boxes and
barrels of trade goods; others sat bunched on benches.
Aurelia nodded and said hello to friends as she maneuvered
to find a place to sit in the overheated, nearly airless room.
She looked up and smiled when Owen, his cheeks red from
the cold wind, came to take a place on the bench beside her.
Zibby had found a spot near the front next to Rachel Walsh;
their giggles joined the general hum of voices.

The meeting commenced and Aurelia awaited her turn. In
the past she had demonstrated her artistry by carving gravestones and mantle pieces from the area's lovely magnesian
stone, and because of that, she had been selected to draw a
layout of the proposed town. She was particularly proud of
the embellishments she had added to the otherwise utilitarian
checkerboard drawing and was ready to show her handiwork.
But Admire Walsh was holding the floor so long, she won-

dered if he would ever finish.

"You know I want a town as much as anybody," Ad, a former cowhand, said. He stood with both hands on his hips next to the stacked bags of flour and beans. "But we ought not put the cart before the horse." His face was flushed with feeling above his black beard. "I say, let's get a railroad line here afore anythin' more is done. A town will grow up natural around a rail-stop. We ship our grain, stone products, and our beef by rail from right here," he jabbed his finger at his boots, " 'stead of wagon-freightin' our goods to Dodge City to be sent by rail on east. Railroad will make money both ways, bringin' supplies to us and shippin' our goods out. Railroad, first, I say." He sat down. Beside him, his wife, Lucy Ann, crisp and neat in lavender gingham, blond braids a coronet around her head, patted his arm.

Only a few close friends knew that Lucy Ann had been brutalized by savages as a young girl, and that her dark-haired ten-year-old, Rachel, was part Sioux. Lucy Ann's brother, Lad, had been half-scalped in the same raid and left mute from the trauma for months. They had overcome the bestial acts on them admirably, although they no doubt had their private nightmares. Lucy Ann was one of the community's founders and finest citizens.

"We do need a railroad," Aurelia stood up quickly to say. Gathering courage, she looked around at the assemblage. "But what if a railroad is a long time coming? Or, as much as we need one, never comes at all?" She allowed her listeners to absorb that. "Must we cheat ourselves of the most ordinary necessities in the meantime, say church services? As it is, we must travel to Dodge City or Spearville to attend church or depend on rare visits from a circuit rider. And—" she took a deep breath, "you all know that Emmaline has done a fine job teaching our younger children, but we need a high school academy right here for older youngsters. Our region is filling up with folks and we need to provide advanced education to those young people who desire it."

She was aware that an academy would not be a popular prospect with hardworking farmers from around the valley; they wanted their children at home to work. She ignored the snort from the back of the room at the notion of such a school, and continued with deep sincerity, "My Joshua and David John have been away all winter, boarding in Larned for their studies. Heaven knows what kind of mischief those boys are into without their mother's eye on them. But more than that, I miss them something fierce. I want them home with me all that can be—'til they're grown men doing their life's work."

Joe Potter jumped to his feet; his eyes were like fire in his ruddy face. He jabbed fingers through his red hair that was beginning to gray. Sprays of spit accompanied his words. "All this book learnin' ain't necessary! Just costs money." His chin jutted. "I only went to school four years my-ownself and I ain't never needed a day more. Youngsters want extry schoolin' for just one reason: to get out of honest work. Like Lad Voss," he snorted, "off to college in Lawrence, and Emmaline's Selinda, up there, too, gettin' their heads full of fancy ideas. They ought to be home, both of them, helping their folks. Emmaline Lee's teaching is all any of them need."

Several heads nodded in vigorous agreement. Aurelia's heart sank. Her first husband, John Thorne, had been a teacher. She and a handful of her friends at Paragon Springs esteemed advanced education, believed that the future for all of them depended on it, but they were grievously outnumbered in their belief.

From the far end of the table where she'd been taking notes for the *Echo*, Emmaline shook her head. Time and loss

11

had put streaks of silver in her raven hair, lines of sadness below her almond-shaped eyes. "For some my teaching is adequate, for others it isn't near enough. Lucy Ann's brother, Lad, and my Selinda have fine minds, needful far beyond my teaching." She said more strongly, "Young folks deserve the best, and most, education they can get."

"I'm of the same mind about schooling for these young folk," Lucy Ann was saying in her shy earnest voice. "I want my brother, Lad, to get all the learning he can. He'll be a fine lawyer someday. Even here out west, we need educated professionals, like Ham Gibbs, the same as we need farmers and common laborers. But that's not to say I wouldn't have liked to've had Lad home with me as long as possible. Instead, after Emmaline taught him what she could, I had to send him off to Larned. Youngsters ought not to have to do that. They need a good high school academy in their hometown, their home valley."

"I'd like to see a nice dry goods store closer than Dodge City," Mrs. Hessler spoke up, tucking a graying strand of blond hair behind her ear. "A drug store for medicines when we need them quick, and a doctor, too!" Beside her, Mr. Hessler held his farmer's hat in his lap and spoke of the need for a well-stocked hardware store and lumberyard, although Meg and Hamilton Gibbs stocked some tools and equipment in the mercantile.

Owen cleared his throat and got to his feet from his place beside Aurelia. She felt a warming of pride and love for her husband. He had become an important part of their small band at Paragon Springs, such a happy change to her life. A former department store clerk from Ohio, he had been brave to come west and marry her, a widow with three children. He had filed a regular claim on Meg's timber section when she relinquished it. Aurelia filed on an adjoining claim, making

12

their farm a full half section north of Paragon Springs proper.

They discarded Meg's high-flown idea of growing *trees* and were raising cattle and grain, not only for their own use but for sale to markets reached via the Santa Fe railroad from Dodge City. Owen assisted Aurelia in the Gibbs' mercantile and post office, too, when necessary. "We need to start building our town," he said, "right here and now. Only other choice we have is to move to one of the other Hodgeman County towns with more to offer. You want to move to Purdyville, anyone? To Kidderville, Marena, *Flagg?* How many in favor of moving away from here?"

From the lack of response, no one wanted to leave. Aurelia smiled a quiet thanks to Owen. More than anyone, he knew her private heartache over loss of her little Helen Grace to deadly croup years ago. Knew she could never remove herself very far from the little graveyard on the knoll above Paragon Springs where her fourth child lay. Owen had found her there one day, the spring after his arrival in their rustic community and ages before they married.

She looked up at him and wiped at her tears. A hot wind stirred the dust on the small grave. "Are you lost, Owen? Or am I needed at the store?" It embarrassed her that he'd found her in such a state, eyes red and swollen, hair a mess, wallowing in grief and angry at the cruel terms life handed her.

"I'm not lost, and you're not needed at the store," he said, his voice gentle and kind. He knelt beside her in the grass where she sat. "I came looking for you. You looked so sad in the store this morning, I thought I'd cheer you up. Can I help? Anything I can do?" He nodded toward the tiny headstone where she had placed a clutch of wild blue asters, his expression was solemn.

Aurelia shook her head. "There's nothing anyone can do,

unless they can bring back my little Helen Grace." She said, her voice angry, "And unless someone knows how to make this country a better place to live!" Her green eyes welled afresh. "Fairfield, Kentucky, the small town near where I was born and reared was a gentle, lovely village where I felt safe. Once or twice a year my family journeyed to Louisville, where my mother had pretty new dresses ordered for herself, my sisters, and me; we attended musicals, watched horse racing, and had picnics in the parks. When I was young, I assumed the whole world was the same, life everywhere as easy and peaceful, and beautiful. Then trouble struck even there, my husband was killed, and I was forced to come to *Kansas*." She spoke bitterly, motioned at the barren rolling country around them, the scrubby makeshift buildings down below. A scurry of wind blew dust over her and Owen, accentuating her dislike of the country.

She brushed dust from her bodice and after a moment turned her attention to Owen, noting how handsome he was. He'd washed at the spring, she could smell his clove soap. His silver hair was neatly combed. She was touched that he'd gone to the trouble before setting out to look for her, felt guilty for burdening him with her troubles. "I apologize for carrying on. You're very kind, Owen, but I won't bother you more." She started to rise but before she could move he took her hand and clasped it warmly in both of his. She waited, startled at his intimate touch, but she was comforted by it. Her heartbeat quickened.

"Paragon Springs may never be another Fairfield, or Louisville, Kentucky," he told her gently, "but it can become a close match, in time. Keep hope, Aurelia. Civilized life will come." He added with a twinkle in his eye, "And someday, if my own dreams are fulfilled, you'll marry me."

It wasn't the first time he'd mentioned marriage. She'd

begged him before not to persist. She pulled her hand from his and jumped to her feet. "I care for you, Owen, but as I've said before, I could never, ever risk losing another husband. It's too painful. I'm fond of you, I enjoy your company more than I can say, but I can't marry you. Can't we please just continue to be friends?"

He didn't answer for the longest while. Disappointment was etched in his face, although he struggled to show good humor. "Of course," he said huskily, getting to his feet. He leaned forward and lightly kissed her cheek. She stood very still and his lips moved to press her own, warm, tender and sweet. Caught in the moment, drawing a sharp breath, feeling apology and a surge of passion, she kissed him back. Her arms slid around his neck as he pulled her close.

Aurelia recognized then that she had fallen in love with Owen, but going down the hill that day she still believed they could just be friends. That was hogwash of course. She wished now she had the years back when she'd held him off, repeatedly turned down his proposal of marriage. Because marriage to Owen, when she found the courage, was the best thing to ever happen to her. She'd been wildly in love with her first husband, but her love for Owen was stronger, deeper, and growing more so with every day, with every struggle they met together.

Owen, as much as she, wanted for her other three children and for the two of them and their friends, the best that could be provided.

Aurelia looked around the meeting room and spoke with passion she rarely showed in public, "Let's put it to a vote. I say we build our town, and not wait another day to get at it!"

"It's gonna take money to build a confounded *town*," Potter shouted back at her. "Some folks will have to borry from the banks in Dodge or beg money off their relatives back east. We got a station here that's good enough, I say we forget a town, go on like we been."

"That's not progress," Hamilton Gibbs answered him, his lanky form unfolding as he got to his feet from his seat on a pickle barrel, "and progress is what this part of the country needs if it's going to survive. We're at a standstill out here, and we all know it. With no hope for improving our lives or those of our children if we don't do something to advance our situations." A warm smile lit his homely face, his voice drummed deeply with encouragement, "This can be done. Our local folk can form a legal town company. They've already offered to donate portions of their land for a town site. Through advertising, lots can be offered for sale to folks with capital who want to establish in a new town with a promising future, in a country with natural advantages already. It's been done in other parts of the west, and I personally feel our project will succeed, probably with better results than any of us can imagine."

"My quarry can supply plenty of building stone," Meg said from her seat on a bench not far from him. She spoke softly so as not to wake the baby in her arms. With one hand she stroked the dark hair of her small daughter beside her. "We can freight in what other building materials we'll need, window glass, lumber. I'll do business on credit as much as I can. I'm sure Dodge City business owners will do the same if they are convinced of an eventual profit."

"The whole thing is damned scary and awful hind-sighted, if you ask me!" Admire exploded, throwing his hands in the air, "but I can see most of you don't share my thinkin'."

Will Hessler chuckled sympathetically at Admire, but said, "Bethany and I have plenty of family who'll come west to help with construction. We're not talking about need for a metropolis, just a small comfortable town with conveniences we now have to do without. I think we can do this, and I think it's time; I sure don't want to leave these parts. I've got a lot invested in my farm already."

Applause and exclamations of "Yeah, let's do it!" easily drowned out the last bit of minor grumbling. The ensuing vote was overwhelmingly in favor of building the town first, attempting to attract a railroad second. It was clear Ad still believed they were taking the wrong approach, but with a tight grin he said, "Aurelia, show us what you got."

She felt a momentary flurry of nerves now that the time had come. She stood up, squeezed between seated folk and merchandise that had been pushed against the wall, and moved to the head of the room. There, her enthusiasm for the project took over.

"As you all know, each landowner in the Paragon Springs circle has pledged to donate a parcel of land to form a town of one-hundred-sixty acres total. If in time that turns out not to be big enough, I'm sure some of us will be willing to make further donations of land. Here is the plat, drawn to scale." She unrolled the large sheet of newsprint she'd gotten blank from Emmaline and held it in front of her. Someone coughed, otherwise the room was silent as everyone strained to study her drawing.

With a bit of noise, Dinah Ambler moved her chair to the front in order to see better. "Sorry," she whispered in Aurelia's direction, an apologetic flush rising to her pretty face.

Aurelia shrugged and smiled that she wasn't bothered, and waited for her to get settled.

Dinah's rancher husband, Jack, had been the women settlers' worst enemy. He left his Pawnee River ranch above Paragon Springs in Dinah's hands, and stayed with his cattle

17

crews down in the Cherokee Strip, away from the home-steaders he hated, away from homesteader law. As much as anyone, Dinah wanted Paragon Springs to succeed as a town, this was her home country now. If she minded her long-distance marriage, there wasn't much she could do about it, except visit Jack in the Strip from time to time.

Now that Dinah was settled quietly in her chair, Aurelia went on, "Most of the residential lots are one hundred twenty-five by twenty-five feet. Some business lots are bigger. Six streets run north and south," she pointed them out, "six run east to west. We can name the streets later. Additional streets can be laid out as we need them." She waited a moment, drew a deep breath.

"Our town will be both functional and beautiful. Here," she tapped the paper, "you can see that public buildings will take up the center blocks along main street. Main Street bisects the town east and west. There will be businesses on each side of Main around an attractive town square with flower gardens and benches and a bandstand." Her voice had risen with excitement and she pointed proudly to where she had sketched them in, in fine detail. Selinda Lee was the real artist in the community, but she was away at college and Aurelia felt she hadn't done too badly with the drawings.

"Now," she smiled at her audience, "dwellings will take up the blocks beyond downtown." She pointed to tiny houses drawn into the front part of each long narrow lot, leaving room in back for yard, garden, outhouse, and stable. "If we can attract manufacturing companies through advertising and Owen's and Hamilton's contacts, we will locate them on the outskirts of town. Additional small farms will continue to dot the perimeter."

The plan was perfection, a dream on paper that could—with hard work from all of them and newcomers they would draw—become reality. A cheery hubbub arose in the room. The enthusiastic response thrilled Aurelia. She beamed as she sat down, her part finished. "Thank you." Tragedy had snatched her from a beautiful little town in Kentucky years ago; now she'd be part of a thriving town again, God willing!

"I nominate Aurelia for president of our new Paragon Springs Town Company," a firm woman's voice spoke up at the same time she shushed her whimpering child. Aurelia gasped. Everyone turned to look at Meg, who added, "Other members will, of course, be the rest of us who donated land." Heads bobbed and there was murmured agreement.

"What? Me? For goodness sakes, Meg—!" Aurelia frowned, but Meg didn't appear to notice as she cooed to her blanket wrapped baby boy, Pauly, cuddled close in her arms. Her little girl, Vesta, a sweet-faced charmer, clung to her skirts. Her husband grinned from where he sat on the pickle barrel.

More than ten years ago, Meg had fled St. Louis and an abusive husband to hide in western Kansas. She was the main founder of the community with Aurelia and Lucy Ann. Later, in a lengthy battle, Meg's lawyer, Hamilton Gibbs, had fought to win her a divorce. Meg and Hamilton fell in love, and when the divorce was final, they married.

Taken off-guard by Meg's nomination, Aurelia continued to squirm and her heart quaked. She was only to draft the plan, for pity's sake. Meg had always been their leader. Turning Paragon Springs into a real town was originally Meg's idea, one of her many grand schemes over the years! She loved to preach to the rest of them that "land is our wealth" and that they were simply "nestled in opportunity" and ought to do more and more. But now Meg expected Aurelia to take the lead just because she'd platted and drawn up a nice picture of their town? Ludicrous!

*I can't,* she thought, and except for guilt she would have voiced that belief aloud. She felt a stirring of compassion for Meg, who, bless her heart, had her hands full. Although Hamilton helped run their farm, the quarry and freight business when he was home, he was often away tending to legal affairs in Dodge City and about the county. He hoped that Meg would eventually act as his assistant. A law office would be necessary to the new town, a wonderful asset.

Aurelia continued to fret silently, thinking that Meg deserved a peaceful family life after all she'd done for the rest of them and after her long struggle to gain her divorce.

Still pondering, Aurelia considered that her own children, compared to Meg's, were older and capable for the most part of looking after themselves. Zibby—who at the moment had her head bowed in giggly conspiracy with Lucy Ann and Ad's pretty ten-year-old Rachel—was eleven and was nearly as helpful as a grown woman. Owen, bless him, helped with the mercantile and post office when he could take time from working their land.

"You would be excellent at the job, Aurelia," Meg broke into her thoughts. "This pioneering honor should be yours. You were here before any of the rest of us."

Aurelia felt her face heat up, remembering, *here very reluctantly,* or had everyone forgotten? She'd traveled to Kansas from Kentucky, a grieving widow with four children, fully expecting security and aid from her brother-in-law who had turned out to be a heartless good-for-nothing. He had traded her to Meg as part of a land deal. If Meg would take in Aurelia as part of his claim, he'd let Meg have his land for next to nothing. As though Aurelia and her children were something to be bartered!

Of course, like Meg, she was changing. She was not at all the same person who had left her old life in Kentucky after her first husband was killed. There was a lot about western Kansas she got angry about, still, but she had to give that country its due for toughening her up and forcing her to use her strength and good sense. As Meg liked to say, "A lot of water has passed under the bridge since Aurelia went out to pick up cow-chip fuel wearing white gloves."

Not that she was anywhere near perfect. Owen complained that she was far too protective of her children and him. He allowed her leeway with himself only because he knew how fearful she was of losing another husband.

But lead them in this town building project, such an important role? She had neither the knowledge nor the experience for such a position. "I can't," she said in a flat, quiet voice. "I'm sorry, but I can't do it." She did her best to disregard the echo in her mind, Meg's voice telling her more than once that she was more capable than she realized, that most women were. But then, Meg was the optimistic one.

At that same moment, Meg was saying, "Of course you can do it, Aurelia."

In glancing away from Meg's smile of encouragement, Aurelia's eyes again caught Zibby. She couldn't even contemplate sending the child, her only living daughter, away for schooling with strangers, the way she had her sons. She did want her to have the same chances, though, girl or no. And bless the angels, she wanted the town and all it would provide! More than anything. If there was a chance, any chance at all of turning Paragon Springs into a *real* town . . .

She hedged, aware she was weakening but still hoping there was some other way, "Why must there be a town company president? We're all in this together."

"Why is there a president of our country or chief of an Indian tribe? Because one clear head, one well-intentioned, honorable soul must lead the rest," Ham Gibbs answered

21

her. Ham bordered on homely, but he had the most sincere blue eyes and engaging grin given to man. He turned that grin on her now, "But you won't be alone. I will assist you with legal matters such as drawing up our charter, getting our townsite registered, incorporated. All matters of importance will be taken to a group vote, but a leader is still needed."

"Take it, honey," Owen urged. "Look at how fine you've managed the mercantile, the mail, and cooking for all those folks passing through the road ranch. Look at your beautiful children, the wonderful job you've done with them under the worst possible circumstances."

*Land, must they come at me from all sides?* Aurelia frowned at Zibby. She had overheard her step-father's praise. She was beaming and preening like a young princess next to Rachel. The children were dearest friends, though, and Rachel didn't seem to mind Zib's momentary air of superiority.

"Because Aurelia will earn it," Meg threw in, "I also suggest that we award three of the town's best lots to her in exchange for her duties."

"Here! Here!" Hamilton said. Others echoed him.

All except Joe Potter, who grumbled, "Don't seem legal or right for a woman to be president of nothin'."

Admire bristled at that, and he turned on Joe, "My wife, and Aurelia, and Meg Gibbs was the first settlers in these parts. It was them built up Paragon Springs to serve the rest of you all. They done a good job so far. If they're gonna do this, they're gonna do it. Let Aurelia be, or do you want the job, Joe?"

"Hell, no. You know I'm too busy on my farm."

"Shut up, then."

"You can do it, Aurelia," Meg encouraged her again, "you know you can."

"B-b-but—" Aurelia sputtered. Beyond Meg's wide smile

she saw the image of the restaurant she had lately dreamed of owning. A high school sprang to life in her mind. Down the block from the restaurant stood a fine, three-story home of white stone. She blinked at a sudden mist in her eyes. Not to live in a dirty, dusty soddy, ever again? To have fine advantages for her children, her friends' children? In that sudden blind moment, seeing the restaurant, the school, and grand house, she leaped to her feet and hands on her hips blurted her answer, "Oh, all right, I'll do it!"

For a frozen eternity she stood there. Finally, with wooden movement she went back to her bench, thinking, *If that isn't the biggest mistake I've ever made, I've never made one! God help me, God help us all.*

# Chapter Two

*Fairfield, Kentucky, July, 1872.*

"I beg you, John, please don't go." Aurelia clung to her young husband's arm. She spoke softly, not wanting to wake their three small children, Joshua, David John, and Helen Grace, in their beds in the next room. It was a sultry evening and with her free hand she wiped her brow with the hem of her apron. Outside, a dove cooed mournfully.

He pried her fingers free and sent an embarrassed smile in the direction of his friend, Karl, a gangly straw-haired fellow who waited and looking grim and impatient in a spill of lamplight by the door, holstered guns strapped around his hips. John took Aurelia's trembling chin in his hand and kissed her mouth. "I have to go, Aurelia, you know I do. The thieves who stole Karl's thoroughbred colt, Red Royal, could get clean away if we don't hurry. Our own pure-bloods could be stolen next."

She understood John's concern. A schoolteacher by occupation, he had a great deal of money tied up in their small horse farm. Karl and John's pride and joy, their dream for the future, were in their fine trotters and racing prospects, and in their brood mares. John was right that the thieves had to be caught and punished. But all day a sense of doom had suffocated her, a feeling without reason until Karl rode in hard wanting John to ride with him. *He mustn't go. She couldn't let him.*

"I have a bad feeling that—that something terrible will happen to you. Let someone else go with Karl." Karl wasn't married, and he had other friends, not family men, who could ride with him after the thieves. John had family, owed it to them to keep himself safe.

Her dark-haired, handsome husband laughed as he strapped on his Army Colt revolvers, "If I paid heed to every 'bad feeling' you have, Aurelia, I'd never leave the house. I couldn't teach my school each fall. I'd have to sit here at home with you and—*knit.*"

Her voice rose in a soft wail, "Don't make light of this." She clutched at him. "I mean it, John! What would I do if something happened to you? The children and I need you." Her hand went to her swollen abdomen. "My time is close. What if this little one decides to come tonight and I'm alone with the other children?" Her heart was cold with fear, not for the birthing, but being without John, never seeing him again. Tears welled in her eyes. Right after the war she'd lost her mama and papa and brothers and sisters to cholera on their way to California; she'd stayed behind to marry John. He and the children were all the family she had. "I can't do without you, please, please let someone else go with Karl."

He shook free of her. "Karl's been my friend since we were boys. I owe it to him to help."

"And we've been sweethearts since we were children, doesn't that count?"

"Aurelia, for God's sake—" He reached the door and frowned back at her. "You'll be all right," he said sternly, "And nothing will happen to me. I'll likely be back before dawn, maybe a little later, depending how long it takes to track down these thieves and recover Red Royal. But this horse thieving has got to stop and I mean to help end it!" He nodded at Karl and they left the house.

Aurelia ran clumsily across the porch and down into the star-lit yard after their striding figures. "John, please—" But

25

he was well on his way to the stables to saddle his horse. His voice floated to her, "Aurelia, go back in the house. Go to bed and get some sleep. You'll be fine, and I'll be back before morning."

The silvery night, as she watched them pound away on their mounts, was heavy with the scent of her jasmine vines. Her stomach roiled and heaved and there in the yard she lost her supper. On legs wooden with fear she followed his orders and went back inside, but not to bed. All night she sat in her rocker by the parlor window, waiting, rocking, praying that John was right, and that she was foolish to worry.

When the sun rose, she went to the kitchen to make coffee. At the sound of horses outside, she stumbled to the window, parted the curtains with shaking fingers and looked out. There were four riders, her neighbors, crossing the pennyroyal carpeted meadow. One, heavy-set Mr. Hartley, held the reins of a fifth horse, John's favorite mount, Raven. As they neared, she saw that it was John's bloody body draped over Raven's saddle, arms and legs dangling. She ran outside, her hands clasped in prayer, her blood icy in her veins.

"Sorry, Miz Thorne, John's dead," Mr. Hartley said gravely, removing his brown hat and resting it on his chest.

Her trembling cry rent the morning. She ran to John and caught his head in her hands. His crisp, curly black hair was soaked with blood, his face slick with it, his eyes unseeing. "No! No! No! He can't be dead, Mr. Hartley. You're wrong! He might still be alive and we can save him." She laid her cheek against John's back as he hung there, to feel if he breathed. There was nothing. She slid to the ground, her face and hands coated with John's blood.

"Get her inside," she heard a voice bark from a distant darkness. "She's with child. Lord only knows what she'll do without John. She's got three other young ones besides this one that's due."

Another voice echoed, "What a god-damn sorry mess!"

There were six bullets in John's body; Karl, also, was dead. The two of them had surprised the outlaws holed up in a cave ten miles south. In the firestorm of gunplay, John was killed, Karl was seriously wounded but managed to ride for help before he died. A posse was formed to find the outlaws, but they escaped with Red Royal and were never caught. It was suspected they fled to lawless country to the west, but no trace was found.

Aurelia lived the next few months in a state of numbness. She buried her husband, gave birth to a baby daughter she named Zibby. The bank took her house and the horse farm when she couldn't make payment. After selling John's horses to pay off their other debts, she was near penniless. With four young children to care for, she couldn't take outside work.

John's brother, Harlan Thorne, had written numerous letters to John about his exciting ranching venture in western Kansas. Her brother-in-law would have to help her in John's place. She would keep house for him, her children would have a home, a good life. She wrote Harlan Thorne a letter, not knowing in the least what she was getting herself into.

That night after the meeting in the mercantile, while Owen snored softly in their bed nearby, Aurelia sat at her lamp table and made a list of town needs. Night-time varmints rustled in the sod walls in accompaniment to her scratching pen. Whatever reluctance she might feel toward taking on a difficult chore, once it was hers she could neither shirk it nor delay attacking it. She had a grip on their plan to build a town, and no one was going to wrest the dream from her.

Not even that Joe Potter, thinking a woman couldn't do this—she'd show him!

Chewing the top of her pen, she worried that a dry town could never succeed. *Water* was a must. The spring couldn't provide for the needs of any larger a population than their small group.

On the other hand, an ample water supply would be a strong attraction to both families and businessmen. When they got their railroad, steam engines would need water, too. They must commence immediately to dig a town well. There ought to be a hotel built right away, also. Newly arrived land seekers and businessmen would need a place to put up while they chose their lots, and later built their businesses and homes.

*Businessmen.* Or businesswomen. She sat back in her chair, thoughtful. The best sort of merchants must be persuaded, somehow, to cast their lot with them, establish their business in the new town of Paragon Springs. Perhaps they should give away a few free lots to the first, especially promising, folk? She would talk to the others in the town company, convince them that a core of good strong businesses would surely attract others.

Next morning, Aurelia was up before dawn. As she washed her face before the little looking glass over the washstand, she studied her reflection in dim lamplight. Gone was the "February face" gloomy and grave and angry that used to look back at her, and a good thing. Thanks were due to her beloved Owen, mostly, but also to the accomplishments she'd managed since moving to Kansas. Her dark golden hair was still thick, but beginning to show streaks of gray. She smoothed her straight winged brows, the crinkles around her eyes below them. She wasn't beautiful, but Owen thought so, and that pleased her. She would ask him to save a dish of cream from the milking tonight to use on her sun-and-wind-dried skin.

They had made love last night after she finally crawled into bed next to him. Now, seeing the sparkle in her large green eyes, she blushed and looked away from the mirror. She had no time to fritter remembering last night, sweet as it was. She had a job to do, and only time would tell if she were up to it, in the way she desperately wanted to be.

At the mercantile later that morning, possessed of a fever to make the town a reality, Aurelia stole a few moments from the store's chores to continue her list, scribbling on a sheet of paper at the main counter. A bank, a dry goods store, lumberyard and hardware store, were of utmost importance. Meg's mercantile carried a little bit of everything, but it was not enough. Until they got the railroad, and even after, they needed a regular stagecoach line operating to and from town. Transportation now was catch as catch can among the settlers. A livery was necessary. A flour mill, grain elevator, drug store, meat market for city folk who didn't raise their own—all would be nice—in time. Why couldn't Paragon Springs become as nice a town as Fairfield, or Bloomfield, back home in Kentucky? Her imagination soared.

Those attending the meeting last night had set the store to rights again before departing, but a few boxes and barrels were out of order. As Aurelia moved them to their accustomed positions, her mind remained with the coming town. She'd build her restaurant as soon as possible. Heaven only knew where she'd find time to run it, but she'd find a way somehow. Thank goodness her family was such good help. She could depend on Zibby.

For a moment Aurelia stood with her finger to her chin and then she picked up a small crate of dried fruit and placed it on the counter where the fruit would be more noticeable. Humming to herself, she grabbed a broom and began sweeping. In a few months Joshua and David John would return home for the summer and her strong growing sons would take some of the burden of work. Unless the Larned high school academy had given them the fanciful idea that honest work was beneath them. No, Potter was a fool. Her boys were raised better than that.

Aurelia swept the dirt out through the open door and off the wide door stone and put away the broom. She sighed with satisfaction. Everything was going to be just fine, she thought.

"I see no reason," she said in a meeting a few days later with Emmaline in the small nook of Emmaline's home that was the newspaper office, "not to advertise our new town in the rosiest of terms. Meg was right when she said of our location that we are 'nestled in opportunity.' I'd like to use that as our slogan."

Emmaline, at her small oak desk, dipped her pen in her inkwell and wrote it down. "I agree. We already have the beginnings of a town: post office, mercantile, a newspaper. Now that the open range days are gone, there's quite a bit of land around that can be homesteaded or preempted for farms." Her dark velvet eyes were contemplative. "No, I don't think we should worry about a bit of puffery in our promotion. You wouldn't believe some of the claims I've read in other papers about new towns. If we don't do the same, we're lost before we begin."

Aurelia's admiration was boundless and over the years she had become very fond of Emmaline, who was part Cheyenne.

For the next hour they played with phrases that Emmaline wrote down. Then the discarding, revising, and rearranging of wordage began. Finally, they had an advertisement that pleased them both:

GARDEN OF THE WEST
"The new city of PARAGON SPRINGS welcomes YOU. Invest now in a first-class site verily *nestled in opportunity*. Located in Hodgeman County, soul of the region, PARAGON SPRINGS is a fine and pleasant place not just to live, but to *prosper*. In abundant supply you will find reasonably priced land, good grass and water, and superior building stone. Nothing will prevent success on a site such as PARAGON SPRINGS. A railroad is contemplated directly through this area. We are destined at an early date to become county seat. PERSONS SEEKING LOCATIONS FOR BUSINESS WOULD WISELY VISIT US BEFORE INVESTING ELSEWHERE!"

"We'll send our advertisement to as many large city newspapers as we can, and let's make circulars to post in towns near us!" Aurelia exclaimed while Emmaline went to prepare tea.

The University of Kansas was situated at the summit of Mt. Oread, the main buildings of white and rose limestone bordered a drive that followed the ridge. Below to the north was the broad green Kansas River Valley, and on the south was the valley of the Wakarusa. The young couple, their attention on one another, were oblivious to the beauty of the warm spring day.

"If you can't stand still, Lad, I'll never finish this sketch." With sketch pad in one hand and charcoal stick in the other, Selinda stood back, squinting at Lad as he leaned against a newly-leafed tree, books under his arm, his legs crossed at the ankles. He was the handsomest subject she'd ever drawn and it was hard to keep her mind on her work.

"Hurry, then," he said with a bedeviling grin. "Unless you don't mind if I fail my law studies."

"Of course I care. That you don't fail, I mean." Her charcoal stick moved swiftly over the pad, her eyes moving back and forth from Lad to her drawing in intense concentration. A warm breeze tossed her dark hair and wrapped her long skirts around her slender figure. In a moment she laughed softly, "All right, might as well call it finished if you're going to badger me into hurrying."

"Wait." He caught her arm as she started to put the sketch pad into her sail cloth portfolio. "I want to see it."

"It's not good." Reluctantly, she turned the sketch pad over so he could see her drawing. There was a shy catch in her throat as she said, "You're much better looking than I've shown you. But it's your fault I didn't capture you, you kept moving." He wasn't moving now, he was standing so close she could feel his breathing and it set her heart to a dizzying pace. She moved aside and took a deep breath. She had known Lad for years, growing into adulthood with him at Paragon Springs, and still he could do this to her.

He whistled through his teeth as he scanned her drawing. "You're wrong. This is very good! I just wish I was half as handsome as you've drawn me. May I have it for my sister?"

"I'd like to send it home to Mama. I send her most of my drawings, so she can see what my life is like here at the University. I've drawn the buildings, groups of students, a professor or two."

"All right, this one can go to Aunt Emmaline and maybe you'll draw another one of me later for Lucy. I know your mother misses you. Especially since—" he broke off. "I'm sorry," he said softly, "I was thinking of Shafer."

She nodded, "I know." Sadness shadowed her lovely face. "I believe it's true that twins are closer than most brothers and sisters, I know I miss Shafer dreadfully. Mama hasn't been the same since his death." She looked off into the distance and shook her head. "Shafer was getting quite wild before he entered that horse race last year and was thrown and killed. I don't know if he could have changed or not. He was happy living life his way." She took the sketch pad from Lad, their hands touched briefly before she put her work in her portfolio. They walked along together, her arm looped through his.

Lad reminded, "We'll be going home for the summer soon. Having you home again will help your mother."

"I can hardly wait. I miss her, I miss everyone at Paragon Springs. And—I need to ease Mama's mind about a project I have." A frown creased Selinda's brow and she chewed her lip.

"That sounds almost ominous. I'll walk you to your room at your boarding house and you can tell me about it. The project is not another fellow, is it?" he wisecracked, holding her closer to his side as they followed the path bordered by fragrant lilac bushes, "because I know your mother favors me. Trouble is," he reflected, "neither of us has time for courting, with all the studying that's piled on us." His expression looking down at her was wistful, his eyes shiny, and for a moment she thought he might kiss her.

Selinda ignored a squiggle of disappointment when he didn't. "I'm not preoccupied with another fellow." *You're the one for me, Lad, and always have been.* Aloud, she told him, "I haven't time for—romance, as you say. And you needn't joke about too many books, Lad. The world knows how much you love college."

"I do, but we were talking about you."

She began slowly, eyes locked on his, "You knew that my father went to the Montana goldfields when Shafer and I were just toddlers, and he vanished? That we waited years, hoping he'd come home, but we never saw him again?"

"I knew. You used to talk about it a lot, a long time ago, and I've heard about your missing father from others, Aunt Aurelia, my sister, Lucy."

"Well, I'm going to find him."

Lad stopped short in the path and turned her to face him. "Find him? You're going away? But you can't—!"

She shook her head. "I'm not leaving Kansas to look for him, at least not anytime in the near future. Mama would worry too much, I'm all she has. For now I'm writing letters. I wrote first to officials in Helena, in Montana Territory—" she drew a breath, "they told me there wasn't mention of my father, Simeon Lee, in court records. No record of his death, or involvement in a crime—nothing."

They walked a few paces and stopped again. Lad said, "That's somewhat good news, but unfortunately many accidents and murders happen that are never made a matter of record—hundreds of incidents, probably."

"I realize that," she answered defensively. "I requested and was sent a list of newspapers located in mining towns that I might write to. There's a rare chance an old-timer will read my story and can tell me something about my father, if something happened to him and he's dead, or if he's still alive. Whatever the answer, somewhere someone surely knows."

"Oh, Selinda," Lad's voice was husky and filled with doubt, "You're not neglecting your studies to write these letters, are you? Because if you are, I think you're making a mistake."

She halted, stung with disappointment. "Mistake?" She

whirled on him. "How can you say that?" Tears sprang to her eyes.

"Selinda, I only meant—"

Lad dropped his books, reached out and caught her about the waist but she wrenched away, her anger flaring. "Isn't it my personal business how I use my time?" She stamped her feet. "Don't you see how important this is to me? You feel that I shouldn't even bother?"

"Selinda, listen to me, please. How long has your father been gone, eighteen years or so? That's a long time. Why now? Do you even remember him?" His glance softened, his fingertips traced her cheek.

"Does that make any difference? I was tiny, yes, but I remember him! I remember the *feeling*, having a father hold me, care for me, even if I can't remember what he looks like. I've always missed him, wanted to know him, hoped for him to come home." A sob caught in her throat. "It was time to *do* something!" She wiped at her tears, only to have them start again.

Lad held her face in his hands, thumbed at her tears. "You know I wouldn't hurt you for anything, Selinda." He pulled her close in spite of her resistance. "I shouldn't have been so blunt, could have been kinder in what I said, and I'm truly sorry. Come," he said, clasping her hand and leading her to a nearby stone bench. "Let's sit a moment so I can explain."

He gave her his handkerchief. "I was thinking of you, Selinda, believe me. I would hate to see you hurt due to this search, that's all I'm saying." He frowned and spoke cautiously, "What if your father left your mother, his family, intentionally? As much as you might dislike the idea, that might be what happened, and he doesn't want to come back. Or— what if he's dead?"

Lad, of all people, didn't see the point of what she was

doing, its importance to her. Selinda gasped with pain at the knowledge and buried her face in her hands. She loved Lad, had always loved him, believed that someday their individual paths would merge, they'd marry and have a family. "Of course I've considered that he might be dead, or that he might not want to return, although I can't believe that. The point is, I need to *know*." She stood up, grabbed her things, and set off at a run, her portfolio banging her leg, her heart splintered and aching.

"Wait, Selinda! I'll go with you. I'm sorry."

"Go away, Lad. I'll see myself to my room. Go away."


At Paragon Springs, Emmaline told Aurelia about Selinda's letter writing campaign to Montana Territory to learn if anyone might have known her father and what became of him.

"My goodness." Aurelia hesitated, her heart hurting for both Emmaline and Selinda. She asked softly, "How long has Simeon been missing?"

"Close to eighteen years. He meant to be back within the year, with enough gold to make us wealthy the rest of our lives. We never saw him again."

"Do you think there's a chance Selinda will find out what happened?"

"I can't see how." Emmaline went to bring cups and saucers, a fresh pot of tea and ginger cookies. "I used to think of going to Montana Territory myself to search for him, to find out what happened. But it didn't seem fair to drag my small children into a quest like that; plus I had Father to take care of, and I needed to keep my teaching job to support us." Emmaline sighed, her expression regretful and sad. "When she was little, Selinda would beg that we go and find him—" her voice broke off.

"Maybe the effort now will make her feel better, even if she doesn't find out the facts," Aurelia said. "She will have tried."

"I suppose there is no harm in the letter-writing itself. What truly worries me is that even though the odds are against it, Selinda believes deep in her heart that she may find her father alive."

"You don't think that's a possibility?"

"Not at all. If Simeon could take so much as three breaths together he would have returned to us or there would have been letters if he were alive but couldn't come home. He wouldn't have abandoned us."

"Poor Selinda. But I suppose she has to try."

"She grieves for her twin, too. If she could bring Shafer back she would, but she knows for certain that *he* is dead." Emmaline's face crumpled with pain, remembering the Dodge City horse race the previous summer that ended in her son's death. She recovered slowly, her voice thick, "I think Selinda would walk away from her studies in an instant and search in person for her father, but she knows how much that would worry me. I suppose I should be glad that she's only writing letters; that she's staying at college."

"I hope she learns news—any kind of news that will bring her peace of mind and ease her heart. We can only wait and see."

"We can only wait and see," Emmaline echoed, but Aurelia thought she'd never seen anyone so concerned. She hoped excitement in executing plans for the coming town would take Emmaline's mind off the matter at least part of the time.

With their advertisement off to numerous metropolitan newspapers, and Owen, Hamilton, and Admire distributing circulars on their business rounds to other towns, Aurelia began to worry about their claim of an "abundant water supply." It didn't yet exist. Although it could.

As she expected, each member of the community she spoke to agreed with her that no time should be lost before a city well was dug. They set a date for the digging to start within the week. Customers to the store were advised of the event and were asked to spread the word. "Tell your neighbors and friends how important it is to give whatever time and effort to the project that they can," she told them. "We will all benefit from the well and the town in every conceivable way. And the sooner the digging begins and we strike water, the sooner we will be finished and can go on with building the town."

They laughed at her when she showed where she wanted the well dug and was told that the well would be where water could be found. She had the last laugh when Will Hessler's witching stick dropped and pointed at the precise spot where she wanted the well.

Two days before the digging was to commence, Zibby looked after Meg's children and Meg looked after the store while Aurelia and Hamilton measured and determined where to drive stakes to mark off the lots and streets within the two-mile perimeter. The second day, after working long in the spring sunshine, Aurelia straightened from driving a stake and rubbed the ache at the middle of her back. She smiled as she pictured the town blooming right out of the prairie around her. Then a moment's panic struck. What if no one came to buy the lots and settle the town? What if Jack Ambler, the rancher who tried for so long to drive them out, was right, and this wasn't a country for civilized people, for a town? What if, although they had many advantages to offer—water, grass, a main-traveled road nearby—businessmen refused their site because there was no railroad, *yet?*

Hamilton saw her frown and she told him what she was thinking. He had already taken care of legal ramifications, preparing forms for titles to lots and drawing up the official plat of survey. He chuckled, "I don't think you need to worry, Aurelia. That was a pretty convincing advertisement you and Emmaline drew up—how can anyone resist at least a look at what we have here?"

What they had was a wide dusty area of several acres sprinkled with stakes and little flags. On the east side of "town" was the original road ranch; everything new would happen to the west and south of that.

On the day the digging was to begin, Aurelia closed the store and joined the group at the well-site. It would take only moments to return to the store if anyone needed anything. Farmers and ranchers alike fell to with pick and shovel in the field of matted grass and like a giant prairie dog hole, the public well began to open up in the center of what would be their town.

The men, shoveling furiously, pouring sweat, and by using a windlass and rope, brought up dirt by endless bucketful. Aurelia joined the other women and the children who grabbed the heavy buckets and dumped the fragrant pulverized earth into wheelbarrows. These were unloaded into their wagons for taking home and spreading on their spaded gardens.

Owen, Admire and Will Hessler and two of Will's sons cut and hauled stone to case the hole. From the top into the bowels of the earth, measure by measure, the stone was laid around the walls with wood pins and mortar, augmenting the sides to prevent cave in and to assure clear water.

At noon, Aurelia broke from the dirt-hauling task to help

some of the women serve lunch from the backs of wagons that had been parked close together. Tired workers drifted to the spring pond in twos and threes to wash up, then sat chiefly silent eating the meal of baked beans and fried chicken, cold biscuits and cornbread. One male worker wished for "skull-varnish" or whiskey to drink, but Aurelia had provided a dipper and buckets of water from the spring and Lucy Ann had made ginger swizzle.

After the meal and a rest, work at the well was taken up again. It was mid-afternoon when a pair of finely dressed middle-aged men drove up in their black buggy. They leaned down to smile and speak to young Rachel at the fringes of the working group and she turned to call, "Aunt Aurelia, these men want to talk to you!"

Aurelia brushed her dirty hands on her apron, smoothed her hair, and walked toward them. The dapper-looking gentlemen were peering out of their buggy at the dusty, flag-specked townsite, and at the workers digging the well in the center. "May I help you?"

They introduced themselves as Luther and Silas Jones. Both were slight of build, Luther looked to be a little older, his dark hair had more gray. "We were in Dodge City," he told her, "looking over prospects to build ourselves a new business, a combination dry-goods store and men's haberdashery."

Silas put in, "We had given up on Dodge, and we were about to return to Kansas City when we saw one of your circulars advertising the proposed town of Paragon Springs. We're here to look it over."

*Dear heaven, already?* Aurelia swallowed her surprise and delight and said calmly, "We welcome you then; please alight and I'd be happy to explain our town. My name is Mrs. Aurelia Symington, and I am president of the Paragon

40

Springs Town Company."

They followed her around as she led the way in her sure-footed stride and pointed out the layout of the town; they stood for sometime watching the industrious well diggers and were introduced to most of them and to their wives and children. When there was nothing more to explain or show the Jones brothers, Aurelia waited quietly for their decision, hardly daring to breathe. They had stepped aside to talk privately. "We like what we see here," Luther told her when they returned to where she waited. "This is where we'd like to invest our capital. You all are so friendly and enthusiastic about your town, it's our pleasure to join you."

While her heart pounded giddily, Silas counted the bills into her hand for the lots they had chosen—one for their store, one for the home they planned to build. "We'll camp here," he told her, "on our lot. When we've changed into other clothes, we'll help with the digging."

"Oh, you needn't—" she started to protest. From the fine look of them, the pair couldn't possibly be accustomed to such work. Both of them shook off her words. "We insist," Luther told her, and Silas agreed with a smile, "We want to do our part."

That night, Aurelia went home and cried tears of relief, smudging her face with dirt from her hands until she was a mess. Luther and Silas Jones would build Paragon Spring's first real business from the outside! After she had dried her tears, she got paper and pen and set about ordering the parts for a giant windmill.

Slowly, the digging of the well progressed. It was wearying for everyone, keeping up with their work at home, and taking their turn at the digging, but no one wanted to see the work stopped, least of all, Aurelia. One day flowed into the next and the digging and packing away of the dirt continued until the day a cheer arose among dirty, weary workers at sight of a dark seep of water down in the hole. The children laughed and danced, the women hugged one another, the men shook hands. They were at one hundred feet. Clear sweet artesian water was reached in ample supply several feet deeper. They had found their water!

As much as Aurelia enjoyed tending the store and post office, she wanted to be outside in the middle of activity at the townsite more. Folks were beginning to come from nearby farms and other towns for a look-see, and she reveled in showing them the planned town. It was hard to be in two places at once and the attempt made her feel as addled at times as a goose flying north in winter.

Meg found her in the store-yard one day, discussing lots with a visitor and at the same time trying to tell a customer inside the mercantile where he might find the rose-colored fabric his wife had ordered. "Far corner away from the window light! I'll be right in and cut it for you!" she called in a harried voice, then turned back to the land seeker. "You might want side by side lots, on the south side—"

After Meg had helped the customer with his fabric, and Aurelia bid her land seeker good-bye—he wanted to discuss his plans with his family before he acted—the women sat down to visit.

"You're working yourself to death, Aurelia," Meg commented.

"Not really, I'm just busy. And I'm enjoying myself immensely."

"Even so, I'll tend the store from now on, after you take care of the mail. I'll keep my children with me, and get help as needed from anyone who might be available: your Zibby or

Owen, or Lucy Ann and Rachel."

"Are you sure, Meg?"

She leaned forward and patted her knee. "Of course, I'm sure. We gave you a job to do with the new town. You can't be everywhere at once."

Two days later Aurelia was outside, replanting stakes errant, playful children had pulled from the ground, when a strange, distant sound caught her ears. She watched the object move slowly toward her across the prairie against a vast blue backdrop of sky. In another few minutes she identified a team-drawn wagon, a tiny driver high on the seat. The sounds coming from the conveyance were like a band: clanging cymbals, whistling wind pipes, the rat-a-tat of tin drums.

She waited, curiosity growing. Then she smiled and clapped her hands. The sight was right out of her Kentucky childhood.

Nearly every inch of the wagon was hung with tin goods such as shears, dippers and spoons. Turners, ladles, pots, pans, and skillets twirled and clanged in the breeze. Wind whined through hanging saws. Down near the turning wheels, buckets and tubs banged. Tied near them were pitchforks, rakes, and hoes. Behind the bewhiskered gnome-like driver, kegs of hardware goods rocked and thumped on the floor of the wagon.

The bright-eyed driver, in shabby dusty brown, hauled back on the reins, slowing his team of gray nags. With a last loud rattle and bang, the wagon came to a stop in front of her. The man hopped down and bowed. "Abel Pennybaker, at your service, ma'am."

Later, she took him home with her to share her family's noonday meal. Over chicken stew she heard his story. For forty years, from the age of seventeen when he accompanied his father in the trade, Pennybaker had peddled tinware goods from New Hampshire to Maine, from Massachusetts to Connecticut, throughout the eastern states. He was not so young, now, and he was tired of life on the road. He wanted to establish his own hardware store in a thriving town.

Eastern properties were more than he could afford so he had wandered west. He had recently heard about Paragon Springs. If they would sell him a lot for a small payment down, he would pay the rest as his business took root and grew.

"Keep your money to build and stock your store, Mr. Pennybaker. We have a few free lots available for businessmen like yourself," she was glad to tell him. "The town company votes who gets the free lots and I will recommend you. We need your goods, as much as you need our town, need a place to establish your business. Of course, according to the rules of our town company, your lot will return to us if not improved upon within six months. A couple of other gentlemen have already paid for their lots, but they've agreed with our plan to give free lots to those we deem trustworthy, whose type business we desperately need, but who are low on funds. When you've finished your raisin pie, I will show you what we have."

# Chapter Three

*Louisville, Kentucky, February, 1873.*

The wharf of the Louisville Packet Company swarmed with noisy activity in the misty cold. Aurelia focused on the steamer before her, the *Harmony Ann*, that would transport her and the children most of their journey to Kansas.

The vessel was at least a half block long and resembled an imposing white frosted cake as it rode the water close to the dock. Up and down the wide gangplanks, roustabouts loaded wood for the boilers, sweated under burdens of trade goods and baggage. Passengers hurried to board, friends shouted and waved and cried their goodbyes. Aurelia watched in envy as elite passengers took the stairway from the main deck to the luxury of the upper cabin deck.

Mr. Hartley, his nose red, and huffing from effort, returned down the gangplank after delivering Aurelia's trunk aboard. Aurelia met him halfway, her bundled baby girl in one arm and her other hand gripping three-year-old Helen Grace's wrist. She was trying to thank Hartley above the racket when the *Harmony Ann*'s twin stacks loudly belched smoke and her shrill whistle pierced the air, the sound reverberating up and down the wide gray-green Ohio River.

Helen Grace screamed in terror, "No!" She yanked back, "No, no!" Aurelia swayed over the water, held tight to both daughters and frantically held her footing. Taking a deep breath, she said in a harried voice, "Please, Helen Grace, let's get on the pretty boat. Mr. Hartley, thank you for everything." Over her shoulder she said, "Boys, stay close to me."

Joshua, age seven, and David John, age six, both wide-eyed with uncertainty, struggled along behind her up the plank with their bundles. Aurelia pulled Helen Grace onto the steamer's pine deck. "There now, angel, we're fine. We're here."

Six-month-old Zibby squirmed awake in Aurelia's arms, poked her thumb in her mouth, and looked at her mother with solemn eyes. Aurelia kissed her and turned to wave goodbye to Mr. Hartley as he climbed into his horse-drawn wagon parked on the wharf. "Wave goodbye to Mr. Hartley, children." He had driven them to Louisville as a neighborly favor after convincing Aurelia that travel by steamboat on the waterways would be cheaper and faster than overland by stage and train. "You'll travel down the Ohio River to where it joins the Mississippi at Cairo, Illinois," with a blunt finger he'd drawn the river map in the air, "From there you head upstream to St. Louis, where the Mississippi joins the Missouri river. From St. Louis you go west to Kansas City on the ol' Missouri. 'Too thick to drink and too thin to plow'," he quipped with a smile about the Missouri. "Of course, you'll have to take the train or a stagecoach from Kansas City to western Kansas."

She thanked him for his advice. It was important to reach Kansas as soon as possible, vital that she conserve her small funds.

The *Harmony Ann* trembled as her boilers heated and steamed. Her whistles blew again, setting Helen Grace to crying anew and grabbing her mother tight about the knees. Zibby, the baby, also began to cry. "Shush, now, both of you. There, there." Holding onto the baby, Aurelia stooped to loosen Helen Grace's arms. "The whistle just means it's time to go, there's no harm to it." As the vessel struck for midstream, leaving a wake behind them, she jiggled the baby in her arms and turned back and surveyed her surroundings. She had bought the cheapest possible passage on the crowded, warehouse-like main deck. Under ordinary circumstances, she would have insisted on a stateroom on the upper deck, but her life was anything but normal since John's death. Remembering him was so painful she wanted to die; she closed her mind to the past.

"Over there," she motioned her children toward a half-moon space among stacked bags of flour, crates of live chickens, a dozen or so barrels marked molasses, and her trunk where Hartley had placed it. Others had claimed the few crude bunks undercover, her family would have to make do with a spot six by four feet as their traveling quarters. "Bring our bundles here," she instructed Joshua and David John. The boys had been cautious about boarding, but from their faces they were now eager to explore these strange new surroundings. She hated to disappoint them, but said, "Fellows, you're going to have to stay close where I can see you. Promise."

Many main deck passengers were ordinary folk like herself, farmers and immigrants, their wives and children. Others were skulking and shifty-eyed—ne'er-do-wells from the look of them and they made her uneasy. Equally worrisome was the fact that the main deck had no outside railing. The *Harmony Ann* could bump a log, roll slightly, and throw her sons into the water to drown. "Stay close by me now."

"Want to go home," Helen Grace sniffled. "Want Papa."

Aurelia's breath caught and her heart constricted. She knelt beside Helen Grace and when she could speak said, "We're going to our new home in Kansas. Papa's not at our old home, remember? He's in heaven."

"Not be in heaven," she pouted sadly. "Want Papa with us."

Tears burned Aurelia's eyes as she stroked Helen Grace's flaxen curls, and gazed into her small tear-marked face. "Papa would be here with us if he could. But he can't be. Papa's dead. Now," she cleared her throat and smiled, "Your baby sister is hungry and needs to nurse. You can be a big girl and help me make our place here on the boat comfy—like a play house. You can help me change the baby's nappy and dress her in a nightie. Shall we?"

Helen Grace nodded and a smile lit up her face. Aurelia heaved a sigh and relaxed for the moment. With her children's help, she retrieved a quilt from their trunk and folded it for a pallet on the deck floor inside their small area. They draped a sheet from stacked flour bags to molasses barrels and had a privacy curtain. Baby Zibby gnawed at her knuckle while she was changed. A short while later she hungrily nursed, and Aurelia sagged tiredly with her back to the trunk. Helen Grace played with her sock doll, and the boys occupied themselves with their slates and chalk retrieved from the trunk. For the next half hour, beyond their crude quarters, came the sounds of the steamer's engine as it steadily plied the Ohio, voices of other passengers moving about the deck.

"H'lo in there." A rosy-cheeked woman's face peeked past their curtain.

"H-hello," Aurelia answered uncertainly. "You can drop the curtain if you like, my baby's finished nursing."

"Going far?" the woman asked, fixing the curtain to the side. "My name is Flory Steinberger." She hustled into the cubbyhole and joined Aurelia on the quilt.

"To Kansas, eventually. I'm Aurelia Thorne."

"Your husband with you? Didn't see him when I watched you, earlier."

Aurelia's voice trembled, "My husband is—dead. The children and I are going to Kansas to live with my husband's brother. He has a ranch there, north of Dodge City. How about you?"

"Oh, I get off in a couple of days at Cairo. Going to help my sister with her baby." Her voice lowered for modesty's sake, "Her time's close." Then she chuckled, sharing privately, "Hope she waits 'til I get there to have the wee one."

"Boys, come back here with me," Aurelia said suddenly, seeing the two of them about to slip away. They looked at her, eyes shifting guiltily, then they came back and took up their slates again.

"Got a nice family," Flory said. "But I reckon they're a handful?"

"My boys would like to roam, and play. It's going to be hard for them to be confined hour after hour, day after day, to this bit of space on the boat. My Helen Grace, here," she stroked her curls, "would rather we'd never left our home back in Fairfield. But once we get to Kansas, we'll be fine. They're very good children."

At supper time, Aurelia fixed meat and biscuit from their food parcel. With a small knife, she sliced an apple for her family to share. During the evening hours, she told the children stories about her own childhood, and about falling in love with their father, and marrying him when she was seventeen. The stories calmed all of them. When the stars came out overhead, Aurelia bedded her children down on the quilt. Later, she slipped under the covers beside them and pillowed her head on the carpet bag containing Baby Zibby's things. She had never felt so alone in her life and tears dampened the corners of her eyes.

As the boat plied on through the night, Aurelia found it impossible to sleep. From the upper deck came the sounds of merrymaking—laughter, singing, shouting. The noise from the steamer's machinery was jarring. She ached with loneliness, yearned for her husband's company, his help on this journey into the unknown. As she tossed and turned on the hard pine deck floor, she thought the night would never end.

Twice next day, the *Harmony Ann* stopped at remote riverside woodyards to take on wood. When they were moving, Aurelia sat on her trunk with her baby in her arms and watched Kentucky pass by. She would never see her home again. But without John there, what did it matter?

Flory Steinberger came again to sit with her and visit. The pleasant company lightened Aurelia's mood; she wished Flory was making the entire journey with her.

"Are we in Kansas?" David John asked excitedly that late afternoon as the *Harmony Ann* chugged into port at the mud-smothered hamlet of Cairo. "Can we get off?"

"We stay aboard," Aurelia said quickly. "This isn't Kansas."

She hugged Flory goodbye, wished her well caring for the new baby and her sister. When the *Harmony Ann* was underway again, steaming and whistling into the brown waters of the Mississippi upstream, Aurelia's loneliness returned stronger than ever. Adding to her misery was the cold weather. She told the children, "Let's go for a walk here on the main deck, but stay back from the edge, mind." The exercise was warming and they walked some distance, weaving in and out of boxes, bundles, and bales of freight, and people grouped in conversation. They approached a woman bundled in brown linsey and seated on a bale of raw wool, her face hidden in the depths of her blue slatted bonnet. Hoping to make a new friend, Aurelia approached her. She put a smile in her voice, "Hello, I'm Aurelia Thorne, and these are my children. Are you going far?"

The woman glared up at her from the shadows of her

bonnet, then looked away without speaking.

"I-I'm sorry," Aurelia said, "I didn't mean to intrude." As she hustled the children ahead of her, embarrassed, Aurelia heard the woman mutter, "Ain't nobody's business where I'm agoin'!"

For most of that next day it rained torrents. Aurelia huddled with her children out of the wind and cold. She was getting little sleep at night, daytimes were spent forcing herself to be alert to care for the children. Fatigue dragged at her.

The second day's travel toward St. Louis from Cairo brought the return of sunshine. Aurelia basked in the warmth after she'd spread their things to dry. She gave the children their toys and, seated with her back to her trunk, fought to stay awake. Her head bobbed from time to time, waking her, but need for sleep was like warm wool beckoning her.

Aurelia jerked awake with a start. Her eyes found Helen Grace cuddled asleep on one side of her lap, the baby napped peacefully on the other. There was no sign of the boys. From the position of the sun, she had slept for an hour. Where had the boys gone?

She jumped to her feet and looked up and down the main deck that was now a confusion of rigged clotheslines, as well as freight and people. She called out, "Joshua! David John!"

A group of children played tag at the far end of the deck, aft, but her sons were not among them. Aurelia bundled the baby, took her into her arms, stirred Helen Grace awake. She forced a state of outward calm, "We're going to look for Joshua and David John," she said quietly.

After fifteen minutes of searching, she could not spot them anywhere on the main deck. The crew members she spoke to had not seen them, nor did anyone else remember seeing them. But there were many children on the boat and her sons were pretty nondescript. With the baby in one arm and pulling Helen Grace along, Aurelia took the stairs to the upper deck, and entered a different world. Wealthy-appearing merchants, planters, and gamblers lounged at the lacy wood deck railings. Richly gowned women chatted. After repeatedly questioning about her sons, and receiving as many negative answers, Aurelia sailed past rows of state-rooms. She'd knock on every last door if she didn't find the boys soon.

She opened a door into a carpeted and lavishly furnished saloon where bluish cigar smoke clouded around a brilliantly lit chandelier. Men relaxed in overstuffed chairs; a few played cards at the tables. One of the card players stood up to tell her, "Ma'am, this is the gentlemen's saloon."

"I see. I was looking for two little boys—"

"Only big boys here," one of the men laughed and splayed cards onto the table in front of him. The first gentleman said kindly, "The ladies' saloon is next door."

Aurelia hesitated, "Thank you." She closed the door and hurried on.

The ladies' saloon was as elegantly furnished as the men's. Aurelia's eyes widened in shock at sight of her sons, Joshua and David John, seated confidently at a table with a lovely brunette lady in an exquisite emerald gown. In front of each boy was a dish of treats: candy, raisins, almonds, dates, and peanuts. They were happily feasting and their lady companion was enjoying watching them.

"Joshua! David John!" They looked up quickly at Aurelia's voice. She asked, "What are you doing? You shouldn't have run away!" Her face warmed as she faced her boys' benefactor, "I fell asleep and they must have wandered off. I'm sorry they've imposed on you."

"They've been no bother at all, they've kept me company.

I'm Pru Gilham." Her satin skirts swished as she stood and came to take Aurelia's hand, "You probably saw my husband out on the deck, smoking with his cronies. I feel I should thank you for the company of these two young gentlemen. We were about to come find you, so you wouldn't worry about their absence. They told me you and their sisters were sleeping, and they didn't intend to be gone long. They only wanted to look around."

"They shouldn't poke their nose where it doesn't belong, though! I'm so embarrassed. And for all I knew," she said, her voice stricken, and frowning at her sons, "they had fallen overboard and drowned."

"We're sorry, Mama," Joshua said, hurrying to her side.

"Sorry," David John echoed.

"May I give the little girl some candy?" Pru Gilham asked.

Aurelia shrugged, "Yes, I suppose so." She gave up trying to identify Pru Gilham's delicate perfume.

"Would you come see me again?" Pru asked the boys, "but not without your mother. Bring her next time. You mustn't worry her." She smiled at Aurelia, "Looks like you have a lot to contend with. Will you and the children come join me, tomorrow perhaps? It'll help the time pass 'til we reach St. Louis."

"Thank you. Perhaps," Aurelia answered, her head swirling in confusion. "Right now we need to get back where we belong. Boys, Helen Grace, thank the la—thank Mrs. Gilham."

The children said their thank yous, and with cheeks and hands stuffed with nuts and candies, they trailed after Aurelia back to the warehouse deck, and their cubbyhole quarters.

Mrs. Gilham didn't wait for them to visit, but that same evening she searched out Aurelia and the children. When she saw their makeshift hovel among the smelly coops of clucking chickens and other freight, she was appalled. "You can't stay here! The children could catch their death here in the open. You all are sleeping on the hard deck floor?"

"It's not as bad as it looks," Aurelia replied, her face warming. "We're quite comfortable and it's not as though we have any other choice." She told her story, how John had died and that they were going to Kansas to live with his brother on his ranch.

"Do you change craft in St. Louis?" Mrs. Gilham frowned thoughtfully.

"You mean take another steamer to Kansas City? Yes, I believe we do."

"As a gift, you must allow me to buy first class passage for you all on the next boat."

Aurelia frowned, "I can't do that. I appreciate your kindness, Mrs. Gilham, but I must rely on my own resources." She added with a wry smile, "I admit I'm dying to be in a real house again and it will be a joy to sleep in a feather bed once more."

Mrs. Gilham argued a while longer, but Aurelia didn't change her mind. "It's not so long before we reach Kansas. We'll be fine."

"Can I be a cowboy when we get to Kansas?" Joshua asked.

"If you like."

"Me, too?" David John asked.

"Of course." Aurelia looked toward Helen Grace but she was busy, her tiny face buried in a fresh sack of candy Mrs. Gilham had brought.

After Mrs. Gilham departed, Aurelia's mind turned to her husband's brother. A year older than John, Harlan had run away from home when he was eleven or twelve to "see the world." He'd written letters now and then, describing his itchy-footed adventures. Like John, as a young man he'd fought for the South in the war. John had been thrilled when word came after the war that Harlan had settled down, had taken land in Kansas, partnering with a man named Ross McCoy. Harlan invited John to join them in his ranching venture, but John was happy where he was. Of course, all that now was changed.

When they docked in St. Louis, Aurelia and the children—aided in carrying their things by Mr. Gilham—changed to a different steamer scheduled for Kansas City. The *Flying Hawk* was almost identical to the *Harmony Ann* in all but its name. Aurelia settled herself and the children on the new steamer, much as she had before, stressing again to her youngsters that they must not leave her side.

For a day and half, the Hawk bulled its way upstream on the wide muddy Missouri, its pennants snapping in the wind. On occasion the boat swerved to miss a snag and plowed on. At each sizable town they put in for passengers and freight; stopped at woodyards to take on fuel. Bull boats floated past, their owners waving.

They had stopped at a woodyard, and Aurelia spotted Captain Phillip Pennywitt giving orders to the roustabouts. The children, tired of travel, badgered her constantly to know if they'd reached their destination. "Boys," she said now, "I'm going to ask the Captain how much longer it will be until we can leave the boat and take the train. Stay with Helen Grace and don't wake the baby. I'll only be gone for a minute or two." Aurelia hurried and caught up with the Captain just as he was about to take the stairs to the upper deck.

"Captain!"

He turned and waited.

"How much longer to Kansas City? I've lost track of time and days, I'm afraid. I need to plan—"

He smiled, "We'll put in at Kansas City day after tomorrow, barring trouble and providing we can hold this speed." He asked, attentive, friendly, "Do you have family to meet you in Kansas City, ma'am?"

She shook her head. "No. In fact my true destination is western Kansas. I'll be taking the train from Kansas City."

He nodded. "Train station isn't far from the docks. A short hack ride and you'll be at the depot. You won't have any trouble."

"Thank you. Thank you very much."

Aurelia hurried back to the cubbyhole and immediately saw that Helen Grace wasn't there. Joshua and David John sat scratching chalks on a slate board in a game of tic-tac-toe, the baby slept in a bundle of blankets. "Where's your sister, where is Helen Grace, boys?" Aurelia's hand went to her mouth in alarm and she looked swiftly up and down the crowded deck, strained to see her little one's golden head, her blue dress. She was nowhere in sight.

Joshua and David John, who had been engrossed in their game, followed her gaze in surprise as they stood up. "She was here just a minute ago. Sissy," Joshua yelled, "Helen Grace, where are you? You hidin'? Come out right now." He began to look behind their trunk and stacks of crated goods that marked their storage space. "Sissy, come on . . . !"

Aurelia rolled the baby in her blanket and took her in her arms. "We have to find Helen Grace, but stay with me."

A plaintive protest played in Aurelia's mind, *Dear God, will this nightmare journey and its troubles ever end? Will my young ones and I ever be safe again?*

For twenty minutes they looked, but found no sign of the three year old on the main deck, or in the ladies' saloon where

Aurelia thought her daughter might have gone seeking someone to give her candy. Leading the boys, Aurelia, now frantic, found the Captain to enlist his aid. Within seconds, a more thorough search was under way, most of the crew and nearly a hundred passengers taking part. Every inch of space—from the main deck to the galley, the upper deck, staterooms, saloons, up to the Texas deck and pilot house—was scoured. Helen Grace was not on the boat.

"Maybe the child wandered down the plank when my roustabouts went after wood," the Captain suggested, "although I've questioned them and no one saw her." The roustabouts were almost finished, they would soon draw up the plank. "Ma'am, I think we'd better search—"

Aurelia, senses reeling, her mouth dry and her heart in her throat, didn't hear the rest. With a whimpering cry, she stumbled across the deck and looked down off the far side into the muddy river. The boat rocked, she felt dizzy. Those ugly, filthy waters had taken her child. She screamed and fell to her knees, screamed her anguish over and over. Someone grabbed her baby from her arms.

Anger at John, rage she'd held in check since his death, boiled from her in a storm. She pounded the deck with her fists. "Why, John? This is your fault." She threw back her head and sobbed at the sky, "You had no right to leave us. I begged you to stay. You've done this, and I curse you!" Sobs tore painfully at her throat, she threw off hands that tried to console and help her to her feet, beat at the deck floor until her fists were splintered and bruised.

Joshua yelled, penetrating her heart's pain, "Mama, stop! Don't swear at Papa, he's dead."

She shook her head to clear the webs, staggered to her feet, struggled for control. She felt strangely empty and as though she'd been away, certainly not herself. Other passengers stood about, staring at her.

"We're sorry, Mama," David John sobbed, fists balled to his eyes.

"Oh, boys, what've I done? I didn't mean it, truly." Aurelia clasped them in her arms. She looked wildly for her baby, Zibby, and took her from a kind-faced woman's arms. "Thank you. I didn't mean to make a scene—"

"No need to be sorry. If your little girl has drowned you got a right to your grief," the woman in cranberry plaid said. "Let us help you, now. Come up to my cabin with me."

Aurelia was about to answer when a distant cry, a child's voice, floated to where they stood.

"Look there!" A male voice behind Aurelia shouted in hoarse triumph. "There she is."

Aurelia looked, saw a spot of blue, hardly dared to believe. On the far bank, coming out of the dank, swampy forest, was a Negro with a squalling Helen Grace in his arms. The roustabouts at the foot of the gangplank cheered.

"Oh, my God!" Aurelia passed Baby Zibby back to the woman in cranberry plaid who'd held her earlier, ordered the boys not to move, and flew down the plank. "Wait!"

On land, she slogged through mud and wood chips to meet the man with her child. Gnats and dragonflies swarmed into the air. Never had she felt such joy as seeing Helen Grace alive. "Thank you," she said, snatching Helen Grace into her arms. "Thank you!"

"Tyke's awful little, reckon she slipped down that gangplank and by all us with nobody seein'," the Negro woodcutter said. "I'se back in the woods, ready to carry out more logs, when I heard her. Chile cryin', lookin' for her daddy she said. Wanted to go home."

Tears coursed down Aurelia's cheeks. Swiftly, she examined Helen Grace. She was wet, muddy, and scratched from brambles, but all right. Her hysterical sobs began to ease now that she was in her mother's arms.

The Captain joined them, smiling, from his wallet he paid the woodcutter a reward. The Captain took Aurelia's arm, and escorted her and little Helen Grace back on board the *Flying Hawk*.

"I reckon you're mighty anxious to reach Kansas," the Captain said gently, when she was rejoined with her sons, the baby, all of her family.

"You have no idea," she told him, trembling from head to toe. "No idea."

Icy particles of early-spring snow swirled into the halted buggy and bit Aurelia's cheeks as she sat beside the driver of the rig she'd hired in Dodge City. She shushed her crying baby, hugging her close as she stared in disbelief. For almost a day and a half they had traveled under leaden skies, through the dreariest, most desolate country she had ever laid eyes on.

Twice before along the way she had noted crude and ugly shelters built into the side of a hill, like the one they faced. The front was made of slabs of sod, there was one dirty window, a stovepipe poked crookedly through the grassy roof. She asked the squat, tobacco-chewing driver a second time, "Are you sure this is Harlan Thorne's place, his *ranch?*" She rocked the whimpering baby in her arms, felt the small fevered cheek with the back of her hand. "There, there." She hoped tiny Zibby was only teething, had not contracted a disease. Her other children, tired, hungry, fussed in the seat behind her.

"Yup, 'tis." The driver spat over the side. "I reckon that's him ridin' this way from that ridge yonder." He hopped from the buggy. "I got to be gettin' back to Dodge, ma'am."

A lean rider loped toward them through lightly falling

snow. From his build and the way he rode he looked enough like John to be Harlan. Reluctance pulled at Aurelia as she allowed the driver to help her down. He unloaded her trunk and bags and set them at her feet.

"Is this Kansas?" David John piped as he and Joshua scrambled from the buggy.

"Yes, David John," she replied in a hollow, forlorn voice, "this is Kansas. Joshua, help Helen Grace down, please." Aurelia fought an urge to cling to the driver, beg him to take them with him. But she had already paid him with her last cent, and where would he take them *to?* The driver reined the rig around, tapped the driving horse lightly with his whip. Aurelia watched him leave, then she turned back, ill with misgiving. Besides her brother-in-law, the only living things in sight were a handful of scrawny, snow-flecked cows.

"Is that man riding over here a cowboy?" Joshua asked excitedly.

Aurelia sighed, "I suppose he is. Your Uncle Harlan."

He walked the roan the last few yards to where she stood, the horse tossed its head, snorted steam into the chill air. "You're John's wife? Aurelia? I'm Harlan." He removed his wide-brimmed hat, revealing a tan rawboned face. Wind tossed his dark hair, like John's. Snowflakes melted on the shoulders of his blanket coat and the thighs of his canvas pants.

"Yes," then she corrected, "his widow. And these are John's children."

"I was sorry to hear about John," he said quietly, clapping his hat back on and swinging down from the saddle. "Hadn't seen him in years, since we were both young'uns. I hoped he'd come out to Kansas, work with me here on the ranch. Ain't never gonna happen now. So these are his boys?" he grinned at Joshua and David John. "Good-lookin' little fellers, pretty little girl," he started to pat Helen Grace's head but she ducked behind Aurelia's skirts.

"I thought you would have a house," Aurelia addressed Harlan as she snuggled her sobbing baby and cooed to it. She stuck her knuckle in the tiny mouth, let the baby gnaw to ease the pain.

"I do!" He stared at her, puzzled, and dipped his head toward the cave in the hill. "Right there, my dugout. Cool in summer, warm in winter, tornadoes can't touch it," he said proudly. The yard was muddy from wet, melting snow; harness hung from pegs on the wall, other horse gear was scattered around.

"I beg to differ," Aurelia said, beginning to be really angry, "but what I'm looking at is not a house. And," she waved her arm at the scrubby acres stretching to the gunmetal skyline, "this is not the ranch you described to John!"

"I wrote him what I planned, that's all. Aurelia, I grant Kansas ain't like back home, but this is my—ranch. If you don't like it, you don't have to stay."

"I have no other choice," she admitted furiously. "None." She called the boys back from where they hopped about in the mud like frogs, trying to catch snowflakes on their tongue. "My baby is sick, my children are hungry, I'm tired enough to drop. Show me your *dugout.*"

The small, low-ceilinged single room was squalid. Battered pots and pans hung from pegs over a mud and stone fireplace where a small fire flickered. A pot of spoiled-smelling beans centered a large dry-goods box used as a table. Chairs were beat-up boxes and kegs. There were two cots covered by rank, shaggy buffalo robes. The floor was hard-packed dirt.

To Aurelia's shock, Harlan grabbed rounds of cow dung from a box and threw them onto the fire, sending up a shower of sparks. *Dung.* She moved closer to the warmth and asked, "Where is your partner?" How on earth could they all sleep, eat, live together as humans, in this close animal den?

"Ross got gored by a bull a while back. Bled to death before I found him. He was the best friend I ever had. We fought in the war together, rode together workin' cattle on a ranch north of here after that. I ain't had much heart for ranchin' since he died."

"I'm sorry." Aurelia was too frazzled, tired, and depressed to comment further for the moment. "If you'll show me where I can lay the baby, and what I might fix for supper, I'd like to feed my children."

"Put the little one over there on my bed," he waved toward one of the hide-covered cots. "Out yonder is my root cellar where I store beans, salt pork, and cornmeal. Might be some squashes. A little past the cellar is the spring where I get my water. Ice will have to be broke on it if this cold gets worse." He started toward the door, putting on his hat. "Be seein' you in a day or two."

"What?" Aurelia was stunned and hurried after him. "Where are you going? You're leaving us here alone?" Fear riddled her spine.

He shrugged, "I reckon you'll be all right. Gotta go to Dodge."

He ducked his head and went out the door. He poked his head back in, "Remember to keep the fire goin' with those cow-chips in that Arbuckle coffee box by the fireplace. That's what we use for fuel out here."

Aurelia was positive that fate had landed her in hell in the weeks that followed. The wind, grime, dust, and loneliness ground into her soul. She and the children ate sparingly, afraid their food would run out and they'd starve. She washed their clothing at the spring without soap, rubbed her knuckles raw. Harlan came and went, continuing his bachelor life as he always had, rarely did he remember to bring the provisions she requested he buy in Dodge City.

Day after day, she paced the hard-packed yard, stared into the vast distance, and searched her mind for a better answer to her situation. The wind laughed at her and threatened to drive her mad, the empty plains taunted. If God had ever listened to her, he did not heed her now. She would leave, go anywhere else on earth, but she had no money, no way to earn her way out to a decent, civilized life.

She never saw another soul except Harlan, and when he returned periodically for a day or two, they argued about everything.

And then one day two women and a boy and girl arrived at the dugout. Aurelia was thrilled to her depths to see them, but mortified to offer them hospitality in a hole in the ground. The old woman was called Grandma Spicy, the younger one, Meg Brennon. The fourteen-year-old girl was Lucy Ann. She and her brother, Lad, had inherited half of the property from their uncle, Ross McCoy.

Shortly after the newcomers arrived, Aurelia went out into the yard from the dugout, surprised to overhear Meg and Harlan making a deal for Meg to buy his half of the property. Meg had goods to trade, he wanted out, badly. "As part of the deal," he was saying, "my sister-in-law stays on here 'til she figgers whatever else she wants to do without me. I'm sellin' cheap on that fact alone."

Aurelia shriveled inside. She and her children—*traded* like sacks of inanimate grain that nobody needed or wanted.

# Chapter Four

"I can see it with my own eyes, and it's still hard to believe how much Paragon Springs is changing," Aurelia remarked to Owen as they strolled arm in arm about the townsite one evening.

"Even though you're behind it all?" he laughed.

"Not just me," she reminded. "Everyone involved in the project is working twice as hard as they've ever worked before and they're all determined to succeed."

Bringing their dreams of a fresh start and future prosperity, people had arrived from other parts of Kansas where life was less to their liking. Many came from long distances by train, first to Dodge City and then by farm wagon, rented buggy, or on foot or by horseback the rest of the way. Some stayed after a look, others had not.

Tents were scattered on the beaten grass, as there was no hotel yet and the road ranch could accommodate only a few boarders in the root cellar and livery shed. Some fixed temporary homes in their wagons. There were men with families, but several newcomers were bachelors; many were a transient population who hoped to hire out as carpenters, stonemasons, freighters. From a half dozen glittering campfires came the homey smell of outdoor cooking. Voices in conversation carried softly on the evening air; someone at the edge of camp played a lively tune on a mouth harp.

"It's different, all right," Owen said, "but you sure hated it here when you arrived ten years ago, didn't you?"

"You have no idea," Aurelia chuckled. "I brought my children all that distance from Kentucky on a most harrowing, frightening journey, then arrived to find that my brother-in-law lived in a *hole in the ground* and the children and I were expected to make that do."

"A dugout. Lots of folks in this country still live in dugouts, in case you've forgotten. Lack of trees, you know."

"To a southern woman at the end of her wits and expecting a real house, it was a hole in the ground! Home for a mole, or some other earth-animal, not humans. Yes, I hated it. It got a little better after Meg, Lucy Ann, and I started the road ranch, and immensely better after you came."

"Mmm, well-said." Owen turned and kissed her forehead.

"Not that it was really his fault, but I was so angry at my husband, John, for getting himself killed and forcing me to leave my home. Although I loved him, it was difficult to even look kindly on his memory. I'm sorry you're the one who had to pay for that, Owen." She leaned into his shoulder as they walked along. They circled a group of children playing tag. "It wasn't fair to make you wait, but I was so afraid of marrying again."

"I wanted you badly those three years, but I knew it would be worth the wait." He added softly, his eyes twinkling with intimacy in the dusk, "I knew that under that proper southern lady exterior lay wonderful passion—for life, for love."

Her face heated and she smothered a laugh, "You knew no such thing, Owen Symington!"

"I did. And you couldn't get rid of me now if you tried."

She held his arm tighter. "Thank you, Owen. I need you more than ever for this new dream of ours." They had reached the southwest corner of their proposed town, an area that had become a natural wagon yard. A makeshift corral had been put up and horses stood bunched and hipshot until fences and barns could be erected.

Aurelia and Owen watched the horses for a while and then

circled back. "Good evening, Miss Mullendore," Aurelia called to a middle-aged plain-looking lady who sat in front of her tent, sewing. "I'd like you to meet my husband, Owen. Owen, this is Maud Mullendore, she wants to establish a combination dressmaking shop and laundry in our new town."

Owen nodded, "Nice to make your acquaintance, Miss Mullendore. Aurelia has mentioned you. We're pleased you're here."

Maud Mullendore stood up, smiling. "No more pleased than I am, Mr. Symington." She grasped his hand. "I look forward to getting my little house and dress shop built."

"You've found someone to help you build?"

"Looks like there's plenty of folks to ask," she smiled over the townsite, "if I need help."

"Don't hesitate!" Aurelia told her, "we're all in this together."

In the days that followed, Aurelia was everywhere, suggesting lot selection—the chief rule being first come first served—giving advice on building plans and ordering supplies, asking for signatures on papers and collecting payments. A few bought their lot on credit; the town company contract required ten dollars down and ten dollars a month payment at two percent interest. Some paid cash, having sold out elsewhere to bring their dreams of a new start in a fresh country.

Most folks had brought with them a milk cow or two to be staked out, a crate of chickens, a dog. The noise of the animals, frolicking children, and men at work was an incessant but not unpleasant symphony that played dawn to dark at the townsite.

Sometimes, Aurelia was so tired she could hardly see as

she returned in the evening to their ranch and her little sod house and the chores awaiting her there. One night, after preparing her family's supper, she was too tired to eat. Owen watched her worriedly as she sat with her fork in her hand, unmoving. "Honey, you need to slow down, not work so hard. Rome wasn't built in a day and our little town won't be either."

"I'll be fine." She tried to smile at him. She made herself take a bite of potatoes and gravy but it took effort to chew.

Zibby offered sympathetically "I'll do the dishes alone tonight, Mama. You go to bed." She hesitated. "Can Rachel spend the night with me, Saturday?"

"Y-yes," she mumbled. She looked at Zibby, wondered if she were neglecting her child too much these days. "Yes, Zib, of course Rachel may spend the night." She stood up slowly. "But now, I think I will take you up on your offer to wash the dishes and I'll go to bed."

Before drifting off to sleep, she found herself thinking of home and family in Kentucky, both of which were no longer there, of course; she had only the memory. What would her mother, Charity Allen, a gentle southern woman, think of her daughter Aurelia's life in a place like Kansas? She would be shocked, she thought, but she'd also be proud that *a town* had become her daughter's passion, like one of her children. She sighed and closed her eyes, another busy day tomorrow.

Aurelia was resting for a moment in one of the chairs placed in the shade outside their old mercantile. Zibby was inside stacking new merchandise. Meg's baby, Pauly, was teething, and Meg had thought it best to stay home today. The sound of hammering rang in the air; three raw pine structures being raised cast a yellow glow on the trampled dusty landscape. Someone was singing as he sawed. Aurelia could hear the *thunk* of stone being unloaded at yet another site. A handful of dwellings and business houses would be built of sod for now, the quickest and cheapest to build, but in each case the lot owner intended to build a finer structure of wood and stone in the future. Several weeks of construction was changing Paragon Springs; Aurelia's and others' dreams blossoming into reality.

Admire Walsh, who Meg had made a full partner in her stone quarry business, had had to hire several men and their wagons to keep up with orders of stone for building. Numerous trips were made to Dodge City to haul lumber and window glass ordered and shipped by train from eastern Kansas. Which gave Ad cause to growl that getting a railroad line direct into Paragon Springs before building would have made better sense.

When Ad was a very young man, he had ridden for the Rocking A as a cowhand. Rock quarrying and farming had never suited him well, although for Lucy Ann's sake he stayed with it. Maybe it was the burden of work he didn't really like that often made him grumpy.

"Don't let Ad's grumbling bother you," Meg told Aurelia as they had watched the bustling construction together one morning. Meg had come out, leaving Lucy to mind the store and Meg's children, to tell Aurelia that Hamilton suggested they draw up a charter of city government soon. "Ad means well, but we're doing the right thing here."

"Oh, I'd worry about most everything," Aurelia had told Meg, "if there was time!" On occasion she worried about the risk of building the town first, but she and others were confident that they would gain county seat and a railroad soon after the town was established. Few dreams came true without taking risks. That country was perfect for raising cattle and grain, for manufacturing enterprise that would bring prosperity to owners and employers alike. One just had to have gumption.

She stood up now from the chair and shaded her eyes to see more clearly the rig rattling up the road. A while later, a buckboard drew up in front of her and a jolly-looking, stout little man leaped down. She told him who she was and he introduced himself as Oscar Wurst, his rosy cheeks plumping up in a smile. "I may be the first Wurst man you ever met, huh?" he joked. He asked more seriously, waving a plump hand at the structures under various stages of construction, and the mercantile at her back, "You think there is room for another store here, eh? Could be?"

"What kind of store, Mr. Wurst?" She motioned for him to take the other chair beside her as she sat back down. "I believe we have plenty of room for new business, sure another store. We have very nice lots available." She'd been promoting enough that it was becoming automatic.

"I think a grocery store to start. Later, maybe a butcher shop and a bakery making good dark bread and cakes. What do you think?" He gave her a wide smile. "I bring my family from Flagg, start up brand new here?"

*Flagg*. She wasn't surprised, actually. Settlers often pulled up stakes and moved to where the grass looked greener. And Flagg as a town was becoming home to more lazy no-goods, gamblers and outlaws than ordinary folk. "Of course you and your family are welcome to settle here, Mr. Wurst. Let me make sure my daughter is able to manage the store and we'll go take a look at what lots we have."

In a day or two Mr. Wurst was back with two wagons loaded with family and goods. He introduced Aurelia to his wife, Josephina, so like him in shape and personality that they could have been matching salt and pepper shakers. Also with him this time was his sister and brother-in-law, Lotta and

Claus Geyer. Claus, taller and more handsome than Wurst, wanted to open a barbershop and bathhouse. He also had experience as a dentist and could pull teeth. He and Lotta, a tiny, shy little woman, had three little stair-step children. Oscar and Josephina had five.

*School,* Aurelia was reminded, not for the first time. They must have a real school, a large school, and soon, for all the incoming children as well as those already living on outlying farms who would make the drive to town. For years now, Emmaline had taught their younger children in her home. That would no longer do. Emmaline was cramped as it was, running the newspaper from her house, too.

Dinah Ambler came to choose a lot in the new town. "I don't have half enough to do," she explained to Aurelia as they strolled the townsite under a bright morning sun. "My foreman runs the Rocking A. It's lonely now that Jack lives down in the strip." She shaded her eyes as she faced Aurelia, "Jack should've left you women alone, not been so determined to harass you into leaving the country so he'd have it all for himself for cattle grazing."

"He hated us."

Dinah tucked a flyaway strand of blond hair behind her ear. Her blue eyes clouded. "It's true he had no love for outsiders, homesteaders. He went too far when he got drunk, kidnapped Will Hessler and threw him onto that cattle car headed east. Will could have been killed, and Jack could have been sentenced to years in prison rather than given an invitation by the judge to leave the country."

Solemnly, Aurelia remembered that when Jack drove a large herd past Paragon Springs on his way south to the Strip, Meg's toddler, Vesta, had almost been run down and trampled. In a turn of character that surprised all of them, Jack had ridden hard and snatched the little girl out of danger. She supposed even a hard man like Jack Ambler could have a bit of good in him, and he was Dinah's husband. "It's over, thank goodness. Do you think Jack will return when his sentence is up?"

"I have no idea. But for now I have to think about myself." Dinah shook off gloom and smiled. "I'd like to have a small millinery shop, what do you think, Aurelia?"

"I think with your clever talents we'd all be lucky if you had such a shop." Her voice grew in excitement, "There is a small lot available on the east side of what will be Main Street." They headed that way.

"I want to be part of this hustle and bustle," Dinah said with a wave of her arm. "But I won't build just yet, I'll give the town time to grow some. I'll pay for my lot now so I won't lose it."

"Good idea. Lots have been selling rather easily, at one hundred to two hundred dollars per lot, depending on size and location. We've saved a few prime lots on Main Street which will sell for three hundred dollars or more, each."

"Just a small lot for me, please. As it is, Jack is going to have a fit when he finds out I've thrown in with you all, in your town. But I won't twiddle my thumbs and sit home on a pillow until he's served his sentence down there and can come home!"

To Aurelia's elation, Will and Bethany Hessler put the work of their farm in their nearly grown children's hands so they could build the first hotel in "downtown" Paragon Springs.

Bethany, her palms flat out in front of her, motioned for Aurelia not to be carried away the day they came to pick their lot. "It won't be a palace, mind, just a nice two-story building of white limestone with as many rooms as we can afford."

"We have family on the way from the East to help build," Will threw in. "And I've ordered materials."

"I'm so happy," Aurelia told them. "I have no doubt the hotel will be very nice and I can't imagine a business that would be more welcome."

From the time they'd arrived in that country years before, Will and Bethany had been better off than many of the settlers. During the terrible grasshopper plague in the seventies, family members back East had sent them food staples, and seed to replant in the spring. Will and Bethany had insisted on sharing with the families at Paragon Springs. Their soddy was one of the bigger and more elaborately furnished ones in the valley, with a real parlor. Aurelia was too fond of the couple to be envious of their good fortune.

Aurelia watched in amazement as the Hesslers' crew—husky, blue-eyed males of all ages, teamsters, stonemasons, carpenters, paperhangers, and general handymen—fell to, tackling the building of the hotel like a swarm of capable ants. Day after day they toiled, dawn to dark. A few weeks later, the modestly designed building stood there as if it had always been and carried the distinctive name, HESSLERS' MARBLE HOUSE HOTEL.

One day while Will and his relatives unloaded bedsteads and wash-stands, Aurelia toured the small rooms with Bethany. Two kinds of wallpaper were used, pink cabbage roses upstairs, and daisy chain and ivy on the main floor with dark wood trim. There were tables to seat more than fifty diners, guests and townspeople, in the dining room. "How wonderful this room will be, for town gatherings, banquets, wedding parties—!" Aurelia said. "Customers to my restaurant—when it's finished—will likely be, by comparison, cowboys drifting through, the farmer or ranch family come to town to trade, the businessman or -woman who just wants a home-cooked meal, nothing fancy."

"That's what I was thinking," Bethany replied as they visited the kitchen with its monstrous-sized stove, coolers and work tables. "Two dining places won't be too many. Will and I planned to wait awhile to furnish the hotel completely," she explained to Aurelia, "but Will's family couldn't see how an unfurnished hotel could succeed and they made donations in exchange for a share in the business. Will and I had savings to pay for the most of it."

Aurelia was as proud of the hotel as were the Hesslers and their industrious crew.

Almost immediately, some tent "residences" left their staked-out lots. Their occupants moved into the hotel to wait out in more comfort the building of their own dwellings. Within two days after opening, most rooms were filled at the Marble House.

With the hotel built and operating, the Hessler relatives, except for a brother and a nephew, departed. Lars, the father, and Dirk, the grown son, decided to establish a construction business in Paragon Springs and immediately hired themselves out. They sent for their families to join them, purchased lots on the edge of town to build their homes and business.

Aurelia, in the middle of it all, couldn't remember ever feeling such high excitement before, nor with it such total exhaustion. Her experience as a mother stood her well in bossing others, in giving directions as she went about her duties. Anyone who looked even remotely idle was given a job to do; sometimes it was giving someone a hand unloading a wagon, or raising roof timbers. Often, the chore was simply to haul water from the well so tired builders could have a drink and a good "wash up."

# Chapter Five

Aurelia laughed and groped under a length of freshly pasted blue and yellow floral wallpaper that had fallen back over her face. "Help, Lucy Ann! I can't see where I'm going."

Lucy Ann chuckled in turn, caught Aurelia's elbow and led her toward the side wall of the restaurant. There she climbed a crude homemade ladder to take over the top of the strip and place it carefully next to the ceiling. Their youngsters, Zibby and Rachel, rushed forward to do their part of smoothing the bottom of the strip in place.

For weeks Aurelia, with enormous pride and excitement, had watched and aided the building of her restaurant on a small lot between the hotel and the Jones brothers' dry goods and haberdashery. When the twenty-four- by thirty-four-foot structure with twelve-foot-high ceilings was completed, she and Lucy and their girls painted all the trim, shelves, tables and chairs a soft blue.

They oiled the plank floor. Owen and Ad carried in her beautiful new Home Comfort cookstove and an icebox and set them in the kitchen area. Crisp, yellow dotted-Swiss curtains awaited hanging at the large front window. Two potted ferns waited in the corner for placement.

Just because folks were in the West, they needn't have to eat in a hovel, she believed. Once the wallpapering was complete, the kitchen utensils and food supplies in place, she would be ready for business.

To combat the overpowering smell of fresh paint and wallpaper paste they had opened the door wide. Now, the soft thud of a horse's hooves and creak of buggy wheels coming from the west along Main caused Aurelia to hesitate in her work. Curious, she plopped her paste brush back into the paste bucket and walked to the door wiping her hands on her apron. Lucy followed and stood close behind her.

The collapsible top was down on the four-wheeled black business buggy drawn by a glistening black horse. The sun glinted off the buggy's crimson wheels and brass mountings. Noticing them watching, the driver, as fine looking as his conveyance, pulled back on the reins, halting the black.

"Forevermore!" Aurelia murmured. They seldom saw a man, or a woman for that matter, as finely dressed as the newcomer. He looked like a department store model, or a peacock, in his teal suit, white shirt, dark tie and pearl-gray Stetson.

"He looks rich," Lucy Ann commented softly. "If he's come to settle a business here, don't you suppose that this is one gentleman we don't want to let get away?"

"Indeed!" Aurelia poked a graying tendril of dark golden hair behind her ear, removed her apron, and went out to greet him. She hoped he was a doctor although he didn't look like one. Doctors were usually more threadbare. A doctor was the one professional she would yet like to see settle in Paragon Springs.

"Good day, sir. May I help you?"

From the shiny leather seat of his buggy he looked up and down their rough new main street. Handsome in a way, his brow above his biscuit-colored eyes was furrowed deep in study. His eyebrows and thick moustache were the same peachy-gray color as the hair at his temples. Around the thin, unlit cigarillo gripped in his teeth, a smile suddenly twisted up the corner of his mouth. He looked at her town like a starving man seeing his first platter of country-fried chicken in ages.

She followed his glance. In spite of raw newness, their town was already looking substantial and promising, she thought. The smell of pine lumber, the song of busy hammers, and rasp of saws filled the air. Three false-fronted frame buildings lined the north side of Main, and two stone and two frame structures sat on the opposite side. Other buildings, mostly two- and four-room residences, were going up on the side streets. Lumber and stone seemed to be piled everywhere.

The town company had officially named the streets and new signs were planted at the end of each. As a founder, Aurelia chose to name a street *Spencer*, for her home county in Kentucky. Meg chose to name her street *Dublin*. Lucy Ann chose to honor her uncle who left her the land and named her street *McCoy*. Other east-west streets were named Willow, Elm, and Locust. North to south streets were numbered, First through Sixth.

The gentleman had come just in time. Lots in the downtown section, if that's what would interest him, were first choice and going fast.

He looked at her but hardly seemed to see her, he was so interested in everything else. "Ma'am," he touched the brim of his pearly Stetson, "I'd be obliged if you'd direct me to the land office. I don't see a sign."

"We don't have a land office as such—" she began.

A fresh light came to his toast-brown eyes, and he gave the slightest nod.

*Profiteer,* she thought, hands on her hips as she sized him up. There was nothing wrong in a person wanting to succeed and accumulate money, but it depended on the person's motives, and equally as much, on his methods. Otherwise . . .

"A town company, then?" The flatness of his deep voice seemed forced, designed to hide his true thoughts, his excitement at seeing her town. But he'd already given himself away.

"Yes, we do have a town company." She nodded, stepped forward, and held up her hand. "My name is Aurelia Symington, Mrs. Symington. And your name, sir?"

"The name is Granville Harris." His tone was impatient as he politely touched her hand. "But everyone calls me Boot. Boot Harris. I saw an advertisement about this place—"

"We did our best." She couldn't keep away a smug smile. She and Emmaline had hoped but couldn't have known that their advertisement would turn out to be as successful as it had.

"The ad was a huge exaggeration," he said bluntly, puncturing her ballooning pride, "but looks like there is some promise here." He shook his head as if in doubt. "Right person might even be able to make the town into something close to the ad's description. I 'may' be interested in establishing here."

She started to reply to that but he raised his hand, "Let's not waste any more time, ma'am. I'd like to speak with whoever represents your town company." He had misunderstood when she had introduced herself. "Or whoever is in charge of land sales and lot selection. If you'd tell me his name and where I can find him?"

She didn't think she could call anyone *Boot* but she supposed she could try. "I can show you the available lots in town, B—Mr. Harris. Is there a particular kind of business you have in mind for here in Paragon Springs? What is your background?"

He looked agitated, like he might drive away. Then he removed his hat, a breeze riffling his thinning peach-gray hair. He told her, "I have soldiered, freighted, prospected. I took a two-year course of study at a pharmacy school back East. Most recently I owned a pharmaceutical manufactory in St.

Louis that was extremely successful, until—" he stopped. "No offense, ma'am," he said tightly as he yanked his hat back on, "but I prefer to speak to the man in charge of land sales and lot selection."

Goodness but he was slow, at least in this regard. She spelled it out carefully: "We do things differently around here, Mr. Harris. You are speaking to the president of the Paragon Springs Town Company. Me, myself, and I, Mrs. Symington, President. And I would be happy to show you what we have. Either on paper, or actual location of the lots, as you prefer. But first, it would be helpful to know what kind of business you intend to engage in, or if you want to build a home, or both!"

His reluctance to discuss such an important matter as real estate with a woman was obvious in his shocked, then mocking expression. Time ticked by before he told her, "I have more than one enterprise in mind, Mrs. Symington. One of them would likely be a drug store. I can come to a decision after I see what's available." He grumbled, "Show me the actual lots, I'll look at your papers later."

"Fine. If you would like to tie your horse . . ." she nodded toward their brand new busy windmill, the big watering tank and hitch-rack, "we'll walk the street." To her the whirring of the blades above them was a sound of progress, optimism. She wondered if he noted that, too.

"I'll drive." He nodded toward the toes of his fine leather boots propped high on the buggy's footrest. "Got bad feet. Corns," he told her indelicately. "I haven't been able to find a decent-fitting pair of boots since I was fourteen. I never walk if I don't have to. Ma'am?" He motioned with his head toward the seat beside him, moved as though he would get down and assist her into the buggy.

"I'll walk, but you suit yourself, Mr. Harris."

They continued his easterly direction along the street and she was sure they looked ridiculous as she strode alongside his buggy, pointing and explaining as he drove slowly. But it was his choice. "The large corner lot next to the Marble House Hotel to our left is still available. It costs," she decided to raise the price from three-hundred, "four hundred dollars. The smaller empty lot just west of it is available for two hundred dollars." When he didn't answer she continued, "Of course, there are many cheaper lots available on the side-streets, but downtown here most of the best lots are taken as you can see. We plan a town square in the central area over there," she pointed to a dusty area where children and dogs played, "so that area is unavailable for building."

She gave him another long study. It was possible that he could provide a very necessary addition to Paragon Springs' businesses. A small oddity or two about him was harmless. But that gleam in his eye was unsettling.

Maybe she only imagined his uncommon greed, his wish to ignore her position? Heavens! Who would have believed she would become so possessive of the role she hadn't in the least wanted in the beginning? But she was letting her mind stray.

"You can see for yourself that we already have one hotel, a dry goods store and men's haberdashery." She nodded over her shoulder. "The small building back there, between the hotel and dry goods store, is a restaurant, which will open soon. That is my establishment." He still wasn't talking but he was looking hard at everything. They came to the east end of Main and she motioned toward the older buildings to her left that made up the road ranch. "There's where Paragon Springs began. Several of us have lived here for ten years. We've made our living off the land and by operating a road ranch, but we've planned a thriving town in this spot from the beginning."

79

His only response was a shrug. She told him, "We'll turn around here for a look at the other side of Main." With a light touch of his whip he turned his driving horse in the middle of the street, the wheels of his rig rolling smoothly.

Harris cracked a thin smile at the sign in the window of Wurst's Grocery Store: *The Wurst Store In Town—The Best Place To Trade.* Next came Maud Mullendore's small dressmaking shop, with her residence and laundry business in back. Drying clothing popped in the wind from a clothesline in the backyard. Maud, as it turned out, was a widow, a friendly woman and a hard worker. Moving slowly, they passed the new combination Paragon Springs *Echo* office and post office. Emmaline had been appointed by the government to take over postmistress duties from Aurelia.

At the end of the street beyond Pennybaker's hardware store were empty lots with small flags waving in the warm breeze. Harris halted his rig and studied those lots for several minutes before they turned back the other way.

Across the street, through the open door of her restaurant, Aurelia could see that Lucy Ann and the girls had moved ahead with the paper hanging. Lucy Ann waved and she waved back, nodding her thanks.

They were passing the general store when Bethany Hessler stepped out, a large grocery basket of parcels on her arm. "Hello, Aurelia," she smiled. She stood looking for a moment at Boot Harris in the buggy, before turning back to Aurelia. "Will you be coming to the hotel later?"

"I believe so," Aurelia answered. She was about to introduce Harris to Bethany but he seemed to have arrived at his decision, wanted only to get on with business.

He pointed behind them. "That lot at the west end of Main, south side past the hardware store, is it available?"

"I'm sorry, no. That lot has been spoken for. A young

couple now living in Dodge City want to establish a saddlery on that spot."

Essie and Ben Reid, who refused to buy on credit, were working to earn the cash to pay for the lot and build. Young Ben worked twelve hours a day at a boot shop, then half the night at a Dodge livery. Essie was a seamstress and hotel maid. They wanted desperately to move from Dodge, and to establish their own business. At first, they had offered Aurelia Ben's pocket watch, and Essie's wedding ring to pay for the land but she had refused.

Instead she had promised to hold the lot they wanted until they could pay, allowing them six months to earn the money. The town company backed her on her agreement with the Reids. The Reids hoped to have the money before the six months deadline.

"*Spoken* for?" Harris's thin cigar bobbled on his lip. "No cash down, no contract?"

She shook her head.

He mocked, rolling his eyes, "Now that's a *fine* way to do business."

Despite being rankled by his ridicule of her methods, she managed to speak calmly, "Essie and Ben are good, hard-working, honest young people, Mr. Harris. The town company likes to see their sort settle here. The Reids will be an asset to our community."

He glared at her, waved his cigar. "Give them one month, make it two, to pay up. If they don't, I want the lot." He shoved the cigarillo back in his mouth, reached inside his vest and pulled out his leather money pouch.

She was about to say that he had no right to arbitrarily change their rules and that he could take his money elsewhere when she saw that the leather pouch was stuffed as full as a Christmas turkey with money. The town really, really could use more funds. *Cash.* Many of the lots were sold on credit. She caught her breath, said nothing.

He motioned with his head to the opposite side of the street. "In the meantime, I want those two lots for sale east of the hotel on the corner and I'm prepared to pay for them today in full."

She was speechless, thinking *six hundred dollars.*

He lipped his cigarillo from one corner of his mouth to the other, his grin acidic. "Now, do we do business out here on the street, Mrs. Symington? Or do you have an office?"

"I have a—place to do business," she muttered. She struck off without another word across the street toward the Marble House, the buggy rattling as he swung it around to follow behind her. Of late, Bethany had let her use a back table in the dining room for paper work involving land buyers. So far, because they had no city hall, important city papers were stored in a locked pantry cupboard at the hotel, which was handier than Hamilton Gibbs' small office in their soddy. Town money, because they had no bank yet, either, was at home under her and Owen's bed-tick. What funds there were, of course. There wasn't a great amount yet.

She was glad not to share any of that information with the stuffy, know-it-all Boot Harris who she was sure would be critical. At the same time, it was better not to put him off. She might not like his attitude but the town could likely profit from his presence, from his investments. Cash was scarce.

A short while later Aurelia sat alone at the table staring at the forms Harris had filled out and signed, the impressive stack of bills near her hand. Bethany walked over beaming to refresh her tea. Seeing Aurelia's frown, she asked, "The fine-looking gentleman's money is good, isn't it? Paragon Springs needs the likes of him, seems to me."

Aurelia nodded. "Mr. Harris plans to build a drug store on

the corner past your hotel, and he's thinking, too, of having a mortgage and loan business. Everything is in order, yes." And it was, and as legitimate as sunshine as soon as she got Hamilton's signature and seal on the papers. So why, with no real cause, did she feel as though she had just made a contract with the devil? Sighing, she mentally scolded herself for her flyaway imagination. She might be misjudging Mr. Granville "Boot" Harris. Who was to say that he had ulterior motives?

She tucked his money into her reticule. The cash was a godsend for the city. Before very long they must establish city government. They would need funds to erect a building to house records and conduct city business and general meetings. They needed to hire a sheriff and he would need an office. Until they set a tax, money would have to come from somewhere to pay him for his services.

They needed a proper school building to accommodate the growing number of children moving into the community. A church and money to pay a minister. And the list went on. She sighed and rose to her feet. For now there was Owen and Zibby's supper to think about. She had a sudden yearning to be fixing supper for her sons, too. For them all to be a regular family again. She wanted to see her sons, have them *home*.

# Chapter Six

"Mama," Zibby called into their new restaurant kitchen where Aurelia was cutting biscuits to meet the evening demand, "Mr. and Mrs. Reid are here to talk to you."

Aurelia glanced at Zibby over her shoulder for a moment, eyes wide with surprise, then she brushed her floury hands off on a towel and went out to greet the young couple. She hadn't expected to see them for months.

Ben's hat was clasped in front of him, his curly brown hair mussed around his large ears. Essie was as plain as a little hen dove beside him. But their manner was electric with excitement, their smiles spoke of good news.

She greeted them with an expectant smile. If they were there to buy their lot, they had beaten their deadline *and* Harris's. She wouldn't have obeyed his request, anyhow—order, really—that she shorten the time limit and sell to him if the Reids couldn't comply. "Hello, Ben. Hello, Essie. You both look fine today." She led the way to a table where they all took chairs. She had been on her feet all day, it was a welcome relief to sit. "To what do I owe this visit?"

"We have our money for the lot," Ben told her, beaming. "And we want to buy two more lots in that southwest end of town, too. We have cash money."

"My Goodness!" Aurelia smoothed back her hair, unable to contain her surprise although she'd guessed why they might be there. "Zibby, would you pour us some coffee, dear?" She asked the Reids, "What's happened? I know how hard you've both worked, but—"

Ben explained, holding his cup for Zibby, "When Essie's

folks back in Sycamore, Indiana, heard about our plans, they wrote that they wanted to partner with us. They sold out and sent us the money to start up. They're on the way here right now. Besides the saddlery, Mathis, he's Essie's Pa, wants us to have a wagonworks. Mathis can repair or build a wagon better'n anybody you ever saw."

"Well, I declare—that's simply wonderful!" She nodded at them over the rim of her cup. "We'll do the paperwork after I close this evening. I can't leave just now, the evening rush is starting." She nodded to where Zibby hurried about like a flushed-face little copy of herself, showing Maud Mullendore to a table. The fragrance of roasting beef and onions had overcome the fresh-paint-and-wallpaper-paste odors of the restaurant.

Maud sniffed appreciatively and waved at Aurelia, "Good evening. Whatever you've fixed this time, Aurelia, it smells delicious!"

"Good evening," Aurelia nodded and smiled. Maud dressed very plain for a woman who could make such beautiful clothing. Tonight she wore a simple, almost drab gray frock, her beaming smile and friendly manner her only real adornment. Which, when one thought about it, were quite adequate.

While Maud studied the menu written on the signboard at the front of the room, Zibby laid out her cutlery. Then she scooted off to clear another table of dirty dishes. The Jones brothers, Luther and Silas, in dark suits and slicked hair, came in at that moment, no doubt for an early supper. Zibby, her small arms loaded, nodded in confusion at them to take whatever table they chose.

Aurelia would help in another minute, but she didn't want to be rude to the Reids. They were her business, too. *Good* business.

"We got everything we own with us right now," Ben was saying. "We'd like to unload before nightfall what we'll need right off." He nodded toward the window. Outside at the rail stood their team hitched to a wagon piled high with a tent, stove, table and chairs, bed-ticks, and other household goods.

"Of course! Go on over to your place and set up however you want. That plot is the same as yours." She saw them to the door and hurried to help Zibby, her mind flying ahead to one of the things the town company might purchase for the community, using the Reids' money.

It would be a good idea, she thought, to have a large bell to hang at the top of the public windmill. She had been wanting to do that from the first. The bell could be used to warn folks of fire, to call them together for news, or for alarm of any sort.

The rush to the new town began to slow. People came and looked, but moved on. A few others bought and settled in.

One day, Aurelia was showing a dark little man named Elliot Charbonneau around town and she could tell he was seriously interested. She had spent nearly an hour with him while they strode about and he, with his eyes, studied and sized the town. Sometimes he would stand in one spot for a full five minutes in deep thought, his arms folded across his chest. He wanted to establish a lumberyard, he'd told her, stocking lumber and other building materials shipped from the east.

He decided on several lots on the southern edge of town. "This would be a good location for the railroad to go through, here on the south side," he told her. She smiled and nodded agreement. She and Owen had also decided the south side was best for their eventual railroad. If it turned out that way, the line would run right along Charbonneau's property. He had chosen well. He explained with a frown of caution, "I'll wagon-freight my wood products in now from a distance, but without a direct railroad to make the freighting quicker and cheaper, I may not be able to stay in business."

"I guarantee we will get a railroad through here, Mr. Charbonneau." Maybe she was wrong to make such a strong promise, but she did it out of very positive feelings. In its turn, they would get the railroad.

He gave her a maybe-yes, maybe-no look, but he pulled out his wallet and followed her to her back-corner office at the hotel.

Her next prospect excited Aurelia so much she could hardly contain herself. As much as any other profession, she wanted a medical doctor for Paragon Springs. Her candidate, Doctor Stuart, a tall, thin, slightly stooped-shouldered man with silver hair and a very serious expression, had arrived in his buggy late one afternoon. After being told that she was the person in charge, he had been sent to her restaurant. He got over his surprise that she was town company president quicker than Harris had.

From the first, though, he seemed disappointed in what she showed him. Or at least not as interested as Mr. Charbonneau had been or Boot Harris before him. He would frown, shove his hands in his pockets, walk quickly on. Maybe, she thought, with deepening concern, he was a man of little vision.

"I truly believe this spot right here would be perfect for your office and home," she told him, showing him a lot on the east side of Main. "All the conveniences of downtown would be right at hand. We're going to have a drug store in short order, right over there." She pointed out Harris's lot across the dusty street catty-corner. At the same time, she managed to bury her personal feelings, her worries, about Harris. Among the wagon-loads of goods Harris had brought in was an amazing number of kegs of whiskey. He dispensed whiskey from his wagon for the slightest ill a worker complained of—which made her desire a qualified doctor on hand more than ever.

Doctor Stuart's steel-blue eyes surveyed the dirt streets, the twenty or so dwellings and businesses in various stages of construction, and he shook his head. "This place is too small, I'm afraid, to support a doctor, it couldn't afford him a decent living."

"You can have a second business, Doctor Stuart," she rushed to suggest. "Many Paragon Springs folks have more than one trade. Our barber will have a bathhouse and he's also a dentist. His brother, Mr. Wurst, our butcher and grocer, has taken up four hundred acres outside town where he also intends to farm."

Land was always a good investment. If not rich, yet, in luxuries, most of the founding women of Paragon Springs had been proud landowners since the early days. "You could have a nice farm or ranch, Doctor Stuart. And I have every confidence the town itself, the population—which at the moment stands at nearly one hundred and fifty—will grow to many times that number given time."

He was direct. "I'm not a farmer, Mrs. Symington, nor a stock rancher. I have no desire to attempt to eke out a living at a line I abhor. I prefer city life. Your town is not what I expected, and I can't afford to wait for it to grow, if it does at all."

"Won't you at least think over the prospects, not decide right away?" she asked, hiding her dislike of his attitude.

He shrugged, finally answered. "I'll think it over. I'm staying the night at the hotel. I'll give you my final answer in the morning."

★ ★ ★ ★ ★

When she arrived at the hotel at the appointed time next day, Bethany informed her that Doctor Stuart had checked out. He had left a message for her that Paragon Springs was not the place for him.

"I'm sorry," Bethany said, touching Aurelia's hand. "I know how much you want a doctor for our town, how much we all do." As Aurelia turned away she grabbed her arm. "Doctor Stuart did make a suggestion. He said that two years ago a law was passed that all practicing physicians must register in *The Physicians Register* at the office of county clerk. According to the law, doctors beginning practice are expected to have completed two years of study at a reputable medical school. On the other hand, doctors who've been practicing two years or more before this new regulation may continue even if they haven't had proper medical training. Stuart believes you may find the right man on such a list."

"Our county seat is temporarily at Flagg. It would be a miracle if they had such a registration list over there! But I'll find out, one way or the other."

Aurelia drove the seven miles to Flagg that same day. As she drove through town, she shook her head at the rundown, shiftless feel of the place. She ignored the stare of a pair of drunks lazing in front of a saloon, drove around a black dog sleeping amidst litter in the middle of the street. When the time came for a serious election, Flagg would be no competition at all for the new town of Paragon Springs.

She drove another two miles to the farm of the county clerk, Wilbur Shaw. He was plowing in the field behind his sod shack and he halted his shaggy brown team with a show of irritation when she flagged his attention with her handkerchief.

He didn't bother to remove his battered felt hat to her, and

89

scoffed when she told him what she was after. "We don't got any list like that, I never heard of such a thing." His eyes in his grubby, bewhiskered face were disinterested.

She hadn't heard that Flagg had a doctor, but she asked him, to be sure.

"No, Flagg ain't got no doctor. Don't need one. Our women tend the ailin'. The other month a fella crushed three fingers between some rocks in an accident. My wife cut them fingers off with my razor and her sewing scissors, tucked the skin in place and sewed it up. Fella's doin' fine, paid us with a chunk of pork," he finished proudly.

After another few minutes of conversation that turned out to be equally useless, Aurelia thanked him with a tight smile and returned to her rig. She wasn't surprised that their county had no such register for doctors. And Shaw was right when he said women normally gave what medical attention was necessary in a community. At home she kept a basket of herbs, tonics, and salves for her family's use and to help a neighbor when called on. She kept such a kit handy now at her restaurant. She had treated two smashed thumbs, some strains and sprains during the recent construction. Harris had treated other ailing folks with whatever nostrums he had, but mostly with whiskey. Without a doubt, they were not equipped—in the absence of a qualified doctor—to treat serious accident or illness. She would keep hoping and looking for such a person to establish his practice in Paragon Springs.

A second doctor came to look them over, and arrived at the same conclusion as Doctor Stuart's—the town's population was too small to provide a doctor a good living.

It took Aurelia days to overcome her disappointment this second time at not gaining a physician. But she would not give up. In the meantime, the hustle and bustle of construc-

tion and general activity in the raw new town continued as
steadily as ever.

For her house in town she had chosen a location on
Spencer Street. It was around the corner and down one block
from her restaurant and the Jones Brothers Dry Goods Store
and Haberdashery. She hadn't the finances yet to build, or
even the time to plan her house. It was hard not to envy Luther and Silas their fine residence, almost finished on the lot
next to hers.

From the first, the dignified gentlemen showed themselves to be a valuable asset to the town. Surprising everyone,
they joined in on the dirtiest jobs, from digging the well to
shoveling manure, although they left the building of their
house and store to qualified carpenters and finishers. They
were very generous with encouragement to those who needed
it, equally generous with credit at their store. They would be
good neighbors. She could hardly wait to have her own new
house. For now she would continue driving each morning
from their ranch, and home again to the soddy at night. It
wasn't so far from the ranch that she couldn't walk to town,
but wild cattle and snakes made walking through the fields
less than safe. Owen had bought her a fast little driving mare
and it was hard to know how she had gotten along without the
sorrel she named Sweet Annie.

Within days after his arrival, Boot Harris had bought up
several claims on the far outskirts of town, small farms from
folks not doing well. There was no dishonesty or particular
trickery involved, some folks were just too lazy for the hard
work necessary to make the land pay, or they were the
"mover" type, who never stayed long in one place, anyhow.
They chose to try their hand yet again elsewhere on Harris'
payment. It was said that he was loaning money to others who

wanted to stay, who were willing to put up their farm for collateral for needed funds to buy new equipment, or stock animals, or seed for spring planting.

He had also bought several lots in Flagg with intentions to also build there. Spreading his wealth, Aurelia supposed. He would want ownership, businesses, in whichever town was made permanent county seat. With some counties, that was a matter that in some instances took years to settle.

She wondered about the source of his money, and decided that it must come from the successful pharmaceutical business in St. Louis that he had mentioned. No one seemed to know any more about him than he'd already told her. But many folks liked him and trusted him. They didn't seem to note, as she did, that he most readily loaned money to those who would have difficulty paying him back and would probably lose their farm to him. To her mind he was building his own personal holdings beyond any one man's needs.

He was building an impressive structure of beautiful white stone on his lot at the corner of Main and Third and when she could no longer hold back her curiosity, Aurelia paid a call at the Harris construction site for a close look and to ask questions. He had mentioned opening a drug store, but he hardly needed such a large building for that. She found him out front, talking with two of his workmen about a problem with the pillars for the porch they were starting to build. The building itself was all but completed. A foundation for a smaller structure had been laid on his other lot next to the Marble House Hotel.

While she waited for him to finish with his workmen, she took in details of the stone building. It was two stories high, with four arched windows in front upstairs. Flanking the downstairs double doors in front were two tall narrow windows. A flight of stairs went up on the far left. She walked around and noted that along each side of the building were six windows, three on the top floor, three on the bottom. He certainly meant to hide nothing, with so many windows!

"Mrs. Symington?"

She started, felt her face warm that he might have read her mind. "I was admiring your building, Mr. Harris." She got to the point, "What business have you decided to carry on here? Will it be a drug store? The establishment is quite large . . ."

His smile was congenial. "I will have a drug store—downstairs in front. Make use of my studies as an apothecary. I'll carry on my mortgage and loan business in back on the main floor. Upstairs will be my living quarters, as well as offices for rent to others."

She didn't know whether to be glad or worried about his intentions to operate a pharmacy. If he ran a straightforward, honest drug store, she could be glad. But if—as was happening in many towns since prohibition was voted in—his drug store was simply a front for selling whiskey, she was going to be upset indeed. "A drug store will be very beneficial, particularly until a doctor settles here in Paragon Springs."

"Afterward, too," he corrected. "Besides tinctures, nostrums and pills, I will carry a full line of notions: perfume, stationery. Paints, oils, dye-stuffs. Tobacco, cigars. School supplies, soda water, licorice sticks—" The wind sent dust twirling by and when it was past he brushed his trouser legs.

"Of course." She nodded. "I suppose you'll be dispensing whiskey from your drug store, to ease pain and as an antiseptic?" She could hardly argue about the practice, although she would hate to see it abused.

Two years before, Kansas was the first state to pass a prohibition law. Unfortunately, the law was largely ignored, especially in her part of the country. Saloons operated openly, catering chiefly to men in the cattle trade, but to others, too. Local sheriffs and politicians simply looked the other way. Or dealt a small, meaningless fine to the saloon owner who went right on operating illegally. Word was that there were twenty-three saloons in Wichita regularly paying fines, and that there were a dozen more places there—drug stores, joints—from where whiskey was easily procured.

"I am a licensed druggist, Mrs. Symington, permitted by law to dispense liquor for 'medical, scientific, and mechanical purposes.' "

Which covered any excuse a man might profess to obtain whiskey, she thought to herself, frowning. She honestly had no objection to men drinking in moderation. Owen liked an occasional peach brandy, a toddy. Her first husband, John, sometimes drank whiskey with his friends. But she was thoroughly opposed to the sort of saloon dives that lined the streets in Dodge City, making it the hellhole it was.

The times she'd been to Dodge, it seemed the majority of the population was sotted with drink and senseless. She could never let that happen to Paragon Springs. Their town would be a good and decent place to raise families or she would die trying to make it so!

To be sure he understood her mind, and that of most of the other townsfolk, she said, "Mr. Harris, though whiskey is required in some medical treatments, I want to make it clear that Paragon Springs isn't the place for free-flowing alcohol."

"You mean a saloon? I believe Paragon Springs ought to have *two or three* saloons if it is ever going to amount to anything as a town."

His proclamation shocked her. "Forevermore, why?"

"There are several good reasons, Mrs. Symington. Men like a place to relax and talk business, drink with friends, play a few card games. I want to warn you, right now: a town without a saloon will never be voted county seat." He cocked his head at her, tucked his hands in his vest pockets. "I believe becoming county seat is Paragon Springs' chief aim? And I don't have to tell you a town *not* county seat won't thrive for long. Not out here."

"You are telling me that a town not providing sinful entertainment can't succeed?" She held onto her hat in the hot blowing wind.

"If you want to put it that way, yes. Exactly."

Besides drinking, most saloons in western Kansas had as sidelines prostitution and gambling. She would rather see Paragon Springs die, than to put up with such debauchery. But, one way or another, she would show him that a town could survive without vice. "You speak poppycock, Mr. Harris. Sin doesn't spell success. We're a community of decent folk and we don't need a saloon. We're just a small farm town—"

"To survive, Paragon Springs will have to be a lot more than just a farm town. Of course whether that happens is up to you and the rest of the citizens." One of his men was calling him, and he excused himself.

"Boot Harris worries me something dreadful," she complained to Owen a few nights later as they prepared for bed.

He undid his tie. "What do you mean?"

"I've watched his actions lately, and I've heard things from some of the wives." She fastened the ribbons at the throat of her nightgown. "Workmen go to him for a dose of whiskey to ease the slightest ill. A smashed thumb, a 'bothered' stomach, a *chill* in summer! Why, the other day a workman fell over a sawhorse and couldn't get up, he was so sotted!"

Owen sighed and nodded that he was aware as he yanked off his boots.

She looked for her hairbrush, found it where it belonged on her dresser. "Providing them liquor illegally isn't all of it, either. He worms his way into folks' confidence. He buys folks out that can't make a go of their farms. He loans ready cash to those who want to stay. People like him."

"Now, Aurelia, loaning folks money isn't a crime." He dropped his trousers, picked them up and folded them over the back of a chair and stood stretching in his shirt and long-johns.

"Don't you defend Boot Harris!" Seated on the edge of their bed, she brushed her hair so hard it crackled. "I tell you the man is greedy as sin. In the guise of kindness, he is gobbling up this town and half the country around it! So that eventually he can run it how he pleases, I'm positive of that! He agrees to cash loans so fast folks don't stop to realize they have just handed to him for security the very things they need to survive: their wagons, stock animals, their homes and land."

She went on, "Not to mention their wife's treasures. Why, Dirk Hessler's wife, Rilda, borrowed money for Dirk on her mother's fine china from the old country. What if she doesn't get her dishes back? What if Boot Harris sells her china to someone else from his drug store? I don't like it one bit. I'm responsible for his being here. I sold him those downtown lots, without really knowing what he might be up to."

Owen peeled off his shirt. He wore a quiet, earnest grin meant to calm her down. "He might not be up to anything. Maybe he is just a good businessman trying to make a profit in land and loans and running a business or two. Sweetheart," he came over to sit beside her and pulled her close into his arms, "these folks selling out to him or accepting his loans, buying a dose of whiskey for whatever reason, are grown people. They are responsible for their own decisions and actions." He kissed her tenderly on the mouth. She melted inside although she still wanted to argue. "You can't," he whispered against her temple, "mother-hen the whole town, Aurelia."

She nestled her face against his chest, drew in the clean spicy clove scent of his soap and thought about what he had said. It was probably true that her duties called for her to simply locate folks. Not mind or care about them further. But that wasn't her way, she could never be like that and she couldn't believe the town would survive under that method. "Oh, yes I can mother-hen this town!" she insisted, mostly to herself. "It's part of what I've taken on."

For the moment, though, what she wanted most was Owen. He—his closeness—had stirred feelings in her the last few moments. She wanted to forget for the time being every other thing but him, but *them* in their bed. She drew away and scrambled under the covers, right smartly, she thought, for a hard-worked woman. "Owen?" She smiled and held out her arms to him.

"Ah, lady," he said huskily, crawling under the covers beside her and pulling her close. "Ah, lady, sometimes I don't know what to make of you, but all the tea in China couldn't buy you from me."

Laughing softly, their lips met.

# Chapter Seven

The Hesslers planned very soon to run a stage-line in conjunction with their hotel. Every two days, the stage would make the trip south to Dodge City, southeast to Spearville, and then northeast to Larned. But in June the only way to transport Aurelia's sons home for the summer was for Owen to fetch them.

Busy though she was, time crawled for Aurelia at the restaurant awaiting their return. Then, late in the afternoon with dusk just around the corner, she spotted their wagon drawing up outside with the boys on board. It was impossible to contain the overwhelming joy she felt.

"My sons are here! Please excuse me for just a moment," she begged Maud and Dinah, Lucy Ann and Rachel, her customers at the moment. They smiled and waved her toward the door.

"Zib," she called her daughter from wiping dishes, "they're here!" Leaving on her apron, which ordinarily Aurelia would never wear out into the street, she grabbed Zibby's hand and tore through the door.

"Oh, boys! Joshua, David John!" She tripped and nearly fell over their carpetbags they had just put down. She grabbed first one son, then the other in a long tight hug. She scarcely heard, over her own cries of joy, their exclamations of "Hello, Ma!" Then their squirmy protests of "Ahh, Ma," at being held so long. She finally stood back with tears in her eyes as the gangly, grinning boys, with shy teasing, greeted their sister.

Rachel had followed them outside and she smiled a quiet

hello. David John turned beet red at sight of her. Although he tried to pretend otherwise, his glance was full of adoration. Aurelia smiled—those two had been fond of one another for farther back than she could remember. Rachel was a pretty little thing in a yellow bonnet and a sheer lawn dress printed with dainty yellow flowers. She was a child, and David John not yet sprouting whiskers, but when they came of age—who knew what might happen?

Surely her sons had grown inches since she'd seen them at Christmas! Joshua at sixteen looked more like his dark handsome father every day. Sandy-haired David John, a year younger, looked like her and he—well, he was handsome, too. How could she ever let them go again, so far, for so long? Her heart ached thinking of it. But now she had them home for the whole summer!

"We brought presents from Larned," David John was saying. "A brooch for you, Ma. A doll for Zibby. And we got Owen—Pa, a cob pipe!"

"Well, come on then! Bring them into the restaurant. Are you hungry?" She stopped and waited, smiling. Both boys were looking around as though they had arrived in a foreign land. "Looks different around here, doesn't it?" she asked softly. In truth, Paragon Springs had changed dramatically in the past few months and although she'd written them letters to describe the process, they couldn't know exactly how it would look until now.

"Sweetheart, I'll put up the wagon and feed the horses." Owen motioned in an easterly direction toward the crude soddies and sheds that made up the road ranch they'd all started out in.

"Go ahead," she nodded, still watching her sons. The original homestead soddies at the east edge of town were all that was familiar for them now. Raw new businesses lined the plowed streets, buggies and horses were tied to spanking-new hitch-rails. Most folks going about on errands were strangers to her sons. Behind the old Thorne place, the Hesslers were erecting a huge hotel barn which would also be headquarters for their stage-line.

The soddy where they had all lived together the first years had recently been sold by co-owners, Lucy Ann and Meg. It was being given a fresh coat of whitewash. The buyers, named Morgan, had built an addition and were operating it as a boarding house.

With a satisfied sigh, Aurelia turned away and within minutes had settled Joshua and David John at a table inside her restaurant—after introducing Maud and allowing Lucy Ann and Dinah a chance to say hello to them. She brought her sons large plates of steaming beef and noodles, piccalilli, and warm yeast buns. Between bites of food they spilled over with stories of school. To them, interesting news had little to do with actual studies, but who had been caught at what prank and forced to stay in after school. David John kept sliding glances toward Rachel at the table with her mother, but when Rachel smiled shyly back at him, he pretended ignorance of her presence.

Joshua said that on Saturdays most everyone turned out to watch the Santa Fe train arrive. Aurelia was stunned to hear that a streetcar line—and the boys could hardly wait to ride—was being laid in Larned. "A streetcar line?" she asked. "Is that true?"

"Sure, mother, a streetcar line," David John said. "Larned is a modern town."

Joshua, older, seeing his mother's face, added, "But Larned will never be as good a place as Paragon Springs." He looked around. "I'll bet Paris hasn't got a café any prettier than your restaurant, Ma. And I know those Paris chefs can't cook as good as you do."

The other women, overhearing, chuckled.

"Thank you, Joshua," Aurelia said. For his world knowledge, knowing a bit about Paris anyhow, she cut him another slice of butterscotch pie.

David John, his eyes on Rachel as he reached for his water glass, accidently knocked it over, spilling water over the table. Trying to mop it up, he dragged his sleeve through his own pie. When Zibby and Rachel burst into a riot of giggles, he flushed and his eyes filled with fury and hurt. A short time later when Lucy Ann and Rachel said goodbye as they left the restaurant, David John choked out, "Goodbye, Aunt Lucy Ann." He looked right past Rachel.

"David John, that was rude!" Aurelia scolded when Lucy Ann and Rachel had gone and her sons were back at their table. "Why would you treat Rachel that way? You know you're fond of her."

"He's sweet on her, that's what," Joshua teased with a laugh.

"I'm not!" David John protested, leaping to his feet. "She's a baby, and she's dumb like Zibby. I don't like either one of 'em."

"David John, that's not true! Maybe they hurt your feelings, son, by laughing at you," her voice softened, "but you need to ignore things like that. I'd like for you to apologize to Rachel the very next time you see her."

He didn't answer, but his jaw set in the same way her own did when she was feeling stubborn. For the moment, Aurelia decided to let it go.

After a few days of being treated like a pair of young princes by their mother, Joshua and David John settled into family life as if they had never been away. They worked on the farm helping Owen plant and cultivate. Meg sold out her mercantile goods to Wurst and Pennybaker and the boys helped move the stock to the General Store and to Abel Pennybaker's Hardware Store. They then helped Hamilton move his law books and furniture into the mercantile building to make it his office.

One Sunday the Symington family drove into town for church services which, until a church could be built, were being held at Luther and Silas Jones' new house.

As they drove along, Aurelia commented that Boot Harris' crew of carpenters had finally completed his second building. It was one story with a false front, smaller than the drug store, and had double windows and a small porch. Oddly, they had painted a large yellow rose on the varnished plank door. In recent weeks she had had a hard time containing her curiosity, half-hoped the place would be an opera house.

David John, in a dark suit, his hair slicked down and looking throttled by his tight white collar, was the first to spot the signs over the door. He gave a glad whoop, "Hey, look, Josh, billiards! In Paragon Springs."

Aurelia gasped, felt herself heating to fury. *Billiard Hall* was simply another name for a saloon! For years, A. J. Peacock's Billiard Hall, along with his other Dodge City saloons, the Lady Gay, the Nueces, and the Saratoga, were known to cater to the lowest clientele from miles around. Resulting in unbelievable debauchery, in shootings and killings. Now, Harris meant to bring the same sort of activity to Paragon Springs? Put an end to the peaceful, picturesque little village she expected the place to be?

"Yeah, I see," Joshua answered his brother with a chuckle. "They got places like that in Larned. Some of the fellas from our school—" he hesitated suddenly, knowing he'd said too much in his mother's presence. He finished, sparing her what she'd be better off not knowing, "Oh, nothin'."

The signs, THE YELLOW ROSE, above, and DANCE HALL & BILLIARDS, below, had to have been hung after she left town last night. Disbelief, then rage built inside her. "I told him! I told him, no! I told Boot Harris plain enough that we would not stand for vice in Paragon Springs. This is a farm town for quiet, decent folks."

"Now, Aurelia," Owen tried to calm her, reaching over to squeeze her gloved hand. "Doesn't look to me like the place is an outright *saloon*. There are no laws against dancing, and playing pool, which is all the man is advertising. A lot of folks favor dancing and billiards as pastimes."

She whirled on him. "What you see is a saloon, Owen Symington, and you know it as well as I do! That despicable Boot Harris doubtless has whiskey and beer piped secret into that place from his drug store. Whole unlawful fountains of liquor, I'll vow." Owen flushed and didn't argue the point. Her rage continued, "And if he doesn't bring in lewd women sooner or later, I'll eat my bonnet! I believe the man would do anything to make a dollar, whether good for the town, or not."

She felt very foolish, now, for believing Boot Harris would put something nice like an opera house in that building. Suddenly, her sons' whispers and snickers caught her ear. Confound her for getting upset and carried away! If she had had her wits about her she would never have mentioned loose women in her children's presence. She turned in the wagon to see a pair of adolescent male smirks vanish to looks of sweet innocence. Zibby simply looked puzzled.

"Boys! You wouldn't—? In Larned, you didn't—? Your father might consider billiards an innocent game, I don't. You two mustn't go anywhere near Harris' establishment, please don't. That place—" How could she describe it to them, in terms fit for their ears?

"Heck, Ma," Joshua told her in feigned agreement, obedience, "we wouldn't dream of it. Anybody can see by your face what you think of a place like that."

"We know we'd get skinned," David John added, fighting to keep his face straight.

"Yes," she said, feeling better, "you would. Remember that. Cheap joints like that are the dens of the devil."

"What is a 'cheap joint'? Why is it a 'den of the devil'?" Zibby wanted to know. Her young face, framed by her best pink bonnet, was scrunched with curiosity.

"Now, Zib—" Aurelia began slowly. Luckily, they reached the Jones' lovely new two-story house and she didn't have to answer Zibby.

She herded her youngsters inside the well-furnished home. "Behave now," she cautioned softly and then she and her family were exchanging greetings with Luther and Silas who welcomed them to Sunday services. In spite of herself, Aurelia could not take her mind from Harris' new dance-and-billiard hall. She studied her gawky long-legged sons, a frown creasing her brow. She could keep a close eye on Zibby, her sons were another matter. Yet, they were good fellows. She sincerely believed they would be good men when fully grown. They'd be like their father, John; like Owen and other men in the community. If, of course, she could keep the evils of the world at bay.

Lad stood back to allow Selinda to proceed as they boarded the train in Lawrence. She had seen him at the college a few times since their disagreement the day she'd sketched him, but their exchanges had been cool and restrained. He touched her arm now as they moved forward. "I'd like to sit with you, Selinda, if you don't mind." His blue eyes on her were keen and friendly.

"Of course." She was glad he'd asked, was afraid he might not. She hadn't enjoyed their spat. They took their seat, didn't speak as the conductor came to take their tickets to Dodge City.

"I hear the Hessler family recently began running a stageline—Paragon Springs to Dodge and back," Lad said. "That's certainly an improvement over the old days."

"Yes. I wonder if we'll recognize home? Mama says the place has changed a lot. New businesses, new people. In a very short while—about three months—the road ranch has spread out and become a town."

"Lucy has told me about it in her letters, but it's still hard to imagine that that shabby little spot is anything other than what it's always been."

"I'm excited to see it."

"I am, too." He sat forward so he could turn and look into her face. "Selinda, I'm sorry about our fuss a few weeks ago. I didn't mean to hurt you."

"It's all right, I know you didn't," she said around a tightness in her throat. "I shouldn't have gotten so upset."

"Have you heard anything more about your father?"

She didn't want to confess about the latest letters she'd received. She chewed her lip, but met his gaze steadily, "It's a pretty personal project, Lad. I think for the time being we should avoid that subject. All right?"

He hesitated. "Whatever you want, Selinda, truly. Maybe we can talk about it later? I'm glad we're leaving the books behind and going home." He added huskily, "You know I think the world of you and always have?"

"I know, Lad." She smiled at him and when he reached for her hand she curled her fingers inside his.

He leaned back, seemed satisfied as the train racketed on.

When Selinda stole a look at him fifteen minutes later, she saw that he had fallen asleep. She smiled and took the opportunity to study his face. He was so handsome—even with his full sensuous lips drooped slightly open—he nearly took her breath away. He combed his sandy hair in a swirl over his strong forehead, hiding the old scar from years ago in Nebraska when he had been partially scalped. He had wonderfully prominent cheekbones that she longed to caress. For someone so young, he sported a luxurious moustache.

She'd heard other young women at college talk about the handsome young law student, Lad Voss. She had listened, wanted to tell them that he was taken, that he belonged to her, or would, someday.

Aurelia's worry over Harris' establishments was sidetracked by the arrival home of Selinda Lee, and Lad Voss, from the University of Kansas in Lawrence.

It was decided to hold a celebration to welcome all of the young people back into the community fold. The gathering would be a chance for Paragon Springs newcomers to become better acquainted, too.

The picnic was set for the area beside the Hesslers' large new hotel barn where the most shade was cast. On the day of the picnic, makeshift tables and benches were set out.

Making their way past tables centered with crepe paper flowers and flags, Aurelia and Owen headed toward the circle of folks around Lad and Selinda. Lad was deep in conversation with Hamilton Gibbs while Meg and the children were off at the corner of the barn, seated on a blanket in the shade from the Gibbs' buggy. Other townsfolk were just arriving.

Across the way, Aurelia spotted Lucy Ann and Admire and noted that Zibby had found Rachel. She waved. Out front of the barn Joshua and David John had found friends their age. The group of young males—most wearing devilish grins—were looking up at the weathercock twirling in the wind atop the barn. She hoped they wouldn't be throwing things at it but you could never tell about fellows their age.

She hesitated, warning them just in case, "Now, you young men, leave that weathervane be, hear?" Several of them turned to grin at her, Joshua and David John looked embarrassed.

"Honey," Owen cautioned, "the boys are fine."

"Maybe they are, I don't care. The Hesslers went to a lot of trouble to put that weathervane up there and I don't want to see it damaged or the fellows in trouble." She called, more friendly, seeing that one of them held a ball and a bat, "Start yourselves a game of baseball." She was gratified to see them move slowly toward the open field east of the stage barn, Rachel and Zibby following a few paces behind. She nodded triumphantly at Owen.

She watched a moment to see how David John reacted to Rachel. He paid her no attention, but then, in the presence of other young men, she supposed that was natural. She hoped he wouldn't hurt Rachel's feelings. She was a nice little girl, and she hadn't really meant to hurt David John by laughing at him that day. He was old enough not to let it bother him.

"I can hardly believe it," Lad remarked to Hamilton as Aurelia and Owen reached the group surrounding Lad and Selinda, "that I am finally realizing my dream to study law under Uncle Jimmy Green, dean of law at the university." Hamilton and Lad stopped talking long enough to nod and smile at Aurelia and shake Owen's hand.

Since Lad was occupied and Selinda for the moment was free, Aurelia went to her. Most of the women present wore plain browns and black and Selinda, in soft apricot, stood out like a sunflower. Aurelia felt toward the young woman as she might a beloved niece. She kissed her cheek and held her hand. "Welcome home, dear. How are you? Tell me about college. Do you enjoy living in Lawrence?"

There was something regal in Selinda's quiet way that only added to her dark beauty. A beauty that Aurelia didn't always remember was so astounding until they were again face to face. Shadows under the young woman's hazel eyes made them luminous. Shafer's accidental death the past year had not been easy for her; she missed her twin. According to Emmaline, Selinda's letter-writing campaign to find her father could only bring her more sadness.

A warm smile slowly overtook Selinda's face. She replied in her soft voice, "Life in Lawrence is quite comfortable and interesting, thank you. I admit to a bit of lazy mind-wandering recently—lilacs blooming all over campus might have been responsible." Her eyes twinkled mischievously, then followed a speckled white butterfly that fluttered between them. She said honestly, "I missed home. I couldn't wait to see Mother, and my 'Aunts'—you, and Meg, and Lucy Ann."

Male students far outnumbered young women students on the campus. Possibly Selinda was lonely there for female company. "Well, I'm sure the classes are easy for you," she said encouragingly.

"Not all of them." She stroked the ribbon from her bonnet and admitted, "I've found that I am not very proficient at mathematics and physics." Her chin lifted. "I believe from now on I'll concentrate on my courses in art and journalism."

"That sounds jim-dandy, Selinda." She brushed a fly from her face, and smiled. "Your mother has been turning out some fine articles in the *Echo* about Kansas women's suffrage struggles. I imagine she will want your views on that matter and on other subjects. I'm sure she will want you to do some writing for her."

Selinda nodded, her expression both eager and thoughtful. "I can't wait. I *do* have strong opinions on woman's suffrage—women deserve to have the vote, should have had it ages ago." She sighed, waved the matter away for the moment. "While I'm here, I'd also like to paint some landscapes, draw portraits of local folk for practice. Eventually I'd like to work as an art journalist for a large city paper like the *Kansas City Star,* or the *St. Louis Post-Dispatch* or possibly for a magazine like *Harper's Weekly.*"

"Honestly? How very interesting!" Aurelia at Selinda's age had never thought of an occupation for herself, had only wanted marriage to John and a family. Few girls of her time did. Of course, necessity later had thrust the mercantile and post office into her keeping. Now, she had her own restaurant.

She envied the confidence shown by 1880's young women, some of them. Admired the way they created opportunities for themselves, dared to branch out from what others expected of them. "Speaking of local folk who would be interesting to sketch or write about, you must meet the Reids. Follow me, dear." In the next few minutes she introduced Selinda to Essie and Ben Reid, then Maud Mullendore, and next the dapper bachelor brothers, Luther and Silas. She looked for Abel Pennybaker but so far the little hardware storekeeper hadn't appeared at the celebration.

"Let's sit down a moment," Aurelia encouraged, leading Selinda to a bench at one of the tables. She took a deep breath when they were seated and said, "I don't mean to pry, dear, and you don't need to tell me anything if you don't want to, but your mother tells me that—"

"That I'm writing letters trying to find out what happened to my father?"

"Yes," Aurelia flushed, "and I'm being nosy. Forget that I asked."

Selinda laughed softly and took Aurelia's hand. "I don't mind talking to you about this, Aunt Aurelia—my goodness, you're like a second mother. I know Mama worries about my project, and I'm glad she has you to discuss it with—especially since she feels that my putting hopes in the letters is a terrible mistake. To be honest, Lad feels the same; it's hard to talk to him about it." She was silent a moment. "As for any success in writing the letters, I can't say that I've had any yet."

"No replies at all?"

"I have had some. I received a letter from a woman who said that she knew my father, but you could tell she was just lonely and wanted someone to correspond with. She wasn't able to tell me one truthful fact about him." She drew a deep breath and frowned, "Another letter came from a man who said my father was trapped in a blizzard in Colorado and ate his companion to keep from starving, then went mad and shot himself to death." She shuddered. "I didn't believe *that* letter."

Aurelia reached over to hug her. "I'm so sorry, Selinda. Maybe your mother and Lad are right. Are you sure you want to continue with this?" Tears of sympathy burned behind her eyes.

"I have to, until I'm satisfied that I've done all I can."

"Then that's what you must do."

Aurelia was glad a moment later to see Lad's tall strapping form and Owen, striding toward them.

Lad was telling Owen that while he enjoyed working outside with Ad on the farm and at the quarry, he particularly relished his time with Meg's husband. "Ham Gibbs promises I can apprentice in his new law office when the time comes."

Aurelia stood up to say, "My, that would be nice, having you both practicing law right here in the new town of Paragon Springs. Maybe you'll eventually be his partner in law?" She was more than a little pleased with the idea. The day was beginning to heat up and she blotted her chin, then her forehead, with her handkerchief. "We're small potatoes now but someday Paragon Springs will be a thriving city, wait and see."

"I'm sure it will be," Lad smiled. His metamorphosis from the boy he had been had amazed them all. He had taken an almost overnight interest in books as a growing boy. He had read all that Emmaline and the others had in their possession, including the Bible, Shakespeare, and well-thumbed almanacs. He had taken his voracious appetite for reading with him to high school, and now to the university.

He spoke so well, one could hardly believe there was a long period as a young boy when, following the Indian raid, he spoke not at all. He was altogether a handsome, smart, fair-minded young man of whom his sister, Lucy Ann, could be very proud. She was doing her utmost to see him acquire a university education.

It was a while before he answered her question. Then he told her, "I'm not sure I'll come back to stay, Aunt Aurelia, I'm not sure of quite a few things. I may even go into politics, eventually. I have joined a Young Republicans group on campus and they've caught my interest." His glance, deeply affectionate but shadowed with uncertainty, swerved to Selinda. "I have plenty of time, I believe, to choose from several plans I have in mind."

Selinda colored. She gave him a soft smile and then said, "I'm sure, Lad, that whatever you do will be the right thing."

Aurelia smiled and favored them with her two cents' worth, "I'm sure, too." Then she took Owen's arm and led him away, allowing the younger pair some time alone.

# Chapter Eight

"Get up!" Aurelia said, stooping to get her hands under the young cowboy's arms from behind and help him rise from where he'd passed out at the door to her restaurant. He reeked of alcohol, needed a shave, his clothes were rank with filth.

"Th-thanks." He stood weaving on his feet; his eyes squinted at the sun. "It's morning? Be damned!"

"Yes, it's morning and you're coming inside for coffee."

He grinned at her in childish apology with his palms turned up, "L-lost all the money I had at the Yellow Rose. Damn cards, thought sure I had a good hand. Don't—don't got a dime to pay you, but I sure would like a cup."

She helped him inside and to a table. "It will take a while for the coffee to brew once I've got a fire in my stove. I'll fix you some bacon and eggs."

"Sure appreciate it, ma'am."

"Yes, well . . ." She couldn't turn him away, or the others who, more and more, showed up at her restaurant hungry and penniless after a night of drinking and gambling at Harris' establishment. Many didn't mind gambling their money away, they'd just earn more working another man's cattle. Some believed they could gamble their wages into huge sums, buy a little ranch of their own. Whatever their reason, they always lost, and Boot Harris profited.

Trade had boomed in Paragon Springs for most of the early summer months and local merchants were thrilled. But the Yellow Rose and Harris' drug store had drawn a lot of that trade to town. Increasingly, a different breed of men from local merchants and farmers began to spend time and money in the new town of Paragon Springs. Hardly noticeable at first, it was as though a dark shadow settled over the community, threatening what it was meant to be.

Aurelia noted with growing concern that most of the men from out of town appeared to be friends with Boot Harris, at the very least were his customers and men with whom he transacted real estate deals. There were cattle dealers in expensive clothes, glib-tongued gamblers, sneaky sorts who looked to be on the run from the law. There were booted and spurred cowboys in off the range and anxious, along with the rest, to spend their earnings at the Yellow Rose. Like the fellow at her table.

She sighed, and in a while brought his plate of bacon and eggs. She poured his coffee. He gave her a lop-sided, red-eyed grin, "You're an angel."

*An angry one.* Aurelia waved the comment away. This boy wasn't the first and he wouldn't be the last to need her charity.

When Zibby came in later that morning to help, Aurelia left her in charge while she made a determined visit to the Harris Drug Store.

Boot Harris was freshly shaved and finely dressed in a dark suit, but he had sleepy-lidded look that told he hadn't been out of bed long. Or maybe he was just bored. Aurelia stood next to a counter of nostrums and told him, "This morning I had to feed a half-drunk penniless cowboy who had lost everything to your establishment."

He shrugged with disinterest from behind the counter. She continued, her anger rising, "And it wasn't the first time someone else had to care for your castoffs after you supplied them illegal whiskey and then took all the money they had."

He grinned mockingly and stooped to look for something

below the counter. "Maybe your cowboy had too much 'medicine'? It's not my fault if my drug store customers take more than the prescribed dosage, you understand. That's not my job to oversee."

Aurelia leaned over the counter, "That's nonsense. You know exactly what you're doing and you can't be blind to the trouble it's causing. Bethany and Will Hessler say they can hear fistfights happening in the Yellow Rose half the night. The racket disturbs their guests, and other folks living in town. Bethany tells me there was a knifing due to one man calling another a liar in the Yellow Rose. You turned the wounded man out onto the street to bleed to death and he probably would have if Will hadn't found him and Bethany hadn't tended his wounds."

He stood and his mouth tightened. "I'm doing this town a favor."

"I won't let you ruin it!"

"Good-day, Mrs. Symington, this chit-chat wearies me."

She hesitated, her fingers itched to grab one of his bottled tonics and throw it at him. Instead she answered quietly, steel in her voice, "Good-day to you, too, Mr. Harris. Know that I mean what I say."

"Zibby!" Aurelia scolded a few days later as Zibby stood holding the screen-door open while she stared up the street, "Close the screen-door! This is a place of business where people eat. We can't allow flies in here." Luckily, it was mid-afternoon and they had no customers. She was busy preparing for the evening trade.

"Sorry, Mama," Zibby said in a sort of daze, "I was watching some pretty ladies in a wagon over in front of the drug store."

"Well, go out to the sidewalk if you must watch, but close

the door." Stopping suddenly in her tracks and laying aside
the onion she'd been chopping, she asked, "What ladies—at
the drug store?"

Wiping her hands on a dishtowel, she hurried out to the
walk to stand beside Zibby. "Oh, dear heaven! Zibby, dear,
go back inside."

"Why, what's wrong?"

"Those women are, well, they're—" *soiled doves, fallen
frails, sporting women*—prostitutes had all kinds of names in
the West. She hesitated while her heart hammered in frustrated anger and her mind scurried to explain to Zibby. She
gave up. "Never mind about those—*ladies*. I'd like for you to
go back inside, tend the restaurant for me if someone comes
in." She ripped off her apron and handed it and the dish towel
to Zibby. "I'll be back as soon as I can."

She strode toward the drug store and billiard hall, forming
in her mind what she'd say as she went. Boot Harris had come
out to hand the women—who looked like gaudy, plumed
birds—one by one down from their wagon.

When she reached them, Aurelia took Harris by the arm
and pulled him aside. "They can't stay here, not in Paragon
Springs!"

"I beg your pardon?" He looked at her hand on his arm
and shook free of her.

"Those women can't stay," she repeated in a low voice,
"not for a minute."

"Yes, they can. They're my employees, I hired them to
dance at the Yellow Rose." This time, he took her elbow and
pulled her toward the gawking women, whose eyes were
shaded against the sun. "Mrs. Symington," he said smoothly,
"I want you to meet my dance hostesses. This is Mollie," he
nodded at a redhead in turquoise velvet who stood with one
hand on her hip looking Aurelia up and down. "The little one

there in dark blue is called 'Sawed-Off Sal.' But that's not a very nice name so from now on we'll just call her Sal." He bowed to a bad-skinned blond in dark rose, "And here we have Franny, my lady."

The women reminded Aurelia of wildflowers that once might have been very pretty but had suffered too much Kansas sun and had dried into thick hard stalks. They were studying her with snooty, tilted grins, as though *she* was the one out of place. She saw no sign of remorse in their faces for their line of work.

"Good afternoon," she nodded stiffly at them, but told Harris, more firmly this time, "You'll have to take them to Flagg. Paragon Springs isn't the place for them."

He grinned at her. "I have five of their friends settled in over there in an establishment I bought. I need these ladies here at the Yellow Rose to dance with my customers." His eyes narrowed slightly. "These women are no concern of yours, you know, Mrs. Symington. They aren't hurting you."

They were hurting her just to look at them! She had never seen so much garish color, so much white bosom and fake jewels glinting in the sun.

"They are going to stay. There are no laws against their being here—"

She stood silent as time ticked by, recognized that for the time being she was beaten. She turned on her heel, skirts clutched in both hands, her face hot with frustration. She threw over her shoulder, "We'll see about that, Mr. Harris. We'll just see about that. Paragon Springs is a respectable town and it's going to stay that way!"

She could hardly tend to her work in the restaurant, she was so preoccupied with the last hour's developments. Harris was right that there was no city law against having hurdy gurdy girls in his place of business. In fact, they had set down no laws of government at all yet. Their legal papers thus far covered such items as the name of their town, property boundaries, and so on. In the rush to build their businesses, most believed that city government could wait. Hamilton had warned them that they must set down a charter so the laws would be there when they needed them. She was wrong when she told him they were all friends and there was nothing to worry about and they'd set their laws in due time.

Their small town had risen in hope and harmony. But there had to be rules and regulations to keep things that way. *Orderly. Decent. Civilized.* They had left the door open for Boot Harris to carry on whatever lawless activity he chose as a means to line his pockets. Rooting out trouble, now that it was here, wouldn't be easy.

The colorful birds moved in upstairs above the drug store and afternoons took to sitting on the sills of their open, top-floor windows, to make bawdy jokes with men on the street. Raucous and cackling like crows, they beckoned them to come back at night for a dance. It cost one dollar to dance with them and the dance didn't last long. Night-time boot traffic on the side stairs of the drug store rarely ceased.

"Harris is making money as fast as he can take it in, the Yellow Rose is the most popular place in town," Emmaline commented one afternoon in Aurelia's restaurant. Selinda, Emmaline, Lucy Ann, and Bethany had gathered to have tea and discuss the troubling situation. "I'm sure he doesn't feel responsible for the lawlessness his establishment spawns, to him that's just an unfortunate side-effect."

"I threatened to bring in the county sheriff for a look at Harris' illegal dispensation of whiskey," Aurelia told the women as she placed small dessert plates and cutlery on the table. "Harris laughed and said the county sheriff was one of his best customers when he came this way. Unfortunately, it's probably true."

Bethany nodded. "I can't see how we can possibly shut the Yellow Rose down, no matter how much trouble it's causing us. It isn't only outsiders frequenting the Yellow Rose. The place is popular with town workmen and some of our own businessmen, good men like Oscar Wurst, Elliot Charbonneau—most of them, in fact."

"Admire goes there once in a while for a drink and to play billiards," Lucy admitted. "Ad doesn't dance or—" her voice lowered, "use the girls. It's a chance for him to see friends he used to cowboy with. He misses the old life sometimes."

"The fact that our own locals enjoy the entertainments Boot Harris offers doesn't mean we can't have law and order," Selinda said with a frown, her fork poised over her chocolate cake. "We just got off on the wrong foot."

"Yes, we did," Aurelia agreed. "And I'm working on a plan for a town meeting. We need some rules and regulations and a peace officer to enforce them. Of course, it will take time to bring all that about."

That same night, Aurelia was late closing the restaurant. She had accidentally spilled a gallon can of molasses and she was a long time cleaning it up. It was well after dark when she grabbed her parasol and shawl and locked the restaurant behind her.

Tinny music, shouts, and laughter came from the Yellow Rose two doors up the street. Aurelia saw a man stumble out the door. She picked up her pace toward the livery to harness Sweet Annie to her rig for the drive home. The sound of the man's footsteps echoed close behind her. Panic threatened to close her throat.

"Girlie—" the stranger called after her. "Girlie." He said something else and from his muddled speech she realized that he thought she was one of the Yellow Rose women. He grabbed her and tried to drag her behind the Jones' store which was closed for the night. The reprobate was offering to pay for her services "after."

She recognized his face in the gloom as a stranger who had been in her restaurant earlier that day. Sudden, intense fury gave her strength. "I am not from the Yellow Rose!" she shouted. "I served you stew at Aurelia's Place restaurant today, you idiot. I'm Aurelia Symington, *Mrs. Symington!*"

As hard as she could she whacked him with her parasol—a dozen times around his head and shoulders while he yowled and staggered. She shoved him off his tottering feet by throwing herself hard and sideways against him. He landed on the ground in the shadows, whimpering an apology for his mistake.

"Don't you ever—!" she panted, standing over him in the dark, parasol lifted—"try that with me again or with any other decent woman in Paragon Springs. Hear me?" He mumbled something that he'd behave and she whacked him again for good measure. "Well, don't forget!"

She stomped across the street to the livery. Hot tears sprang to her eyes. She glared back in the direction of the noisy Yellow Rose. It wasn't right that a decent woman had to be subjected to such depravity on the street at night. It hadn't been like that in the beginning, a few months ago. Everything had been good and decent, but that was before Harris came! Who built the town in the first place, if not the women? Who had better right to walk safely when they needed to be about?

At first she was too angry about the incident to tell Owen. She rationalized then that she hadn't really been hurt and to tell Owen would only worry him, but she did tell Emmaline and Selinda what had happened when they came into the restaurant for their noon meal and for details about the upcoming town company meeting.

Emmaline looked shocked. "I'm so sorry, Aurelia. What if you hadn't been able to fight him off . . . ?"

Aurelia colored. "I was so angry! God willing it won't happen again. But let's not talk about the ugly incident anymore. About the meeting, I've decided to have it here at my restaurant after hours this next Thursday. We need town government in operation as soon as possible."

Emmaline made notes on a pad of paper. She said, "We've worked too hard to build Paragon Springs to allow it to be taken over and ruined. Of course Boot Harris would like to see Paragon Springs turned into another hell-hole like Dodge City has been since the trail-driving days, ten, fifteen years ago. Fortunes were built from trade with cowboys, gamblers, buffalo-skinners, and soldiers. From all who frequented the numerous saloons, the liveries, the bath houses, and barber shops. The brothels."

"It's a quandary, for sure. Some of our own people won't want to lose the added business the Yellow Rose has brought us all, but whether the establishment stays or goes—" Aurelia freshened Emmaline's tea, "the ugliness, dangers, and lawlessness have to stop."

Governing wasn't part of the town company's role, but they were the only leadership the community had so far. Shortly, a town meeting with *all* citizens present to voice their opinions would be held. As a new town in trouble, they would have an election to vote on rules and regulations, and officers to carry them out.

In talking around the last days before the meeting, Aurelia and her friends learned what they'd already guessed: that although there were other concerns, what worried folks most was violence stemming from the Yellow Rose.

High in their minds was a very recent incident in which two cowboys clashed in a heated argument over the favors of Sawed-Off Sal. Guns were drawn but local citizens managed to stop the altercation before anyone got killed. They put the culprits, both suffering minor wounds, on their horses and ordered them out of town. Sawed-Off Sal was invited to leave, too, but Boot Harris defended her, claiming the incident was not her fault.

The day after that, a peevish loser at cards at the Yellow Rose attacked Abel Pennybaker at his hardware store and beat the poor little fellow severely in order to rob him of five dollars. Children browsing in the store witnessed the latter event and were very frightened.

"It goes without saying that most of our citizens want decency and order," Aurelia said, as she served slices of lemon pie and cups of coffee at the town company meeting that Thursday night. "But it's clear this won't just happen, it has to be worked for, fought for. We must set some laws and hire a sheriff to see that they are obeyed."

They had all managed to be present: Meg and Hamilton, Lucy Ann and Admire, Owen and she. The children were under Joshua and David John's keeping at the ranch. Emmaline and Selinda were present to take notes for the *Echo*.

Meg said, "I heard that those children who witnessed Abel's beating were very worried for him, and frightened for their own lives. My own children are too young to know what's happening, but other youngsters see the most degrading sights when passing the Yellow Rose. They hear language unfit for anyone's ears. Must they be dodging bullets next?"

Ad saw no reason to get *rid* of the Yellow Rose, although he said it might be 'tamed some.' They all agreed it was past time to form town government, to elect a mayor, a clerk, and council to carry on city business, as well as a marshal to carry out the law. The community was growing faster than anyone would have guessed. Serious problems already at hand needed to be taken care of before they grew worse.

"I've talked several times with Will and Bethany Hessler and like the rest of us they are worried," Aurelia told the others. "They have a cousin who they believe would make us a fine city marshal. His name is Bert Holberg. Will and Beth say he is a giant of a man, weighing two hundred and fifty to three hundred pounds. He was once an army scout and he spent several years as a freighter. Right now he takes occasional jobs in fine carpentry in Emporia, but he would like more dependable work. He's a stable fellow, a regular church-goer. Bethany says he is quiet and shy but confident in his abilities. Will says Bert is strong—mentally and morally as well as physically—in the face of violence. They believe he would be the right man to protect the peace and dignity of Paragon Springs, to curb the lawlessness coming from the Yellow Rose."

"Sounds like Mr. Holberg is just that," Hamilton said. "I vote that we send for him as soon as a wire can be sent."

Owen smiled, the lines crinkling around his eyes. "Thanks for speaking up, Ham. Now I can say I agree with my wife without sounding partial." He winked at Aurelia over the rim of his coffee cup.

"I like you partial," Aurelia joked back at him.

Ad thought more than one man should run for marshal, to make it a regular election. He would ask young Ben Reid, the saddler, if he would be interested in running for city marshal.

They discussed other matters, of lesser concern than troubles stemming from Harris' establishments, but important: the garbage in the streets, stock animals running loose, the possibility of fire danger and the need to be prepared for such an event.

It was a long evening. But members of the committee left feeling they had made strides in the right direction and none too soon.

Notice of the upcoming election was printed in the next issue of the *Echo*. Nominations were requested to fill the offices of Mayor, four councilmen, city clerk and treasurer. Suggestions for ordinances toward town improvement were also asked for. Two meetings were scheduled. Besides deciding on ordinances at the first meeting, persons running for office would speak, present their platforms. At the second meeting, a week later, a slate of officers would be named by vote and the business of the town could really begin.

After the report of the upcoming election appeared in the paper, there was talk of little else. Selinda remarked to a group of women conversing in the dry-goods store, "Maybe we women can't vote, yet, but we can express our opinions on important matters that involve us—to anyone who will listen!" Her comment brought a chorus of "Amen!"

Aurelia agreed that this was not the time for nonsense propriety, receding to a "woman's place." She voiced her mind regarding the town's problems at every opportunity. She spoke out on the street, in the stores, while serving tables at her restaurant, at home with Owen. She knew her women friends, most of them, were following suit. She hoped that in the not too distant future women would be voting legally right alongside their men.

A few people argued that the town company was moving too fast, having the ordinance meeting and election of officers in such a short time.

"We've waited too long already," Aurelia was firm. "Take a good look at the mire piling up in our new streets. Yesterday I was nearly run over by a stray cow! Pigs loose and rooting everywhere. But that's not the worst of it. Look at Boot Harris' place and the foolishness stemming from there. It's only a matter of time until someone gets killed by a stray bullet from some cowboy only having 'fun' and getting a little 'rowdy.' Do you want your wife, your child, your man, to take that bullet? We need laws, and enforcement of them now."

Boot Harris' response to the notice in the paper, to all the talk, was to nominate himself for the office of mayor.

As much as his nomination infuriated and worried her, Aurelia wasn't surprised. She was glad when Owen offered to run against him. They waited, anxious for other nominations, but Owen was the only other candidate for the chief office. Luther Jones, Lars and Will Hessler, Mr. Wurst, and Able Pennybaker—still bandaged but recovering, agreed to run for council seats. Silas Jones would be the only candidate for city clerk.

There probably wasn't a soul in town who didn't recognize the importance of the mayor's race. Owen stood for peace, dignity, and growth for the town. Harris, in Aurelia's estimation, stood for one thing: lining his pockets as thickly as possible with foolish men's money. Unfortunately, he provided a very popular commodity toward that end.

Each customer to Aurelia's dining room was served a heaping vocal helping of her husband's fine qualities, his qualifications for office, along with the food she served. Of course Owen's honorable and dependable qualities were already known to most.

Emmaline interviewed both mayoral candidates for the

*Echo.* If her written report on Owen was a little more glowing than that written about Harris, it was doubtless intentional.

The day for the first real town meeting arrived. It was hot outside and the windows of the meeting room at the hotel had been opened to let in air. From the moment she arrived at Owen's side, their children trailing, Aurelia sensed the tension among those gathered. Or possibly it was just her own anxiety she felt as she took her position at the head of the room. She discreetly patted her brow with her handkerchief.

Lucy Ann, with both of their daughters in tow, smiled and waved from the back of the room. David John and Joshua leaned against the wall, watching, waiting. Aurelia drew a deep breath. Then Meg sidled by and whispered, "You ought to have a medal, dear, for all the hard work you've done and are doing for Paragon Springs. You're the one ought to be named mayor, legal or otherwise." Meg stopped as though the idea had just registered with her in that second and she said, "Someday, when we women get the vote, I wager you will be mayor of Paragon Springs!"

Aurelia hoped not, truth to tell. At the moment a nice long rest appealed more than anything. But there was still a job to do and as president of the town company and leader of the citizenry until a proper mayor could be elected, she'd been chosen to conduct the meeting. As folks found their chairs, she called the meeting to order.

The question of necessary ordinances came first on the agenda. Although Aurelia led the meeting, she let others do most of the talking. It was their town and they needed to express their concerns, their desires. It was generally agreed, following discussion, that the streets were not the place for loose livestock. A few residents grumbled at the extra effort it would take to keep their pigs, chickens, and milk cow, penned, when they had plenty of other, more pressing work to see to, but the loose stock measure passed.

A regulation was set forth and passed that shopkeepers must give thought to ladies' hems and sweep their sidewalks clean, and haul away the piles of horse manure from in front of their shops.

When the matter of hiring a marshal and building a jail was brought up, Joe Potter leaped to his feet to strongly disagree. "Why spend money we ain't got?" he argued. He looked around the room for signs of support; his graying red hair practically stood on end. "We can be our own vigilantes to take care of troubles. Somebody breaks the law, we lock him up in a feed bin or chain him to a stall at the livery, till he learns better. We don't need to pay no sheriff, build no jail. That means taxes and I sure can't afford to pay none."

Nearly everyone there knew that Potter was miles from poverty row, that it was his nature to be against anything that cost an extra dime. By driving his large family mercilessly, he had built his holdings into a large and successful grain farm. Recently he had opened a store in town, Potter's Feed and Seed, putting his thin, brow-beaten but business-wise son, Lloyd, in charge.

Aurelia knew relief when the gathering paid little mind to his objection. Not even Joe bothered to suggest they call in the county sheriff in case of troubles. Sheriff Finney lived too far up in the northwest corner of the county to be of timely help. He kept his office in Flagg only part time. He was lazy and a coward, wouldn't care much about Paragon Springs' troubles anyhow. They needed a local lawman.

"I want to introduce Bert Holberg," Aurelia announced.

The blond, blue-eyed, sandy mustachioed giant had arrived in town the night before and he was all the Hesslers had claimed. Now, he stood up in the far corner of the room and with a quiet smile and in a no-nonsense, deep-voiced rumble, he promised to uphold the law in Paragon Springs to the best of his ability if elected.

Ben Reid promptly withdrew as the other candidate for marshal. "Be a waste of my time to run," he said, "anybody can see who is the better man for the job."

Aurelia knew, also, that Ben and Essie were hoping to have a child. They likely didn't favor the prospect of Ben risking his life, possibly leaving the child fatherless.

Owen suggested that the new city council, when formed, could legally appoint Holberg as peace officer, there was no need to take it to a vote. The contingency nodded agreement, and after considerable discussion, it was agreed to raise a tax to pay him, and to build a small jail.

Aurelia was deeply disappointed when the majority felt it would be too expensive to build a new school at that time, which would increase the taxes already agreed upon to pay Bert Holberg. They voted instead to build a new room onto Emmaline's soddy for the time being, and to buy a few new books and materials. Aurelia had suspected this would happen, but still it was a let-down that made her feel almost ill. For another year and maybe more, she would have to send her sons away, along with other older children who needed advanced studies Paragon Springs couldn't provide. With difficulty, heart-sore, she turned her attention back to the meeting.

# Chapter Nine

One by one, Abel, Oscar, Lars and Will Hessler, Luther and his brother, Silas—all seeking city office seats—were recognized. They stated simply that they would do their best to follow the people's will and lawful regulations to keep town affairs running smoothly.

"Now it's your turn, Owen!" Joe Potter shouted. "Let's hear it for Paragon Springs' next mayor!"

Joe liked her husband. That was one of the few good things, maybe the only good thing, Aurelia could say, at least at the moment, about Joe Potter.

"Now you all probably think," Owen began with a twisted grin, "that I do what my wife, Aurelia, says I have to do." He waited for the chuckles to die down. "That's mostly true." His grin grew wider while Aurelia's face warmed and she listened with amused affection. "Aurelia told me I should run for mayor. If elected," he grew serious, "I promise to do all I can to get us the railroad we all want and need. And the county seat. Now, we all know what a pickle this county is in as it stands, as it has been for a long time. The county commissioners are off farming, the county sheriff off drinking and yarning with his friends, the County Treasurer forgets to collect taxes or 'misplaces' the tax money when he does—"

There was a lot of head-shaking, nodding and grumbled agreement.

He went on, "We're going to change all that. As a town, Flagg doesn't deserve to be county seat. Paragon Springs does!" He seemed to have said all he was going to say and the gathering, mostly the women, shuffled restlessly in their seats, looked at Aurelia, then at Owen, then back at Aurelia. She waited patiently, sure of him. Owen finished in a strong voice, "There is an answer to the episodes of violence, the scenes of degradation our fair village has been subjected to of late. If elected, I'll make sure that the state law against prohibition is strongly enforced in Paragon Springs. Have no doubt about it!"

The women sighed in satisfaction. The chorus of male resistance was like a deep roll of thunder through the room. The grumbling came for the most part from Harris' cohorts and supporters. But it also came from good men like Admire and Mr. Wurst. Men who simply liked their whiskey, medicinal or otherwise, and were willing to put up with what they saw as minor disturbances because of it.

"Hell," Mathis Tuttle, Essie Reid's father said, "are we going to be tied to women's apron-strings so's us gents can't have a drink occasionally? Next gol-darned thing you know we'll be wearing flowery ladies' hats and saying 'la-de-da'."

The room burst into laughter. Aurelia shook her head, recognizing, not for the first time, how very difficult it was going to be to enforce the no-saloon law.

Although from the beginning he hadn't voiced an opinion either way, Boot Harris was beaming innocently.

His was the final speech. He made no reference whatsoever to his establishments or the troubles they had caused. Like Owen, he said they must get the railroad and become county seat and he vowed to make it happen if elected. "Both are imperative to the town's success, to future prosperity. To your good and to mine. But equally important, let me say *more so*—considering the future not just of this town, but the future of our whole beloved country—we must provide the finest grist for the mill of *education*."

His remark took Aurelia by surprise and she was suddenly wary and on guard. She sat forward, and her throat dried.

Potter yelled, "You talkin' about a new school? We got that all settled. We're addin' on to Emmaline's school. Just shet up on that."

"I don't deny that a well-equipped school will cost money," Harris nodded sympathetically at Potter. "You will be taxed enough to build the jail, to provide Mr. Holberg's salary, and make other city improvements that demand attention. Therefore, I promise," voices and shuffling in the room stilled, "that regardless of the outcome of the vote next week, I will donate land for a school site."

At the rush of exclamation he said, "I will also build the new school at no cost to anyone but myself." His voice rose with what might have been taken for honest sincerity, "A building large enough to accommodate both grammar and high school students on their home ground. I will see that all the educational needs of our precious young folk are met with the latest styles in factory-made school furniture, blackboards, ceiling lamps, maps, globes, dictionaries, and—other schoolbooks. Only the most qualified teachers will be sought and imported—"

The room burst into glad cheers, excited talk, and laughter.

"Wait, wait," he said, his expression mockingly serious behind effusive good humor. "I must ask for something in return. I would like your new school to be named for me." His face broke into a wide, twisted smile. "How does HARRIS SCHOOL sound to you?"

Aurelia felt like she had been caught in the jaws of a steel trap, then hit by a railroad car. He had defeated her by pledging the one thing she most wanted. If he owned the school, he owned the students. And their parents. Everything.

Others applauded and stomped the floor with booted feet. Shaking with indignation, a chill chasing down her back, she glared at Boot who was smiling directly at her.

She had no doubt he would fulfill his promise. Whether or not he won the election was only of minor importance. Building the school would be his down payment on owning the town and shaping it to his own design, defeating her dream. And he still might win the office of mayor, now, with promise of the school on top of everything else.

From the excited talk around her, she was the only one who felt as she did. Others saw him as a kind and generous benefactor. Not as a coyote greedily rampaging a gentle prairie dog village, the way she saw him.

"Is something the matter, Aurelia, dear?" Bethany asked a week later as they stood on the sidelines watching a riotous wheelbarrow race down Main Street. She strained to add above the happy shouts and laughter, "This is our first celebration of our first city elections and Owen _won_ the mayorship. You're frowning like it's the end of the world."

"I'm sorry. My mind is wandering." She forced a smile, "I don't mean to be grumpy when everyone else is having such a good time." The voting had taken place earlier in the morning. The tallying of votes and announcement of the winners was followed by speeches and toasts, an anvil fired, and now—under a blazing August sun that few seemed to mind—a succession of games. "Of course I'm glad Owen won even though it was by only a handful of votes. I can't help feeling sore—can't get it out of mind, though—that it is Boot Harris' ill-begot money, not our own city funds, that will provide our new school. The way folks feel about Boot, it's a wonder that Owen won the mayor's race at all!"

"We would've had to wait a lot longer for a proper school

building," Bethany reminded, "if Mr. Harris wasn't going to build us one. He's promised to begin construction right away. Maybe eventually we'll be able to buy the school away from Mr. Harris."

"That's what I'm hoping for." In the meantime, his reputation had boomed and would probably continue—along with his accompanying influence in the town. She smiled and waved at David John trundling Rachel by very fast in a wheelbarrow. "Hurry, youngsters, it looks like you might win!"

When the games were finished, the population walked in a body to the east end of town. Earlier, tables had been placed outside the Hesslers' big hotel barn; the dance would be held inside later on. While the women set out the food: fried chicken, corned beef, roasting ears, slaw, beans, platters of sliced bread and bowls of butter, doughnuts, cakes, and fruit cobblers, Zibby and Rachel stood at the end of the table singing duets. Aurelia hesitated in her tasks to listen to the words of Samuel Woodworth's *Old Oaken Bucket*. She fanned her flushed face with an empty tin plate and smiled at the sweet voices singing in unison:

"How dear to this heart are the scenes of my childhood,
    When fond recollection presents them to view!
The orchard, the meadow, the deep-tangled wildwood.
    And every loved spot which my infancy knew;
The wide-spreading pond and the mill that stood by it;
    The bridge and the rock where the cataract fell;
The cot of my father, the dairy house nigh it,
    And e'en the rude bucket which hung in the well!
The old oaken-bucket, the iron-bound bucket,
    The moss-covered bucket that hung in the well."

The girls were well into the second verse, Aurelia tapping

her foot and humming along with them, when the sound of sobbing brought the singing to a faltering stop. Aurelia jerked around and saw that it was Essie Reid's mother, Hannah, weeping over the peach pie she carried, "I'm sorry. I'm sorry. I had no idea I was homesick for Indiana 'til those little girls started to sing. I'll stop my crying this minute, don't mean to bring no sadness on a day like this."

Some of the women went to give Hannah a smile and an affectionate pat. "It's all right, mother," Essie—petite and plain in brown calico—spoke quietly, "we all feel that way sometimes. But this is Kansas, our home now."

Hannah put the pie on the table and wiped her eyes on her apron. "I'm just fine, now. Let's call the children and menfolks over here to eat."

After the food and gallons of coffee and lemonade had been consumed, the men rested in the shade, smoking their pipes, or chewing tobacco, while the women cleared the table. Folks visited for another hour and a half, waiting for the evening to cool however much it would before heading inside the barn for the dance.

A makeshift platform had been placed at one end of the area cleared for the dance. On the platform the musicians, a fiddler, a second man with a mouth harp, a third using a pitchfork for a triangle, and a string-bean fellow thumping an empty keg for a drum, were soon ringing the rafters with song. Happy dancers swayed and swung to *Golden Slippers*, then hopped and kicked furiously to *Old Dan Tucker* and *Jimmy Crack Corn*.

Aurelia spotted Joshua dancing with one of Bethany's daughters and the girl's blond pigtails were flying. Several tunes later, David John, who hadn't spoken more than a half-dozen words all summer to Rachel—before today when they paired for the wheelbarrow race and a three-legged race—

awkwardly squired Rachel around the floor. When Aurelia privately praised him, he turned crimson and declared shyly that he asked Rachel to dance only because she looked silly dancing with Zibby dance after dance. She told him, squeezing his broad young shoulders affectionately, "But you're having a good time and that's what is important."

It amazed Aurelia, smothering a yawn hours later, seated on a goods box at the side of the dance floor—babies and younger children long since put down to sleep on pallets along the wall behind her—that folks had so much energy after the day's frivolities. Of course a celebration such as this one might not happen again for months. Some folks had traveled thirty miles or more to attend and wouldn't start home until the dancing ended at dawn. She was glad to see that folks were having a good time, even though with the advancing hour the men slipped outside more and more to visit the whiskey jug behind the barn. She could smell whiskey in the air, on the dancers' breaths and clothes, and she could see it in their eyes. Some of the men, unable to handle the horses or stay awake on the way home, would be roundly scolded by their wives when they had their senses back.

The musicians began to play slower, more lilting tunes: *Carry Me Back to Old Virginny*, and waltzes, and Aurelia was only too happy to slip into Owen's arms and dance with him. "Hello, Mayor," she said in his ear, giving him a squeeze. "I haven't really had a chance to congratulate you."

"Doesn't matter. I've had more folks congratulate me on my clever and beautiful wife than on my election to mayor."

She chuckled at his fib and smiled into his eyes. As they were swinging around the floor, she caught the sounds of a commotion near the door and turned to look that way. A cowboy she recognized as a regular from the Yellow Rose had come in, swaying on his feet. He was leering and calling

134

something to Selinda and Lad as they danced by. "I hope this isn't trouble," Aurelia whispered to Owen. Yellow Rose customers hadn't been told to stay away from tonight's party, but neither had they been specifically issued an invitation. Boot Harris had been around at the day's activities, but she hadn't seen him tonight. She could feel Owen's slowed breathing as he watched, ready to intervene if necessary.

The cowboy lunged onto the floor, yanked Selinda from Lad's arms, and rushed her over the floor with all the care and finesse of an animal in the wilderness. Aurelia started to break away, but Owen held her and said quietly, "Let's wait a minute. Lad is being a gentleman about it—you can bet if he thinks the gent is harming his girl, he'll stop it." Selinda appeared to be speaking calmly to the drunken cowboy as they danced, albeit wildly, to the music.

It was hard for Aurelia to relax, but she knew it could just as well be one of their own young men creating a scene; some of them were as pie-eyed as the Yellow Rose cowboy.

In the midst of the next waltz, Lad tapped the cowboy on the shoulder and reclaimed Selinda. Scowling, the cowboy stumbled toward the door, hauling an amber bottle from his vest as he went. He disappeared into the starlit night, to Aurelia's relief. Then, two quadrilles and a Virginia Reel later, the cowboy was back. This time, Selinda shook her head with an apologetic smile and moved closer to Lad. The cowboy's voice rose as he argued that she should dance with him and get rid of "the city tenderfoot."

"Little does he know Lad or how he grew up or he'd not be mixing with him," Aurelia muttered.

Lad must have convinced him to leave them alone because the cowboy staggered away, shouting epithets over his shoulder. In a moment he was back and from food tables he had found an ear of corn which he threw as hard as he could, striking Selinda in the head. Lad looked to see that she wasn't seriously hurt and then he went after the cowboy. Grabbing his shoulder and turning him around, he drew back and planted his fist in his face. The cowboy recovered dizzily and swung back, his fist arcing wide from the floor and connecting with Lad's jaw. Lad reeled and struck again.

"Stop them!" Aurelia cried. "Where's Sheriff Holberg?" Her hands crept to her face as Owen raced toward the brawl that now involved several other men. Just when she was sure someone would be killed, Sheriff Holberg's huge bulk stepped into the wild, fist-swinging fracas, and he hauled the cowboy out of it. At the sheriff's order, the rest of the men one by one fell back, shaking themselves, examining their torn sleeves and bloodied fists. To Aurelia's chagrin, several of them were laughing.

"What are you going to do with him?" she hurried to ask the sheriff as he escorted the cowboy outside.

The sheriff told her over his beefy shoulder—the cowboy had collapsed against him like a rag toy—"Can't put him in jail since we don't have one yet. I'll probably lock him up in a stall at the livery until he wakes up to good sense. Maybe before I let him go I'll fine him for disturbing the peace."

"Good." She took a deep breath, "And I'll see that a crew of men start on the jail."

"I know *you and the Mayor* will," the sheriff looked past her at Owen. With his free hand he tipped his hat. "Goodnight, Mayor, goodnight, Mrs. Symington."

Taken aback, she stared after him. Clearly, she'd been put in her place. "Goodnight, sheriff." She turned to Owen, "I'm sorry, I didn't mean to speak out of place. But I can't stop fighting for what's right for this town, myself, just because you're mayor and for all intents and purposes the town company is dissolved."

"No one expects you to, sweetheart. Now come dance another dance with me before this shindig ends."

"Thank you, Mr. Mayor." She took his hand. An understanding husband was just about the best thing a woman could have!

A few months later on an autumn day when the sun was fading, Aurelia drove past her lot on Spencer Street. Because so many other things required her and Owen's time and money, her dream house was yet to be built. The lot would probably remain vacant for some time. Sighing, she drove on two blocks west and drew Sweet Annie to a halt in front of the new school building under construction. Boot Harris had had the basement dug for the school right after the elections. Still without a roof, the school was a grand building of white stone. There were two rooms in the basement—one to be occupied by the janitor and his wife, four rooms on the first floor, three rooms and a supply closet on the second floor. The many windows, each with two panes of glass, reflected the fading light. Word was that the high school rooms had a capacity for eighty students. Unfortunately, Joshua and David John had had to return to Larned for their schooling until this one was finished.

It was impossible not to admire the structure and all it would mean for their young people, Aurelia admitted to herself as she tapped the reins over Sweet Annie's neck and drove on. She wanted the school. She'd always pictured a school just such as this one for Paragon Springs. But part and parcel with this wonderful school came an unvoiced agreement that citizens must condone Harris' corruption, granting him license to form a sewer of the rest of their town.

Against the pressure of Kansas prohibition law—enforced in Paragon Springs by Bert Holberg since elections—Harris had changed his tactics only a little. With his bulk shipments of roots, herbs, leaves and bark he used for mixing, mashing, and measuring into medical dosage, and along with ready-made patent medicines, he continued to receive large amounts of whiskey to liquefy his potions. Lawfully, unfortunately.

In an immense ornate sign in the drug store window he advertised GILBERT AND PARSONS *PURE HYGIENIC* WHISKEY for Medical Use. He suffered no shortage of customers for it. Far too regularly, Bert was forced to toss the drunkest and rowdiest of the dosed into their small new jail to sober up.

Whenever a rare case was actually proven against Harris that he was dispensing whiskey illegally, he paid the fifty-dollar fine, which he could well afford and went on about his business.

Although the Yellow Rose continued to be a hangout for confidence men, gamblers, and thieves, he now called the establishment a "restaurant." She grimaced at the thought. The Yellow Rose's tough steaks and greasy potatoes hardly drew competition from her own place and delicious foods served in the hotel dining room. His courtesans, Franny, Mollie, and Sal, were now billed as "café singers." Gambling tables had been moved to a back room marked "Private."

On the surface, Harris met the law just enough. He continued to maintain, at the same time, that whiskey selling, gambling, and the dance hall should be allowed to continue if they were conducted properly, orderly, and decently. Which was hardly the case. The town council and sheriff's best efforts to the contrary, the red glare of his dance hall "restaurant" was anything but extinguished and still spawned trouble. He was slick, powerful, and making a great deal of money. With a certain element, he was very popular.

Over at Flagg, he continued to operate his two so-called drug stores, a dance hall, and billiard hall, with fewer regulations brought against him there. As Aurelia's concern climbed, she hoped the lawless element would move altogether to Flagg, but as yet it hadn't happened. Harris, like a persistent noxious weed, was a strong, ever-growing presence in Paragon Springs.

Aurelia had rarely felt so defeated and worried as she drove on toward home, but she knew she couldn't give up fighting to make their town safe, comfortable, and smoothly run—a place of pride for its citizens. The right kind of growth for the town, versus the shady, was a dead-heat horse race.

On the favorable side, Owen had recently used his mayoral influence to encourage two new industries to build in Paragon Springs. Located on the far eastern edge of town, the small cheese factory would buy milk from surrounding area farmers and turn it into several kinds of cheeses. Next to the cheese factory a furniture manufactory was being built. Besides furniture, the latter would also provide coffins and undertaker's goods. The new businesses would serve not only the needs of townsfolk and those passing through—as in the case of the cheese factory—but hundreds of others living in outlying areas. No other town in the county had either type business. Such progress enthralled Aurelia, countermanded somewhat her worries about Harris.

At the University, Selinda hurried along the snowy path to the lecture hall where she'd find Lad. The first months of winter had passed fairly uneventfully but now she'd received a letter that had her terribly excited. Bundled in her coat, she hopped up and down in front of the hall to warm her feet. Lad was due out any second. The door opened, and chattering students spilled out onto the sidewalk. Selinda spotted Lad and ran to him.

"Selinda! Is anything wrong?"

"No, something is very right. Come for a walk with me, I have something to show you." Leading the way, she fairly danced along the path until they came to a gazebo cleared of snow. She leaped to sit on one of the benches, motioned Lad to take the other, then changed her mind and moved to sit close to him. With her mittened hand, she reached in her coat pocket and brought out the letter.

"You have news?"

"Yes, my good man, Lad, I do have news." She waved the letter. "This is from an old miner in Montana and it concerns my father. I wired Mama about it and she agrees with me that the letter holds truth. The fellow describes my father accurately. He and my father dug for gold together until my father, feeling Montana Territory was too crowded, followed the goldfields to Oregon."

"That's a very real clue, I'm happy for you, Selinda. What now?"

Her face grew quiet. "Well, the old miner says that was the last he heard of Simeon Lee, that he'd gone off to the goldfields in Oregon, but I'm not giving up. This is the first real news we've heard about my father, and I know it's leading me to the truth, to what really happened. I'm so pleased, you can't know how much, Lad." Impulsively, she threw her arms around his neck and kissed his mouth.

Lad drew back in surprise, a glowing grin on his face. "You're pleased—!" He exclaimed and pulled her to him for another kiss, and another.

"Will Selinda start all over with letters to Oregon?" Aurelia asked when Emmaline told her the latest news.

"I'm afraid she will, although it's a hopeless cause," Emmaline's smooth forehead wrinkled with a sad frown and her eyes clouded. She added, "I have to admit, though, just hearing this bit about Simeon is more than we've had before, for our memories of him. Selinda is very excited, and yes, she's writing letters to Oregon with renewed vigor. I—I wish sometimes that she'd marry Lad, settle down and be an ordinary housewife, but this search is so important to her she can hardly think of anything else. She's not giving up hope that she'll find her father alive." Her voice caught and she started to cry. She finished with a wry, wet smile, "Mrs. Potter reminded me the other day that my daughter is well beyond the usual marrying age and Lad might start looking elsewhere."

"Rubbish!" Aurelia took Emmaline's hand. "They care very much for one another and it's only a matter of time, to my way of thinking, until marriage becomes their priority. Selinda is different, that's all, but she's different in a very nice way. I'd be proud to have Zibby grow up to be just like her. Mrs. Potter perhaps doesn't know that it's possible for a girl to have dreams of her own or how it feels to have the father you hardly had a chance to know simply disappear. Not know what happened to him, or if there's something a person could do to rescue him and bring him home."

After a while Emmaline wiped her tears. "Thank you for understanding, Aurelia. I'm sure everything is going to be fine."

A few days later, Aurelia was thinking about Lad and Selinda, hoping for the best for the pair as she stood at the window of her restaurant idly looking out on the mid-winter day. Her attention perked at the sight of an old man on a beaten-down mule plodding up the street. He made his way through the street's slush and mud to tie at her hitch-rack outside. It had been a slow day for business; bad weather was keeping most diners at home. Her mind quickly tallied what she might serve him as the man approached her door, moving slowly from stiff and half-frozen limbs. He carried a satchel that he was evidently afraid to leave outside. Below his battered hat, frost clung to his mutton-chop side whiskers and shaggy hair. He tracked snow inside on his dirty scuffed boots, but Aurelia had such sympathy for his condition that she didn't mind. "Come in, sir, come in! Sit over here, let me bring you some hot coffee to warm you." Cold air had followed him inside.

He mumbled something and fell into a chair at the table she pointed out. He took off his hat and dropped it on the floor, placed the battered satchel on a chair next to him, and brushed tiredly at his whiskers and moustache.

"I have hot soup," she told him as she poured his coffee, "it'll warm you up in no time." His placid cow-brown eyes looked at her gratefully as he wordlessly drank the hot coffee. She studied him further as he ate his soup. He was the most pathetic looking soul she'd seen in a long time. He wore a dirty brown-checked coat over a tattered black suit with several buttons missing where the cloth stretched across his wide girth. "I've never seen you in Paragon Springs before," she said when he was somewhat revived. "You must be new in town."

He nodded, his double chin jouncing. "More," he said, holding out his empty bowl. She brought him more soup. When he'd finished that he said, "Thank you, ma'am, you're very kind to this unfortunate old man, you're an angel from heaven."

She smiled, "I've heard that before, and I'm really not. I'm just Mrs. Symington, and this is my restaurant. And you, sir, what is your name?"

"Beal," he answered, "Doctor Erastus Beal. From Arkansas."

Her breath caught. "Did you say *Doctor* Beal?"

"Is there pie?" he asked. "Yes, I'm a doctor." He patted the satchel. "My medical books, instruments, and some tonics."

Aurelia rushed to fetch the pie for him. She waited for him to finish it. "Are you looking for a town to practice in? Because we need a doctor hereabouts desperately." Her heart thumped anxiously.

He stroked his moustache and took on a look of importance, "I am seeking a place to practice, Mrs. Symington, and I must say even in the dead of winter, your town looks inviting. My friend, Raffles, is waiting for me just now but later we can discuss the matter." He stood up, looking a trifle embarrassed. "I'm short on funds at the moment—"

"Oh, it's on the house! Anything, Doctor, that you need, just ask. You're very welcome here. Who is Raffles?" Did he have a companion, an assistant perhaps, who hadn't come in with him?

"My mule. Raffles is my mule." As if on cue, the ratty looking gray animal outside brayed loudly sending steam clouds into the chilly air. "Coming," Beal said, "coming."

Aurelia, with only slight misgivings, watched him leave to put up his mule at the livery. She poured herself a cup of coffee, eyes squinted in thought. She should not judge the man by his appearance. Cleaned up and patched, Doctor Beal would probably look as dignified, and professionally able, as any doctor. Traveling a long hard trail in winter would make anyone look like a tramp. She could hardly wait for his return so she could inquire about his qualifications and experience and ask for references.

Although he'd promised to come right back that same afternoon, Aurelia didn't see Doctor Beal again until the next morning when he willingly sat down with her to talk while he ate his oatmeal, flapjacks and ham, and drank his coffee.

"I've lost my paper credentials so I can't show you those," he explained, "but I assure you that I've had years of experience treating every illness, ailment, and accident known to mankind. Beginning," he said, "with my experience as a young orderly to a doctor during the War Between the States."

"Of course, I'm impressed," she told him, and added respectfully, "Even so, I must insist on seeing your credentials. I will write to the medical school that gave you your license, and I'd also like to contact the last town where you practiced." She waited, trying to quell little worms of suspicion and doubt in her mind.

He smiled at her confidently, "I received my two-year course of medical studies at the St. Louis School Of Medicine. I last practiced in Paragould, Arkansas. I understand your concerns, ma'am."

She smiled in relief, her suspicions faded. "Thank you. I'll write the letters right away. In the meantime, while I wait to hear from the medical school and the officials in Paragould, you may as well begin your practice." She told him soberly, "We seem to have more than our share of sickness and accidents in and about Paragon Springs. I vow you'll have more patients than you can count as soon as word gets out that we have a doctor in town. Until you begin collecting fees, I'm sure the Morgan family will give you room and board on credit at their boarding house, or you could stay at the Marble House Hotel and take your meals there or here in my restaurant—if you like."

He shook his head at her suggestions of where he might stay. "I engaged a room," he told her, "above the pharmacy. That will be very handy for me, and I'll see my patients there."

"But that's—" Aurelia began, and then she said, humbly, "all right." She supposed it made sense for a doctor to room and see his patients in the same building that housed the pharmacy, but her disappointment drove deep. Not twenty-four hours had passed and the doctor was already a Harris man. But he was a doctor and that alone was a small miracle—given all the effort she'd put into trying to find a physician willing to practice in Paragon Springs.

# Chapter Ten

A silk purse couldn't be made out of a sow's ear and time soon proved that Doctor Beal would never fit the qualifications of a physician such as Aurelia had hoped for. He wasn't always available, meaning he often wasn't sober. Records sent her from the medical school indicated he had been a mediocre student; Paragould officials indicated that Beal had practiced there only a few weeks and they had no firm opinion about him, either for or against.

Aurelia decided that he had to be better than no doctor at all; he did have training and experience in medicine. But she was uneasy regarding him and his qualifications. If she could find someone better to replace him, she wouldn't hesitate.

They had a spate of illnesses in the community and roundabout the area the rest of that winter and spring: colds and flu, rheumatism, malnutrition, and one isolated case of typhoid that fortunately didn't turn into an epidemic. And one gunshot wound, and then a broken arm from being thrown from a horse. Doctor Beal, according to reports, treated cases—whatever they might be—with two main panaceas: a massive dose of calomel, or blood-letting by either lancet or the use of blood-sucking leeches. Blood-letting was a practice many doctors and patients were beginning to doubt was beneficial.

Aurelia wondered if Beal's patients survived despite his care and not because of it. But he was the only doctor they had until they could find a better one. She worried particularly about Essie Reid. The soft-spoken little woman had already suffered two miscarriages and she was expecting again.

Ben was asking around where the best doctors were available in western Kansas. He would take Essie to Larned, or even Garden City where they would take a hotel room. A doctor in one of those towns could look after her and attend her delivery. Aurelia felt guilty that Paragon Springs couldn't provide reliable medical care but Essie's was a special case. Most women felt they needed only a female friend or relative to attend them.

Aurelia was locking up on a rainy spring evening when a voice cleared suddenly behind her. She whirled. "Ben!" His face was pinched with despair and worry; he drove his hand through his curly brown hair while his hat hung limply in his other hand. "Oh, Ben, is it Essie?"

He nodded, cleared his throat again and found his voice, "She's very bad. The baby wasn't due for another three weeks, but—Essie's in labor."

"Someone's with her?" she caught his arm and frantically studied his face in the downpour.

"We got Doctor Beal, and her mother is with her, too. But the baby won't come, and Essie's in pain and very weak," he explained as they hurried down the street toward the little house in back of the saddlery. "Essie was fine this morning, although she's felt a little blue lately. She wanted to go for a walk and see the sunrise. Wasn't rainy then, it was a nice morning."

"I saw the two of you walking when I drove into town to open the restaurant. Essie seemed fine."

"She was, then. After we got back from the walk we cleared the breakfast dishes and I left for the furniture factory to order a rocking chair to be built for her. We were all packed to leave for Garden City so the doctor there could attend her and the baby. I was a little long at the factory, telling just how

I wanted the chair designed and built while we were away. I stopped at Wurst's store to buy a few vittles to take with us on our trip and when I got home about eight-thirty Essie was in labor. I fetched her mother to stay with her and I went for Doctor Beal."

"She's been in labor almost twelve hours?"

Shivering in the rain, he choked, "I thought maybe with you and her mother both there, you could think of something, do something, to help her." He swiped at his eyes with his fist. "Doctor Beal told me to keep out of the way and wait. I've been walking around, praying, but I can't stay away."

"Of course, and she'll be all right," Aurelia said, breaking into a run and holding his arm to keep from falling in the slippery mud. "We'll see that she's just fine and the baby, too."

When they burst into the small sod shack, Essie's mother was coming out of the curtained bedroom, eyes flooded with tears, and carrying a small bloody morsel on a towel in her arms. "He's dead—Essie's baby boy is dead. I'm so sorry, Ben."

Ben bolted for the bedroom, almost crashing into Doctor Beal who had come out at the sound of voices. With a bloodied hand Beal let the curtain drop behind him. He barred Ben's way. "Your wife wants to see you, son," he said, his hand on Ben's rain-soaked shoulder, "but let the women clean her up a bit first. I'll see to the dead infant." He took the baby from Hannah's trembling arms. "There's a lot of blood," he told her, looking puzzled and somewhat guilty, "see what you can do."

Aurelia fired him a look of disbelief, suggested gently to Ben that he dry off, and then she followed Hannah into the bedroom. Essie looked at them from the bed. She was very pale, and there were blue shadows under her eyes. Pain was written in her expression and her voice was almost soundless from exhaustion, "Mama. Aurelia. My baby—" Her tears spilled over.

"Shh, now, girl, shh," Hannah crooned to her daughter, her tears welling fresh.

"We're going to take care of you," Aurelia said softly, keeping her sadness and worry from her voice as much as possible. "So Ben can come in." Essie's face when Aurelia touched it was warm and beaded with perspiration. She had almost no pulse. Aurelia turned back the coverlet and smothered a small cry. Essie's thin, nightgown-clad body lay in a river of blood.

Working together with tender concern, Aurelia and Hannah washed Essie and dressed her in a fresh nightgown. They changed her bedding, placing extra padding between her legs and under her. But she was in obvious pain and she continued to flood.

She told them feebly, "I'm afraid the d-doctor has killed me. I heard him say that the cord was b-broken when he tried to remove the afterbirth when—when I couldn't get it out by-by pushing. I—asked him to wait, I was just r-resting." Tears swam in her eyes. Her face was ghostly pale. She licked her lips and whispered, "I don't have long; bring Ben here to me, please."

"I'll get him," Aurelia told Essie, tears of sympathy, as well as fury at the doctor, choking in her throat, "but you'll be fine, Essie, we'll get you through this."

Essie smiled wanly, her eyes closed. "Thank you, Aurelia, but I feel so—so weak. What happened—wasn't right. My poor baby first, and now I'm leaving Ben . . ." A tear trailed down her pale cheek.

A harried Ben entered at Aurelia's bidding. He bent to kiss Essie's brow, his mouth trembling, then he took her hand and sat down by her bed. "How do you feel, angel-darlin'?"

Essie tried to raise her head from the pillow but made only slight movement. She sighed, her limp fingers loose in his big hand, "I don't feel good at all, Ben. I'm so sorry."

Aurelia could hardly see for the tears swimming in her eyes. "I'm going to talk to the doctor for just a minute," she said softly. As she went into the other room, the first thing she saw was the tiny blanket-wrapped form of the baby lying in a small box on the table. For a moment she couldn't move, her heart felt like it was breaking into pieces. She clutched the edge of the table, watched the doctor alternately drinking coffee and looking for something in his medicine bag. When she had control, she kept her voice low but she was direct, "Hannah showed me the afterbirth in the pan on the floor in there; to both of us it seemed like precious little. Is Essie bleeding because there is still afterbirth in her womb and the cord broken?"

His eyes shifted away from her and he spoke defensively as he rummaged in his medicine bag, "I'm a doctor but I'm not God, Mrs. Symington. Essie was too worn down and weak to expel the afterbirth so I helped and the placenta tore. I'd used manual pressure and friction on her abdomen over and over, at least fifty times, trying to get her to push and expel the afterbirth. She doesn't seem to have the necessary strength."

"Mother of God! That's because she's weak from losing so much blood!" Aurelia's voice was hoarse with anger and despair, "I don't expect you to be God, Doctor Beal, but I do expect you to do your best for Essie and save her! What are you going to do? She's bleeding to death in there." Rain drummed on the ground outside adding to the tension.

He brought out a green bottle, examined the amount of the contents and swirled it. "I'm prescribing ten drops of fluid ergot every two hours. The tonic should stimulate her womb. The rest is up to Essie." He pushed past

Aurelia and returned to the sick room.

Aurelia went to the stove, stirred up the fire, and made fresh coffee. She considered fixing some food, then decided no one felt like eating. A while later, Beal came out of the other room. He put on his coat and hat, picked up his satchel, and headed for the door.

"Where are you going?" Aurelia was aghast. "You can't leave!" A sudden thought struck her. "Is Essie—is she—?" She leaned back against the cupboard, forgetting her frantic search for something that might nourish Essie, help her regain her strength until the bleeding could be stopped.

"She's not dead, if that's what you're asking, but there's nothing more that I can do for her. I gave Mrs. Tuttle directions for giving liquid ergot. Essie should be kept warm and allowed to rest. There's nothing else can be done, but I'll be back to check on her after I've had a chance to have supper and rest a bit, myself."

Aurelia watched in numb disbelief as he went out into the rainstorm. Walking softly, she hurried back to the sickroom. Hannah, her face embedded with worry, was arranging and rearranging the coverlet over her daughter for lack of something constructive to do. Ben sat by the bed looking at his still wife with teary eyes, his hand on her hair.

"I want to try to help her—" Aurelia waited for Ben's nod and then she took his arm and leaned over him, "You should get some coffee, Ben. I made sure that it's nice and hot." He sat without moving, as though he hadn't heard. When Aurelia sighed and spoke again, he moved mechanically to obey. As he left the room he looked over his shoulder at Essie, his jaw trembling, his eyes haunted.

For sometime Aurelia massaged Essie's abdomen gently, hoping the womb would contract and expel the contents. She stopped when the manipulation seemed only to encourage

151

the hemorrhaging. Asking Hannah's help, she changed and washed Essie, exchanging fresh padding and bedding for that which was soaked again with blood. Essie was like a lifeless doll, her breathing short and weak, her color gone. Her perspiration had grown cold. She was close to losing consciousness and still the bleeding continued. They found extra quilts to cover her and keep her body warm. Outside, the sound of wind and rain continued.

By the end of the first two-hour period, they could not revive Essie enough that she could swallow another dose of ergot and it dribbled down her chin. "Nothing seems to work!" Aurelia lamented in frustration.

"We can pray," Hannah said wearily, but hopefully, from her place at Essie's bedside—she lifted Essie's limp hand to kiss it—"and that's what I'm doin'. I'm askin' God's good grace to save my child—" her voice broke on a soft sob.

Beal did not return but sometime in the middle of the night one of the girls came from the Yellow Rose with a dish of ice the doctor had sent. Aurelia stared at it dumbfounded and said nothing. The girl misunderstood and thought Aurelia wondered at its origin, "One of the ranchers keeps an ice-house, Boot buys the ice from him. The doctor says to put the ice—well—inside the lady, it might help her womb contract."

At the sound of a wail of sobs from the other room, Aurelia left the woman standing with the bowl of ice in the open doorway, silver streaks of rain behind her against the blackness of night. In Essie's room, Ben was on the floor on his knees, his head on Essie's lifeless body, his shoulders heaving. Hannah was sobbing at the other side of the bed, her hand caressing her daughter's brown hair over and over. Hannah looked up at Aurelia, "She's gone. Her pain is done. My Essie is with God."

★ ★ ★ ★ ★

The rocking chair Ben had ordered special for Essie was replaced with a coffin. The town's new undertaker dressed Essie in a white shroud and placed the infant beside her in the long narrow pine box. At the funeral service, those attending sang *Abide With Me*, their hearts crying out for God's help in dealing with their grief. Essie had been one of their beloved own, and she would be missed. And Aurelia would believe to the end of her days that Essie's death, and possibly the infant's, too, might have been avoided with decent doctoring.

Doctor Beal came into the restaurant for supper a few evenings after the funeral. It was hard for Aurelia to be civil as she served him. Noting her manner, he brought up the subject of Essie's death and tried to defend himself, "I did the best for that poor young woman that I could." He broke a biscuit, then shoveled his fork into the thick, steaming beef stew and began eating as though that settled the matter.

"I believe you did, Doctor Beal. The trouble is, your best is not good enough for folks here at Paragon Springs. I can't in good conscience even pretend you are a physician; I could not send anyone to you in the belief they'd receive reliable treatment. I suggest you either leave town, or find another profession that doesn't harm people." Her hand shook as she poured his coffee, inside she was so furious she would have liked to drive him from town with a horsewhip. "I will advise the town council to prevent you from carrying on a medical practice here, do you understand me?"

A few weeks later Aurelia heard that Boot Harris had put Beal to work in his pharmacy by day and to dealing cards in his back room at night. If anyone went to him for doctoring, she didn't hear about it. Most folks believed they were safer dealing with their medical concerns themselves, than having

Beal treat them. She next heard that Beal had left town altogether. She experienced intense relief at the news, but hoped that wherever he went, others would know him for his quackery sooner than she had.

It was hard to set aside her feelings of sadness over Essie Reid's death, and her guilt that the community couldn't provide better doctoring. But gradually as summer came on, by throwing herself into daily tasks, she returned to her normal strong self. She appreciated—counted like gold coin—the simple ordinary days that came and went with no serious troubles occurring. She treasured the small moments—loaves of bread fragrant from the oven and browned just right, a rosy sunset, a friendly smile from a person she hardly knew—and she drew those moments into her soul. They were patches of healing against past pain, reinforcing muscle against whatever strife the future might bring. If experience had taught her anything, it was that life never stood still and anything could happen—especially in a land just beginning to feel its way toward true civilization.

Selinda bent and threw more papers on the small fire she'd built in her mother's backyard. It blazed up and she watched in sadness, coughed when she breathed in smoke. At the sound of a horse and buggy coming to a halt out front of her mother's small cottage, she left the fire and ran to the street to meet Lad.

She had been expecting him. Every evening that he didn't have to be out of town on a case with Hamilton this summer, he'd come to take her for a ride in the country. Often the moon was high and it was after midnight before they returned from the ride. For both of them, being separated was growing more and more difficult.

He leaped from the buggy, grabbed her and kissed her. "I

saw smoke as I drove up the street. Are you burning rubbish?"

"Some letters and newspapers that I ordered. Come to the backyard with me." She took his hand and led the way around the cottage to the small fire. "I'm almost finished. I don't want the fire to get out of control, the whole country has been like tinder this summer."

Lad rifled through some of the newspapers in a chair a few feet from the fire. "These are from Montana, Colorado, and Oregon. And letters—what are you doing, Selinda?"

"It's over, I'm giving up the search for my father."

"But why? Things were going so well. You had the tip that he'd gone to Oregon. I don't understand why you're giving up?" He grabbed her hands and held them tight.

"I've heard nothing from Oregon except for a few radical letters. Some of the letter writers claim they knew my father and he owes them money and I'm to pay what's owed. Some propose marriage because women are few in Oregon." She looked away from him, pulled free and fed more papers into the fire. "You and Mama are right, I've thrown myself into a useless cause that I never should have begun."

"I know you, Selinda, and you wouldn't mind receiving a hundred crazy letters if in the end you found your father. I wish you weren't doing this . . ."

"All right, I don't mind the letters except that they are no help. I'm heartsick to give up the search, but for Mama's sake I must. My pursuit of my father's destiny keeps her constantly upset and I never wanted to hurt her. I won't be writing any more letters. It's enough that she lost my father in the first place. And then my brother . . ." She swallowed tears. "I'm all the family she has."

With a murmur deep in his throat, Lad slipped his arms around her waist from behind and pulled her back against him. He kissed her neck. "I'm sorry you're giving it up, Selinda," he said in a low voice, "because I know how much it meant to you to find out about your father. As far as your mother is concerned, however, I can be her family."

Selinda squirreled around in his arms, and her heart raced. "Lad Voss, what did you say?"

"I said I could be your mother's family, her son-in-law. Without much effort, we could probably provide her a whole flock of grand-children."

"Speak for yourself! From what I've heard, you'd have the easy part!" Her face flamed, but she felt a deep stirring of happiness. "I'm assuming your remark constitutes a proposal?"

"I love you so much, Selinda, I'm not sure I can finish my studies this last year, unless you're my wife."

"Mama will be so excited, she loves you, Lad, and always has."

He chuckled, "My sister Lucy will be thrilled, too. In fact, let's don't tell anyone the news just yet. You know this town, these people. In their delirium they'll want to take over our plans, our lives."

She laughed, "They'd do it out of pure love—they care about us, very much. What about our plans, then?"

"Let's finish with your little bonfire, then we'll take a ride and discuss our incredible future."

"And really truly blackboards!" Zibby told Aurelia in breathless excitement. It was a month before classes would start and Zibby had been at the new school building that summer afternoon, watching the unloading of a large wagon filled with school supplies. Aurelia would have liked to have seen the unloading for herself, but couldn't leave the restaurant. Zibby continued, "Mama, they carried in a piano, and music books! Something called a-a microscope. And storybooks, and study books. Desks and tables, and a clock and a globe for each room." If Zibby had seen fairyland her eyes couldn't have reflected a fraction more delight. "Mr. Harris has some men planting tree seedlings on the grounds—box elder, mulberry, and soft maple." She giggled, and whispered, "There are *two* outhouses, one marked for boys, and one for girls."

Aurelia drew her daughter to her and hugged her. "I'm glad you're happy about the school, Zib. I'm—" she drew a deep breath— "I'm happy about it, too." Joshua had declared his high school studies at Larned were all he wanted or would ever use. David John had wanted to quit the same time as his brother but at Aurelia's insistence he would continue his studies at the new high school for a year and maybe two. She had hoped Joshua would want to go on to college—she would have been more than pleased if he chose to study medicine— but both of her sons were natural-born farmers and wanted only to work the land. She wished sometimes now that Lad had studied medicine instead of law. They had Hamilton to see to their legal problems. But Lad was cut out to be a lawyer, and she had no right to wish otherwise. She'd simply have to continue searching for the right doctor for them.

The new teachers arrived soon after the supplies and this time Aurelia slipped out with everyone else to watch their arrival in town.

The stage drew to a dusty stop in front of the Marble House. Harris was there to introduce them to the crowd in his friendly, booming voice. Again, Harris appeared to have kept his promise to provide the best teachers that could be found. Aurelia liked the looks of both women. Miss Myra Otto was the taller of the two, plain of face, lean and angular. Her light brown hair, worn pulled back in a bun, was surmounted by a large horn comb. Under her shawl she wore a blue plaid dress with the teeniest bit of lace around her high tight collar and the cuffs of her long sleeves—nothing showy. She was brisk of manner and somewhat fidgety, but her gray eyes were friendly as she was introduced. Her attentive, loving manner toward the children was entirely satisfying.

Miss Carolina Marshal was as different in appearance from Miss Otto as night from day. She was short, plump, and pretty with flaming red hair worn loose about her face and in a thick knot in back. Her corseted full figure was encased in corded pearl-gray bengaline. She had lively green eyes, an adoring care for the children in the crowd—far more than for the adults—but overall there was a firm, no-nonsense manner about her that closely matched Miss Otto's. Both women looked to be careful with their clothes, and probably with their money and reputation as well. All told, they suited.

Emmaline would devote herself from now on to her duties as postmistress, publishing the *Echo*—the circulation having grown to three hundred paying subscribers. Paid advertising in the *Echo*, and printing circulars for businesses supplemented her income and she would also fill in at the school if one of the other teachers fell ill or needed to be away for any reason.

Two gentlemen teachers followed on the next stage, a Mr. Haywood, who would be the superintendent as well as teach classes in United States history and advanced mathematics, and a Mr. Rutan who would conduct the remaining high school classes—in physiology, literature, grammar and spelling, and basic mathematics. Aurelia believed them to be equally qualified to teach and guide the fifty youngsters of Paragon Springs and twenty or more children coming in from surrounding farms and ranches.

She still hoped to buy the school out of Harris' hands, but

it couldn't happen any time soon. The community was building a small, long-desired non-denominational church on the hill close to the cemetery. Plus, several members of the community, Owen and herself included, had made the decision to pool their funds and start a small bank as soon as possible—to compete with Boot Harris' nefarious lending methods that left so many folks destitute. Once again, the building of her house in town had to be postponed.

At home at the ranch, Aurelia worked long hours into the night, after the restaurant was closed, sewing new school dresses and bonnets for Zibby and shirts for the boys. She bought a fine new hat for David John from the haberdashery, but Joshua said he had no need of anything so fancy where he'd be spending most of his time with Owen in the fields.

Then school started, and for most of each day the town was reasonably quiet. Aurelia was at the restaurant, taking the last of four pumpkin pies from the oven one day when Emmaline burst through the door. It was during mid-afternoon lull, between dinner and supper, and the only customers were a rancher and his son who'd been passing through and stopped for pie and coffee. They were getting ready to leave. Aurelia took their money, with a smile bade them to come again, and when the door closed after them she turned to Emmaline. "What is it, for goodness sake, Emmaline? You look like you've seen a ghost!"

Emmaline had the strangest expression: half sad, half relieved and maybe a little glad. There was evidence of recent tears on her cheeks. She asked on a deep sigh, "Can we sit down?"

"Of course we can. I've been baking all day and don't mind sitting down at all." She motioned to a table, wiped her perspiring brow with her apron and sat down. "Now tell me what has you all a-bother, Emmaline."

"It's Selinda. When she got back to college there was a letter waiting for her—and a package, too. She sent them on to me, with a letter from her, of course, explaining." Emmaline licked her lips, "My throat is awfully dry, it's hard to talk. If I could have a drink of water—"

Aurelia held up a hand. "Wait. I'll get us some coffee and pie." She flew at the tasks, dying to know more of Emmaline's news. She sat down again, her hand gripping the handle of her steaming cup. "Go on."

"The letter was addressed from Baker, Oregon, and was written by a man named Hap Goode who said—he knew— Simeon." Emmaline stared at Aurelia for a moment as though lost in a dream, then she took a sip of coffee. "He wrote that Simeon and a fellow named Oblinger were partners in a rich mine in the Greenhorn Mountains of Oregon, close to a townsite called Robinsonville. He said Simeon and Oblinger had found deposits of gold in rotten quartz— gold so rich it looked like nut candy." Her eyebrows rose in some doubt at that. "Right after they discovered the gold, Simeon disappeared and it was generally believed he had taken his share and returned to his family—as he'd often talked about." A glimmer of tears showed in her eyes. She wiped them away and lifted her coffee cup to her trembling lips.

A shiver traced down Aurelia's back and she held her breath. Simeon hadn't returned so something else had happened. She waited for Emmaline to regain her composure.

"When Oblinger died of natural causes—this was years after they struck gold—his cabin was torn down and the ground around it was dug up by men who believed Oblinger's share of the find was buried there somewhere." Here Emmaline spoke so quietly Aurelia could hardly hear her as she said, "No gold was found, but a-a-the skeleton of a man was. The size of the skeleton was the same as—as Simeon's would have been. Simeon's gold pocket watch, with his initials entwined with mine, was found in the rotted cloth of his vest pocket. Hap Goode has kept it all this time."

The hair on the back of Aurelia's neck stood up. She stared at Emmaline, her throat emotion-filled for her friend. When she could speak, she asked, "They concluded that Oblinger killed Simeon for his share of the gold?"

"Yes. And they are convinced that Oblinger, a miserly sort, hid all of the gold—his and Simeon's—somewhere else. It has never been found." Emmaline opened her drawstring bag and with a shaking hand brought out a pocket watch on a small chain. She said in a choked voice, "This was Simeon's. I gave it to him for a wedding present." She caressed the engraved initials on the back with the ball of her thumb and her eyes filled with glittery tears. She blinked at them and dug out her handkerchief.

Aurelia's hand covered Emmaline's on the table. "You believe, then, that the skeleton that was found was Simeon's?"

"Yes, I do. There was no one to prosecute, since Oblinger was dead, and the truth of what actually happened died with him. But, Aurelia, I know in my heart these are the facts, the truth of what happened to my husband. I've known all along that he was dead; if he were alive he'd have sent for us or returned to us years ago."

"Is Selinda satisfied she's finally found the answers to what happened?"

Emmaline's expression cleared, and softened, "She's sad, but satisfied. As I am. The man's story was believable, and Simeon's watch clinched his story."

Aurelia said on a deep breath, "Well, then, I'm glad it's over and done. Even if the ending could have been happier."

"My Simeon's at rest, and in my heart I'll always love him.

He went away to help us, not hurt us. It was fate that altered our lives."

The remainder of fall and the first months of winter that might otherwise have passed in dreary sameness, was an exceptionally enjoyable time for the women at Paragon Springs as they prepared for the Christmas-time wedding of Selinda and Lad. The announcement had been sudden, and yet no one was surprised. The women hustled the men of the community into finishing the little church and furnishing it with benches and a pulpit. They formed an evening sewing circle strictly for the purpose of creating a trousseau of household linens, aprons, and pretty undergarments for Selinda. When they gathered, the women coaxed Emmaline to tell her story and Simeon's over and over—they never tired of it. The best part was seeing his watch that had come home to stay, their names entwined on the back.

Lucy Ann had been working on a wedding ring quilt for a year or two, intending to give it to Lad and his bride when the time came. The women helped her finish it. Cookies and candies were made and stored. Admire, who claimed he had to go anyway on a business trip, took his wagon and team and drove sixty miles north to a stream where he cut down two cedar trees, one to decorate for the church, and one for the hotel where the wedding supper and dance would be held.

A few days before the wedding, Aurelia and Meg were decorating the Christmas tree at the church with red bows and strings of popcorn. "Remember our double wedding?" Aurelia asked Meg, "when you married Hamilton and I married Owen in the same ceremony?"

"Do I! It was outdoors in July and the heat and flies were terrible. The minister was days late and folks who'd come for the wedding danced until the wee hours every night and ate up all the food we'd fixed for the wedding supper. We were lucky to still have cake." Both women burst out laughing and put their arms around one another.

"The most important thing," Aurelia said, "is that we got married—each to the wonderful man who had captured our heart."

"Amen," Meg answered, then teased, "Although you were the stubbornest thing about getting married for a long time, Aurelia."

"I didn't want to lose another husband. I still don't. Owen is the wonder of my life; I wouldn't trade our years together for anything else on earth."

They finished tying cedar garland with red and white ribbon and draping it about the walls. Later, after they'd fastened tiny candles to the many branches of the cedar, they stood back and admired their handiwork. The rich scent of cedar, a rarity in their part of the country, filled the room. "We'll light the candles on the tree for the church service in the morning, and again in the evening for the wedding ceremony," Meg said.

"And keep an eye on them every moment so that an accidental fire doesn't spoil the day," Aurelia added.

There was concern that the bridal couple might be held away due to bad weather, and then, as though even the fates were in favor of the wedding, they arrived home on the Hessler stage, cold but otherwise just fine, the day before Christmas.

The next day dawned clear and bright. Under a sky of dazzling blue, a blanket of snow sparkled as far as the eye could see. All over the community, breakfasts and baths were hurried through to attend church for Christmas morning services. Once there, citizens fidgeted and time seemed to drag as they listened to scriptures and preaching from their minister, young, cherub-faced, Reverend Smithall. One and all, they were primed for a wedding and time was simply standing still. Reverend Smithall, after a frustrated hour and a half trying to preach and save their souls, conceded. He led them in singing a final rousing hymn, and then with a sigh he released them until evening.

Selinda had selected her wedding dress in Lawrence. It was a simple but elegant gown of lace-trimmed, ivory brocaded satin that highlighted her dark beauty. As she and Lad stood facing one another before the congregation that evening—repeating their vows after the minister—Aurelia thought she had never seen a more beautiful bride, a more handsome couple. Lad stood tall and erect in a black suit, his adoring gaze on Selinda's face. Her smile, looking up at him through her sheer veil, was radiant.

Aurelia was so happy for them—and for Emmaline and Lucy Ann, too, that she could have burst. It was so right that Selinda and Lad were the first couple to be married in the community's new church, by the first minister that was truly the town's own!

Dark had fallen when it was time to leave the church. The Hesslers had purchased three sleighs to add to their fleet of hotel conveyances, and the horse-drawn sleighs were lined up outside, lit with bright lanterns, waiting in the snow to take the wedding guests to the hotel for the wedding supper. When it came their turn, Aurelia snuggled close to Owen, laughing lightly as their sleigh, with the horses' harness bells tinkling, flew smoothly over the snow and ice, down the hill, and along the street to the Marble House. When Owen took her into his arms and kissed her soundly—the night starlit all around them—she wasn't surprised. "I've wanted to kiss you, too, all evening," she whispered, her cold nose against his ear.

"I suppose weddings do that to people who are already in love."

"Absolutely," he nuzzled her cheek, then helped her from the sleigh so she could hurry inside and help lay out the wedding feast.

Emmaline and Lucy Ann had arrived in an earlier sleigh, and with aprons over their best dresses they were setting out the food on long white-clothed, candle-lit tables. There was roast turkey, beef, and ham, oysters, corn pudding, sour cream potato salad, many kinds of bread, pumpkin pie and mince pies, fruit cake, ginger cookies, and candy. And a tall, snowy white wedding cake.

When Aurelia had helped Lucy Ann and Emmaline, she went to assist Meg who was setting out cups, preparing to serve hot cider.

"If every day in Paragon Springs could be like this one," she marveled to Meg, "what a blessing it would be!" With a high heart, her eyes followed Selinda and Lad. The newly-wedded couple were holding hands, their young faces shining as they moved about the crowded room to speak to first one guest and then another. Contentment and happiness were as thick in the room as soft cotton, and Aurelia could only wish there was a way to preserve it, for all time.

# Chapter Eleven

Months flowed one into the next. Paragon Springs lay quiet behind Aurelia on the summer morning she made her way up to the cemetery. Ahead, against a pink-tinged sky, a flock of larks circled the spire of the little white church.

She carried a jar of water filled with carefully nurtured fragrant cornflowers for Helen Grace's grave. In the deepest recesses of her heart she still missed her first girl-child more than she could ever describe to anyone. Although her thoughts were often with Helen, hard work and shortage of free time prevented her visiting the cemetery as often as she would like. Today she had stolen the time, would open her restaurant a tad late.

With the years, other graves had joined that of Helen Grace's. Her heart ached over each one: the recent small graves of a mover family's three youngsters who, like Helen, also died of childhood disease. Almost as new was the grave of Essie Reid who was buried with her tiny infant. From the old days, the grave of Grandma Spicy—such a dear old woman they had all loved; the graves of Emmaline's father, Old Professor, and Emmaline's son, Schafer, Selinda's twin.

As she left a flower on each grave, insects sang in the grass around her ankles, and caught on her long skirts. Finally, she came to the burial place of the drifter shot last New Year's eve in a gambling dispute at the Yellow Rose. What a way to end the year, after Selinda and Lad's beautiful wedding! No one knew the drifter's real name, but some thought he came from Texas, and *Tex* was carved on his tombstone. Good sense and abolishment of Harris' hangout would surely have prevented his death. Proper doctoring, she was positive, could have saved some of the other lives.

That she hadn't yet been able to find a qualified, permanent doctor for their community angered her, frustrated her, was her almost constant worry. She would keep trying to find the right doctor for them, and one way or another, she would succeed.

She knelt and yanked weeds from around Helen Grace's monument. The morning began to heat up, cooled only slightly by the wind, and she wiped her brow on her sleeve. With the plot cleared of weeds, she placed the remaining flowers in the jar of water at the head.

If not for her child's grave here in the Lord's good earth, she reflected, she would have been long gone from this place. She touched the stone she had carved herself, so carefully, years back. "Helen," she whispered, "my child. I would near give my soul to have you with me still." Helen would be approaching young womanhood now, had she lived, she'd have been a beautiful young woman she was sure. Ignoring the fact that she must get back to town, she sat for a long while in the companionable company of her child's spirit.

Because of Helen Grace, she had brought this town into being. Not alone, of course, but she had had more to do than anyone else with making the place substantial, a real town. Just two years old—and as if they had always been there—false-fronted shops and stores edged the criss-crosses of dusty downtown streets. In the town square, a few thin elm and cottonwood trees thrived, home for locusts that sang on hot afternoons. Geraniums bloomed in window boxes at her restaurant, at Dinah's millinery shop, and at Maud Mullendore's dress shop.

In a while, still thoughtful, she made her way back into town. As usual, a few old men with nothing better to do and the day hardly begun sat on the bench in front of the Harris Drug Store. Near them, younger fellows, drifters and no-goods for the most part, lazed back on one heel against the walls, chewing, spitting, yarning. Blatantly they sipped at bottles of whiskey-laden bitters for their so-called "stomach troubles."

With irritation she tore her gaze from Harris' unpleasant establishments. She looked beyond downtown where dozens of dwellings lined side streets, as though sprung from the prairie. A few were stately stone or frame structures of two stories, including Meg and Hamilton's new place in town, the Jones brothers' house, and next door, her and Owen's house finally being built. Most residences, though, were small, white-washed board and batten cottages or sod houses with pink and red hollyhocks blooming by the door. The result, in any regard, pleased her.

Down the road to the west and on the opposite side from her house was the two-story school of polished stone. Out back, spanking white in the morning sun, were twin out-houses in a grove of young trees. As Harris had promised, the school was well-equipped and well-run.

As much as she liked having her children attend school close to home, it scared her to have Harris *own* every stick of it, the life of the school in his hands. Should he become dis-gruntled with acts of the town council—say stronger effort to curb his illicit businesses dispensing alcohol and providing girls for prostitution, he could take the school away from them. He could turn it into whatever sort of business ap-pealed to his gluttony for money.

She desperately wanted it to be a city-owned school, truly belonging to all of them. Of course, even if they raised the money to buy him out, Harris had to be convinced to sell.

On the far eastern edge of town were the newest industries, the cheese factory and furniture manufactory, that they'd gained thanks to Owen's efforts as mayor. He had won the mayorship in the first election by a frighteningly narrow margin over charismatic Boot Harris, but this spring, thanks to excellent leadership, Owen won the second term more easily. Naturally, he often teased her that he was only a figure-head, that she and her women-friends really ran the town. She couldn't argue the point altogether.

Owen was as instrumental as she, on the other hand, in convincing a group of citizens to pool funds to form the Paragon Springs Community Bank. Their own house might have been built sooner had they not invested their time and money in bringing to fruition the small but impressive stone bank across the street east from Wurst's General Store.

If their banking concern cut into Harris's loan business as she'd hoped it would, it was hardly evident. There were still many who went to him for easy money, rather than see a tough time through. Invariably, in turn, they lost most everything they had to him.

Regardless, she was sure that the bank—along with the other industries—would strengthen the drive to attract a railroad. Would improve their chances to see the town named county seat. She also saw them as counter balance to all that Harris owned, as his holdings continued to grow—including their school.

From their homes and farms around Hodgeman County, lax commissioners were still "thinking over" Owen's request—which had recently turned into a demand, for an election to name a new county seat. Flagg certainly wasn't suitable. She had no intention of letting the matter drop, and alongside Owen, would continue to push to get the county seat question on the fall ballots. She just wished she, all women, could personally vote.

Remembering that she had to stop at Wurst's for a parcel of sausages for her restaurant, she abandoned her thoughts and picked up her steps.

One sultry evening in August, about seven o'clock, Aurelia had served all but the last of her supper crowd and was beginning to wipe down tables. Only Luther and Silas Jones remained, eating leisurely, talking quietly at a corner table.

The restaurant was successful, was making money, but it was hard work and took up so much of her time. She was tired, anxious to be with her children at the ranch.

For nearly a week Owen had been traveling the county to talk to folks about voting bonds for a railroad. It was a hard argument to sell. Town residents of Flagg and other small communities believed the railroad would benefit only Paragon Springs so they felt no need to help pay for it. Luckily, many of the farmers and ranchers in outlying areas were in favor. The matter would simply have to be brought to a vote and then they would see.

Today Owen was canvassing the northwest section around Kidderville. She was anxious for him to be home in another couple of days and tell her what he learned from up there.

At first she took no more than little note of the odd light outside the front window. She had thought the day's storm, lightning and thunder followed hard by hail and rain, was over.

She brought Luther and Silas their apple cobbler and a small pitcher of pouring cream. Then, as she swept the kitchen area, she noted that their faces and clothes had taken on an odd coppery hue from the outdoor light flooding in. Everything in the restaurant was turned copper-colored.

She mopped her forehead on the back of her arm and wondered if the muggy heat she was feeling had something to do with the copperish air? Her dress under her arms was wringing wet. It was hard to breathe. The temperature had ranged in the neighborhood of 102–105 degrees for days now. They had needed rain, but the downpour earlier in the day had dried almost as soon as it touched the parched soil.

She thought irritably that Kansas weather was capricious at best, a terrorizing destroyer, a killer, at its worst. Summer brought searing heat, winter typically brought blizzards. Idyllic weather was rare in Kansas. There was no in-between. Whatever the weather brought, it was either too little or too much. Or too late.

This past spring a rainstorm began with a horrendous thunder and lightning storm, followed by pounding hailstones the size of hen's eggs. She had been held captive in the restaurant long after closing hours. The ruts of main street turned into rivers. All over the county, hail had cut to bits kitchen gardens and field crops, as it surely had done today. The Pawnee River, Buckner Creek and Saw Log Creek had flooded, nearly destroying many small homesteads. A farmer, attempting to drive his stock to higher ground, had drowned in White Woman Creek.

His wife packed their wagon with what few belongings were spared, took their children and left the country. There were no other casualties, only minor injuries. Boot Harris bought the vacated White Woman Creek property, put another family there on shares.

She hurried to finish her sweeping, then put up her broom. She went to the door to look outside. Wind rolled clouds of dust up the quiet orangey street. The doors of most businesses were closed for the day, their owners at supper with family.

★ ★ ★ ★ ★

Tinny music and off-key female singing could be heard from the Yellow Rose Restaurant, otherwise there was little sound. There was something wrong, though, with the look of peace. She moved out onto the boardwalk, gazed up and down the street. Then she saw it. Alarm rose in her throat and stuck there.

In the distance, southwest of town, the sky was as black as death. The base of the black cloud was eerie green. From it more thunderheads bulged downward like huge balloons. From every ridge and draw in that direction, what must be dust and debris spun into the air, formed dusty, sky-climbing masses.

As she watched, a tunnel shaped cloud separated from the rest, a long dark arm reached for earth. For another second she remained frozen, saw the black funnel cloud's narrow mouth sway and bend and bound along the horizon, stirring into enormous clouds whatever it touched. It was maybe ten or fifteen miles away . . .

She came to, then, knew she had to move fast. "Cyclone!" she shouted back through the open door at Luther and Silas. "Twister coming from the southwest!" Unless the monstrous sucking funnel turned, the town was in a direct path of danger, not to mention farms along the way.

A cyclone generally traveled about forty miles an hour, she had heard. But one never knew what to expect. She might have five minutes to warn folks to find shelter. Or much less. When you could *hear* a tornado, and she couldn't, yet, you had only seconds to safety.

"Take this side of the street," she told Luther and Silas, tight-lipped. "There will be folks at the hotel and at the Yellow Rose, and maybe the Harris Drug Store. There will be people at the boarding house. The cheese factory and furniture factory will need to be vacated, those folks work after hours. I'll take the other side of the street." She gathered her skirts in her fists and took off at a run. Starting at the livery stable, she hesitated in the open door just long enough to shout, "Cyclone! Find cover!" John, the livery boy, gave her a drop-mouthed stare followed by a frantic wave that he had heard.

On she went to Reid's saddlery, and the wagon works, taking only enough time to shout a warning when she saw Ben's father-in-law, Mathis. She raced up the backstairs to Mr. Pennybaker's living quarters above the hardware, the store itself was closed for the day. She pounded on the door but he didn't answer. He had to be out in the country, he often delivered hardware to a farm customer. She prayed he wouldn't be caught in the cyclone.

She found Emmaline working late at the newspaper, alone. "Dear God!" Emmaline cried, hearing the frightening news, "Selinda is home fixing supper. Lad's in Garden City on a legal matter for Hamilton while Hamilton and Meg are in Missouri. Lad isn't expected home for a day or two."

"Go to Selinda. And on the way grab anyone who has no other place to go and take them with you to our old dugout and the root cellar over there." Emmaline nodded.

Aurelia chastised herself for not remembering sooner the fire bell atop the city windmill. She grabbed up her skirts and ran for it. She leaped at the rope, pulled it hard, over and over, setting off a great clanging. Even a warning of a few minutes or seconds could save lives, but where to find shelter?

"Cyclone!" she shouted over and over, as people came rushing out to the street. Lars Hessler, hearing only the bell and not her voice, ran from his construction office carrying a bucket of water, ready to put out a fire. "Twister!" she shouted at him, "find cover."

There were few cyclone cellars in town. Most residents meant to dig one but hadn't yet gotten around to the task. Their business, their home, and shelter for their animals had to come first. There was a dugout behind the boarding house, a root cellar, too. Were those and the rest of the few cellars enough shelter for everyone? They would have to be.

Maud Mullendore ran out of her dress-shop still carrying a flatiron she'd been using to press a garment. Hearing the warning, she went back in with it, and rushed out again to Aurelia's side. "What would you like me to do?"

"Check the general store and meat market. Mr. Wurst might have taken his wife and children and his customers to the cellar under the store. But make sure. And you stay there with them, Maud." Maud nodded.

Dinah Ambler, white-faced, her eyes wide, had run to join them. She urged, "You come, too, Aurelia." Her skirt whipped in the wind. In her arms she clutched the small speckled pup she had recently acquired. The puppy was shivering, whining, wriggling to be free.

"Not yet, thanks. I'll find a safe place. Hurry, Dinah, Maud, and don't worry."

Thank God school was closed for the season, parents would know where their children were and would look out for them.

A quick frantic glance showed that the funnel cloud making the huge dusty mass on the ground was maybe five miles out now, or less. *Dear God!* It had to be tearing up Ad and Lucy Ann's place! And now—the cyclone boiled its deadly path toward town.

She couldn't bear to think that Lucy's family hadn't found shelter in time. They had to have. In their root cellar, or under heavy furniture. Somewhere.

She wasn't sure if the roar in her ears was the sound of the storm or her own panic. Part of the noise was the frightened cries of others, out on the street now, running toward safety in whatever direction they believed they might find it. They were a blur of folks she only half recognized in their hurry. Among them she thought she saw the women from the Yellow Rose.

Owen ought to be safe at Kidderville. The boys were raking and stacking hay out at the ranch, Zibby helping them. They would be safe if they saw the cyclone in time and went into their dugout cellar. The cyclone could turn suddenly, too. A twister often cut a zigzag path. Or touched down, lifted, touched down somewhere else. She knew she had to be with her children, warn them, see that they were truly safe. Be with them, in any case. Most townsfolk seemed headed for cellars, what shelters they could find.

There might be enough time. She thought if she rode at a right angle to the twister, she could outrun it, reach home. But she had to have a horse, although there wouldn't be time to hitch up Sweet Annie. She turned and struggled back in the opposite direction toward the livery, breathing hard, determined. She had never worked so hard to run, yet moved so slowly. It was partly her bones, no longer a young woman's limbs, holding her back and partly it was the hard pulling wind. Her hair, combs lost, blew about her face. Her chest felt it might burst for need of air. She pushed on, frantic that precious seconds passed.

After an eternity, she reached the shelter of the livery, through its wide-open door and out of the worst of the wind. At the same moment, Abel Pennybaker arrived, a bewhiskered, dwarf-like figure atop his gray nag. She sucked air into her lungs, fought to keep the gusty wind from sending her crashing into him and his horse as he climbed down and

175

she struggled toward him. She forgot trying to hold down her skirts in modesty. Pennybaker had lost his hat, his hair stood on end in the wind, his face was set as he fought to control his frightened horse, so much bigger than him.

"Mr. Pennybaker," she struggled to make herself heard above the roar of the wind, "Let me use your horse. Give him to me, I'm going to the ranch." She grabbed for the animal, saddled and ready, but Pennybaker backed it from her reach.

From his whiskery, walnut-wrinkled face, his worried eyes looked at her as though she were daft, and maybe she was, but she had to make sure her children were safe. The cyclone could rip through town, then swerve a little and hit their place. "Please," she screamed, "I have to go now, Mr. Pennybaker." She tried to wrest the reins from his hands but he wouldn't let go of them. Her hair swirled wildly about her face.

"You can't, Miz Symington," he shouted in a crow-voice, "you'd be killed. There's no ti—" The climbing wind, like a train roaring at them, tore whatever else he was about to say from his mouth. He tied his horse quickly to the hitch-rail. Then he dragged Aurelia down to the ground, forcing her hands to grab onto a hitch-rail post and hang on for her life. He wrapped his arms around the other post a few feet away.

In the next instant they were in the middle of swirling winds, the boiling black cloud. She hugged the hitch-pole as tight as she could. The wind whipped her up and down like a bed-sheet on a clothesline, hair flying. She held on until her arms ached. She screamed, but made no sound in the caldron of wind.

Dirt streamed through the air. The sound of the twister was like the roar of hundreds of locomotives. She could feel the sound vibrate the air against her eardrums, throb against her cheek. She thought her eardrums would burst, she protested in a cry that wouldn't be heard.

Vicious brilliant blue lightning lit up the hideous darkness. Wide-eyed with shock she watched as around her debris flashed upward: splintered wood, tar paper, crockery she thought was from her restaurant. A wagon flew by, and a porch without a house. The air was filled with chunks of mortar and stone.

A few feet away, the side of the livery crashed in as if driven by a giant sledgehammer.

As the twisting winds took on incredible strength she knew she couldn't hang on much longer. Her body was being whipped, banged, thrown about. Her arms were growing numb, felt as useless as strands of thread.

She looked to see how Pennybaker was faring and saw that he was gone, torn away from his post. She screamed for him in the blackness. There was no answering sound, only the terrible roar as she was sucked at, then yanked free of her own hold. She felt herself flung and rolled about like a ball in a dizzying whirl. Twice, a dozen times, she felt something strike her head, her arms, her body. She was swallowed by the roar, the crunching, crashing sounds, the flying dirt and debris.

She came to buried in broken boards. She lay still, felt like she was in a trance, the world an alien place. The turbulence had waned. She was alive.

The storm had dropped her some distance from the livery. The walls of the stable were gone except those pieces covering her. She stared, wondering if she were dreaming: within the foundation of the livery, nervous horses still stood unhurt in their stalls where they were before the storm hit. Beyond the horses, Pennybaker's hardware was a pile of rubble. She was unable to see further except through a film of red as her eyes filled with sticky matter she recognized as blood.

Everything was horribly quiet. Then the silence was broken by the sound of crying from down the street. A man's call, an answering shout. Had the storm occurred over a matter of several minutes, the eternity it seemed, or the snap of a finger? She didn't know. But it was over.

She freed her right hand from the rubble and wiped her sticky eyes, brushed back her hair. She began to push aside the debris covering her, ground her teeth in pain when she tried to use her left arm. It took a while, using only her right hand, but finally she was free. Through a haze, sitting up, she saw that she was covered with dirt and blood. Her right eye began to refill with blood from a gash she found on her head. She blinked, trying to see. She caught her breath when she saw a man's body in rubble a few yards away in the street.

"Mr. Pennybaker? Abel!" She managed to balance herself on one hand and her knees. Her mouth was filled with dirt and she spat. Holding her injured arm against her, she crawled. A few feet from the body she saw that it was a mannequin from Jones Brothers Haberdashery. She rested a moment on her side, sobbed her relief.

Disoriented, in a trance-like state, she got to her feet and carrying her left arm in the other hand stumbled along the cluttered street. She skirted hills of rubble and stared. This was not a place she had ever been. She felt very alone.

Across the way her restaurant and the dry goods store were gone, every stick of them. The hotel's roof was missing. On the side where she stood the *Echo* office and Maud's dress-shop seemed untouched. The windows of Wurst's store were blown out but the building seemed to be otherwise spared. Inside the store she could see odd objects: the bench that usually sat in front of the drug store, corn stalks with ears of corn, a footed tub, other, nameless debris.

Again, she looked across the street. The buildings she

would like to have seen smashed to smithereens, the drug store and dance hall, stood as solid as ever; hard against her wishes like Boot Harris himself. The only difference was the wagon blown to land on the drug store roof.

She began to laugh hysterically. Then, as quickly, her laughter died in her throat. As she crossed the street, she had to walk around Dinah's little speckled pup, dead with a large splinter of wood driven through it.

# Chapter Twelve

The debris-littered street slowly filled with townsfolk emerging from shelter. Most were silent as they walked a short way, stopped to stare in disbelief, and then moved on. Dinah, blond hair mussed and her face begrimed, stumbled toward Aurelia in a dazed state wanting to know, "Have you seen Speck, my little dog? He got away—" She broke off to stare. "You're hurt, Aurelia. My goodness, you—"

"I'm all right, just a little messy." She took Dinah into her good arm a moment, the other heavy and numb, then turned and pointed to where the little dog lay. "I'm so sorry, Dinah. Are you all right?"

"I think so. Yes, I am." She wiped at a tear as she walked toward her pet. "Poor thing. I'll take him home, bury him there." She turned in a circle, as though momentarily losing her direction, then finding it again, she said huskily, "I need to see how my help are, and our herds out at the ranch. The cyclone looked like it went north. I pray that it died before it got to our place."

"I pray that it did, too." She called after Dinah, "Maud was with you, wasn't she? Is she all right?"

She answered over her shoulder in a quivering voice, "We took opposite directions to warn folks. I didn't see her after that, but I think she went to shelter below Wurst's store."

She nodded. She wanted to find Mr. Pennybaker, she was worried about him. From down the street she heard Rilda Hessler's glad, tearful cry, "Dirk! Oh, Dirk, there you are!" Both were spattered with blood and limping as they went into each other's arms. She could hear others, calling the names of their loved ones. She prayed silently that one and all would be reunited, safely.

Franny, the Yellow Rose woman, picked her way across the street to her. Her blue satin dress was torn and her bad-skinned painted face was smudged with dirt, otherwise she seemed unharmed. "Are you all right, Mrs. Symington? You look—badly hurt. Your arm—"

She drew back. "I'm fine." She reconsidered her blunt answer. "I'm sorry, I didn't mean to be rude. I suppose I do look a sight. It's just that—I'm looking for someone in particular. I'm worried about Able Pennybaker; he was with me when the cyclone hit. I'm afraid—"

"I ain't seen him. He could be down in somebody's hidey-hole, or helping out somewhere. But Mrs. Symington, you ought to have yourself looked after, let somebody else find the hardware man."

She shook her head, stumbled on, coming abreast of Boot Harris who was talking with a group of men in front of his drug store as they gestured up at the wagon on the roof.

She silently cursed his good luck, then was relieved to see beyond his store that the whole east section of town was untouched except for various pieces of debris.

*Thank God.* Some of her town—most of it—was still standing. Meg and Hamilton, who were on a visit to Missouri, would come home to find their house, on the east side, just as they'd left it.

Across the way, Mr. Wurst stepped out of the general store through the window where the pane was blown out. His wife and children followed by the door, stepping over objects in the way. Then, two or three people, customers at the time the storm hit, probably, came after the family, but no Maud. All of them stood on the littered boardwalk and stared dumbfounded. Wurst waddled fast on plump legs to Aurelia.

"Have you seen Maud Mullendore?" he asked. His usually shiny cheeks looked gray and he didn't smile. His eyes were worried.

Her alarm picked up anew. "I thought she was with you at your place."

He shook his head. "She was there, and I told her not to leave, but just before the cyclone hit she ran out to find her cat. She never came back."

Aurelia shook her head. Those poor lonely women with pets that were like children to them. Dinah. Maud. She tried to see if Maud was among any of the huddles of folk still forming along the street. There was no sign of her.

She clutched Mr. Wurst's arm with dirty fingers. "We need to spread word for everybody to gather in the center of town for a head count. We have to know how many people besides Maud and Mr. Pennybaker are missing, then quickly organize a search for them. Start—digging." She looked at the giant piles of rubble on the west end of town and her heart sank. *God in heaven,* she thought, don't let anybody be under any of that mess. Aloud, she said to Wurst, "We should hurry, help me, please."

As it turned out, most everyone could be accounted for. Those who were hurt were given rushed and—unfortunately, without a real doctor on hand—crude medical attention. Tourniquets were applied, splints were made from scraps of lumber, and torn sheets.

Nobody seemed to know what had become of Pennybaker and Maud. They had vanished. Also among the missing was Joe Potter's son, Lloyd, who minded Potter's Feed and Seed.

"I'll get on over there to what's left of the feed store." Bert Holberg moved away as he spoke. "Knowing how hard Lloyd tries to please his father, he is probably there trying to set things aright already." His huge form bustled down the street.

Aurelia made her way to the worst of the storm damage—on Spencer Street—wanting to help, wishing she had two good arms. Instead, her body was wracked with pain that seemed to radiate from her arm. She clenched her teeth and fought an urge to vomit.

Dark descended earlier than they might have wanted. Lanterns and lamps were lit to provide light for searchers so that they might see as they dug into the debris.

Jones Brothers Dry Goods store had been blown almost a quarter mile north from its original location to land in a pile of rubble, part of which was her restaurant. Dirk Hessler and his search group examined the huge pile of debris. Slowly they began to dig, and to remove the clutter piece by piece.

"Over here!" Dirk shouted in a tone of disbelief. "Damned if we haven't found somebody!" He was exultant, "A woman's under here. I think—yeah! I've uncovered Mrs. Mullendore's hand and she's not dead. I can hear her."

The watching crowd pushed forward with a unified glad murmur. Faint mewing could be heard under the splintered boards. Moving with the others, Aurelia prayed that the sound was Maud, but it could be her cat.

Dirk was telling his crew, "If we don't carefully remove the blamed stuff that's all over her, the pile will shift and kill her." His expression silently added, *if Maud is alive*. Word that the sound they heard might be her cat had traveled through the crowd.

"Is there anything we can do?" Aurelia's injured arm throbbed so she was afraid she might faint.

Dirk addressed her and the rest of the watching crowd. "Let's form a chain, folks. We're going to lift each piece of rubbish carefully and then pass it along to the next person." She nodded as he took the head of the line.

He examined the situation intently before choosing a board and passing it to Oscar Wurst who was next in line. As the board passed along, and Dirk picked up another, he spoke encouragingly to whoever or whatever was beneath the wreckage, "We be getting you out, shortly, you just hang on there. We're comin' to you, yeah, we are. Just hang on now—"

Was the mewing from a cat? Or was it Maud? The sound was like a cat's, but the hand could be Maud's.

Methodically, and at times collectively holding their breath, rescuers removed large and small pieces of debris—boards, stone, stuff blown from houses and barns, tinware from the hardware store—from the pile burying Maud. No one made a move or took a step that wasn't carefully evaluated first, even as they hurried.

"I see her head!" Dirk shouted after much of the pile had been moved away. He said over his shoulder, his teeth white in a wide, dirty-faced grin, "She's alive, dammit, and lookin' at me for sure!" He turned back to work, more eager than ever. "Wait a minute, Maud. We'll get you out." He knelt, brushed at her exposed face to help her breathe the fresh air. Lamps and lanterns were held high, making a glowing oasis of light in the otherwise darkening night. Her face was a smudged white moon in the rubble.

Maud's rescuers continued to work carefully, but now with more speed. When Maud lifted an arm voluntarily, a shout of joy went up. With great care, Dirk helped her to sit up, pulled her free and lifted her dirt-covered form into his arms.

Bethany, beside Aurelia, called to Dirk, "Take her to our hotel. We'll put her to bed there. Any other injured folk can be taken to our place, too." She repeated, loud, "Anyone who needs medical attention, come to the hotel. We'll make it a temporary hospital. Care for everybody in one place. Will," she directed her husband, "go on with Mr. Harris to his drug store and bring everything you think we might need. Laudanum, bandage, splints, salves."

"Thank you, Bethany," Aurelia touched her arm with her good hand. "We needed a central place to see to folks' injuries. You can't manage it alone, though—"

"Aurelia, I want you to come."

"Of course I will."

"I don't mean come to help. A body can tell you're just barely managing to stay conscious and on your feet. That left arm of yours is clear broke, or I miss my guess. It needs a splint and binding. You're a bloody, dirty mess. Come on, now. There's plenty of others can see to things the rest of the night."

"Someone needs to look for Abel Pennybaker. He was with me when the storm hit, and I haven't seen him since. I'm afraid for him—" She drew a breath, tried to hold steady her body that wouldn't stop weaving. Her mind was such a fog. She asked uncertainly, "Did we see Emmaline and Selinda, were they among the counted? I can't remember—"

Bethany answered, "They are fine. They went ahead to my place to get things ready. We'll find the missing, too. Now come on, Aurelia, and stop your worrying. It doesn't do a body any good."

She didn't want to leave the street, fought her body's seeping pain and weariness. Rather than argue which she hardly felt up to, she let herself be steered toward the hotel behind Dirk carrying Maud. At the hotel she refused to be looked after until she knew the extent of Maud's injuries.

It turned out that Maud had severe bruises over most of her body, a deep cut on her left breast, but no broken bones. It was a concern that she might later develop dust pneumonia or some other lung malfunction from the long hours she was buried and breathing dirt. She would be watched and in the meantime her wounds would be treated with stitches, tinctures and bandage. Bed rest hopefully would do the rest.

"Now, you, Aurelia," Bethany said, leading her into a bedroom where three women were making up extra cots beside the big double bed.

"What are *they* doing here?" Aurelia asked in shock, seeing that the women were Mollie, Franny, and little Sal from the Yellow Rose.

"They wanted to help," Bethany whispered close to her ear. "Now, don't say anything, Aurelia. They cleaned up good, we probably wouldn't catch anything from them, anyhow. And we can use their help."

Aurelia leaned back against Bethany, her mind fuzzy, trying to think of a good reason why the women should not touch her or anyone else. She couldn't think of any, but then she was tired and hurting badly all over. "All right," she whispered finally. "All right, let them stay." She dropped to the nearest cot and stretched out, barely aware as Franny, brassy as a fall moon, leaned over her with a wet washcloth.

With an amazingly gentle touch, the Yellow Rose woman washed the caked blood and dirt from her face and hands. She examined her head, chiding as she might to a child at the same time, "Oh, this isn't good, Mrs. Symington—your poor scalp torn thisaway and the dirt in the cut, My Lord! Got to be cleaned, good. But you know, I think we can bring the edges together tight, and tie some of the hair from each side across the cut. Yessir, that'll hold it together 'til it's healed. Might need some carbolic but no need for a plaster. Now then, look at your arm! I vow it's broke in two places! Oh, sweetie—I know everything happened so fast, but you ought've seen it looked after before now. The flesh is swollen. It'll be harder to set but we'll do the best we can."

It spite of Fran's gentle maneuvering, the pain of having her arm examined left Aurelia out of breath and barely conscious. From far away, feeling she was sinking, she heard Fran say, "Drink this, Sweetie Pie, so I can go to work on your poor head and your arm." Only after the liquid went scalding down her throat to warm and turn her into jelly did she realize she'd been given a strong jolt of whiskey. And then it was too late. Fran was pulling on her arm, calling for splints. Someone screamed, she thought maybe it was herself, and then darkness sucked her away.

When she woke, her arm was firmly splinted and tied in a sling with a snowy hotel dishtowel. Her head ached something fierce and seemed to be bound in cloth. Emmaline was sitting by her bed looking solemn, Selinda in a torn and dirty red dress stood by the window. "You two are all right," Aurelia said through a dry throat. "I was so worried about you."

"Us?" Emmaline reached out a hand to touch her face. "We were worried about you! You fainted out dead cold when Franny and her friends were working on you. Of course we are all right. We got to the old dugout in time. After the storm we saw Bethany and she said to come here, make sure there was plenty of water on to heat, soap laid out, bandages and splints ready to take care of the injured."

"How is Maud?"

"She's holding her own. Coughing up a bit of dust and pretty badly bruised, but we think she is going to be fine."

"I wonder about my children— They probably went to our cellar, but they were alone. Owen is up at Kidderville."

Selinda came over to the bed, took her hand. With her beautiful smile she told her, "Your children drove in this morning in their wagon, worried about you. Bethany is feeding them breakfast downstairs in the dining room. They were up here to see you but you were asleep."

"Has anyone heard from Lucy Ann and Ad? Are they and Lad and Rachel all right? Are they safe?"

"All fine. Your young Zibby come through all right with them, too," Selinda told her.

"Zibby?" she questioned, puzzled. "She was with Joshua and David John out at the ranch. What do you mean?"

Emmaline explained. "Your boys took her to play at the Walshes' yesterday, right after you left the ranch to come to town. She begged, and they took her to play with Rachel for the day."

"She was there when the storm hit? She was in that cyclone?" She tried to rise, felt weak, then, staggered by the pain, she fell back.

"Yes, she was with the Walshes. Safe. Safer than you were in the storm," Emmaline said emphatically. "She hid out in their root cellar with the Walsh family."

She whispered to herself, thinking of how she had lost Helen Grace, "I would have died a thousand deaths, had I known."

"Well you didn't know," Emmaline said gently, "and she is just fine. Josh and David John drove over and picked her up on their way in to town to see how you fared."

"But no one at the Walshes' was hurt?" she asked a second time, wanting to be very, very sure. Watching the cyclone hit their location, it was hard to believe they could be alive.

"Well, there was plenty of damage to the place, but none of the family were injured. Ad lost his windmill, his barn, and two cows were killed. The Walshes are lucky, of course, although Ad doesn't seem to realize that, yet. He's mad as thunder about the barn and the cows."

Poor Ad. He struggled so hard to succeed as a farmer. But the dividends he reaped so far hadn't begun to measure up to the long hard hours of work he put in. Only occasionally did he seem to be the same happy-go-lucky cowboy who had come to court Lucy Ann.

Something seemed to eat at him. Maybe it was not getting ahead as he expected and worked for. She didn't think it was the old matter of the Indians and Lucy Ann, and Rachel's true parentage, bothering him. But it could be. Only Lucy Ann and Ad would know that for sure, and it was a matter neither had spoken of in years. Nor had anyone else, to her knowledge.

"What else? Anyone still missing? Was anyone else—hurt?" She wanted to hear that everyone was accounted for, that there were only injuries that could be healed and forgotten and that damage to property could be repaired or rebuilt.

"Several folks have cuts, scrapes, and bruises that don't appear to be serious. Boot Harris is providing at no cost all the medicines needed. You and Maud were the worst hurt so far as we know now. Lloyd Potter, Joe's son—" Emmaline frowned, seemed unable to finish.

"What about Lloyd?" She pictured the spindly, pimply-faced young man who was always in a fearful rush to please his father and usually failing. Emmaline tried to speak, couldn't, shook her head.

"I'll tell her, Mama." Selinda came to stand with her hand on her mother's shoulder. "Lloyd," she said quietly, "was at the feed store when the storm hit. Their store got hit pretty hard. Nobody is sure how it happened, but Lloyd's back—we think it was broken. When he came to and he guessed how bad off he was, he grabbed the sheriff's gun as Bert was trying to help him. He said—his father wouldn't want to put up with a cripple. He killed himself before Bert could get the gun away."

"Dear heaven, no! Oh, poor Lloyd." For several minutes she was silent, letting the horrible fact sink in. She wasn't sure she wanted to hear more, and yet she wanted to get all the worst details over with at once. And then take care of them. "And Abel Pennybaker? Was he found?"

"He's dead, too," Emmaline told her in a voice filled with sadness, and quiet disbelief. "The wind just up and blew that poor little fellow into Luther and Silas' house. He had so many broken bones—he seemed to be broken up inside, too. Maybe if there had been a doctor closer than Dodge City, he might have been saved. He lived a while. But—he's dead, Aurelia," she repeated.

"No, oh, no," she whispered, clutching at Emmaline's hand. Tears flooded her eyes. That nice little man had been her savior, truly. If she hadn't held onto the post as he made her do she would be dead. And if they had a doctor, he might be alive.

She started to lift her trussed arm to mop her eyes and then remembered to use her good hand. "I hope to heaven there is no one else—?"

"That's all of the injuries and the dead that we know about," Emmaline spoke solemnly. "There's been a lot of property damage. But it could have been worse, Aurelia, so much worse. The whole town could have been destroyed, there could have been many more deaths from the storm."

She nodded from her bed. She wished Owen was back from his trip. She wanted to see her children, wanted desperately to see something bright, alive and wonderful. "Send my children up now, Selinda, would you, please? No wait," she said as Selinda started for the door, skirts swishing, "I'll go downstairs to them." To Emmaline's frown she answered, "Like you said, it could be worse. My arm is bound, I'm a little stiff and sore—well, truthfully I feel like I've been whipped by the blades of a windmill. But I don't want to stay abed. I want to go down to them." With a tight groan she couldn't prevent, she rolled off the bed and prepared to venture downstairs.

Besides seeing the children, there were folks she must thank, such as Franny and the other Yellow Rose women. She needed to thank Bethany, Dirk Hessler, and so many others. She supposed she must thank Harris for providing medicines at no cost to those who needed them. Unfortunately, his offerings likely included free whiskey in a gesture of good will toward future trade. She chided herself for her small-minded conclusion, correct though it no doubt was.

In any event, she was thankful the injured had all been seen to as far as the community's limited medical knowledge was able.

Heaven's to Betsy, how badly they needed a doctor! She appreciated Harris's generosity, but Paragon Springs still needed an honest to goodness real doctor. They couldn't continue to meet crisis after crisis without one. She had a new idea, though. As soon as the mess of the tornado was taken care of, she meant to pay a call to a medical college or two and search for a candidate.

Next day, everyone who was able turned out for the joint funeral of Able Pennybaker and young Lloyd Potter. The August weather was very warm, it wouldn't do to keep the bodies above ground any longer than necessary.

Joe Potter wept openly over the grave of his son. Perhaps he cared more for Lloyd than any of them had had any idea. Sadly, it was now too late for Lloyd to know his father's feelings. Perhaps it had taken his death to bring them out.

There was a brief meal after the funeral, then everyone went home to change back into their work clothes. Salvageable debris would be set aside for use in rebuilding. Rubbish would be loaded on wagons and driven to a ravine west of town to be dumped there.

Aurelia, her arm in a sling and her head swathed in bandage, was directing the start of the cleanup when Owen arrived back in town. She was standing in front of the shattered remains of Aurelia's Place, heartsick, dirty, and tired. There was little that could be saved except for her big old cookstove, a table or two. The beginning of their new house was gone, every stick of it blown across the plains.

For a long moment she and Owen just looked at one another. Then, ignoring the crowd at work in the dirt and rubble around them, he scooped her up tight into his arms. She held onto him as dearly. And then she gasped, "Oh, Owen my love, I'm so glad to see you home." Her voice faltered, "It's been . . . times like these . . . I need you so, beside me."

He seemed unable to speak, but from the pounding of his heart against her, from the look on his face, she knew how glad he was to find her safe.

At dinner they discussed the cyclone, knowing now that the twister had lasted about eight minutes or a little more. In a path two hundred feet wide and twelve miles long it had scoured the ground of grass and every other obstruction, demolishing all before it. It had swerved further west after hitting Spencer Street, then east again outside town where, several miles away, it petered out. The Rocking A north on the Pawnee River hadn't been hit.

"We could see it was stormy in this direction, but I didn't know how bad it was until it was over," Owen lamented. "I got here as soon as I could. I was so afraid of what I'd find—"

"It could have been much worse," she said to him over the

rim of her coffee cup. She took another sip and it was hard to swallow. Over and over that phrase had run like a shining ribbon through the community, a reminder to be glad for what they still had. *It could have been worse.*

But simple words, even feelings of gratitude for all they were left with, were not enough to remedy the pain and loss. It was going to take work, a lot of hard work, and scraping together of finances, to rebuild again. The individuals they had lost could never be replaced.

There were those who were discouraged enough by the storm to want to leave. She must do everything to encourage them to stay. Let them know the community would help them rebuild and go on. If she didn't, Harris would be providing them with "leaving money" in exchange for their land. Yet, wherever else they might go, they could be worse off. She needed to be sure they were aware of that.

She pushed her half-eaten meal away and stood up. "Well, it is time to get back at it." She could see that Owen didn't want her to leave, felt she should get some rest. But they both knew that she would carry the town on her back if she had to, until it was again on its feet and once more moving forward. "Do you want to come?" she asked softly. With an exasperated sigh he nodded, yes. He was so different from most men. That he allowed her the freedom to do what she felt she must do, along with his concern for her, made her love him all the more. "Come then," she reached for his hand, "let's go see what folks need."

# Chapter Thirteen

In early September, Aurelia and Owen left the rebuilding to others and traveled to eastern Kansas.

"Would you look at that!" She turned on the rented rig's seat beside Owen as they traveled along Topeka Boulevard in the capital city. "Bustles are back and I didn't even know it. I do believe you could hide a small table under the back of that lady's dress, the lady in blue!"

Her glance fed on every woman on the street. Particularly catching her eye was a finely-dressed lady in sage green silk who swept by, a tiny child's hand in her own. The woman was slender, but still there had to be at least twenty yards of fabric in her bustled frock.

For a few seconds Aurelia's mind flashed back to the fine clothes she had brought with her to western Kansas years before. Lovely, fashionable dresses long since disintegrated. She pulled her mind away. That was then and this was now. Her best black dress was perfectly fine. Still, she felt a touch of envy as her buried interest in fashion stirred briefly to life.

"Did you see the lady in green, Owen?" she asked over the clanging of a passing trolley. "And look, now, at the other one just come out of that store, the lady in plum. Bustles, again!"

Owen looked and tried to sound interested, "Hmm. Nice."

He had a lot on his mind. But while she could, she meant to enjoy the sights of the city. On either side of the street, store windows had brilliant displays of everything from incredibly tall stacked bonnets to lace-festooned parasols.

Bright-colored theater bills on signboards advertised the latest plays, boasted the names of actors and actresses brought in from New York. On the corner a cornet band played for a small, foot-tapping group of listeners.

She smiled, then, at Owen. Of far greater interest to him than the sights were their reasons for coming to Topeka in the first place. Causes just as important to her, that filled her with excited anticipation. They had been elected by the community to urge regional officers of the Santa Fe Railroad to extend the Santa Fe line from Larned into Paragon Springs and possibly on west to Colorado. It was a day that they had long awaited, that they had worked very hard to bring about.

After the meeting with the railroad officials, nearer supper time, she would interview a young man fresh out of medical college. Provided he suited, she meant to persuade him to set up his first medical practice in Paragon Springs.

The railroad meeting came first, however. In past weeks Owen had canvassed not just the town but a wide area beyond Paragon Springs on the matter. The *railroad plan,* it was called in constant conversations at home. Coinciding with Owen's forays, Emmaline had written article after article in the *Echo* on the necessity of securing a railroad, extolling Owen's arguments, in addition to reasons gleaned from all and sundry folk she talked to on the streets and in the stores.

The railroad would open up the country, she wrote. It would establish manufacturing, draw much more trade to Paragon Springs. Trade which would otherwise be lost to the towns of Larned, Spearville, Dodge City, which were nearer railroads. Farmers around Paragon Springs would gain profitable markets through the railroad. Teaming supplies forty to fifty miles wasn't profitable enough for anybody. The railroad, she wrote repeatedly, would add thousands of dollars of taxable property to county wealth. And certainly not the least of it, a railroad would mean sure victory in the county-seat contest against Flagg, which had no railroad. Yet.

*VOTE THE IRON TRAIL, THE STEEL NILE,* Emmaline's weekly headlines ran.

In response to the newspaper articles, to fevered street-corner speeches, and to meetings held for such discussion, most area residents seemed to be in favor of the railroad. Others were more cautious. Railroad companies had cheated settlers before, accepting charters for railroads never built, never intended to be built. Such railroad fraud of the eighteen-sixties and 'seventies was still strong in many minds.

There were serious determinations before them: Would the railroad be financed through private capital? Some kind of local aid? Through some sort of government subsidization? Or by issuing bonds in exchange for company stock?

Penny-pinching Potter argued that the railroad was just as apt to come whether or not bonds were voted. He was not alone in the belief that railroad barons would realize that the west was a chiefly untapped source of riches in cattle and grain trade, in limestone and other products. In addition, some area residents claimed the county wasn't big enough to warrant bonds. They wanted the railroad plan dropped.

But town leaders had persisted, eventually gaining sufficient support. Most citizens agreed with the issue of voting bonds as inducement to the Santa Fe Railroad Company to extend a line from Larned to Paragon Springs. The line from the east to Larned had been laid some years back but stopped at that point.

It would surely help that Elliot Charbonneau had promised a gift of land to the railroad for a depot in Paragon Springs. Situated on the southeast edge of town near his lumberyard and proposed coal yard, the generous gesture of a depot on his land was a wise investment. Although in a town the size of Paragon Springs, every citizen stood to profit from having the Santa Fe line through town.

The railroad company office was different from any room Aurelia had ever been in. It was cool, and smelled musty and unpleasant due to several well-used brass spittoons. Little of the light gray walls could be seen for the numerous charts and maps showing endless spider webs of railroad lines. More charts, and books and papers, held down three huge mahogany desks. Behind each desk sat a man dressed in a dark suit and string tie. One fellow was young and thin, the other two were older and corpulent.

Owen introduced himself and Aurelia. He stated their reason for their visit. The youngest man, at the nearest desk, adjusted his spectacles and took his attention almost reluctantly from his work. The other two men—one was bushy-haired and salt and pepper bearded, the other was bald and clean-shaven—were quicker from their seats in spite of their excess weight.

A bit of meaningless small-talk, chiefly about the weather, filled the next minute or two. It became clear, finally, that the commissioners were waiting politely for Owen to ask his wife to leave; at which time they could commence real business. Instead, Owen brought a chair from its place by the wall and held it for Aurelia where the men waited. She thanked him. Then she hid a smile as the railroad men moved back to their desks, seeming rather uncertain of how to proceed.

"My wife is as involved in our railroad plan as anyone," Owen explained simply as he moved a second chair for himself. He took the papers Aurelia drew from her bag, their precious signed petitions. Leaning forward, he explained to the men what they were seeking: A branch line, thirty-four miles of track, from Larned to Paragon Springs. A roundhouse and depot on donated land. At least that.

"Although," Aurelia threw in, "you might want to extend the rail line on past us to Ravanna, the town farthest west in the county. Folks in Ravanna hope that you will." If they laid lines that far, they might as well run them on into Colorado. The line would likely bypass Flagg by a couple of miles north of it.

After absorbing her suggestion, the men seemed to set aside the fact that she was a woman and plunged into full discussion.

However, the figures they quoted made her head spin. At a cost of $21,000 *a mile,* just their short-line route of thirty-four miles would require more than $700,000 in bonds! She preferred to think of the cost in simpler terms, $4.00 per foot, which it also was and didn't seem nearly so outrageous. She felt better still when she learned the Santa Fe would bear half of the cost.

Of course it would take a lot of money. There was a roadbed to build up and prepare. Stone and gravel for ballast to be paid for and hauled. Wood ties and steel rails to be bought and shipped from the east. Workers to be paid as the rail line was laid over a period of several weeks.

Building the railroad would furnish work, also, to local men who could use the money. Their horses and mules would be needed for hire to do the grading. There would be an immediate market at good prices for food to feed both men and animals. Her restaurant, the bakery, the meat market, would all profit. Anyone who wanted to cut wild gramma grass for hay could sell it to feed the stock.

After further deliberation, the head commissioner, the older, bearded man, conceded, smiling, "We'll send a surveying crew out to you folks' region as soon as we can. Please understand how busy the company is, though."

The youngest man supported his comment, "We're laying trunk and feeder lines all over the state."

Aurelia's glance returned to the charts on the four walls, webby muddles of information that she thought with study she might understand. She turned her attention back to the railroad men. The clean-shaven older fellow was speaking this time.

"Heard the other day," he was saying with a money-rich smile, "that this railroad boom in Kansas is greater than in any other part of the country. Which of course 'booms' the rest of the United States. A regional tail wags the national dog, you might say."

From the webby charts she could believe it. Almost every railroad company in the country was laying track to and through and 'round about Kansas. Every small town had their dreams for a railroad, dreams that in many cases were coming true. That dream would surely come true for Paragon Springs.

She did her best to push aside small doubts that nagged at the back of her mind. There were some farmers who had been reluctant to give up right-away across their land. Would they go back on their word to do so? Too, with little doubt, the expense of a railroad was going be a hardship until its services started paying off. But surely folks could hang on?

A while later, as she and Owen were leaving the Santa Fe office, they were told by the men that if the railroad plan succeeded, a subsidiary company of the Santa Fe would do actual construction of the track. "Expect the Kansas, Chicago, and Western," the youngest railroad officer told them, pushing his spectacles up the bridge of his nose as he shook first Owen's hand and then Aurelia's. "They're doing most of the work in western Kansas right now."

She asked on the ride back to their hotel room, "It's a little frightening, don't you think, Owen, now that we're close to getting our railroad? The huge expense might scare off a lot of folks from voting for it." She watched in abstract a variety of traffic around them. Ahead of them a pair of gleeful ragged youngsters chased after a dripping ice wagon. A cyclist on a high-wheeler rolled by. A garishly painted patent medicine drummer wagon hitched to a team of white mules and parked on a side street made her think for just an instant of Boot Harris and how much she wanted him replaced by a true doctor.

"It's not nearly so scary when we keep this in mind, Aurelia: the savings of the cost of coal alone can pay for the tax Hodgeman County will have to levy to issue the bonds."

His assurance lightened her fears. She said with a thoughtful smile, "Next, then, is the campaign and election to raise those bonds. We've done well, today, I think, meeting with those railroad men." Underlining her words was the distant, industrious-sounding whistle of the Santa Fe train chugging into the Topeka depot.

"You bet. And we have to make it clear to folks those bonds don't have to be issued until the railroad is actually completed. So there is no risk to vote them. No interest will be due until the road is finished. But *taxes* can be assessed on the railroad before that time. This long-time dream of ours will happen, Aurelia, and a very good thing for folks, too."

She nodded. One of their main arguments to those against having the railroad was that the railroad could lower taxes per person, as well as lower prices for goods folks must buy. At the same time government service would be increased.

She smiled at Owen and he answered by covering her hand

with his own and clasping it tight.

Lining the streets, interspersed with tall brick business buildings, were stately homes with gingerbread trim and pretty shutters, each with a carriage house. Black, decorative iron fences protected well-kept lawns. Someday, Paragon Springs could be every bit as fine, she reflected longingly as she looked around her.

The long hard days of rebuilding all that the tornado destroyed would revive their town. Some people had a small savings in the bank to start over on, others had to borrow funds, and, of course, every usable particle of material salvaged after the storm was being used. Paragon Springs would be better than ever. Dirk and Lars Hessler were rebuilding her restaurant. The hardware store had been demolished but the site remained. She was keeping the Pennybaker name in his memory for the new hardware store going up back there at home.

They were recovering slowly. More improvement was to come for their town this evening, if her meeting with the young doctor turned out as she hoped. She had done everything possible in past times to convince a good doctor to settle in Paragon Springs, each effort meeting with failure. This time she must succeed.

He was awfully young. Aurelia tried to recover her pang of concern. She and Owen stood in the entryway of the small school off Washburn Street where they had agreed to meet their prospect. Slight of build, blue-eyed, sandy-haired, he didn't look much older than her Joshua.

But what did she expect of a fresh graduate of the Kansas Medical School of Topeka? A man portly and gray-haired like old Doctor Cooper back in Spencer County, Kentucky? "We are the Symingtons. You are Rodney McLean?"

"*Doctor* Rodney McLean," the young man smiled as he corrected her, not brash but forthright, and proud. His outward appearance belied, she thought now, inner strength, and strong character. "I have my certification from a three-year course of medical study. And," his smile quirked deeper, "I graduated in the top third of my class."

"Of course. Doctor McLean. I'm sorry." She asked, "Would you like to join us for supper, Doctor McLean? We saw a café down the street within walking distance. Owen—my husband, here, said a few minutes ago that he is hungry enough to eat a coyote."

"Well, that would save the coyote eating calves then, wouldn't it?"

They laughed. "Did you grow up on a farm then, Doctor McLean?" Owen asked as they took the sidewalk toward the café. In the street the sound of buggies, large rumbling freight wagons, and the clanging trolley, nearly drowned out their words as they walked along.

"No. My father was a small town doctor; his office was in Harveyville, Kansas. We treated many country folk in the Flint Hills. Doc—my father—was occasionally paid with meat instead of money. That is, when coyotes hadn't riddled the beef herds and there was meat to spare."

At the café, over a delicious dinner of roast chicken and stuffing, he told them that he was his father's apprentice from a young age. "You'll want to know my background," he said, his expression sincere, serious.

He related that his father had brought him as a baby west to Kansas from New Hampshire and raised him alone. He couldn't remember his mother. He thought possibly his father had escaped a bad marriage, that his mother left them for another man. "Doc would never say. Whatever the reason, his past was too painful to talk about. I will never know the facts, now, but I don't mind not knowing. In every other way, he was the best sort of father a boy could ask for.

"He was a darn good man," he declared, "indefatigable, selfless, honorable, hard-working." He hesitated while savoring a bite of chicken, "He was an excellent doctor. Underpaid, of course. Overworked. He took too often to whiskey against the drudgery, and exhaustion; against his hidden pain. He died two years ago of liver disease."

"We're very sorry," Aurelia sympathized, and Owen nodded with her. She wondered for a second if McLean might follow his father's alcoholic path, then decided that he would not.

"I miss him still," McLean was saying, his face quiet. "I'll always be grateful for what he taught me. They were things the school couldn't teach: compassion, patience, the ability to listen and know what the patient was really trying to say. On the practical side, I own his fine library, his superb surgical instruments. Some equipment and furniture—examining table, special chairs. A little money, to set up practice."

"What would you like to know about Paragon Springs, Doctor McLean?" Aurelia pushed back her dinner plate, and pulled closer a small dish of applesauce.

"Tell me first about the town, size and so on."

Aurelia was happy to do so, in full detail, from the fine springs for which the town was named, to the many well-built establishments and the good people who made up the population. "We have fourteen substantial businesses including a bank. We have a beautiful new school," she said with a slight drying of her throat, thinking of Boot Harris who owned the school. "Paragon Springs has a permanent population of about three hundred, and a transient population—cowboys in off the range, movers who want to rest awhile—of about twenty-five to fifty more at any given time. It is the finest town in Hodgeman County and improving every day."

"She tends to embroider a bit," Owen cautioned. "Paragon Springs is like one of her children."

"I didn't embroider at all. Paragon Springs is a grand place." To herself she added, *simply nestled in opportunity.*

The young doctor grinned. "I'm sure it is a wonderful place. Now tell me, because it will be helpful for me to know, are there particular diseases locals suffer, have died from? Are there illnesses or types of accidents more prevalent over others in your area? It makes a difference, area to area. I'd like to be prepared."

With a weighted heart, and anger still, Aurelia told him of the unnecessary killing stemming from activities at the Yellow Rose. "We're doing our best to curb rowdiness from our wilder element, but a gunfight still breaks out on occasion. I wish I could say we have no such thing as gunshot wounds but that would not be the truth."

She went on quietly, her mind counting gravestones in the cemetery, "We have had two deaths from childbirth, the mother and the infant. Not to mention some difficult deliveries that could have been easier had we had a doctor to tend the poor mothers."

Owen added, "There are cases of childhood disease, measles, diphtheria. Some children from a family passing through died of diphtheria, there have been frightening close calls with others."

Aurelia fingered her napkin. "My own child died from serious croup years ago, before the town was built. We struggle constantly to keep a clean town; there have been no typhoid epidemics."

They told him about the tornado, those deaths, and how injuries had had to be taken care of.

"That's how your arm was injured? How is it?"

"The bone seems to be knitting," she nodded down at her arm in a sling. "I'm a little impatient with the healing time; if it could be speeded up—?"

"Broken bones take time to heal, but I'll be glad to have a look. If the bones are set properly, so that the arm doesn't have to be rebroken and reset, we'll probably just leave it alone. Keep watch 'til it is fully mended."

In her mind, Aurelia voted for leaving her arm alone, regardless.

In further discussion she learned that he was an advocate of sterilization, proper cleaning of wounds, instruments and bandage. He felt that *prevention* of disease was extremely important and could be had through better hygiene, clean water, fresh air and good ventilation. He had many ideas for improved sanitation that he'd want to implement in any town in which he practiced.

"I'm in full agreement with all of that!" Liking him better and better by the moment, Aurelia leaned forward. She had to know, before she got her heart totally set on him, "With your qualifications, Doctor McLean, why have you chosen not to set up practice here in Topeka or in some other big city?" *Why would you even consider Paragon Springs?*

He answered thoughtfully, "My father enjoyed his small town, country practice, as did I, working with him. At the same time, I intend to do what I can to make a decent living. I think prospects for that might be better in the West. I'd like to take up land, perhaps raise cattle on the side. I want to combine my practice with my own drug store—"

"Oh?" She drew a quick sharp breath, and told him, "Paragon Springs has a drug store, already, Doctor McLean. But," she hurried on, "I'm sure the community, the surrounding country, can support two of them. We're about to get a railroad. We're going to be the county seat." Owen gave her an astonished look that she would promise so assuredly what was not reality, yet. "There will be quite enough business for a good living, I'm sure, Doctor McLean."

She wanted Doctor Rodney McLean badly enough for Paragon Springs that she would promise him the moon.

Boot Harris wouldn't like the competition, but she would be blessed if she'd let that stop them getting the doctor they had sorely needed for so long.

"Did I understand from our previous correspondence that you will have a building to house my practice?"

She nodded, having a hard time pulling her mind from the matter of Boot Harris. She listened as Owen described the small but well-built three-room building that would be the doctor's office.

The fine little frame structure had been built next to the community bank, by a tramp printer named Stephens. He wanted to settle down and operate a rival paper to the *Echo*. Which might even have been good for the town. But his taste for drink and spending time at the Yellow Rose was greater than any drive he might possess to travel around the area to obtain paid ads and subscriptions for his paper. It wasn't long before he admitted failure at the new venture, chose to return to the life of an itinerant printer that he'd always been. This time, Dinah Ambler beat Boot Harris to the punch and she bought the Stephens building expressly to house the practice of the doctor they hoped to find.

McLean nodded that the building would surely do, then turned the subject back to the drug store. "I remember Doc, my father, being paid in potatoes, cabbages, cord wood, chickens—when what we sorely needed was cash money. He seldom complained, but I feel I must take a different approach from the beginning. The drug store will give me a second source of income, and will also solve my office and supply problems. I prefer to mix my own medicines from drugs ordered from reliable companies. There are obstacles enough to healing without putting up with fake medicines and expensive drugs of doubtful efficacy."

*Drugs of doubtful efficacy.* She was suddenly remembering what Emmaline had found out, searching old St. Louis newspapers for information about Boot Harris' past.

Harris was truthful when he told her he had owned a successful pharmaceutical manufactory in St. Louis. What he hadn't mentioned was that four children had gotten drunk on the heavily alcohol-laden cough medicine he produced. Sotted, the children had gone out into sub-zero night-time temperatures in their thin nighties to play. They had frozen to death while their parents believed them to be safely abed. Their angry families and neighbors set fire to his company, would likely have hung Harris if he hadn't left St. Louis in a hurry for the West.

She had no evidence that he still dealt in dangerous drugs other than excessive, illegal whiskey he doled out to adults. But just in case, she was glad they were going to have Doctor Rodney McLean to attend the community's ills.

Feeling triumph she could scarcely contain, she told him, "If at all possible, if you have your equipment and belongings ready, we would like you to accompany us on our return trip to Paragon Springs, doctor."

Aurelia and Owen had driven by team and wagon as far as the livery in Dodge City and from there had taken the train to Topeka. When the trio arrived back in Dodge City, they loaded Rodney's crates from the freight car into their wagon and headed the last twenty-four miles home. They would spend the night on the way with Ma Jewett, a kindly woman who gave bed and board to travelers.

In spite of the long tiring trip, Aurelia was enormously pleased. They had their young doctor in tow. They had promise of a railroad survey and probable costs. It was up to them, now, to see that the railroad bond issue was on the ballot and voted in.

They were perhaps five miles south of town next day when Aurelia saw a cluster of figures out on the prairie some distance off the trail. She recognized Pauline Schlissel, a tiny little woman in faded calico, and her children. Stooped with tote sacks, Mrs. Schlissel and her brood moved slowly as they picked up "prairie fuel"—cow chips. A larger boy stacked his gather in a wheelbarrow he pushed along.

"Owen, stop for a minute, please! I want to talk to Mrs. Schlissel." He was surprised, but "whoaed!" their team to a halt. Without waiting for his help, she piled off the wagon-seat, somewhat clumsily due to her bad arm. "I won't be long." She trotted across the bumpy prairie, skirts in her good hand, toward Mrs. Schlissel and her children. They stopped to stare and to wait. A range cow trundled out of her hurried path. Grasshoppers whirred up in front of her flying feet.

She took a few moments to talk with Mrs. Schlissel and then returned to the road where Owen and Rod waited by the wagon.

"For heaven's sake, woman, what was that about?" Owen asked when he helped her into the wagon.

"About the railroad." She was near breathless as she settled herself. "I told Mrs. Schlissel that if we got our railroad, tons of coal could be shipped in cheaply and regularly. It would be as readily available as it is back East. She and her children would never have to pick up cow chips again or burn fires of twisted weeds. She'll persuade her husband Edward," she said to Owen's amazed expression, "by voting time."

★ ★ ★ ★ ★

Their new doctor had scarcely advertised in the *Echo* and hung up his shingle before patients lined up in the entry of his office and along the boardwalk leading to it. "Doctor Rod" was seen as a sudden miracle in that medically deprived country.

They came from miles around hoping for relief from old ills; lumbago, bronchial catarrh, carbuncles, and quinsy—ailments that had previously been accepted as part of life. Patent medicines and home remedies were set aside in favor of the doctor's recommendations. Injuries suffered from the tornado and not healing at last received professional treatment that would speed recovery. Some pregnant mothers saw a doctor for the first time in their grown lives.

Aurelia consented to allow Rod to check her arm. She knew great relief when he pronounced the limb was healing fine. He wanted to know who had set her arm so well and when she told him, he said, "I wonder if she'd like to do some nursing for me? I can use help from time to time."

She hesitated, then told him, "Fran is a kind woman and she did do a good job with my arm. You'll find her at the Yellow Rose." She left the rest up to him.

Boot Harris waited in the summer evening twilight for the last patient to come out of the new doctor's small office. When the stout little woman emerged, he alighted from his buggy, careful how he landed on his feet. "Mrs. Tuttle," he said around a cigarillo clamped in his teeth. He tipped his hat.

"Fine young man in there," Hannah Tuttle motioned over her shoulder. "Treated my corns. My feet already feel much better. You have foot trouble, too, don't you, Mr. Harris? Good thing you're seein' the doc about it." She fluffed away down the street.

*Disgusting old hen, they had nothing in common.* Harris rapped sharply on the door and went in. He hid his surprise at the doctor's youth—talking this one into joining him would be a cinch—and smiled expansively, "Doctor Rod McLean, I've looked forward to making your acquaintance. I've heard many good things about you." He shook his hand. "Welcome to Paragon Springs! Are you finding everything you need? Sorry you weren't given finer quarters, a roomier place to practice, but that can be changed in no time. I'm Boot Harris."

"Mrs. Symington and her husband, Owen, have done quite well for me," Rod responded genially. "I like it here. Is there a medical problem I can help you with, Mr. Harris?" He motioned toward a pair of chairs in the small tidy waiting room and they sat down.

"No, no medical problem." Harris leaned forward in his chair, elbows propped on his knees, his expression benevolent. "I'm not here on my own behalf, but yours, doctor. I'm here to make you an offer."

"Oh?" Rod McLean sized the man, his fine clothes, his polished aloof manner, shallow friendliness. This kind rarely thought of anyone but themselves. He nodded, "I'm listening."

"You can take time to think about it, of course, but I'd like to take you in as partner." He waited but got no readable reaction from McLean. The doctor removed a dead leaf from a plant by his chair as Harris continued more forcefully, "I operate a successful drug store but I would like to expand. You can move your practice into my building, I have two large, well-lit rooms available. If you'd prefer separate offices, a new hospital building, that can be arranged. I have the funds to back you. We could—"

"I don't have to think about it, Mr. Harris," Rod answered

quietly, shaking his head, "and I don't want to waste your valuable time so I'll answer you directly: I intend to have my own drug store right here in this building. For now, the space is adequate for my needs. I don't need backing. Working together with you might be the wiser, more profitable plan, but I prefer to work alone. However, you're very kind to make such a generous offer and I appreciate it."

*Damn young fool. Both of them could make more money working together.* Harris maintained his composure with difficulty and smiled around his clamped cigarillo, "Are you serious in your plans? I can't change your mind?" The clock on the wall ticked loudly, agitating Harris' nerves.

"Yes, I'm serious. I've known what I wanted to do from the day I started medical school. I like mixing my own medicines; there's so much fraud in the pharmaceutical business, isn't there? You'd know that, being in the business." He met Harris' eyes directly, spoke seriously, "Our customers, our patients, deserve fair and decent treatment, safe medicines. I intend to give them that."

Harris didn't answer as inside a cold rage churned. His cigarillo tasted bitter and he removed it from his mouth. The cocky young idiot was doomed for failure and it was his own fault. Harris stood up, smiling, and reached for Rod's hand. "The offer stands. If you change your mind, let me know. If not, I wish you good luck. No doubt a second drug store will be good for the town."

"I believe it will." From what he'd heard, the Harris Drug Store was more saloon and bawdy house than pharmacy. Rod had no intention to be a pauper, but even that would be preferable to being roped together with dangerous scum like Harris. He saw him to the door. "Come see me any time you have a medical problem, Mr. Harris. It was nice to meet you."

Harris gave his horse the whip as he turned the buggy in the street back toward the Yellow Rose. He'd gone about a half block when he threw back his head and laughed. Young McLean was no more to him than a mosquito bite to a buffalo. And mosquitos had short lives.

"I heard that Boot Harris paid you a call, Doctor McLean," Aurelia said to him when he came to the restaurant early next morning for breakfast, her only customer. "Mrs. Tuttle thought he was seeing you for his foot problem?" It was none of her business but she burned with curiosity.

Rod chuckled and buttered a biscuit. "He didn't mention problems with his feet." He explained Harris' offer. "I told him I operate alone—sorry for the pun."

"I'm glad you saw through him," Aurelia said in relief. She vigorously wiped the next table. "Harris is not good for Paragon Springs, but he manages to get around our laws. He's fined regularly for selling alcohol illegally but he simply pays the fifty dollars each time without complaint and continues as always. 'Overhead costs' he considers it. I'd like to see him arrested and jailed but his many supporters, and some of them are Paragon Springs' leading citizens, would surely break him out before the cell door closed. That could lead to worse, to bloodshed." She sighed heavily.

Rod shook his head, frowned as he sipped his coffee. "There ought to be an answer to end the lawlessness he's built around him."

"We haven't found it yet," she answered worriedly. "I keep hoping he'll eventually tire of the restrictions of 'Petticoat Town' as he refers to Paragon Springs. He continues to add to his holdings in Flagg. Two of the three saloons that operate openly there, despite prohibition, belong to him. To my mind, Flagg better suits his taste for the wilder side of life, yet

212

he keeps a foot in each town. Waiting to see which community gains permanent county seat."

Everyone understood that the loser, as had happened to so many towns in western Kansas the past five to ten years, would "dry up and blow away." Hating the thought, Aurelia shivered and rubbed her arms.

# Chapter Fourteen

Following Aurelia's suggestion, the city council ordered a small stone courthouse to be constructed in the center of the town square. It would help to have the building ready for when they won the election.

Further efforts toward gaining the county seat for Paragon Springs, as well as the railroad, began to pay off that early fall. With petitions laid out before county officials and the governor's approval to proceed, the commissioners agreed at long last to set an election for selection of a permanent Hodgeman County seat.

There was immediate dissension from residents of Flagg. Wanting to keep the seat and accompanying advantages—main of which was survival of their community—they set out to contest a new election. But it was already underway and legally there was nothing they could do to stop it. As though in a shiftless, over-confident sleep, they had assumed that they had no real competition among other towns for county affairs. During that same time, Paragon Springs' folk had worked hard to build their town into as decent a place as possible, and had taken additional steps to establish a railroad.

"Listen to this," Emmaline said one day, coming into the restaurant waving the *Flagg Bugle*. There were two pages to the newspaper, most of the space given to patent medicine ads.

Just finishing lunch were the Jones Brothers, Doc Rod, Elliot Charbonneau, and a pair of drifters passing through. They all looked up and Aurelia came from the kitchen.

Emmaline stood next to an empty table set with spoon jar and sugar bowl and read, " 'Every citizen in Flagg welcomes the upcoming election. Little does the petticoat town of Paragon Springs realize the fight it has on its hands.' " She turned the paper so the heavy black print could be seen. It said, **FLAGG WILL WIN ELECTION BY HOOK OR BY CROOK AND FOR ALL TIME WILL RETAIN COUNTY SEAT.**

"It would have to be by crook," Silas Jones said quietly, touching his napkin to his mouth. His brother gave a gentlemanly nod of agreement.

Elliot said, "I've done business there, delivering lumber I didn't get paid for." He shook his head, "You'd have to look hard to find an honest soul in Flagg."

Aurelia hadn't been impressed with Flagg on the occasions she'd been there, it was an embarrassment for county seat, rivaled the worst of Dodge City. "It worries me that the contest could turn ugly and violent as has happened between other Kansas towns fighting for county seat," she voiced aloud, adding more strongly, "but we won't let them intimidate us, not in the newspaper or otherwise."

Emmaline sat down, laid the paper aside, and accepted a cup of coffee. "God willing, Hodgeman County men will decide the issues they believe in at the ballot box and not by violent means. It can be a frightening, deadly situation when two communities pit against each other in civil strife, we simply can't allow it to happen here."

Aurelia leaned to say quietly, "I'd have more confidence in the whole affair if women were voting." Emmaline's brows rose and she nodded, smiling.

Later, after her customers paid and departed, Aurelia went from table to table, gathering up dirty dishes, her mind filled with thoughts of the election.

Besides a slate of county officers vying for election or re-election, also on the November ballot would be the bond issue for the railroad. The railroad line had been surveyed in late September. If November's bond issue succeeded at the voting table, the Chicago, Kansas, and Western, subsidiary of the Santa Fe Railroad Company, would begin construction in the spring. The line would stop at Paragon Springs but might in some future time continue on west for service to towns there.

Having the railroad issue on the ballot was a victorious beginning and Aurelia was elated. A railroad for the town, she decided, could be compared to seeing your child learn to walk. A miraculous sign of progress. Up on its two good feet. *Progress* that would grow and grow.

But first, the election must take place.


Owen had driven a wagon-load of corn to Dodge City and was driving through town toward the railroad yard when he saw a group of men in loud verbal battle, arms waving, near the city well. Two of them were Admire and Will. The six men facing them he took to be from Flagg, considering their shouted epithets and he also thought he recognized a couple of them from earlier trips to Flagg. He drew up to the group to listen and watch.

"Wasn't no need to call an election," a big beefy man shouted. "County seat is right where it ought to be and where it's stayin'. You got no real saloon over there," he said in disgust. "Boot Harris doles whiskey at the Yellow Rose like it's a swaller of medicine. Flagg's got three saloons, and barkeeps that ain't afraid to sell you a drink."

Another man, thin and with greasy hair stringing down from under his black hat, stuck his face in Admire's. "You got that new law over there that says you can't carry a gun," he scoffed. "That's against nature. Carrying a gun is a man's right, and right-thinkin' men ain't goin' to vote for no town where you can't carry a gun."

Admire, who probably agreed in principle to both men's arguments, stepped forward to argue, "Now I'll tell you gents why Paragon Springs will win. We got a bigger population over there, and the town is central in the county." He ticked off on his fingers, "We got more businesses and services than Flagg, we got a smart young doctor, we got a fine new courthouse bein' built. We're gettin' a railroad, it'll be on the ballot. Hell, Flagg ain't got a chance." He spit at the booted feet of the stringy-haired fellow, and the man's face flamed with anger and he lifted a fist at Admire.

Will barred his way, saying, "Not every man in the county lives by a gun, or believes a town thrives on whiskey. You gents might be surprised how many men will vote for a peaceful farm town."

"Then mebbe they need a little persuadin'," the heavy-bodied man bulled forward. He stood with legs spread and stroked the gun strapped at his hip. "Might as well start with you two."

"Wait!" Owen shouted as the man started to draw. "Don't be a fool." He leaped off the wagon, his whip in hand, ready to crack skulls with the handle if need be.

"This don't concern you," the giant snarled. He seemed to be the leader, the others stood back waiting for him to act, their own hands hovering above their guns.

Owen grinned and shook his head. "You're wrong there. I've got a vested interest in Paragon Springs. My beautiful wife considers it heaven on earth or that it can be. Also, these two you're sparring with are my friends. Now, why don't we all go on about our business before somebody gets killed? The election's coming, you can vote what you think, then."

"You all know that my friend is right." A pocket gun spun into Admire's hand, and leveled on the bull man's heart.

There was a long, tense silence. The big man's prominent brow glistened with sweat, his thick upper lip twitched nervously. Then he said, "This ain't done. C'mon," he motioned to the others, "these petticoat kissers ain't goin' to make no matter. Flagg will win. They's ways to get votes. We got nothin' to worry about."

Owen heaved a heavy sigh and watched the Flagg supporters retreat toward the saloon back up the street. "You two come help me unload my wagon." He nodded in satisfaction when Ad put his weapon away.

It was no surprise that the issue of which town should have the seat continued to be hotly debated in area newspapers, as well as on street-corners, alongside country roads, in the stores. It was all the talk, throughout the county, and as tension and tempers rose, Aurelia hoped the issue would end with talk and by legal vote. Many male voters would be in favor of the town where they could drink as they pleased and carry a gun. How many there were of such men, compared to peace-loving farmers, was anyone's guess. The answer would likely dictate, in part, the outcome of the election.

It didn't bother her that Paragon Springs' efforts were being referred to as the "Petticoat Fight." The country was changing. A lot of people were in favor of a more peaceful way of life than in the past and she banked her trust in that.

Then, seemingly overnight, her hope and trust began to fade, to be replaced by very real fear and anger.

There were incidents, as time for the election neared. Farmers in outlying areas were ordered to vote for Flagg, or not show up to vote at all, if they knew what was good for them. There were threats of barn burnings, crop destruction, loss of stock. No other reason needed to be given for voting for Flagg. As example for those who might resist, some farmers were pistol whipped. The beatings intended to assist them in "changing their minds."

Drifting cowboys who had no stake in either town and didn't care who won, were paid a small daily wage by Flagg leaders to stick around and vote the Flagg ticket.

The possible outcome terrified her. There could be bloodshed, open warfare, if matters weren't calmed down. She prayed for cool heads and decency to prevail. She went to the county and town sheriffs to plead with them to maintain control. They promised to do what they could. There was talk that it might be necessary to bring in the militia to keep order, but surely it wouldn't come to that.

One day, five loud, talkative men showed up at her restaurant and ordered dinner. Two of them appeared to be businessmen by the suits they wore, they smelled of stale drink. The other three were well-dressed, but rough-looking farmers or ranchers. She wasn't sure she had seen them before although one of the men wearing a suit and string tie seemed familiar. She thought he might be the County Treasurer, Carter Treadway, but she hadn't seen him enough times to be certain.

Overhearing their conversation as she took their orders, poured their coffee, and listened from the kitchen as she fried their steaks, she realized that all of them were Flagg men. They were in town to test the voting waters and sway the tide their way. She felt grave concern as she wondered what means they might try to achieve that aim?

Perhaps they thought she was deaf, or that a woman who couldn't vote was of no concern. They did nothing to conceal that they saw Paragon Springs' Yellow Rose regulars and old men and other loafers in front of the Harris Drug Store as easy marks, sure bets to their cause. Persuading the rest of the male voting population could be only a little more difficult.

"Hell, most of 'em can be bought with a free bottle or a little pocket money," the man who seemed to be their leader said with a chuckle as he wolfed his food. He was a big man, his ox-like shoulders nearly burst the seams of his tan suit. A rattlesnake skin formed a band around his doe-colored hat. The others agreed with him. "But free votes are better," he laughed, and they all agreed with that, too.

"Before we leave this town, every man here will be beggin' to vote for Flagg," another of the men said as he wiped his sleeve across his mouth to remove the glistening grease. He was a horseman from his garb, either a gunfighter or a rancher. Greasy hair stringed down from under his black hat; incongruously, he had the most beautiful long eyelashes Aurelia had ever seen on a man. "Beggin'," he said again, patting the gun strapped to his hip. "Funny how a good hard tap on the skull can clear a man's thinkin'."

Aurelia looked at Dinah Ambler seated at a table nearby. Below her rose-bedecked hat Dinah's face had paled and she only pretended to eat.

Although Aurelia wanted to take a skillet to the Flagg men, tell them exactly what she thought of them—plus remind them of the no-carrying-of-guns sign at the edge of town—she later calmly accepted payment for their meals, thanked them, and watched them leave. It amazed her that they had ridden right into Paragon Springs to do their dirty work, would go ahead with it if not stopped.

She told Dinah, "Watch the restaurant for me for just a while, please? I'm going to find Sheriff Holberg."

"Aurelia, be careful. I heard those men. They've got guns

and they sound dangerous." Dinah got to her feet, clutching the edge of the table.

"They are dangerous. Which is why I have to find Bert."

Sheriff Holberg's office, across the street east from Doctor McLean's, was empty. She found no notice up as to where he might have gone. She turned about, hoping to find help at Wurst's store or at the hotel. She wouldn't ask at either of Harris' businesses, for all she knew he could be in cahoots with the men from Flagg.

Retracing her steps, she saw that the Flagg group had cornered two old derelicts, known only as Hank and Fleeber, in front of the Yellow Rose and were arguing with them. As she hurried in that direction, the broad-shouldered ox-man drew his gun and poked it under Hank's scrawny chin, lifting his head up unnaturally. He spewed orders at the quaking old men, but she couldn't hear his exact words.

Hank was a reedy, shaggy-haired old fellow who could have been anyone's grandfather. As she came up she saw that fright was razor sharp in his faded blue eyes. His friend, called Fleeber, a tattered soul no bigger than a mid-sized child, was shaking with fright even as his whiskery chin jutted defensively.

Both old men claimed to have no taste for alcohol, yet were constantly intoxicated from bottle after bottle of "tonic" Harris supplied them. Paragon Springs' town drunks the old gentlemen might be, she was not going to let them be mistreated.

She hurriedly circled the group to confront the bully holding the pistol under Hank's chin. "Leave him be!" Hank's adam's apple bobbed in his scrawny throat but there was sudden hope in his eyes. She ordered the Flagg men, "Let them go. They are helpless old men."

The contingent looked at her and laughed. "Go home,

lady," the one she thought was the County Treasurer, Treadway, said, "and mind your cookin'. Mind your own business."

"I am minding my business." They had no idea to what degree Paragon Springs was her business, though it might not have mattered to them, anyway. "I want all of you to leave, now. We have a gun law here in Paragon Springs in case you didn't see the sign when you rode into town. Go back to Flagg before you get into serious trouble."

"You want to take it off me?" In a wobbly turn, the big heavy man in tan leveled the gun at her left breast. "Pow!" he mouthed. He was teasing but he seemed equally serious and itchy-fingered. Old Hank had slid down against the wall, eyes closed, bony knees up and shivering as if from a chill. Fleeber had scooted down the street unseen. With devilish interest the men's eyes were on her and their leader. "Try an' take my gun," he said. He moved closer in disgusting invitation.

She stood her ground although her heart hammered in her chest. "Don't be an idiot. Just take your weapons, your horses, and get out of town. Now."

"Or what? You'll do what?" The tan ox grabbed her by the shoulder of her injured arm in a hard painful grip. She struggled and her hair loosened in its combs. He swung her around, the gun buried against her chest. She was frozen in his fierce grip, afraid the gun would go off, even accidentally if she moved. Suddenly, Sheriff Holberg's voice barked, "Turn loose of her or get shot!"

She was released so quickly she almost fell to the boardwalk.

"The rest of you stay where you are. Did they hurt you, Mrs. Symington?" The sheriff took her good arm gently and pulled her out of harm's way to stand next to Fleeber who must have gone to find him. She shook her head that she wasn't hurt, tried to do something with her hair, and explained the situation. "They were trying to force votes. Bullying poor Hank and Fleeber into voting at the polls for Flagg."

"You can't wear guns in this town," the sheriff informed the miscreants, "and you sure as hell can't mistreat a lady or our old fellas. You'd best be showing some dust back to Flagg. Unless," he looked at her, "Mrs. Symington wants you all arrested for assault and battery and thrown in jail?"

Their leader blustered, "We were only funnin' the old goats. We wouldn't have hurt 'em or the woman. We didn't do nothin'."

"And it rains in western Kansas every time it's needed!" the sheriff retorted in disgust. "Don't talk to me like I was born yesterday. It gets my dander up! Aurelia, you want me to arrest them?"

"Let them go this time."

"Don't ever show yourselves in town again," the sheriff said as he herded them toward the five horses at the hitchrail in front of the Yellow Rose. "We won't look on it so kindly next time. You just might find yourself locked up, you try harming any of our townsfolk."

At that moment, Boot Harris came out of the Yellow Rose, Fran, in garish orange velvet was at his heels. On a couple of occasions Fran had assisted Doc Rod, but for the most part she seemed to prefer her regular job singing and dancing at the Yellow Rose. "What's going on, Sheriff?" Boot Harris took in Aurelia's mussed appearance, looked a little shocked. "Mrs. Symington?"

She wondered if Harris was involved with the Flagg men. He seemed to know them from the way he nodded greeting in their direction, but then he would be acquainted since he owned businesses in their town.

Maybe his ploy was to stay uninvolved in the actual fuss between the towns; to wait and see and at the right time swoop down on the best pickings. Let others fight the fight, shed the blood. "Explain to Mr. Harris what happened here, please, Sheriff," she said in a cool tone, "I have to return to my restaurant."

When Owen heard about the incident that night at home, he was furious at her for putting herself in danger. They sat at the table after dinner, drinking coffee. "We're involved in a dangerous fight out here," he told her. "There are men ready to kill to win that county seat because they are positive that their lives, their futures, depend on it. We have to be extremely careful until the vote is in and folks come to accept it as final and the way it's going to be."

Her coffee sloshed as she set the cup down hard. "We can't allow them to bully the vote their way, though! Heavens, Owen, they came right into Paragon Springs bold as brass." She controlled a shiver.

He sighed, reached out to cover her hand with his own. "I know, I know. I just don't want you hurt, Aurelia. I beg you to take care. Watch what you say. Don't go anywhere alone 'til this is over."

She studied his face. She could hardly argue with his worry or the facts: the success of a town, the lives of its inhabitants, lay in the hands of what took place at the polls. And unfortunately, there were men who would do anything, use force and guns if necessary, to obtain the voting results they wanted.

"All right, Owen." Short of hiding behind locked doors, neglecting business and family, she would do her best to stay out of harm's way. Today she involved herself only because she couldn't find the sheriff, she reminded him. And then she told him, "You must be careful, too, Owen. Heaven knows you're in this as deep as anybody." She left her chair to lean down to kiss his forehead and he in turn took her in his arms, pulling her onto his lap.

"Owen, my Owen, what did I ever do without you?" She kissed him soundly on the mouth, stroked his face, his hair, fitted herself tightly against him.

He kissed her back, a long, lingering kiss that she felt in her very center. She smiled to herself, snuggling her head under his chin as he stood up with her in his arms.

"You missed what we're about to do," he answered her huskily against her temple, "but we can remedy that."

It was after dark two nights later. Aurelia had been home for some time but Owen still hadn't returned from a visit to a farmer over east who needed further convincing to allow the railroad across his land. She threw on her shawl, took up the lighted lamp, and went out into the yard. It was chilly and quiet, there was faint light on the land from the early November moon. She walked a piece down the dark road, looking for him. "Owen?" she called, "Owen—?" *Nothing.*

She went back to the house. She told the children to go to bed but Joshua refused, saying, "I'll fetch Sheriff Holberg if you want, Mother."

"Not yet. Owen might have had a late supper at someone's house and decided to stay the night." But it wasn't like him to do that unless there was a storm that prevented travel altogether. He liked to be home with them and to sleep in his own bed. The night air was chill and gloomy, but that wouldn't prevent travel. "I'd welcome your company though, Joshua, if you'd like to sit up with me. He may come in at any time."

Sometime later when she heard a muffled sound outside that she couldn't identify, she looked at Joshua to see if he had heard. He was asleep in his chair, his head pillowed on his arms on the table. "Josh," she whispered. "Wake up. There is something outside. Stay here and guard your brother and sister while I check the yard."

She took down Owen's Spencer rifle from its rack over the door. Cautiously, she pushed the door open. Owen's horse, Sam, stood snuffling in the yard—Owen sagged sideways from the saddle.

In the light from the open door she could see that he had been beaten bloody. With a cry, she rushed to him. He fell from the saddle into her arms. "Aurelia—" his voice was barely audible.

"Oh, Owen, how could they do this to you?" With her arm around his waist, she kept him on his feet, and they made their unsteady way inside. She helped him into a chair and rushed to warm a pan of water on the stove and bring from the cupboard her few medicinal supplies.

After putting Sam in the barn, she spent most of the rest of the night cleaning Owen and tending the cuts and bruises on his head and shoulders, and later, watching him sleep fitfully as she sat in a chair by his bed. In the morning, he was improved.

Aurelia had hardly got a wink of sleep herself but she felt sharply awake due to the anger burning like fuel inside her. "Was it Flagg men who did this to you? Were they getting back at me for having the sheriff run them out of town?" He looked dreadful as he sipped his coffee. Her heart caught. Both of his eyes were blackened, cuts on his face were raw red.

He nodded. "It was Flagg men who ambushed me, I had a run-in with them before and recognized them. Seems they are part of the gang trying to force farmers over east not to allow the railroad across their farms. Maybe they had it in for me, followed me over there, I don't know. My guess is that they were also out on a foray to force men to vote their way. They made it plain they meant to stop my campaign for Paragon Springs for county seat, and for the Santa Fe railroad, or else. They are serious, Aurelia, they mean to win one way or the other."

"What can we do?"

"We can be careful. Keep watch for skulduggery at every turn from now 'til election day. We won't give up. Tell you one thing, honey, I'd rather lose in a good honest fight than turn tail and hide under the porch like a whipped dog."

If anything happened to him, as it had to John, her first husband, she thought she couldn't live. In a stricken voice she said, "Don't let them hurt you again, though, Owen, please. Thank the Lord we don't have that long to wait for the election. You've done all you can, don't you think? Maybe it's time to stay home and look after the farming." *And stay safe.*

As much as Aurelia would have liked the voting to take place in Paragon Springs, facts were Flagg was the recognized county seat for the time being and the elections were set to be held there.

She chafed, riding in silence as they traveled in the wagon as a family for the election-day activities in Flagg, that besides voting, would include a potluck feast and dancing. She wished she could vote, help change the poor governing that had taken place for so long.

She looked around her as they drove through the abandoned town of Peavy on the way. Most of the buildings had been taken down and moved. Tumbleweeds tossed by the chill wind rolled along the empty rutted streets. She shivered. What happened to Peavy could be Paragon Springs' fate if they didn't win the county seat vote, or find some other way to keep the town alive. A western Kansas town without either the county seat or a railroad invariably died. A slow death sometimes, other times quickly.

# Chapter Fifteen

Aurelia had been to Flagg on only a few occasions, once to a farm equipment auction, twice to county celebrations—harvest fairs that turned into drunken brawls, and the day she drove there to ask Wilbur Shaw, county clerk, if the county had a *Physician's Register*. The town's corruption depressed her. Flagg couldn't possibly win, she thought, as she and Owen and their children arrived on election day.

A larger number of carousers than she had ever seen at home jostled noisily along the rough boardwalks, although Flagg was a smaller hamlet than Paragon Springs. Shabby, false-fronted buildings lined the rutted main street. Piles of manure badly scented the breeze that tossed dust and litter about.

On the other hand, Harris' new bank building seen ahead was finer than any structure they had in Paragon Springs, except the school which he had also built and owned.

Paragon Springs had the Yellow Rose, but Flagg, with a string of busy saloons, was *livelier*. Tinny music poured into the street leaving a person's head ringing. Customarily, saloons closed on election day, but not here where the citizenry, numbering less than seventy-five, adopted their own laws. Main Street and two of the cross streets were jammed with moving rigs. Other wagons and buggies were parked haphazardly wherever they stopped. Aurelia preferred Paragon Springs' streets any day.

As they drove along, looking for a place to tie up the team and park their wagon, she noted that, like Owen, many male voters had brought their families to take part in the potluck

229

supper and dance following the voting. The aroma of pork and beef, roasting in pits off to the side of the general store, wafted on the cool fall air.

Today would be an opportunity for visiting between neighbors. Lonely folks scattered about the county on remote farms and small ranches would seize the chance to socialize, to discuss crops, cattle prices, and weather predictions. Although it made little sense to many women, it was also an excuse for menfolk to drink heavily with their friends. Aurelia's glance followed a pair of would-be voters holding one another up as they staggered and stumbled toward the ramshackle hotel where a crude sign said the voting was to take place.

Owen parked their wagon in the last available spot by the livery and went to join other Paragon Springs men gathered in front of the shabby hotel, awaiting their turn at the poll box.

For safety's sake as well as decorum, non-voters—namely women and children—were exiled to the schoolhouse. Aurelia and her youngsters accompanied the others to the school. Until the election was over and votes counted, ugly confrontations and violence were real possibilities at the core of voting.

As the hours of the afternoon ticked on, Aurelia sat at a small schoolroom desk with her nerves crawling and did her best to interest herself in the other women's conversations. The latest patterns of crockery, the subject of whether or not a child should be weaned from its mother's milk before age five, didn't interest her enough to overcome her worry that Owen, or Ad, or other of their friends might get hurt at the polling; and equally the effect today's voting might have on her town's future.

Owen and Will stood together inside the hotel room off

the lobby where the voting was taking place; the air was blue with cigar smoke and smelled of unwashed male bodies. "Would you look at that, Will! That fox-faced fellow with red hair turning in his vote, has voted three times already!"

"At least three times," Will agreed in disgust. "I've seen others get in line over and over. I heard one man bragging and laughing that he was using a different name each time, names he took off gravestones. The present county commissioners, who're supposed to keep the election fair and legal, look on— or rather look the other way—and don't do a damn thing to stop the cheating."

"All afternoon I've seen money passing hands, men being paid to vote the payer's way," Owen growled, angry. "That voter near the front of the line right now," he motioned with his head, "the fat gent with mutton-chops, everybody knows lives in Ford county, not Hodgeman. And he's not the first non-county resident to vote. I complained to the commissioners about the fraud taking place, and they just said they were sorry they didn't see it and would keep better watch."

Will snorted, "Well they sure as hell ain't doing it. They want this election to be a fraud, so they can declare it void and throw it out, wait and see!"

"I'd like to call a halt to the whole thing, start over and do it right, but only an official can do that. And talking to them is like talking to a wall. You're right, Will, the officials don't want a fair election."

Admire came in and stood for a few minutes with Owen and Will. In a moment he headed for the voting line. Owen followed and grasped his shoulder, "What are you doing, Ad? You've already voted."

"Yeah, and I'm votin' again. I figured it would be this way, and I brought me some extry names. You got to fight fire with fire, Owen, so don't try to stop me."

231

"This isn't legal, Admire. C'mon, come away."

Ad shook free of Owen's grip. "No, it ain't legal. But it's the only way to fight back against what's happenin'. I've got friends doin' the same as me, votin' for Paragon Springs as many times as they can get by with."

"Cowboy!" a voice yelled suddenly, "get out of line, you voted already." A commissioner in a rusty black vested suit, belly hanging over his belt, barreled toward Admire. "I said get out of line, you voted."

"Need some help, commissioner?" The red-haired Flagg man who had just finished voting for the fourth or fifth time, bolted over, grabbed Ad, and tried to throw him off his feet. Ad was ready, and his fist came up from the ground and connected with the fox-face in a sharp thud. The man fell back, holding his jaw and cursing, then he dove at Ad. Owen and Will leaped into the fight, tried to pull the men apart, but others joined the fracas and fists flew.

Mutton-chops' ham-sized fist came too fast for Owen to duck and it collided with his jaw like a sledge as a bullet whined past his ear.

"Order!" a voice bellowed. "We'll have order, damn it!"

Outside noises had seeped into the school building most of the afternoon, and late in the day, Aurelia thought she heard gunshots. "It's probably just drunken fools celebrating," one woman said, motioning for calm, "an' nothing we women can do about it if it's not."

Aurelia hated waiting. A severe ache settled inside her skull. She felt immense relief when Owen walked through the school's main door an hour or two before she expected to see him. Evidently the polls had closed early. Families would have their dinners while county officials counted the votes.

As he approached, she noted the expression of anger and

disgust on his face, and a swollen red blotch on his jaw. She asked, feeling a chill, "What happened?"

"The voting was a sham," he told her sadly as he caught her hand and squeezed it sympathetically in his own. "Some men voted several times but weren't stopped. They used names they took off gravestones when they voted for their second, third, and fourth time. Money changed hands time and again as men paid others to vote the result they wanted. Residents of Ford County voted, claiming they had moved to Hodgeman County. It was a disgrace." His eyes met hers in general apology and his tone was regretful, "Some of our folks from Paragon Springs were cheating, too. Admire Walsh got beat up by a Flagg man when he tried to vote more than once, using names he got off a hotel register." He rubbed his jaw that still ached.

"You were fighting, too?"

"Not willingly. Will and I were trying to stop it."

"I know you would do that, Owen." She hesitated. "I thought I heard gunshots?"

He nodded. "Several men were ready to draw their guns, but what you heard was a commissioner firing into the air to end the brawl."

"What happened, then? What about the election results?" This was worse than anything she might have imagined.

She trembled as Owen told her, his voice deepened by disappointment and anger, "The present county commissioners, who stood by and did nothing to halt the illegality going on, then refused to count the votes when it was all done. The four of them declared the election *void* on account of fraud."

They stood, heart-broken, grimly silent as outside the sounds of jubilation from Flagg folks grew to a deafening din.

"Present commissioners will remain in office, then," she

said huskily, chiefly to herself, "and Flagg remains county seat." It might be months, even years, before a request for another election would be fulfilled. If years, Paragon Springs could die, fade to a memory. People wouldn't stay long in a town they didn't believe could become county seat, residents couldn't survive indefinitely without the benefits of a railroad.

And the baby thrown out with the bath water in the voting today was the railroad-bond issue. She was as devastated over that loss as missing the chance for her town to be county seat. It was almost too much to bear. She took Owen's arm, called to their youngsters, and went outside.

Admire Walsh, dirty and bruised, clothing torn, joined the Paragon Springs contingent who had gathered by the schoolhouse to discuss the matter and share their deep disappointment. A cold wind whipped around them. "Now, you women," Ad explained to the wives, trying to make apology for himself, "this ain't total unexpected. Honest elections are near unheard of in this country, anyhow, you know. You gotta fight their fight or not get nowhere. We just gotta try again."

It was all Aurelia could do not to wring his neck. If Lucy Ann weren't one of her dearest friends, she might have given him an earful. Lucy Ann looked mortified as she begged Ad to take them home, not stay for the supper and dancing. Meg and Hamilton were already loading up to leave. Most of the women around them were stirring uneasily, expectant of more serious trouble.

Aurelia's throat was so dry she could hardly speak. "I'm not hungry, Owen," she told him. "Do you mind if we don't stay for the potluck?" At his nod of agreement, she and Zibby retrieved her dishpan of fried chicken and her chess pie from inside the schoolhouse. When her sons looked like they might protest, she told them, "We'll eat it ourselves, all by ourselves, on the way home."

Within days of the voided election, Boot Harris proceeded to move—lock, stock, and barrel—from Paragon Springs to Flagg. Workers partially dismantled his drug store, loaded what would fit onto wagons, and moved it seven miles southwest to Flagg. The smaller Yellow Rose establishment followed.

Boot Harris spotted Aurelia watching the exodus from her restaurant one day and strolled over. "What are you waiting for?" he asked with a smile after he'd tipped his hat to her. "Any businessperson with good sense would be right on my tail, moving to Flagg."

"I don't know why," she said stiffly, looking past his shoulder.

"Of course you do," he laughed. "It's only a matter of time before this place looks like Peavy, a few abandoned buildings, wind blowing sagebrush along the empty streets, maybe a stray cow or two poking around."

"You're wrong."

"I'm right. And that's why I've decided to throw in my lot with Flagg, help build it up, help it gain permanent county seat. I've got no use for a town sick and dying for more saloons—lively entertainments that are the life-blood of a town. I'm tired of fighting to run an ordinary business here."

"What about the school?" She held her breath but tried not to show her worry.

"Raise the money and I'll sell it to the town. I have no use for it. Nor will any of you, in time," he chuckled.

To the depths of her soul she wanted to argue the survival of her town, but if she caused him to doubt his conclusion, what he'd come to believe so strongly, he could change his mind about selling, or raise the price of the school building. So she played dumb. "I'll see if the money can be raised, find out if that's what others want to do."

"You go ahead," he touched his hat. "They'd be fools and so would you but that's your concern not mine."

To her surprise, Franny came to tell her goodbye. "I already told Doc Rod I can't help him no more. You got a nice town here, Mrs. Symington, right nicer than Flagg is. I wish you all good luck. But I got to go with Boot." Embarrassment or simple shyness, seemed mixed with her apology. "Him and me have kind of an understandin' and anyhow, I like workin' for him."

"I wish you good luck, too, Fran. And I'll always be grateful to you for setting my arm that time. Doc Rod says nobody could have done it better."

Fran beamed at the praise. She gave a small wave, then she was climbing into the wagon with the other Yellow Rose women, on her way to Flagg, away from Paragon Springs.

To Aurelia's dismay, several others—good folks like Ben Reid—left, too. Ben hadn't been the same after the loss of Essie and their child. His father-in-law Mathis, also went. They apologized, but explained that they had to carry on their trade where their chances to make a good living were most favorable and that was in a county seat town. They believed that would always be Flagg, no matter how many elections were held.

Oscar Wurst stayed, but his brother-in-law moved his barbershop and bathhouse back to Flagg. Others, with small farms and residences on the edge of town, moved as well.

For days, Aurelia watched the exodus with a heavy, angry heart. Business at her restaurant slowed dramatically. Other businesses choosing to remain, Wurst's General Store, Jones

Brothers' Mercantile, the Marble House Hotel, Maud Mullendore's dressmaking and laundry business, suffered the same. Some days, there was nothing for any of them to do but watch the moving.

One night, Admire Walsh and a few of his friends came to the ranch to discuss the matter with Aurelia and Owen. "What we ought to do," Ad proposed, "is go on over to Flagg and just take what county records there is, by force if we have to, and bring them to Paragon Springs where they belong."

Aurelia spoke up for herself and Owen. "No. We will ask for another election, an honest election, by spring if not before. We're not resorting to thievery, or violence, though by no means are we giving up."

Admire didn't like the decision not to steal the records, but he accepted that Aurelia and Owen, town leaders, for the time being had the say.

On a day not long after, he came to the restaurant to see her. His expression was accusing and angry. Having no customers, she had watered her plants, had given her kitchen the best cleaning it had had in months, was now giving her glassware an extra polishing.

In answer to her greeting, he stormed, "Boot Harris is building a fancy, two-story courthouse in Flagg!"

She was devastated at the news, but she was also baffled that Ad could be so angry at what was an obvious action since Flagg had retained the county seat. "That isn't surprising," she said.

"Dammit! That ain't all. He's campaignin' to get the Missouri Pacific railroad to run a branch line down from Salina into Flagg and on southwest, skippin' Paragon Springs altogether!"

She was stunned to hear that, but she felt there was more to Ad's raving even so than she was hearing. "I don't understand what this is about, Admire. I hate what Boot Harris is doing as much as you do. I know Paragon Springs is in trouble. It pretty much always has been." She set out cups. "Would you like some coffee?"

He shook his head.

"Why are you so angry with me? I didn't even get to vote!" She tossed the dishtowel aside, stood with her hands on her hips. "It was you men who made the election a blessed mess, ruining everything with crookedness and cheating, losing it for us!"

He didn't seem to hear, his mind on his own argument. He shot back, "If you hadn't been so unfriendly to Harris, if you'd let him have a regular saloon like every other town out here has got, he would have helped Paragon Springs win the seat. He has the power and money to help us here but you wouldn't have it. He never did nothin' wrong. You just didn't like him."

"I didn't like what he did, what he was doing to this town, Admire. Your darn tootin' I'm not in favor of illegal free-flowing whiskey, lawlessness, gunfights, killings—turning a town into a dangerous place for decent families. Not counting that, the man could have stayed here 'til Kingdom Come and I wouldn't have minded!"

"I have half a mind to pull up stakes and move on myself."

"You wouldn't—" Her heart quaked at the picture of him, of all people, taking his family and leaving. "Please don't, Admire. You and Lucy Ann are very dear to us, we would miss you terribly, things just wouldn't be the same here. Rachel is Zibby's best friend. Lad is a son of this town, always will be. He and Selinda belong here."

"What am I supposed to do, then? What is any of us supposed to do, if we stay?"

"Have faith and hang on, Ad, that's what we all can do.

And fight, but fairly, honestly. Do everything we can to get a railroad in here. Do whatever we can to build and grow. Order another election. But not give up, be quitters."

"Lord-God, Aurelia, you sound just like Meg Gibbs."

She smiled. "Meg has been my teacher." Privately she hoped she hadn't been taught a futile lesson. Speaking softly, encouragingly, she told him, "We're going to have another election, and next time Paragon Springs *will* win!" She didn't mind at all losing Boot Harris to Flagg. Except that he was going to be a more formidable foe from there than he ever had been as a member of the Paragon Springs community.

"Oh, awright." He waved a hand. "We'll try and hold out as long as we can. Lucy Ann don't want to move. Rachel don't, either."

He had already discussed moving away with them? She was shocked.

He glared at her, practically spitting his words, "Keeping food on the table, clothes on our backs, is going to be harder than ever to do in a place goin' nowhere. And forget tryin' to set a little money aside for the future. I already owe the bank more than I'll ever see comin' in." He put on his hat, yanked the brim low.

With sadness, she watched him go, his eyes on his boot-toes as he scuffed angrily down the street. She understood his frustration, the worries of all of them. At the same time, she believed hanging on, not giving up, was the right thing to do. The only thing.

With Emmaline, Selinda, Lad, and the Walshes as guests, Aurelia and Owen and the children spent a quiet Christmas at the ranch. To take their minds off doom and gloom resulting from the ruined election, they talked after dinner of other affairs: the exciting ditch-irrigating systems developing all that year in western Kansas, chiefly the Eureka Canal through Ford County. That seventy-mile-long canal, fed by the Arkansas River and financed by New York millionaire, Asa T. Soule, was predicted by next spring to "make the desert bloom."

It was being discussed in Topeka the possibility of *electric* street cars replacing those drawn now by mules and horses and they wondered if Paragon Springs' first street cars might be electric? "And electric street lights, too, can you imagine?" Selinda added.

They couldn't, very well. But if that was the way the world was progressing, that would be Paragon Springs' way.

When the women began to talk about suffrage, the continuing struggle for women's right to vote, Owen begged to be excused. He declared good-naturedly that he agreed with whatever their feelings were but he had to go out and smoke his pipe and see that the stock were bedded for the night. He motioned for Admire and Lad to join him. With smiles of apology, and claiming they agreed with Owen, they followed him.

Later, as Aurelia and Owen were bidding goodnight to their guests, she suggested, to everyone's agreement, "Let's have a New Year's Eve ball to boost folks' spirits. Times like these, we need a distraction from our troubles."

The New Year's Eve dance and supper at the Marble House Hotel was turning out to be all Aurelia had hoped for. From the most staid old gentleman to youngsters just learning to walk, folks were having a fair good time. They filled the room with happy chatter, laughter, and very active dancing. This was the first community amusement since destruction by the tornado and loss of the election, it was time for such an affair.

They were dancing the "Varsouvienne" more simply called "Put Your Little Foot" with Doc Rod teaching them. Then followed the Virginia Reel, and the always popular square dance. Oscar Wurst was the caller shouting with his accent, "Almon right!" and, "Grab your honeys, don't let them fall, shake your hoofs and balance all," to the music from the Rocking A's cowboy band, organized by Dinah.

Selinda and Lad, Aurelia noted, danced nearly every dance together, smiling at one another, in a world of their own even after a year of marriage.

Sharing chit-chat with Lucy Ann as they sat out a dance, Aurelia wanted to ask how she and Ad were faring, whether they might still entertain the idea of leaving the area for other parts. Rather than chance ruining the evening for herself and for Lucy Ann, she didn't ask. It was a time to enjoy.

Toward morning, Owen drew Aurelia into his arms for a waltz. He sounded tired but contented as he said softly in her ear, "I'd better be heading out to the ranch with the children. The cattle and horses don't know it is a holiday. They'll need tending."

She said, looking up at him, "I'll be out later. It's been quite a night, hasn't it, Owen, love? And not over yet. Some of the bachelor folk and families from out of town would like to have breakfast at the restaurant before they start for home. Some of the women have offered to help me cook and serve. When that's done, I'm going to close up for a few days. I'd like some quiet time at the ranch with my family."

"Business will pick up again, honey, as soon as folks overcome the shock of not winning the county seat."

"I know it will."

She walked him and the children to the hotel door. Outside a lovely morning showed pink in the eastern sky. A grand start to a new year, she thought, waving to her family as they

241

walked across the street for the livery to harness their rig for the home trip.

There was an even bigger rush at breakfast than Aurelia had expected and it took hours to cook and serve everyone. Lucy Ann, Meg, Emmaline, and Selinda were a great help, right down to washing and drying the last dish and cleaning the last smear of spilled egg and bacon grease from her Home Comfort range. While they worked the women caught up on their visiting, with a lot of teasing and laughter mixed in.

It was nearly noon when she thanked them and saw them on their way. She noticed that a few clouds had begun to darken the sky that had been so pretty earlier.

Preparing to leave herself, humming a song whose words she couldn't remember, she wrapped a thick woolen scarf around her head, pulled on her overshoes, and shrugged into her heavy coat for the trip to the ranch. Better to be safe than sorry, she thought, although she was already too warm in the heavy outer garments.

Leaving the livery, she shook out the reins of her sorrel driving mare. "C'mon, Sweet Annie, let's hurry." If they could make good time, there was no reason not to drive a few miles out of the way for a short visit to Lena Crowley.

She clicked her tongue again. Sweet Annie swung into a trot and the wheels of her small hack rattled hollowly in the empty street.

Doctor Rod had mentioned at the ball that Lena could use visitors, that she was very lonely since her husband had abandoned her. The Crowleys hadn't been in the area long, so she didn't know Lena well. Recently, though, when Lena came in to town to buy supplies and to see Doctor Rod for her chronic "touch of consumption," she sometimes stopped at the restaurant for a small meal.

She seemed to be a shy woman of few words, frail, plain in looks and dress. Aurelia felt sorry for her. Word was that when Mr. Crowley left for greener pastures he believed his sickly wife would only die on the way so he left her behind. Her few coins of income came from milk she sold to the cheese factory, dried corn and pumpkin that she sold door to door from a sack on her back, and mittens rudely made from heavy grain sacks.

As Aurelia drove, frost crunched and squealed under her wheels and Sweet Annie's hooves. The wind was brisk and chill, the day gloomy. The only life to be seen for the most part were large herds of cattle fenced in by barbed wire strung between stone posts.

She thought of the women she knew whose husbands had abandoned them. Remembered a few men whose wives had left them. She herself had been abandoned by a brother-in-law who left her dependent on others' mercy. But no matter, she and Meg and Lucy Ann had done well together. Were still doing fine enough, although sometimes she worried about Lucy Ann. Admire was so restless.

Sometimes Admire reminded her of a wild horse waiting for the starting gun so he could bolt. But even if he took off, he would never leave Lucy Ann. He would go someplace else, take her along. She was sure of that.

She approached the Crowley place which consisted of a few poorly-fenced acres, a drab-looking dugout home, and a shed. A whisper of smoke lifted from a thin pipe from the dugout's roof into the wintry air. Surveying the barren, poor look of the land and house, she decided it was a wonder the poor woman survived at all. How a man could just walk away and leave his wife in such a predicament was beyond her.

# Chapter Sixteen

The Crowleys had migrated to Kansas from the back country of Massachusetts. Now that Lena was alone, Aurelia wondered, would she go back there?

"Thought I heard something." Lena, a brown shawl wrapped around her head and shoulders, came from the dugout into the windy yard as Aurelia climbed down from her buggy. She looked surprised but glad to have a visitor. "Please come in, Mrs. Symington, come in by the fire." The chill air seemed to bring on Lena's cough and she covered her mouth with her hand.

"Call me Aurelia, please. I'll take care of my horse and be right in." She waved the woman back inside, then led Sweet Annie into the near-by open-front shed out of the rising wind. She unhitched, gave her mare a bit of oats from the small grain box she kept stored in her buggy, then she shoved her way against the wind to the house. Inside, she peeled out of her heavy outer garments. "We missed you, Lena, at the New Year's Eve ball. I brought you some of the delicious little raisin cakes Selinda made." She handed her the cakes wrapped in a dishtowel. "There were so many left over."

"Thank you." She smiled her quiet smile. "I would have liked to have come, but I've had this pesterful cough. Feeling a little poorly." Lena looked not to have an extra ounce of flesh on her, and it appeared to pain her just to move.

"Do you have medicine?" Aurelia asked worriedly. "I could return to town for some. I could get Doctor Rod to come—"

Lena smiled, "I have medicine. Doctor Rod gave me some

cod liver oil, iron phosphates, and quinine when he rode out to see me last. He said the medicines needed to be used up before they got old and went bad. Don't know if that really happens; of course, he was just being kind. He won't charge, but he agreed to take some squashes or a loaf of bread in exchange. I can't imagine a nicer man than that young fellow. He thought I should move to town with someone to look after me, but I told him no, I'm fine right here for now."

With slow careful movements, Lena stirred up the fire in her tiny stove. Using her apron to pick up thick cow chips from a box, she poked a couple into the sputtering flame, then stopped to cough. "We'll have tea with the cake," she gasped for breath, patting her chest. "I make the tea from boiled pumpkin seeds and a dribble of molasses. It's nothing like store-bought tea from China, but I like it."

Aurelia studied the room—which looked church-mouse poor—as she waited. There was only a rickety table, a bench, and the chair where she sat. By the stove where Lena made tea were some near-empty shelves fastened to the wall and in the corner a pathetically ragged bed. A torn curtain at the single small window was the only adornment.

She hadn't seen much in the way of fuel in the shed, either, although there was a box of dried cow dung here in the house by the stove. She wondered again how the woman could go on? She was sick. Alone. With little means of support, how could she survive?

She contemplated taking Lena back to town that day or home with her. Either option might take some persuading. She would give Lena a little time to relax. It was an opportunity for the two of them to become better acquainted before she broached the matter.

It was pleasurable as they ate in front of the fire. The pumpkin seed tea was not so bad, improved by the spiciness of the cake. They talked of many things, the New Year's Eve ball, the winter weather, the hopes for a fine spring. They skirted the issue of Mr. Crowley's cruel disappearance in October, although Aurelia was curious. As they talked, Lena's desperate circumstance fermented at the back of Aurelia's mind, flooding her heart with compassion.

She subtly mentioned that she might need help in the restaurant if Lena was interested in a job. Which was a bit foolish. Business would have to improve considerably to keep the restaurant operating with even a small profit. But she couldn't let the poor woman starve. And business might pick up in a month or two as spring approached.

"I do thank you, Mrs. Symington," Lena said with a tilt of her head, a smile. A paroxysm of coughing hit her and it was another minute before she could talk. "I'd say yes . . . to your offer . . . like scat if I was staying in Kansas," she panted. "But I have decided to go back to Massachusetts where I have family. My sister, Jennie, has offered me a home with her. She takes in boarders, could use the household help." She coughed again. "Soon as the weather clears, I'll be going."

"Of course, and I understand. I'd really like it, however, if you'd come home with me until then . . ."

Lena shook her head. "I thank you, but I need to stay here and look after my cow until I can find someone to buy her; don't know how much luck I'll have—she's a thin old thing despite the fact she's carrying a calf. The man at the livery gave me some feed sacks free, I want to make a new dress from them for my trip back to my sister's. I will be fine. As soon as good weather sets in, I'll perk right up—feel lots better. You'll see."

Aurelia agreed reluctantly, "All right. But when I get to town in the morning, I'm telling Doctor Rod to come see you. He'll know if you need a different medicine, and I'm sure myself that you need to stay in bed as much as you can and build your strength. You'll do that, won't you?" She still didn't like the idea of leaving Lena.

"I will."

"And I'm going to send you some nice healthy meat from the butcher's. Some potatoes and rice and dried fruit."

"You're very kind, Mrs. Symington."

"Pshaw, I'm just being neighborly," Aurelia waved her hand.

They visited quite a while longer. Aurelia was sure Lena was lonely with few friends and it was difficult to make a move to leave. But as evening approached, she knew she had to reach home before her family worried about her. She felt a riffle of concern that she would be driving in the dark with only her small lantern. But it wouldn't take long, from Lena's it was only five miles or so. "We were having such a good chat," she said, taking Lena's hand, "it has gotten later than I thought. I have to leave now, but I'll come back to see you as soon as I can."

In spite of Aurelia protesting that Lena stay inside by the stove, Lena followed her into the yard. The light from Lena's lantern showed light snowflakes starting to fall, glistening white against the dark. Aurelia turned back, "Are you going to be all right, Lena? I can stay—" Snowflakes swirled about the other woman's slim, stooped figure in front of the shadowed dugout.

"I'm fine," Lena panted, after a sharp hard cough left her near breathless. "I sound worse than I really am, and anyhow, I've got my medicine and I promise to see Doctor Rod. Maybe he will have a soothing syrup for me. Mrs. Symington—Aurelia, I enjoyed our visit very much. You remind me of my sister, Jennie. She's a strong, very kind woman, always looking out for other folks. I'll be so happy when I can be with her again, have long chats."

Aurelia, clucking like a mother hen, said with a wave of her hand, "Scoot back inside to your fire out of this snowfall, please, dear, before you catch your death! Thank you for the tea. I enjoyed this afternoon, too. If you're sure you will be all right, I'd best be getting on home while I can." She rushed to hitch Sweet Annie again and turned her buggy toward the ranch.

In a matter of minutes the snowflakes fell in a blinding rush, causing her scalp to crawl with concern. The wind rose in a gale that threatened to tip her buggy over. Her small lantern swung wildly in the whining wind, the flame flickered, threatened to extinguish. She grabbed the lantern from its hook and placed it on the floor of her buggy near her feet. Everything about her was dark beyond a ghostly white curtain. The lantern now illuminated only her skirt, boots, and floor of the buggy, was faint in the area around her conveyance. If there was warmth from the light, she didn't feel it.

She drove into the storm, seeing little but believing that she was properly on the road. She touched Sweet Annie with the whip when the mare tried to turn back to the comfort of the Crowley shed, the companionable warmth of Lena's cow. Ice and snow stung her cheeks, her eyes watered. Clouds of steam rose from her mare's nostrils as she plodded obediently along with her head down.

Aurelia peered for landmarks to verify her location, but there was nothing but snow and the terrible keening wind. Although she lived with the wind daily, she had never known it to blow so hard, except in the tornado.

She drove on for what seemed hours in numb, blind, misery. She ought to be reaching home after so long. But she could see nothing. Sweet Annie was flagging in harness, working hard to make even a little distance when she wasn't wanting to turn.

It felt like a full eternity passed as they continued to drive into nothingness, seeming to get nowhere. Possibly they traveled in circles. She fought panic. Were they near home? Headed back to town, or to Lena's place? She had no way of telling in the blowing snow and shrieking wind.

If they didn't find shelter soon, both she and Sweet Annie were going to freeze to death.

Teeth chattering, so cold she was sure she could never be warm again, she faced the fact that she did not know where she was, that she had gotten turned around and was lost. Deciding to let Sweet Annie have her head, she hoped the mare's instinct would lead them in the right direction. Providing, she thought, she herself hadn't delayed too long to put trust in the animal's knowledge.

They moved in a slow crawl for what seemed a lifetime. Then, Sweet Annie slowed and stopped, would go no further. Half-frozen, hoping to learn where she was, Aurelia climbed down stiffly, falling face-first into snow. She struggled up, tried to see some kind of landmark. Through frosted lashes, she made out a shadowy lump, the Crowley dugout. Teeth chattering, and with a whimper of gratitude that they had at least found shelter, she hugged Sweet Annie, caught her halter and led her into the snow-covered shed. With frozen fingers she unhitched and grained her next to Lena's thin cow, made sure there was water in the trough, wished for a real barn to shelter the poor animals. Maybe the storm would stop soon. They could dig out and be on their way.

Lena quickly got over her surprise at seeing her again. "I never should have let you go in the first place," she reprimanded herself. "But a couple of hours ago the weather was nothing like it got since. I filled the water trough in the shed just in time, it's apt to freeze solid but we can break the ice as often as need be."

She nodded, teeth chattering. She tried to assist as Lena's thin, blue-veined fingers began to peel off her outer clothing that was heavy with snow and ice. She let herself be led to the chair by the stove where Lena draped a blanket around her. Shaking so hard her teeth rattled, she plunged her frozen fingers into the bucket of cold water Lena brought and thought surely her hands would break off with the fiery pain. The remedy was correct, however painful. Tears stung her eyes, she ground her teeth into her lip as she later put her bare feet into the water, to thaw them, experiencing more unendurable pain.

"D-don't th-think I ever saw such a storm," she was finally able to say through chattering teeth. It had been bad the night Helen Grace died, equally bad years ago when a neighbor, Mary Hague, and her little boy, Ollie, got lost in a blizzard and froze, but not so bad as this.

Still cold to the bone, she shared a small supper of biscuits, boiled beans, and more pumpkin seed tea with Lena. She hobbled to the window every little bit on aching feet, hoping to see the storm abating. Instead, the wind howled on and on. There was nothing but swirling white through the window glass. They were being buried by snow. *Buried alive with little food or fuel.*

By ten o'clock that night, unable to sleep, they knew they were in the grip of the worst blizzard either of them could recall. Aurelia worried about the poor cattle, and other animals, and of course, folks, caught out in the open. She prayed most plains folks were home safe and warm in their beds.

She thought of Owen and the children. They would have expected her to arrive at the ranch hours ago. She hoped they would stay where they were and not set out on an impossible search for her in the blizzard. As long as she stayed where she was and she and Lena stretched the food and fuel to last, she was safe. But, of course, they couldn't know what had happened to her. She remembered with guilt that she had decided to stop at Lena Crowley's without anyone's knowledge. Nobody had any idea where she was.

Maybe Owen would think she had been held in town longer than expected and when the storm came up she had decided to wait 'til morning to make the trip to the ranch. She could only hope that was what he believed. That he wouldn't strike out to find her and become lost in the blizzard himself. Life had been dreadful after losing her first husband, but if anything happened to Owen . . . Her heart constricted and she forced the thought from her mind.

The cold grew more intense with each passing hour 'til her bones ached. Throughout the night, she took her turn fueling the tiny stove, yet she could feel little heat emanating from it. Shivering, she lay side by side with Lena under the quilt. Chill from the storm outside seeped under the covers, it was impossible to be warm. Before dawn they both arose, teeth chattering, and formed a blanket tent around the stove, and huddled there together for warmth the remainder of the night.

A dugout would normally be warm in winter, but this storm, this cold, was anything but normal. When they stirred from their place by the stove, freezing cold permeated the small hovel to an impossible degree. It amazed Aurelia that she and Lena had survived the night.

Even so, Lena looked so poorly from the ordeal that this time Aurelia helped her to dress in every piece of clothing she owned. Then she helped her back into bed and brought all the blankets to cover her. Lena protested, wanted to share the clothing, the blankets. Aurelia told her to save her strength and not try to talk. She would wear her overcoat and boots in the house, keep her shawl over her head. She brought Lena her medicine.

Later, she tried to open the door. It was built—probably by an inexperienced city fellow with no carpentry skills or good sense—to open outward rather than inward and now the snow was packed high and heavy against it. Shivers of alarm at this further complication ran through her. She shoved and shoved, finally managing to push the door out less than a foot. "I have to dig out," she told Lena. "I have to get out to the shed and take care of your cow and my mare. Bring in more fuel."

She got a large kettle from the kitchen shelf and began to use it to shovel snow, sometimes packing it to one side, other times tossing it to the top of the drift over her head. By slow inches she tunneled outward and upward. It took nearly an hour to reach outside the door and be able to close it again.

She tied a rope to the door and wrapped the other end around her waist and continued digging. It seemed miles to the shed. When she reached it, she found Sweet Annie and Lena's cow had shifted from time to time and were standing on top of the drifts that had blown in and piled up from the open front. Sweet Annie was standing with her head low, she couldn't raise her head under the roof which was just inches above her mane. Her sorrel color was whitened by snow, her nostrils were frosted.

After wiping Sweet Annie down, talking soft encouragement to her, Aurelia began to dig around both animals' legs to lower them. She would have to melt snow to water them.

Locating their feed was another matter. Once she had freed them, she commenced to dig again, found the feed bin under three feet of snow, gave each animal a portion of grain, and wild hay from the stack. She found an iron pin and mallet, likely used to stake the cow out to pasture, and she used them to break the ice on the water trough. The cow was dry, expecting a calf, so there was no need to milk her. Seeing a stack of old burlap bags and twine on a shelf, she took bundles of bags and placed them over the animals, then tied the covering in place with twine.

She filled another of the bags with cow chips. Then she tightened her belt and filled the waist of her garments with more cow chip fuel. Then she filled her pockets. There was a time, she thought grimly, she could hardly bear to touch a cow chip with her *gloved* hand. Now she carried them next to her body. Tying the other end of the rope to the shed post, she started back for the house.

In the kitchen, she built up the fire and fixed them a thin cornmeal gruel for breakfast. Lena, in the grip of exhaustion and without appetite, could take little. Her cough sounded as though it would rip her chest apart. The phlegm she brought up was profuse and rusty looking, her tongue red and furry. Like the blizzard, she had worsened over the long night.

All morning it snowed. Aurelia fed the fire, worried about the scanty amount of chips left in the shed, the twists of grass in the basket in the corner of the small room. But most of all she worried about Lena.

Her own breath made small clouds before her as she tallied Lena's food supply. There was no more than a cupful of dried beans, less of cornmeal, the molasses jug was empty. Lena's pumpkins and winter squash were outside buried in snow. If no one found them soon or if she could not get out and go for help, for food, they would be without anything to eat in a very short time.

Lena began to sweat in spite of the cold, she tossed restlessly. Aurelia wished hopelessly for medical attention from Doc Rod, but it was too risky, too dangerous to try and reach town. She would probably lose her way and Lena would die then for sure, and herself as well. The medicines, difficult for Lena to swallow, didn't seem to be doing her any good when she did get a little bit down.

She was afraid that Lena had galloping consumption, a sickness that was almost always fatal.

She melted snow in a large kettle, kept the water boiling on the stove, hoping the steam would help Lena's infected lungs. Every so often, she plied her with hot pumpkin seed tea with small results. She resisted thought of her well-stocked larder at the restaurant and at home on the ranch and at midday fixed them a scanty meal of bean soup thickened with a tablespoon of cornmeal. No matter how she pleaded with her, Lena was unable to take more than a spoonful of the soup.

That evening, with the rope to guide her and carrying the kettle to dig with, she made her way out to the animals again. This time it took all her strength and she was afraid more than once she couldn't make it there and back. But she struggled on, knowing that keeping Sweet Annie alive was their only chance of getting out for help when the storm finally abated.

The blizzard, the bitter cold, continued into the third day. This time, no matter how she tried to force the door, it would not open. She thought of removing it, but was afraid the snowbank would cave into the dugout and smother them. Clearly they were froze up, could not get out. She fought the door, over and over, to no avail. She made a mental note to *never* have a door that didn't open to the inside.

There was no doubt that day that Lena's condition had grown critical, possibly she had developed pneumonia in addition to consumption. She spoke very little and that in a faint raspy whisper. She had no appetite. Passing water was very distressful.

She was hot to the touch. Aurelia's fingers felt singed when she stroked Lena's forehead, her cheeks. Her cough and abundant expectoration continued, she had difficulty catching her breath although Aurelia massaged her chest, and her back. Her legs and loins pained her and from time to time Aurelia massaged her limbs, before covering her again to keep her warm.

She would have given anything to be able to go for Doctor Rod for Lena.

She used the last of the cow chips later that day. Her hands were bruised from trying to open the door and not budging it. *This is the only thing I can do,* she thought, reaching for a chair and chopping it up with a hatchet for fuel. The pieces of chair would keep the fire going for a while. If she couldn't keep Lena alive, it wouldn't matter about the chair.

Burning only a small amount of the chair at a time was not enough to keep them warm. She looked for other items to burn. She had to keep them from freezing until they were found, or until the snow melted enough that she could dig her way out for help.

She was sitting practically on top of the stove that evening when she thought she heard a sound outside. Relief flooded through her. They had been found! She jumped to her feet. "We're here, we're here!" She grabbed at the door, tried to push it outward. She put her ear against the door, detecting now the snuffling of an animal. Whatever was outside, it wasn't human. Maybe it was a wolf trying to get into them to fill its own starving stomach.

"Go away!" she shouted, and then, knowing how foolish that was, she leaned against the door. She pounded her fists against it in frustration, at the same time wanting to scare the critter away.

The snuffling and pawing continued. As she turned away,

there was a sudden crash and bellow behind her. She ducked, covering her head with her arms as something huge hurtled by her. In shock, she saw that a young range steer had crashed through the window and half of the wall. The steer sat on folded legs in the middle of the floor, dazed and flinging its head back and forth. Its eyes were nearly frozen shut. Frost and icicles hung from its nostrils.

In another minute, it would be restored to its senses and on its feet. And she would be crushed, everything in the room smashed. She reached behind the stove for the hatchet. She brought it up over her head, hammer side down, and with the strength of her whole body crashed it onto the steer's head, between the eyes. She lifted the hatchet, hammered it down again and again.

With a gurgling groan, the steer rolled onto its side and was still. Aurelia waited, sick at her stomach at what she had had to do. And then, before she could lose her courage, she slit the steer's throat to make sure it was dead and not just dazed. Blood gushed and she shoved the large kettle under the steer's head to catch the crimson liquid.

Swallowing repeatedly at the gorge in her throat, for the next hours she worked over the steer. Lena's butcher knife flashed in Aurelia's hand as she skinned the animal while it was still warm. The freezing wind blowing in through the smashed window and the hole in the wall drove her to hurry. When she'd freed the broad hide from the flesh she made a slit in each hairy, bloody, corner. She hacked a rung of the chair into four pegs, then took the hide and spread it over the opening, pegging it into the earthen wall one corner of the hide at a time. Warmed from the hard work, gratified that the cold wind was stopped from blowing in, she slumped down by the bloody animal, covered her face with her arm, and wept.

That evening, there was steak and hot broth for their meal. Lena sipped feebly at the beef broth, got down a few swallows. Aurelia was heartened. She believed greatly in the nourishment of broth. Surely now Lena would recover, and they'd be found.

# Chapter Seventeen

Aurelia struggled to drag the steer carcass against the far wall out of the way. They would not starve. They had meat enough for a very long time.

She was forced to admit that it was doubtful the food would do Lena enough good. Lena was dying in spite of all Aurelia's efforts to save her. She showed no signs of improvement from the beef broth or from the medicines. Her breathing grew more labored, her pulse was feeble. Each weak cough seemed to bring her nearer to death.

Close to tears, praying for a favorable change, Aurelia refused to give up on Lena. She spooned warm broth between her purplish blue lips only to see it spill down Lena's quivering chin. She wiped perspiration from her fevered brow, begged her not to give up. She kept blankets tucked close around her, stoked the fire with pieces of furniture and the shelves built against the wall.

Near dawn of the fourth day, Lena took her last shuddering breath and was still. Aurelia was overwhelmed by a sense of failure, and anger at being so imprisoned by the snow that she could not get help. She couldn't stop thinking that Lena would not visit her sister Jennie now. Which seemed almost worse than her death itself.

She washed and dressed Lena's body and combed and fixed her hair as she would for a Sunday outing. To keep from crying she hummed a hymn. As she arranged the body on the bed, she sang softly, out loud, teeth chattering: "I come to the garden alone, while the dew is still on the roses—" She drew a breath "—and He walks with me and He talks with me—"

When the song was finished, her tears spilling, she drew a blanket up over Lena, covering her face.

She got a blanket for herself and for a few moments sat shivering on the floor in front of the stove, gathering her strength to dig out past the hole the steer made in the wall. The last stick of furniture, not counting Lena's bed, was burning in the stove. She wanted to absorb that heat for the hard journey ahead.

When she mustered to her feet for a look beyond the hide, she cried out, and her hope faded. Snow, packed thick and deep and high, walled her in, a prison. "Dear God, Owen, I don't want it to end like this, it can't end like this!" She clawed at the snow, sobs catching in her throat. She got her kettle and dug more frantically, time having no beginning, no end. Once she heard muted voices and knew fearfully that she was losing her mind. When the male voices came again, she listened more carefully. Someone *was* outside, more than one person, digging in toward her.

She was nearly frozen when she fell into Owen's strong arms. Through a fog of emotion—love and thankful tears—she heard him explain how he'd found her, that the search party he was with had made a systematic sweep of the prairie, checking every remote farmhouse, sod shanty, and dugout where they might be of help to save lives. "My prayers have been answered, Aurelia," Owen said huskily against her temple, "Sweet heaven, they've been answered—you're alive!"

In days to come Aurelia was to learn further particulars of that dreadful blizzard of January, 1886, which was actually two terrible storms one on top of the other and a few days apart. All of Kansas had frozen solid, nearly one hundred people had frozen to death, though none of them were of her personal acquaintance.

Cattle in the tens of thousands were destroyed by the freezing cold, the herds frozen in drifts at fence-lines, leaving the last few large cattle ranchers impoverished. Although it was not the way she would have wanted it to happen, the blizzard of 1886 ended the cattlemen's open range war with farmers.

Her own personal experience in the storm was too painful to dwell on for any length of time, she was not even sure it was a story she would someday want to share with her grandchildren. An address for Lena's sister was found, and Aurelia wrote to her in Massachusetts and told her what had happened.

Then she turned her attention back to her community. Would it always be two steps back for one step forward? Along with the rest of western Kansas, Paragon Springs faced another year of salvage, of trying to recoup devastating losses, of simply finding ways to struggle on. Would the day come, she wondered, that they would pull so far ahead, be so firmly established and roots so deep, that any trouble would be only minor annoyance?

She wished she had the answers. For now the main problem for one and all was simply to survive through the rest of winter.

At home that spring, on a pretty Sunday in May, Aurelia slipped a fragrant pan of cornbread from the oven. They were having a very special dinner: roast beef, potatoes and gravy, dried apple pie. Humming happily as she worked, she put a pot of water on the stove to boil for the succulent young greens Zibby and Rachel had found growing by the river.

Tomorrow a new election would be held and it was hard to contain her joy over the matter. This time would be different.

Her mind pondered events—fair and foul—of the past few months.

The snow had hardly melted off the ground that early spring when Carter Treadway, County Treasurer and leading citizen of Flagg, absconded with every penny of county funds. Although a posse tried for weeks to pick up his trail, recover the money and bring him to justice, Treadway was never seen again. He left a county struck hard by winter blizzards in even worse straits.

On the positive side, his criminal act, added to general disgust with the way county affairs had been mismanaged for too long, outraged right-thinking county residents to the point that they didn't hesitate to sign a petition seeking a new election. A United States Marshal would be present to make sure it was performed honestly and legally. Four new commissioners, Owen among them, would be listed on the ballot.

Next day in Flagg, although they couldn't vote, Aurelia, Lucy Ann, Emmaline, Selinda, and Meg insisted on being given a spot to witness the election from, in the lobby of the shabby Flagg hotel. Their children were out of harm's way at the schoolhouse under the care of kindly Hannah Mathis.

Long lines of sober-looking men, hats in hand, lined up in front of the voting table in the smoke-filled room off the lobby. The governor had sent not one but two U.S. Marshals. One posted himself near the voting table, the other at the doorway to the room.

"Looks like the men are all behaving themselves and voting properly," Lucy Ann commented.

"And hadn't they better!" Meg responded with a wry smile, nodding toward the marshals. "If women voted, it wouldn't have to be this way."

"We should have had the Federal officers present at the

first election, then we wouldn't have to be here today," Aurelia lamented, "but better late than never."

"When Selinda and I arrived today, a fellow was paying another to vote his wishes, but he was caught by one of the officers," Emmaline commented.

"The Federal man refused to let either man vote then," Selinda said, "Flagg lost both of those votes."

The women smiled.

When the voting was finished that evening, the votes were counted by selected clerks, the U.S. Marshals watching over the process. Aurelia listened carefully to the announcement of the results, read by a less than happy commissioner who had lost in this round.

"Railroad bond issue—passed."

"County seat—Paragon Springs by two-thirds vote."

Loud cheering exploded and Aurelia barely heard that Owen was overwhelmingly voted one of the new commissioners. She ran to him and held him tightly as happy tears spilled down her cheeks. "Congratulations, my darling, congratulations!"

He swung her in an impromptu dance, "Congratulations to us all!"

Emmaline rushed up to them, her face distraught. "Owen, there's trouble! I just overheard some Flagg men talking and they don't intend to let county records be removed from Flagg. They will hold them at gun point. A whole group of them rushed out of the hotel as soon as the election results were read."

"They won't get away with it. Keep the women and children here in the hotel where it's safe," Owen ordered. "I'll let the marshals know what's going on." He kissed Aurelia's cheek, grabbed Will Hessler as he walked by, and hurried out the door. At the hitch-rail in front of the hotel, the Federal men were saddling up for their ride back to Dodge City and a homebound train. "It's not over," Owen told them, "Paragon Springs won fair and square but Flagg holdouts say they won't let the county records be removed from here."

The taller of the marshals swore under his breath. The other, a stocky, well-muscled man, said, "We'll see about that."

Aurelia tried to watch from a window but Owen, the marshals, and several other men with them, moved out of sight in the direction of the bank where it was said county records were stored in a vault. After a tense, interminable time, she heard a spattering of gunshots, like grease popping in a wet skillet. She started to run outside but Meg held her, "Wait, Aurelia."

"Stupid, stupid fools!" Aurelia said in anguish. She tore free and went to the window. Meg's husband, Hamilton, approached the hotel in a swift stride. She yanked open the door, "Ham, what's happened?"

"Stay calm and stay inside." He motioned her back, pushed in after her, closed the door behind him. His face showed strain but he spoke calmly, "Everything is under control, ladies, but please stay here in the hotel until we give you an all clear signal. The marshals are forming a posse, including Sheriff Holberg and Mike Fitzgerald, the new county sheriff and they've taken possession of the county records from the Flagg bank. The records will have an armed escort to Paragon Springs."

"Thank God!" Aurelia said, relief rushing over her in a flood.

"We heard gunfire, was anyone hurt?" Emmaline asked.

"One bull-headed Flagg man who wouldn't put his gun down was wounded by one of the officers. He'll live."

"Why didn't they just give up?" Aurelia asked no one in

particular as she paced. "The voting couldn't have been more fair and honest. Paragon Springs won legally. Why can't the matter end right here and now? We need peace."

"The trouble is over for the moment," Ham told her, frowning. "But I doubt it will last. There is rumbling out there from Flagg toughs that they mean to take the records back by force, destroy Paragon Springs' courthouse in the process if they have to, but under no circumstance do they intend to give up the county seat, legal vote or no."

Aurelia shook her head, unable to find words to express her dismay, her sorrow.

"Then it's not over?" Lucy Ann asked softly, frowning.

Ham shook his head. "I wish it was."

Aurelia's scalp crawled with tension as she and Owen discussed the matter further at their kitchen table that night. Owen told her, "Leader of the Flagg die-hards, now that the ex-ex-County Treasurer has taken himself from the fray, is the ox-built man who gave you so much trouble that time in town when you stopped his bullying poor Fleeber and Hank. His name is Arch Lawler, he's a failed, poor-boy Colorado farmer who, in an attempt to get rich, runs shady businesses in Flagg that include a saloon, racetrack, and gambling hall. Lawler was less than a nobody where he came from, they say, but in Flagg he is a big fish in a small pond. He sees removal of the records and county seat as robbery."

"Why don't they just let it be?" she bemoaned, then asked, "Do you think Boot Harris is involved, is he a cohort of Lawler's?"

"No real evidence either way, that I've heard. For all we know Harris may be behind all of it."

A shiver traveled Aurelia's spine, and she shook it off, and sat forward in her chair. "Owen, I'll tell you this: Lawler,

Harris, or the two together, can't be any more determined for Flagg's survival, than I am for Paragon Springs'! This town will prosper far into the future," she smacked the table hard, "will be a thriving place to live for my children, and my children's children, and their children!"

His hand covered hers and he grinned, "I know, sweetheart, I've never doubted the fact, and I'm with you." He brought her hand to his lips and kissed it. In a moment he said, "Until Flagg troublemakers get it through their heads that they've lost for good, we'll post a well-armed guard around-the-clock at our new courthouse."

"We won't have the U.S. Marshals' protection after today, will we?"

"No. They were sent to oversee the election, make sure there was no corruption, their job is done. Now it's up to each individual in the county to go forward with a cool head and common sense."

She rolled her eyes, doubting the certainty of that.

In the days following, besides having an armed guard over the records, Aurelia suspected that most newly elected county officials carried secret pocket guns for protection, although Owen refused to do so. He had more faith than she did that the majority of Flagg supporters would get used to the idea of losing, that they would adjust their lives accordingly, and county affairs would run smoothly. It was a frightening time and she worried constantly.

"They're back," Owen came into the restaurant to say one day, smiling broadly.

"What do you mean?" Aurelia lay a damp towel over the cinnamon rolls she had just formed and set the pan on the warming oven for the rolls to rise.

"Come outside and see."

Two well-loaded wagons rolled into town from the west, trailing a cloud of dust. "It's Ben Reid, and Hannah and Mathis!" She cried out, recognizing their old friends. She chuckled with pleasure. "I am so glad!"

"I saw them as I was coming into town myself," Owen told her, slipping his arm around her waist. "Rode out to meet them and talk. They're moving back. Ben wants to reopen his saddlery, Mathis is back to run his wagon works. Others are coming, too. Quite a few will be first-timers to live in Paragon Springs."

Aurelia wasn't really surprised. For most folks, the reasonable answer to the county seat question was simply to situate themselves in the town that held the seat, the town with a future. "They're certainly welcome. All of them, except Boot Harris." Harris had sold the town his lots when he sold them the school. Mathis and Ben had been undecided about their lots and now they were back.

"I'm sure Harris knows he'd not be welcome, Aurelia, that the proverbial gates to the town for him are the same as locked."

"He'd better know it." She leaned into Owen's shoulder, saying quietly, "Everything is so perfect now for Paragon Springs. I pray it continues that way. I'm so excited over the building of our railroad I can hardly think."

Large crews of men, those regularly employed by the Kansas, Chicago and Western railroad, plus locals who contributed however many days' work they were able, had begun construction. One crew was building the bed and laying line from Larned, the other from Paragon Springs, to meet in the middle. Owen, Joshua, and David John—most Paragon Springs men, helped when possible.

Several members of the rail company crew stayed at the

Marble House Hotel and Murphy's Boarding House. They went out each morning with pick and shovel, by horse and wagon, to the work site. There were also two camps of men along the surveyed line who only came to town now and then.

In town, construction on the depot had started on land near Elliot Charbonneau's lumberyard.

Aurelia's own business was revived to the point she could hardly handle it all and she was kept busy dawn to dark on week days. She fed the working men breakfast, made lunches to send with them, had their suppers ready when they returned to town at night.

In the dead of night, at the western edge of Paragon Springs, Boot Harris sat in his buggy, his face faintly lit by the burning tip of his cigarillo. Beside the buggy was a wagon-load of men, Arch Lawler on the seat and holding the reins to the team. Others among the group were the greasy-haired outlaw, Morgan Cox, the fox-faced redhead known as Shep Stoker, and a half-dozen other roughs.

Harris chewed the cigarillo and keeping his voice low asked, "You all know what you're supposed to do?"

There was a rustle of sound. "We send two men, Shep and Morgan, in on foot," Lawler answered in a guttural whisper, "them two take the guard captive, gag and hold him until the rest of us come with the wagon. We make the guard open up the courthouse, and we load up the safe holdin' the county records."

"You got to be as quiet as death," Harris warned. "The town is full of railroad workers; you never can tell who might be up even this late at night. Make sure you're not seen. Slip in quiet and after you tie up the guard, take the wagon around to the back of the courthouse—you know which building that is?—it's the small stone structure in the middle of the town square." If it had been built of wood, he'd order it burned down once the records were taken. Another night, they could blast it to Kingdom Come.

"Just a minute," an eighteen-year-old named Wiley, rose to hang over the edge of the wagon. He whispered fearfully, "Hadn't we ought to be wearin' masks?"

"Pull your damn bandanna up over your face," Harris ground the words between his teeth, "if you think you'll be spotted. Or do you want to be identified?"

"After we get the records, what then?" Wiley whined. "Don't seem logical to go to all this trouble, maybe get gut-shot," he shuddered, "over a bunch of papers."

"You idjit!" Lawler hissed, "keep your mouth quiet. We keep the papers, that's what."

Harris fought for patience. These men were ignorant clods, but on the positive side, they had nerve, would follow his orders, would kill if necessary. "We take the records back to Flagg and hide them," he explained quietly. "We order another election, or simply declare Flagg county seat as it's always been. It doesn't matter. We'll take care of that after the records are in our possession." His eyes roved the inky darkness that smothered the cluster of buildings forming the town. "We've wasted enough time. Go on in."


Sheriff Holberg kept to the darkest shadows, close to the buildings that lined Main Street. Every nerve in his body tingled as he sensed something about to happen. Each night since the records were brought to Paragon Springs he had paroled the streets periodically, in addition to having a guard posted at the courthouse.

In the past half-hour suspicion had arisen in him like hackles on a dog. His eyes scanned for movement in the inky darkness up and down the street. He saw nothing, yet they were out there, he could feel it. He thought about going for extra help, Will Hessler, some others, then decided there might not be time. With his heart beating against his ribs, he moved, light-footed for a heavy man, from building to building in the direction of the courthouse, hoping to God he'd be on time.

Slipping along on foot in deep shadows, Morgan and Shep had arrived a few feet from the courthouse without mishap. Morgan flipped his hair back out of his face and crouched low next to a tree in the square, straining to see in the dark. He nodded to Shep, who stank of nervous sweat, "I can make out the guard, he's sittin' in a chair outside the door. Looks like his hat is down over his face—"

"He asleep?"

"How the hell would I know?" Running quietly on the balls of his booted feet, Morgan crept toward the guard. He slid to a stop just two feet away when a voice bellowed out of the dark, "Hold it there! This is Sheriff Holberg. I got aim on you, mister, if you move another step you're dead."

Morgan cursed under his breath, sweat ran down his face and his mouth went dry. He looked for help from Shep and couldn't see or hear him. He was afraid to reach for his own gun for fear the sheriff would detect the movement and fire.

Sheriff Holberg held his rifle steady and moved slowly from around the side of the courthouse. "Jim!" he yelled at the guard, "we got company!"

"Heard 'em comin'," Jim chortled, "they make a sound or try to move, I'll fire this buffalo gun I'm holdin', my trigger finger's been itchin' the last five minutes."

There was a scuttling sound as Morgan dove toward the ground and in a crab-crawl made swift retreat. The sheriff fired at the sound, heard a curse, a voice yelp, "Shep, you god-damn coward, where are you?"

The sheriff shouted, "Both of you, halt!" He fired again at the sound of two pairs of booted feet running away in the dark. There was the sudden sound of wheels rumbling, brakes screeching, horses neighing, as a wagon turned in retreat. "Wait for us, damn it," a voice shouted, boots pounded along the street, the sound gradually faded.

At the edge of town, hearing the commotion, Boot Harris turned his buggy, cracked his whip, and drove swiftly along the dark road leading away from Paragon Springs. Rage at the group of fools he'd engaged, their failure to accomplish a simple job, burned inside him. *If a man wanted something done right, he had to do it himself.*

In town, the guard lit a match as the sheriff approached. "They got away? Shall we round up a posse to go after them?"

"They were Flagg toughs, I figure, after the court records. They didn't get away with anything, hurt anybody, this time. We'd have no cause to hold them. Hope they have the sense not to try again or somebody will get killed."

Sheriff Holberg wearily hefted himself into a chair at Aurelia's restaurant next morning.

"You look tired, Sheriff," she said as she poured his coffee.

"I am, Miz Symington." He rubbed his hand through his thinning hair and told her about the events of the night before.

Stunned, Aurelia dropped into the other chair at his table. "They were here—in Paragon Springs? Flagg men came to steal the records?"

"They didn't give their names or announce their intentions," he said wryly, "but I don't know why anybody else would sneak in here at night except Flagg toughs after the county records."

"How many? Was Boot Harris one of them?"

"It was dark, Miz Symington. I figure there were two on foot, another bunch of them in a wagon; don't know about Boot Harris. If I was puttin' money on it, though, I'd say he was involved."

She nodded. In the past three years Harris had invested deeply in Flagg. That he had given up too soon on Paragon Springs would not sit well with him. It would be incomprehensible, forcing him into making a desperate move to turn the matter around, before too late—before Paragon Springs finished building the railroad and was established for the long run. Before her town became unbeatable.

She waited for the sheriff to drink more of his coffee, then asked, "Do you think, whoever it was, that they learned their lesson? Do you think they'll try anything else?"

He shook his head tiredly. "My job would be easier if I knew the answers to your questions." His eyes narrowed thoughtfully, "If the bunch who came here last night are who I think they are, we're dealing with desperate men. A few of them have criminal minds bent on evil—to destroy Paragon Springs, if they can't have their way. Some of them are as dumb as blocks of wood, which is just as dangerous. Who knows what they might try? I don't think they'll get away with anything, though, if we all stay alert."

"All of us," Aurelia agreed reflectively, cold fear gripping her heart. "Thank you, Sheriff. Let me get your breakfast."

# Chapter Eighteen

Joshua, broad-shouldered and muscular, pushed back his felt hat, wiped the sweat from his forehead on his sleeve and squinted eastward to see if he could make out the tracks being laid from Larned. "There they are, David John, look!" Joshua leaned on his shovel and pointed.

David John barely glanced in that direction. He scratched the golden stubble on his jaw and answered, "Mirage." Panting from the heat, he struggled to drive his shovel into the hard sun-baked earth. Swearing, he threw down the shovel, grabbed a pick, and swung hard, over and over, this time breaking the ground deeply. He moved on, repeated the process. Later, stone ballast would be smoothed over the bed, providing stability, drainage, and an even distribution for the railroad ties.

"It's not a mirage." Joshua followed after David John, slicing the fragrant earth clods with his spade. "If you look real careful, you can see the sun glinting off the rails and some tiny little ant-people, the graders working this way. Only a few days now and there will be tracks laid from Larned to Paragon Springs." He grabbed his pick and said, "Let me go ahead for awhile, Davie, and you break up the clods." He and David John were part of the grading crew of eight men, preparing the roadbed for the line stretching from the west. Experienced railroad men toiled behind the graders, placing the ties, laying the track, spiking down the rails. The chief engineer's goal was for them to lay a mile of track a day, but in the intense heat of deep summer, nobody could work that fast and hard.

"The Chinese and the Irish did the work we're doing, twenty years ago when the transcontinental railroad was laid from the East Coast to the Pacific Ocean," Joshua panted. "Now that had to be a job, grading and laying track through mountains, across gorges and for hundreds and hundreds of miles."

"Don't see any damn Chinese or Irish here," David John snorted as he stabbed his shovel through hard clods. Sweat streaked down his dirty face.

"No, just David John Thorne making his fortune," Joshua laughed, and slapped his brother on the back.

A while later, a foreman whistled and shouted that it was time to head back to the railroad camp and supper. "Grub time!" echoed up and down the line.

Along with the others, Joshua and David John loaded their picks and shovels into their wheelbarrows and trundled them west against the setting sun. They had been working since sunup, had ceased grading briefly at noon to eat their sandwiches, drink a few swallows of beer provided by the railroad men in charge. During the day the graders sang to the beat of their busy picks and shovels, by sundown they were bone-weary, silent men.

They walked a mile and half of prepared roadbed, reached the end of the gleaming rails stretching from the west, followed the rails another mile into camp. There were a half-dozen tents for the use of the chief engineer, the foremen, and some of the other long-time railroad workers. The others, including the Thorne men, kept bedrolls under the grub wagon, rolled them out under the stars at night. Several horses and mules were picketed at the edge of camp. Three wagons held railroad materials: spikes, rails, fishplates, bolts.

Joshua headed for the water wagon and from a water barrel drank several dippers full, dashed some over his head, spitting and sputtering and wiping at his begrimed face. David John followed suit.

At the campfire with the other men, they spooned into plates of beans and fatback. "I miss Mama's cooking," David John grumbled. "Sometimes I think if I see another plate of beans, I'll puke."

Joshua teased in a high squeaking voice that was supposed to sound like their mother's, "David John! I beg you not to use the word 'puke'."

David John slung his fork at Joshua who ducked just in time.

Almost immediately after the meal, stomachs full, the crew went to bed. Joshua lay in his blankets, exhaustion like lead in his veins.

"What're you going to do with your money, Josh?" David John asked him sleepily after a while.

"Is that all you can think about, the money we're earning?"

"What else is there?"

"You don't think it's important we're helping to lay the first railroad into Paragon Springs?"

"I like the money."

Joshua chuckled deep, then heckled, "You're going to buy Rachel a bauble, I reckon? You better, Rachel's going to be an old maid if you don't speak up pretty soon, Davie boy."

"Shut your damn mouth!" David John searched the ground for a clump of dirt, heaved it as hard as he could. Joshua laughed tiredly, closed his eyes, and yawned. He shouldn't make fun of Davie about Rachel. He had no girl, himself, but he was looking.

Hours after the crew had bedded down, Joshua woke from a deep sleep thinking he'd heard something. He lay quietly, peering into the dark. His scalp prickled as the shadows of at least two dozen men edged into camp from every direction, moonlight glinted off gun-barrels. "Wake up!" he yelled hoarsely. "Trouble!" His hand clawed the ground to find a pick or shovel, something to use as a weapon, he had no gun. Around him, the night exploded: foremen charged from their tents shouting orders, workers sprang from their bedrolls on the ground, the exchange of gunfire was like zigzagging lightning. A man screamed.

"Wh-what's happening?" David John said groggily and started to sit up.

"Davie, no!" Joshua yelled. He threw himself forward over his brother, and was slammed backward by a slug. A numb bee-sting in his shoulder, then deep pain, radiated through him, weakened him, made him feel sick. He said close to his brother's face, "Davie, I've been hit."

Aurelia had gotten to sleep close to dawn—after yet another night lying awake worrying that the Flagg gang would return for the records—when Will Hessler appeared at the ranch, shouting for Owen, pounding on their door.

She flew out of bed, pulled her wrapper on over her nightgown, was close on Owen's heels when he lighted a lamp and opened the door to Will.

"What's wrong, Will?" Owen asked, holding the lamp and guiding their panting friend inside with his other hand. "What's happened?"

"God-blast those Flagg devils!" Will tore off his hat and threw it aside. "They've done it now!"

"Our records, they got our county records?" Aurelia asked, incredulous. "But how—?"

"It's not that, they didn't get the records. They probably thought that would be easy pickings next."

"What, then?"

Will ran his hand through his gray hair and dropped into the chair Owen brought him. Normally he was a calm-natured man much like Owen, but at the moment he was red-faced with fury. "They got back at us where we didn't expect it, they hit *our railroad.* They've destroyed what we got built of the line, just tore it up all to hell. Sorry, Aurelia," he apologized for swearing.

"The railroad?" Her heart hammered. "Joshua and David John are working on the line this week!"

"Your boys are fine," Will said quickly, palms up. His glance slid away from her to Owen.

"Don't lie, Will," her voice was thin, her throat dry. "Tell me what happened." She clutched her wrapper tight at the neckline.

"Joshua got nicked by a bullet in the shoulder, he saved David John's life—I swear they're fine. David John stayed on the line to help clean up the mess, Joshua is at Doc Rod's for a while."

"Thank you, Will," Aurelia said quietly, finding a chair when her legs threatened not to hold her. She had recognized for some time that her sons were grown men, strong, capable fellows, but in a part of her mind they'd always be innocent little boys, their father viciously shot to death, the responsibility suddenly hers for their safety.

"We'll get dressed in a minute and go see them," Owen said gently and she nodded. "Will, what happened?"

"The Flagg men sneaked out to the line last night. Not just them, the ones we know, they must have hired a hundred others, gun-toting riffraff from Dodge and God knows where. They struck both of the camps. Knocked guards out cold. Held everybody else at gunpoint 'til they were all tied up. Then—then, they went out and tore up more than half the line we got laid. Used crowbars to pry up the rails, axed the

276

ties to pieces, bent the rails out of shape with sledge hammers. *Under cover of night of course!* Nobody in town knew what was happening so they could stop it."

"Was anyone besides Joshua hurt?" Aurelia asked. Her scalp crawled painfully and she held her breath.

"One of the railroad boys in the west camp fought back, they shot him dead, after he killed Arch Lawler. Lawler is that big fella' that leads the Flagg gang, him and probably Harris. Don't know if Harris was there. I do know Lawler is dead. Another of the railroad boys is wounded. He was brought in to Doc Rod with Joshua. Doc says he will live."

Although she had been prepared in her mind for further trouble, Aurelia was stunned. Destroying the rail line to Paragon Springs was damage to the town itself: was possibly only the first of planned actions to ruin them and return the county seat to Flagg. Her insides churned. This morning two men were dead and others wounded—her son included—because Flagg men wouldn't let the matter rest. "They're sure Flagg men were involved, besides Lawler?"

"He's the only one anybody could identify among the culprits. They only knew it was him after he was dead and they pulled the sack off his head. The ruffians all wore sacks on their heads, with eye-holes. You couldn't tell who was who. Besides, it was dark. But we know it was Lawler and his bunch. Maybe Boot Harris was with them, a sack hiding his identity. But after they did their deviltry, they all got away. Except for Lawler who got killed by the railroad boy."

Aurelia nodded to Owen, "I'll get dressed. Zibby can mind the restaurant this morning while we investigate."

At Doc Rod's infirmary, Joshua was stretched out on one of the two cots in the back room, his head propped with pillows. He was pale, his shoulder thickly bandaged under his loose, unbuttoned shirt. Aurelia's eyes welled and he told her, "Now, Ma, don't do that—! Owen, Pa, make her stop."

"Your mother has a mind of her own. How are you, son?" Owen patted Joshua's good shoulder.

"I'm not crying," Aurelia insisted, "I'm just glad you're alive and I'm very proud of you. Will says you saved your brother's life."

He quipped with a wide grin, "Rachel would have held it against me if I hadn't!"

"Oh, Joshua!" She hugged him with extra care.

The young man on the other cot, more seriously hurt with gunshot wounds to his right arm and thigh, was asleep. Doc Rod told Owen and Aurelia, "He'll be all right, his wounds are clean and no bones broken. When he's awake he's in good spirits, shows a lot of bravery after the fact. Joshua can go home, but you might have trouble keeping him there, he wants to be out on the railroad building site with his brother."

"He can't, can he?" Aurelia was aghast.

Doc Rod laughed, "No, if he tries he'll find the only thing he's capable of for a week or two is rest."

Aurelia felt renewed determination to end the violence between Paragon Springs and Flagg, and not another day lost. Not a single soul more must be wounded or killed in the name of county seat business and that was that.

Owen drove the two of them out to view the scene of destruction and find David John. It was worse than Aurelia had imagined. As far as the eye could see across the windy sunscorched prairie, the steel track was a shambles, turned into useless litter. Wheelbarrows and wagons had been smashed and burned and lay in charred, smoking piles.

David John ceased work at piling debris only a few moments to assure them that he was all right. "But Ma, would you bring us out some pies?" He motioned, "The workers who camp out here all the time have no idea what good food tastes like."

She promised and kissed his grubby stubbled cheek despite his gruff request for her not to fuss.

They visited with other working railroad men, later found the chief engineer, an intelligent-looking, well-built fellow in his mid-thirties. Owen told him, "We're going to do everything we can to assure your men's safety. A wire has already been sent to the railroad officials in Topeka to let them know what happened."

He thanked them, shook hands, and went back to work directing the clean-up.

Owen and Aurelia visited the ruined rail line again a few days later, in the company of a Santa Fe officer. Holding his bowler hat on his head against the blowing wind, his face perspiring from the heat, he sat in their wagon and stared. "This won't happen again," he said stoutly, fire in his blue eyes. "No cowboy outlaws are going to fool around with the Santa Fe Railroad Company and get away with it, nosiree!" His pale chin quivered in indignation.

By himself, he personally couldn't frighten a prairie gopher. But the Santa Fe Railroad Company he represented, Aurelia felt, was indeed a force to be reckoned with.

She wondered what they might do. Owen and she explained that the only recognized culprit was dead, it would be hard to prove who the others were.

"Are your town officials willing to join the railroad company in ordering a full-fledged investigation of the damage and shootings, put a stop to this nonsense warfare over what town gets a courthouse or not?"

Owen answered, "Of course we'd be in agreement with that."

Aurelia bristled but nodded. Didn't it go without saying that they'd want the troubles investigated and stopped? At the same time, the drive for county seat was not nonsense at all, only the illegal or violent acts to get it were wrong.

By another dawn, a company of militia had arrived in Paragon Springs from Fort Dodge. Uniformed soldiers carrying arms were everywhere, on the streets, in the stores, camped around the courthouse. There were two more camps at the entrances to town and lines of soldiers guarded the railroad construction sites where cleanup of the damage was underway.

Along with most others in town, Aurelia hated the feeling of being in the middle of a siege, but she was willing to have the militia's presence if their just being there would keep the peace.

Although in the passing weeks it couldn't be proven who besides Lawler was involved in destroying the railroad, the seriousness of the investigation along with the military presence, had its effect.

Most remaining residents of Flagg packed up hurriedly and left for other parts, among them most of those suspected of taking part in the violence. Word came that Boot Harris remained in Flagg but was selling out his holdings there, bit by bit, for whatever he could get. Aurelia did not expect him to leave quietly. She'd worry until he was out of that country for good.

It took time to clean up the ruined track and haul away the debris. There were delays in ordering and hauling in all the new materials needed. Then the work laying new track had to begin all over again. Although it was believed that most of the troublemakers against Paragon Springs had left the country, the militia remained on hand as inch by inch, mile by mile, the track was laid. By early fall the line was complete and stretched shiningly intact from Larned to Paragon Springs.

Folks not just from town but from all around the county came to witness and celebrate the arrival of the first train from Larned. Aurelia and her friends arranged to serve free coffee, lemonade, and sugar-doughnuts from her restaurant.

Most other businesses had closed for the day and clusters of people waited in high excitement around the turntable and small frame depot for the locomotive's arrival. When someone bellowed that they could see it coming, the chatter, the laughter quieted as all eyes turned toward the northeast.

At first the train was just a small black moving shape, growing in size very gradually, the cowcatcher just a red dot in front, smoke from the engine a smudge in the clear blue sky. As it came nearer, riders a-horseback went out to wave welcome from both sides of the track. Youngsters shrieked in excitement, jumped up and down, were warned by their mother's sharp tongues to stay where they were or be killed by the wondrous black monster steaming toward town.

A quarter of a mile away, the train's whistle blew and blew, its smoke roiled into the sky like a banner, and a great cheering rose from the waiting crowd. Aurelia, watching from where she stood with a group of friends, smiled, could say little, but she thought her heart would burst. *By heaven they had done it, they had their railroad and their train!*

The engine sounded one last plaintive wail. Laughing cheering people cleared back a few yards from the track as the train chugged into the station and hissed to a stop, wheels squealing on steel track. When the dust and steam cleared, the gathering surged back for a better look, some shaking hands with the engineer and fireman as they hopped down from the train.

Compared to many trains, it wasn't a long one, though it was impressively new. Behind the shiny black engine with its bright red cowcatcher was an open tender loaded with coal, then a combination mail and baggage car, two passenger coaches, and then the caboose.

Several men and ladies from Larned alighted from the passenger car to visit friends in Paragon Springs. Others had ridden along just because the train was new, and they wanted to be part of the celebration. Aurelia, Owen, and their friends went out to meet and greet as many of them as possible and point out the tables in the shade where doughnuts and drinks were being served.

Owen had gone with Ad Walsh and Ham Gibbs to climb up into the engine and talk with the engineer, when Aurelia turned suddenly to find Boot Harris at her elbow. His ornamented, crimson-wheeled buggy and black driving horse waited a few feet away, the horse's tail flicking flies. There was so much commotion she hadn't heard Boot arrive.

She did her best to hide her shock at seeing him. She had half-hoped of late that he *had* left the country, skulked away like the snake he was. It unsettled her no little to find he was still there. She managed a tight smile of greeting in spite of her climbing alarm.

He tipped his hat. "Congratulations on your railroad, Mrs. Symington. My many doubts about your goals for this burg would seem unfounded as it turns out." His words were considerate enough but his eyes were flat, empty gold pools. His coolness was more frightening than outright anger.

She controlled a shiver and didn't answer. He went on with a tight-lipped mocking smile, "Since you seem to be such a believer in lost causes, maybe I can sell you some property in Flagg?"

Her voice when she found it came steady. "I think not. I

have all the property I need where I want it."

"Ah, yes, yes, indeed. Of course you know I was only joking, anyway. I've sold out, all that's going to sell. I'm heading further west, to Oregon, or California—possibly Idaho—to the best prospects I can find, anyhow. Maybe my future will be in timber, maybe in gold."

She had no idea why he was telling her this, although she was glad to hear that he was leaving, providing he spoke the truth. She could hardly keep from breaking into a happy smile. She gave a quiet nod. "Fine." She would be blessed if she would wish him well, though. Not after all the trouble he had given her.

"Western Kansas was never much of a proposition, anyway," he was saying.

"For some, perhaps not. For others, it is." She wished he would leave. His presence frightened her deeply. She wanted to find Owen, suggest that they take the train to Larned when it made the run back there, and then take the one after that home again. Maybe Meg and Hamilton would like to go, too, and Lucy Ann and Admire. Lad and Selinda. As many as could get on the train . . .

He tipped his hat a final time. "It was nice knowing you, Mrs. Symington. Congratulations again on completion of your railroad."

She nodded and chewed her lip as she watched him climb into his buggy. Something was very wrong but she couldn't figure out what it was. With difficulty, she turned her attention back to the train.

Acquiring the train was a completion, an enormous success, but it was also a beginning. Advantages of having the railroad were many, but as with everything new and different, there normally came a variety of new troubles. And in her experience she had found there was little use to hope they would be small ones.

She turned to look again in the direction Harris had taken. His buggy was disappearing down the street in a rise of dust, headed west. She heaved a deep, satisfied sigh. He seemed to be gone, really gone. *Now to find Owen.* As she worked her way through the crowd, she stopped every few minutes to visit with someone and joyfully discuss the new train.

The sudden explosion hurt her ears, shook the earth under her feet. Aurelia was too stunned to move; she wondered at the sound, like a cannon at time of war in Kentucky. People began to scream and shout. "It's the courthouse!" a male voice yelled. Another voice shrieked, "No, it's the school."

Horror washed through Aurelia when she saw the huge cloud of dust climbing into the sky above where the schoolhouse stood. She fell in with others racing across town in that direction. *Dear God, their school!* It was closed, but children often played tag in the schoolyard, or played on the swings. Where was Owen, where was her family?

The entire front of the school was blown away, exposing the interior rooms, leaving stone rubble, shredded books and papers, and flying dust everywhere. She spotted Owen and Will talking and gesturing, Zibby and Rachel were there, clinging to each other. Joshua, his arm in a sling, and David John stood with a group of other young men staring at the disaster. Near what used to be the southwest corner of the schoolhouse, now a gigantic chaos of broken stone, Doc Rod, in his shirt-sleeves and hands moving rapidly, bent over a figure on the ground. Aurelia ran, and with a frantic heart knelt beside the doctor. "Who is it?" she panted.

He groaned, or perhaps the terrible sound came from the person he dealt with, Aurelia wasn't sure.

Doc Rod, his face grave, answered, "Harris." Aurelia

gasped as he lifted the blood-soaked scarf he'd been using to stem the flow of blood from numerous gashes about Boot Harris' face and head. Doc's coat covered Harris' chest and blood was seeping through, a crimson flood. A large blood-stained stone that had smashed into Harris' chest and Doc Rod had removed, lay off to the side.

"Dear God!" she exclaimed, realizing Harris was behind the explosion, that it was his buggy she'd spotted barely visible behind the twin outhouses.

Harris' glazed eyes found Aurelia and turned as mean as a badger's.

She recoiled for an instant, then leaned forward, "I thought you'd gone," she whispered, "why didn't you just leave?"

He shuddered as though from freezing cold. "Meant—to be gone," his mouth hung open, he breathed in short bursts, "One last—*payback*. Do it myself. Not enough fuse—didn't —move fast enough . . ." He cursed, a faint sound.

*Sorry your bad feet let you down, Mr. Harris, but this didn't have to happen.* "Surely you knew that destroying the school to satisfy your ego for revenge—whatever your reason, wouldn't stop Paragon Springs? You should have just left!"

She addressed Doc Rod, "Is there something I can do?"

He replied indirectly, "We'll do all we can." His face showed frustrated defeat and anger. "Over here!" he shouted, looking past her shoulder.

With her hand at her breast, Aurelia stood aside as Owen, Will, Lad, and Hamilton brought a blanket to use as a hammock for moving Harris to the infirmary. With care, they lifted his bloody body onto the blanket. He cried out, and then slipped into unconsciousness. They took up the four corners and set off to follow Doc Rod.

"Harris appears to be the only casualty," Owen told

Aurelia. "We're fortunate the children and everybody else was more interested in the train."

Boot Harris took his last breath as the group crossed the empty lot where the Yellow Rose once stood. Aurelia, following, heard the jangle of saloon music in her mind; she shook her head and it was gone.

# Chapter Nineteen

The coming of the railroad brought Paragon Springs several years of reasonable prosperity. Now, those brief sweet years were being destroyed by months of a severe drought and accompanying depression.

Sweltering heat had enveloped the country for months on end and in the August twilight of 1893, it still lay like a hot shroud over the town. The only sound was the dizzying chirrup of locusts.

Musing, Aurelia slowly rocked on her vine-wrapped porch on Spencer Street. The movement stirred the air, bringing slight relief from the heat. Her hair, her dress, were wringing wet with perspiration. Weary and heart-sore from her reading, she let her newspaper slide to the floor.

News of the run for free lands in the Cherokee Strip, *the last free lands,* they were called, had spread through the country like a rampant, however happy, disease. More Paragon Springs folks than she wanted to think about had caught the contagion, the fever for The Run, Admire Walsh main among them.

According to her paper the Cherokee Outlet was a band of Indian land two-and-a-half miles wide that extended 276 miles along Kansas's southern border. After cattlemen began cutting through and using what was meant early on to be the Cherokee's outlet to hunting in the west, it was simply called the Strip.

Long before that in 1817, the Cherokees were persuaded by the white government to trade their very desirable eastern lands in North Carolina, Georgia, and Tennessee for equal acreage in Arkansas. Yet another move west into the new "Indian Territory" followed in a short time. To placate the Cherokee in 1828, the government by treaty granted them a perpetual hunting *outlet* to the West from their assigned lands. They could not live in the outlet but could use it as a route to western hunting grounds.

The vast area consisted of more than six million acres. Drovers, pushing their herds through the Territory and through the Outlet into Kansas talked greatly of the beauty of that land they passed through. They described crystal streams running through luxuriant grasslands. Wooded areas along the streams boasted willow, cottonwood, and elm trees. There were hackberry, mulberry, walnut, pecan, and oak trees in the lower areas. Game was plentiful it was claimed—deer, antelope, quail, wild turkeys, and prairie chickens, not to mention that the streams were full of fish.

When farmers began to fence the plains in the late 1870's and 1880's, Kansas cattlemen pushed their herds onto the Outlet's lush pastures to graze. According to "cow custom" the Outlet was one more area of open range, free for the grazing of cattle.

The Cherokee people, deciding this exploitive use of their Outlet was unfair, began to charge the ranchers for grazing their cattle. One dollar per head at first and finally regulated at forty cents. Many cattlemen, drifting their cattle, managed to pay nothing. At the same time, disagreement over fences put up by some of the cattlemen heightened tensions between whites and the Cherokee.

As a partial answer, a cattlemen's group, The Cherokee Strip Live Stock Association, was formally organized in Caldwell, Kansas in 1883. The Association managed, as a group and through Dennis Bushyhead, principal Chief of the Cherokee, to lease the entire outlet for a five-year period for

$100,000 per year, payable annually. Organization gave the cattlemen better means to protect their cattle, improve breeds, record marks and brands of animals owned by members.

Settlers, seeking to homestead and failing in other locations, had agitated the government for years to open the Outlet to settlement. The rush to Oklahoma Territory in 1889 stirred even greater interest in the Strip, and the cry from railroads, farmers, border towns, and newspapers became "On to the Cherokee Strip!"

The Live Stock Association's lease on the Strip had expired in 1888. The Cherokees approved a new five-year lease with the association for $200,000, but to no avail. The government had decided to yield to pressure. The government would purchase the Outlet and open it for settlement.

An offer was made to the Cherokee by government commission. Cattlemen were ordered to remove all cattle from the Outlet by October 1, 1890. In 1891, congress passed a bill to pay the tribe $1.25 per acre for Outlet lands—with no further negotiation. The Cherokee, believing the Outlet might be taken from them anyway, in late 1891 ceded the Outlet, or Strip, to the government for $8,595,750.

On August 19, President Cleveland issued a proclamation: The Outlet would be opened for settlement at noon on September 16, 1893.

Aurelia lifted her apron to dry the perspiration from her face. She had tried, tried so hard to convince folks to stay here. Might as well whistle in the wind. Within days, Ad and Lucy Ann would be leaving Paragon Springs forever. With other good friends of long years standing, they would head to Kansas' southern border to wait until September sixteenth and the Strip Run. All the talk was about the rich grazing lands there and of the lively new young towns—Alva, Enid, Perry, Woodward, Guthrie—towns born in the earlier land rush to Oklahoma Territory back in April of 'eighty-nine. Places that were very like Paragon Springs in the beginning.

Although she wanted to, it was hard to blame a soul for wanting to go. Hard times had hit the entire country, maybe western Kansas more than anywhere else.

She leaned forward in the chair, thinking she had heard something from near the lilac bush. Owen had given her the lilac for their anniversary, shortly after they moved into the house in town three years ago. She doubted the lilac would survive this latest drought although she watered it faithfully with dishwater each time she finished in the kitchen. She listened, sitting quietly, but heard nothing more. Maybe a poor sun-scorched prairie rodent was seeking shade under the bush.

The drought had hurt everyone, hurt them severely. Without ample rainfall a farmer or rancher could not raise a crop. With no money coming in for what he tried to grow, his mortgage went unpaid. His wife couldn't purchase food, clothing, medicines—whatever family needs the town stores could provide for a price.

Population in most western Kansas counties had dropped dramatically in the recent past. Contracts of all sorts were left unpaid as the creditors left the country to try anew elsewhere.

Without customers to buy the goods he stocked, the town businessman had no way to continue. More railroads than necessary had boomed into Kansas in the 1880's. When, due to the drought, the anticipated bumper crops and new industries didn't materialize, the railroads were left in poor financial condition. Many, still on paper, would now never be built.

The land-office business shriveled as stories of western

Kansas' hot winds, raging blizzards, and violent county-seat wars, filled eastern newspapers. Civilization? It hardly seemed so to those reading the wild stories and they chose not to migrate there.

The vicious circle continued without end. Western Kansas folks who had settled there years before, expecting every dream to materialize, lost confidence. And lack of confidence more than anything else contributed to the depression.

Aurelia could hardly blame the others for what they were about to do. As it was, she and Owen just scraped by. He had had to sell off most of their cattle. Her restaurant was open only four days a week, offering a lot of cheap bean and potato dishes. She mended and patched. The whole family conserved or went without.

Luckily, they hadn't mortgaged as heavily as some, but instead paid as they went. They had a small savings they refused to touch.

Owen had asked if Aurelia would like to move, too—join the rush to Oklahoma and make a new start. She had been shocked, and hurt, that he would even ask. Her answer was sharp, "Of course not. I'd no more leave this town than I would leave our marriage. My faith is in this place, right here from start to finish—whatever happens." *Up down boom or bust.*

Snapping at him wasn't kind or fair. Owen was the love of her life and he'd only been thinking of her. Likely any reasonable person would be pulling up stakes for what did seem to be a grand opportunity. Nail the shutters, lock the doors, and leave; nosirree, that was not for her. It just wasn't in her to start all over again. No, she would stay and work, and wait for the good times to return.

Ad had sold the last chunk of his place a week or so ago to a man from Dodge City, one of the few men in the country with cash to spare. Their other property, the rest of the homestead Lucy Ann and Lad inherited from their Uncle Ross that wasn't part of the town, had been lost to the bank some years ago. The same was about to happen with Ad's homestead, before he sold. In past years he had borrowed heavily to buy new machinery, then was unable to repay the loans. He had had to sell out before he lost it all.

In a couple of days there would be an auction at the Walshes to sell their stock, machinery, and most of their furniture. The money would finance starting over in the Strip.

She hoped they would succeed in Oklahoma. To Ad it was a last chance. He was convinced he would finally have the ranch he had always wanted and a lot better than his farm southwest of town. His scheme sounded good: he and fifteen or twenty of his aged, out-of-work cowboy friends would make the run and take every claim in a valley thirty miles or so into the Strip and north of a bend in the Cimmaron River.

Together they would have an empire. They even joked about naming their ranch and a town *Empire*. His friends knew the area well from running cattle there in the days before the government ordered them out. Best of all, he felt, he would be working with cattle and horses again, not struggling to make a living behind a plow or cutting stone.

Even as she wished them well, she was dying inside to think of them leaving, being gone. How could anything be worse than never seeing Lucy Ann, Rachel, and Ad again? She had known them for twenty years, since she was a young woman and Lucy Ann was a girl of fourteen bearing her baby girl, Rachel. Ad was a dark-haired cowboy, then, who married Lucy Ann soon after her part-Indian baby's birth, making them, with Lucy Ann's brother, Lad, his family.

Lad and Selinda, she thought, might stay. Her mother was

here and wouldn't be going. Selinda had exchanged her youthful dreams of a journalist in a large city to apply herself with Emmaline in building the circulation of the *Echo*, and improving the focus. Lad worked with Hamilton in his law office, but how long would that last with folks hard put to pay them? Some folks she knew had already departed, were on their way to camp in one of the border towns. They wanted to be first in line to register, be ready when the starting gun set them on the Run.

Missing these folks who had become so dear to her heart wasn't all; the Run could be the final ruin of Paragon Springs although she refused to accept that. Two-thirds of the population planned to go, mostly poorer folks but some business folk, too, like Ben Reid, Elliot Charbonneau, and others. A kernel of a town would be all that was left. And there was nothing she could do about it. The losses of the recent past in western Kansas, the forces from outside for new opportunity were just too great.

She was sleepy, ought to go in to bed, but it was so blessedly hot. She closed her eyes and thought about her family, as she always did at bedtime.

Owen and David John would already have turned in out at the ranch. Normally they came home to town at night, but sometimes, when there was a particular job they wanted to see to, they stayed over at the ranch. Joshua would have returned home to his wife, Anna, on their small farm, after a hard depressing day trying to harvest the shriveled grain from the fields.

Joshua had met Anna on a trip to Topeka four years ago, when he was twenty-three. They had married soon after meeting. Anna was a city girl, but they were deeply in love and she was adapting well to farm-life, hard as it was.

So far, David John lived at home, a young bachelor, although she was convinced he had been in love with Rachel for years. She thought Rachel might return the feeling. And why not? David John was an honest, dependable, hardworking man. His only fault, if it was one, was that he was tongue-tied shy. She prayed that one of these days he would speak his heart to Rachel, before too late, before she moved to the Strip with her folks.

Zibby was spending these last precious days with Rachel at the Walshes. The young women would be helping Lucy Ann prepare for the auction lunch.

Suddenly, a sound out in the darkened yard brought her fully awake. After a second's fright, she ordered, "Show yourself! I know someone is out there." She leaned forward in her chair, struck a match, and quickly lit the porch lamp on the table beside her. She had blown out the lamp earlier because she had wanted to keep insects away and conserve coal oil.

A man walked out of the shadows and up the front walk toward her. His silhouette, his height, the way he moved was far-back-in-the-mind familiar. *John?* John Thorne, her first husband? But of course it couldn't be. John was dead. Another, smaller shadow followed the first man.

"Who are you?" As he stepped into the light from her porch lamp, she gasped, threw her head back for a better look at him. "Harlan? Dear heaven, is that you, Harlan Thorne?" She stood up, stunned.

"It's me, Aurelia."

*Where have you been, you rascal cowboy? Why didn't you come back for us?* A storm of recrimination exploded in her mind against her drifter brother-in-law, angry words that got so tangled in her head she couldn't speak. Then, as abruptly, she calmed. It was long ago he had fled and left her stranded. And as it turned out, leaving her there in that lonely dugout on the plains was, in many ways, one of the best things that had ever happened to her.

"What are you doing here?" She faced him stiffly. The hot night wind felt suffocating.

"Passin' through. Thought I'd stop and see how you're doin', sister-in-law, if you was still here. Went first to the old dugout. Lord, everything's changed! A man on Main Street told me the only lady named Aurelia lived here on Spencer Street. Wasn't easy to find your house in the dark, but he give good directions. I'm surprised you stayed . . ."

*I didn't have much choice!*

"Things ain't been so good out on the ranges and on the road for me and my partner, here." He motioned a crone of a little cowpuncher out into the light. "This here is Knob. That's the only name he goes by. We've been partners for quite a spell."

At least he was faithful to somebody. Her eyes traveled over the small, mustachioed man he called Knob and decided he was harmless. She turned back to Harlan. "I suppose you're hungry?" she said. Coals of anger flared again giving an edge to her voice. Who did he think he was to waltz back, after twenty years, like nothing ever happened?

"Thanks, Aurelia." He sounded greatly relieved. "We haven't et an honest-to-goodness meal in—what—three days, now, Knob? Sure was surprised to see me and Ross Mc-Coy's old place had growed up into a town. Nice for you, Aurelia, that that happened. We saw a restaurant downtown, closed up, called Aurelia's Place. That yours?"

"It is."

"This house, too! Very fine." Harlan shuffled up the steps, hesitated to remove his hat. "It's hot as a scorched boot," he commented, running his arm across his face. He motioned his friend, Knob, to come along. "You've done pretty good for yourself, Aurelia."

She didn't answer that she could lose every bit of it in two shakes flat, was hanging on to what they had by a thread. She held open the screen door.

"Married a man could provide well for you, looks like."

That stopped her short and her mind raced. *I married a fine man, thank you, but he did not do all this for me the way you think.* She and Owen were a team, had carved a good life together. They would hang onto it together. Hers was no small part in what they'd accomplished and Owen would be the first to tell this no-good drifter that very fact.

She reprimanded herself for being touchy. "Come on in. I'll show you where to wash up while I fix you something to eat." Both men were covered with road grime and smelled of sweat, horses, and God knew what else. She led the way to the sun porch at the back of the house, pointed to the wash bench where she kept a blue granite wash basin, pitcher of water, and soap in its dish. A clean towel hung neatly from its bar above the bench.

"Thank you, Missus," Knob said politely as he hobbled past her. He looked weary enough to drop and she couldn't help feeling sorry for him. When he came back into the kitchen from the sun porch he looked somewhat revived. His wiry gray hair and moustache were slicked and wet. His collar-less shirt, buttoned up tight around his scrawny, rooster-like neck was damp-dark from the wash-up. She motioned for him to take a chair. Harlan, slicked and water-groomed, ambled into the kitchen a moment later and took the second place at the table.

She set out cold buttermilk, cornbread, and sliced roast pork. While they ate, she told Harlan about Owen. He seemed happy she had married again, after loss of his brother John, but he found it hard to believe her children were grown up men and a young lady. "Zibby teaches school," she told him. When he looked blank, she reminded him that Zibby was the baby in her arms when she and the children came to Kansas from Kentucky.

He barely remembered her dear friend, Meg, although he had traded his ranch to her. Only with reminders did he recall Lucy Ann, and Grandma Spicy, the dear little old woman who had traveled west with Lucy Ann and Lad.

Well, Aurelia thought, he hadn't been around them long. As they talked, she studied him in the light from her lamp. He looked a lot older, and worn down. Still lanky and lean, though. She supposed she could forgive him although she might give him a piece of her mind yet, to set him straight.

She felt his eyes studying her for several minutes after she stopped talking. Finally, he said, as though it had to be some kind of joke, "Down at the livery they said you are Mayor of this place." He looked embarrassed at what he guessed was a fabrication.

She hid a smile, thinking that maybe, after all, what she had accomplished over the years was revenge enough for what he had done to her. "Yes. I am Mayor of Paragon Springs. Owen was our first mayor—served several terms, then I took office after Kansas women were given the vote in municipal affairs in 1887. There are three women on my council now," she told him proudly.

Not that her role was that different from what it had ever been from the day the town was laid out. Present difficulties aside, she was proud, as Mayor, to have brought several town improvements to pass: a well-equipped fire department, a sorghum mill, a theater where both local and out-of-town performers could present entertainments.

She asked him, doing her best to be friendly to her first husband's brother, "And yourself, Harlan, how have you been? I suppose you've seen a lot of interesting country, had adventures?"

"Sure enough saw some country. Climbed Pike's Peak! Lord, Aurelia, if you think Kansas is hilly, you ought to see the Rockies!" He was silent for a moment. "For a while me and Knob traveled with a Wild West Show, ridin', ropin', showin' what real cowboyin' is like." He lost his boastful air, suddenly, like a balloon losing air. He finished soberly, "Whole country is hard hit by bad times now, though. Cattle raising business won't never again be the way it was. If I can get myself another piece of land, I'll hang onto it this time. Be a farmer, raise corn and chickens, or maybe set me up a little store. Made up my mind to make the Run for the Strip."

Of course that would be his reason for passing through, he and nearly everyone else, all determined to make "the Run for the Strip." She swallowed a bad taste in her mouth, took a sip of cold buttermilk.

She offered them beds for the night but Harlan said they had already made arrangements to sleep at the livery. He had a fast horse stabled there. He wanted to stay close to the animal and look after it himself, make sure it was in prime shape for The Run. "Besides, we're not used to the comforts of a real house," he said, sitting back and wiping a foamy line of buttermilk off his mouth. "No use to change now."

"No," she muttered under her breath, "I suppose not."

# Chapter Twenty

"Great day in the morning, Lucy Ann! Have you cooked up every last bit from your larder?" Aurelia couldn't refrain from remarking as she stepped into Lucy Ann's kitchen the day of the auction and saw the loaded tables. The small room was as hot as a furnace but smelled heavenly. Outside it was barely light. Lucy had to have worked for days, plus all night last night.

Lucy Ann, busy at the dry-sink working buttermilk from a fresh-churned bowl of sweet butter, smiled and shrugged by way of answer.

Aurelia felt a touch of guilt; she ought've held her tongue. Lucy Ann and Admire had to be feeling a deal of sorrow today, selling out to leave.

Every available space in the kitchen was covered with either pans of baked hams, or golden brown loaves of bread set out on dishtowels. Aurelia motioned Owen into the steamy crowded kitchen with the peck basket he carried. She had lined the basket with a small tablecloth and loaded it with sugar cookies she had baked for the lunch today.

Owen nodded a cheerful greeting to Lucy Ann, now working the butter with a wooden paddle. "I'll join the men," he said, heading for the door, where, outside, Admire's other friends were bringing tools and machinery from the barn to display in the yard.

"Rachel and Zibby helped a lot," Lucy Ann nodded at the food. She took a moment to lean back against the cupboard. She wiped her hands on her apron, swiped tendrils of damp blond hair away from her glowing pink cheeks. There was exhaustion in her pale blue eyes, but she still looked younger than her actual years.

She added, "We didn't do the cooking by ourselves, however. Look at all the cookies you've baked, and in this summer heat! Bless you, Aurelia. Bethany Hessler baked some of the bread for me, too, brought it over last night." A bit of concern touched her eyes, then she rushed on, "Ad said we might as well use up our hams. Mr. Eastman, the auctioneer, said if we put in our auction notices that there would be a free lunch, a bigger crowd would come to the sale. And the more bidders, the more money. He said we might see a hundred people here today or more."

Aurelia nodded and smiled. She withheld her opinion that quite a few people from around the county would be there for the free lunch and a chance to visit, not to buy. Lucy Ann would know that, anyway. Few folks had money to spend. Many had already had their own sales and would be leaving soon for the Run with the barest possible goods to get by on. For Lucy Ann and Admire's sake, she hoped they would have a good sale.

Rachel and Zibby came from Rachel's room, dressed up for the occasion. Aurelia was glad to see them smiling, chatting, although she knew how difficult the coming separation would be for them. She was sure they were hiding inside how they really felt. They'd been as close as sisters since they were babies.

They were both pretty. At twenty and twenty-one they were unmarried yet neither had a shortage of beaus and could marry tomorrow if they so chose.

Today Rachel wore dark blue gingham, her raven hair was tied up in a ribbon. She had a slim regal build, compared to Lucy's shorter comeliness, and she had a warm, giving personality like Lucy Ann's. She was a teacher in the Paragon

Springs district. She taught the youngest children.

It plagued Aurelia that her David John could be so much in love with Rachel, and yet not tell her so. He had known Rachel from the day she was born. He had played with her when she was a baby, kept an attentive and fond eye on her when she was a girl growing up. Maybe it was her beauty, now that she was a woman, that struck him dumb with shyness. Or maybe he worried—because he had no farm of his own yet—that he had too little to offer such a nice girl.

Zibby was a picture of Aurelia's younger self: the same honey-colored hair, large green eyes and slender figure. She had helped Aurelia in the restaurant until the time came one person could manage the scarce business alone. She worked in the bank, then, until it closed. This last year, Rachel had convinced Zibby to take a teaching job.

"Want us to form a work-line, Mama?" Rachel asked Lucy Ann and she nodded.

The women quickly fell to, with Lucy Ann slicing ham, and Aurelia slicing bread. Rachel and Zibby buttered the bread and put together the ham sandwiches, stacking them in a clean washtub.

Joshua and David John were among the men carrying furniture from the bedrooms and the parlor, out into the yard. Each time they passed through the kitchen, David John's panicked glance found Rachel, then quickly slid away. Aurelia wished he would speak his piece, before it was too late, before Rachel left the country. But one thing a mother couldn't do was meddle in the romantic affairs of her son's heart. Hadn't she tried for years? It was up to David John now.

The women were finishing, cleaning up the crumbs, when Meg and Hamilton and their youngsters, Vesta and Pauly, arrived. "You won't believe it," Meg said, "but we've brought ice for the lemonade. *Ice.* Had to order it brought in on the train, but won't it be nice to have?"

Lucy Ann gave Meg a squeeze. "Thanks, Meg, dear. Have Hamilton bring the ice inside. I'll get Ad's hammer to break it up. I already have the first run of lemonade mixed in one of my water barrels."

"Can we make ice cream, too, Mama?" Vesta, Meg's thirteen-year-old asked, as she played with the big blue ribbon holding back her brown curls. "It'd be yummy and we have ice." The delicious frozen dessert was fairly new to Kansas, but was becoming a favorite.

"No, darlin'. Won't be enough ice for that. But ice-cold lemonade is going to taste good on this scorcher of a day. Can she have a sugar cookie, and one for Pauly?" she asked, and then gave each of them one without waiting for an answer.

For the next hour or so, buggies, spring wagons, and buckboards rattled in a line up the lane to the house. Some men, Harlan and Knob and Ad's cowboy friends among them, arrived on horseback. The yard began to fill with a crowd.

It was hot and dusty, and the hot air smelled of cows, pigs, and horse dung. Flies were everywhere. Lucy Ann's furniture, a quite nice pie safe Ad had made for her from packing crates and punched sheets of tin, her walnut quilt frame, tables, chairs, and a small, rosewood parlor organ, looked strange sitting out by the barn. Beyond the household goods were piles of tools, and an assortment of odds and ends including worn saddles, old wheels, a stone barrow, plus implements such as a hay rake, and a corn planter.

The stock they would sell was corralled, and waiting. Grazing in the side pasture were the horses they were keeping, the team Admire and Lucy would use to pull their wagon, and a new bronc he had invested in for the race.

Before long, most of the men were in the pasture with Ad, admiring his riding horse, an Indian paint that he claimed was as fast as it was pretty. The lot of Ad's friends had fast ponies if not much else, Aurelia was thinking. Maybe that's all they felt they needed to make a new life in Oklahoma.

She spotted Harlan and Knob among the group, talking, laughing, gesturing. Joshua and David John had been thrilled to see their Uncle Harlan. Owen had met him and didn't see much wrong with him, but that was Owen's way. She didn't see much good and maybe never would.

The auctioneer, Eastman, arrived. He walked around awhile, looking over the items for sale before walking to Lucy Ann's iron triangle hanging on the porch and began to strike it repeatedly with its wand, sending out a rich *twanging*. "Sale!" he bellowed, "sale's about to start. Come on up here in the yard, folks. Sale is a startin'!"

He began with the furniture. "Now here's a fine, fancy bench. Mrs. Walsh, will you tell us somethin' about it?"

"Well, it's a settee, my—" she seemed to choke a bit, "rosewood parlor settee." Aurelia knew that Ad and Lucy had bought the piece four years ago when times were best.

Eastman's chant rang out, "Who'll make a bid, make-a-bid, what-am-I-bid on this fine—settee?"

The rosewood settee finally sold for probably a quarter what Lucy Ann and Ad had paid for it. The bidder was a lanky farmer from Ness City whose blond wife was a girl half his age.

Lucy Ann looked like she was choking on rocks to see her treasure sold. Her normally light blue eyes were dark with unshed tears. She managed a smile as Aurelia moved beside her, Meg on the other side. Piece by piece, they watched Lucy Ann's life being sold to the highest bidder, with few bids very high.

Although she couldn't afford it and really didn't need it, Aurelia bought Lucy Ann's mantel clock. Someday, when she could return it in a way that would spare Lucy Ann's pride, she would give it back. Meg bought her bedroom dresser and Aurelia would have wagered that she had the same thought in mind.

Sometime later, when the sale moved to the machinery, most of the women drifted back to the house. They made coffee for those who would want it rather than lemonade. They took tablecloths and covered the makeshift tables Ad and Owen had set up on sawhorses in the thin shade of the hackberry trees, then put rocks on the cloths to keep the ever-present wind from blowing them away. Selinda and Emmaline carried great stacks of tin plates, and some of white china, out from the house to the tables. Eating utensils were brought out. Lucy Ann had borrowed cups from almost everyone she knew and Rachel and Zibby arranged them on a separate table, next to the barrel of lemonade.

None of the women seemed to want to discuss what was happening. They spoke instead of how to best take geranium cuttings for their window-pots, and how to make banana ice cream, the new rage—providing you had banana extract, ice, and plenty of eggs and cream. Meg cautioned them not to let her Vesta hear them talk of ice cream. Since her first taste she could have eaten ice cream for breakfast, dinner, and supper.

Selinda, arranging the forks and knives, smiled, "Better not let Lad hear you either, he loves ice cream."

From out by the barn came the steady sing-song of the auctioneer, his chant punctuated now and then by a loud burst of male laughter at some joke he made. After an hour or so, Aurelia went once to see how the sale was progressing. Owen told her most everything was selling to the farmer from Ness City, and to a rancher from south of Dodge. Selling at a fraction of what the machinery and animals were worth.

"The money will add up, though," he told her, "be a big help to Admire and Lucy when they get to Oklahoma."

"I could wring Admire's neck," she muttered under her breath, "for taking Lucy away from us, away from here!" Her glance found Lad and Selinda, arms around one another's waists as she joined him to watch the sale. Lad would miss his sister, and Lucy Ann—who'd mothered Lad from the time she was a girl and they lost their parents—well, she didn't want to think about it.

"Now, Aurelia," Owen cautioned. He looked worried as his eyes scanned her warm face. "Maybe you better go back to the house with the women. Find some shade, sweetheart."

She took him at his word, afraid if she stayed where she was she would say or do something she would regret. And yet, when she reflected on the matter, she recalled that all day, whenever Lucy caught Admire's eye, she gave him a relaxed, genuine smile. He was happy to be leaving, and she liked making him happy.

After another two hours the sale was completed. Lucy Ann rang the triangle this time, to bring everyone to the tables of food. The men took their filled plates and drink and stood to eat, but the women took theirs and went to sit on chairs that had been sold, on cushions removed from buggies, or on blankets placed around on the ground, in shade where they could find it.

Soon after the meal, the rancher from south of Dodge and his hired man got on their horses to begin the long drive home of the stock they had bought. Some of Ad's neighbors helped the start of the drive.

The Ness City farmer left soon after, in much the same fashion. His young wife had already left with most of Lucy

Ann's furniture in her wagon.

Then one by one, other vehicles in a continuing cloud of dust filed down the lane toward the main road. Some of the rigs had an item or two from the sale roped in. At the end, Ad and Lucy Ann had given away pictures from their walls, feed bags, a sleigh with a broken runner, and other items that hadn't sold, that they couldn't take with them.

Their closest friends, Aurelia and Owen, Meg and Hamilton, Emmaline, and Selinda and Lad, stayed behind to help clean up the debris from lunch and the sale. They helped Ad load his wagon for tomorrow's pre-dawn departure for Kiowa where they would camp and wait for the Run.

At last, before any of them were really ready for it, the time arrived for goodbyes.

With teary eyes, Meg hugged Lucy Ann a long time before she finally gasped, "I have to go. Pauly ate too many sandwiches and he is throwing up all over the place." She hurtled away, nearly falling because of her bad hip.

Aurelia took her turn to tell Lucy Ann goodbye. As she held the small plump woman in her arms, she whispered, "God go with you, Lucy Ann, with you and your family. You've been the dearest friend a body could ask for, have meant so much to my life. Dear Lord, but I will miss you so . . ."

Both Rachel and Zibby were having trouble keeping back tears. Aurelia hugged Rachel, who she had hoped might soon become her daughter-in-law, and give her grandchildren. Now, it was hard to know what might happen. David John was standing like a statue with his brother and the other men. He stared at Rachel like a drowning man seeing his last chance for survival disappearing from shore, and still he didn't move.

Then his feet came unglued from his quagmire of shyness.

He went to Rachel, touched her arm, whispered something in her ear that brought a bright, relieved smile to her face.

It sounded as though he said, "Be seein' you. A ride to Oklahoma ain't so far."

It was a long way to go to propose! Aurelia thought.

Lucy Ann walked to the wagon with her, her arm around her waist.

"It's what Admire wants," she said for perhaps the thousandth time since the Run was announced. "You know I wouldn't go, Aurelia, if Admire didn't want this so much."

She turned and caught Lucy Ann's shoulders, and smiled. "Everything will be all right, Lucy Ann." She repeated David John, "Oklahoma isn't so far." *Maybe there would be a wedding soon, in one of their homes.* Her heart lifted at the thought.

Lucy Ann was looking past her in the direction of town, and for the first time her expression was raw, truly stricken. "I can't leave," she choked out, "unless I know that place over there will always be there, for me to come home to when I want to visit—" She stopped and swallowed. She had a haunted look as she returned her gaze to Aurelia's face. "We've gone through such hard times, such good times, all of us together. It's even harder to leave than I thought it would be. If the town was to just dwindle away in time and vanish, like so many others in this country . . ."

"That town will always be there!" Aurelia answered adamantly as she caught Lucy Ann by both arms and shook her a bit. "Paragon Springs will always be your home, as well as down there in Oklahoma. I promise you, Lucy Ann Walsh, Paragon Springs will stand until the end of time and me with it 'til my bones turn to dust."

Lucy nodded, her expression changed to a faint, weary smile.

Aurelia added, "You come back whenever you can, hear?

We'll all get together some Christmas. Or we'll get together to celebrate a Fourth of July and they will hear us carrying on in the next six states!" She heard the thin panic behind her own voice, realized she spoke harshly to buoy up herself as well as Lucy Ann.

The two younger women, Rachel and Zibby, had grown quieter as the afternoon wore on. They stood by the Symingtons' wagon, and then, as though they were still little girls, they removed their hair ribbons and exchanged them. Then each one reached out to wipe the other's tears away.

Aurelia felt sad for the younger women, for David John with his eyes full of love and dismay as he watched Rachel, it was hard to recognize, give abeyance, to her own pain. Then the whole world took on a blur as she climbed into the wagon with Owen and her grown children for the trip to town and home. When she looked back over her shoulder as they rolled away, Ad still bustled like a man much younger, intent on the work of leaving the country.

She couldn't tear her gaze from Lucy Ann and Rachel, two forlorn figures standing in the blowing wind, watching them drive away. When Zibby, then David John, their faces pinched with pain, turned to look back, too, Lucy Ann and Rachel both waved.

"This feels like a real goodbye but it isn't," Aurelia said staunchly to comfort her son and daughter. "We'll see them again. Lucy Ann, Admire, and Rachel are a strong part of Paragon Springs and they will always be a part, somehow, someway. This isn't over, I vow it isn't."

# Chapter Twenty-One

Only nine o'clock in the morning the first part of September and Paragon Springs sweltered under the sun. In spite of the business-folk who had ignored the Run and stayed, the town felt empty to Aurelia as she walked to the grocery store. It was quiet, as though the life of the town had been sucked away. A town's soul was its people, and many were gone.

The buildings were not old, as in most ghost towns; the paint on some was practically new. But many windows were boarded up, and sightless. Weeds, scorched brown by the sun, blew along the sidewalks, with no one to sweep them up.

All who were taking part in the Run had departed, creating days and days of flying dust on the road south from town. Elliot Charbonneau and Maud Mullendore who was now Mrs. Charbonneau, were some of the first to leave. Mathis and Hannah Tuttle had gone, Ad and Lucy Ann, of course, and so many others. It hurt to think about them.

Meg and Hamilton would stay on as long as possible, as would Lad and Selinda. Emmaline was still at their home place. The Jones brothers felt they weren't fitted for such as the Run and would stay. They believed as she and Oscar Wurst did, that they had worked too long and hard to build their businesses to simply walk away. But without enough customers, it was only a matter of time before they would have to close their doors.

Inside Wurst's grocery store minutes later, Aurelia noted that shelves stocked full in better times, now were skimpy of goods. She could guess at Mr. Wurst's reasoning: Why invest in a huge stock of goods that would only gather dust for lack of customers?

There was no sound in the store except for the rattle of Mr. Wurst's newspaper as he sat reading it in a chair behind the near-empty candy counter. She moved about quietly, selecting her groceries, mentally counting her change as she put items in her basket.

Yet she would buy what she could, whenever she could. They had to help one another stay in business until conditions improved somehow, and they would.

"How are you, Mr. Wurst?" she said, speaking to the back of the newspaper he was reading.

He jerked, put the paper down. "Beg pardon, Mrs. Symington. Sorry not to hear you come in." He got to his feet. His hair was darker at the temples from perspiration, his skin shiny and beaded. "Thought it might be another day with no customers. You finding what you need, *ya?*"

"Yes—well, I could use a bottle of lemon extract."

"Sorry, I let my supply run out. I will order it for you special."

"Thank you." She put her basket on the counter so he could total her purchases.

Although his mind seemed elsewhere, he jotted the figures, his pen scratching, then he gave her the cost. He motioned over his shoulder at the paper he had abandoned in his chair. "There won't be enough," he said.

"Beg pardon? *Enough?*"

"Enough free land for everybody who has gone down there to make the Run. Paper says thousands have come from all over. Ladies, farmers, tramps, doctors, gamblers—all waiting in the heat and dust in the border towns to register for the Run. Those towns are too small to accommodate thousands of folks. There's no place to sleep for most, except on the ground. Not enough water to drink. Not enough food. And in the end there won't be enough land to go around. Sooners are already there hiding in the ravines as I hear it told. They will take the most of it, they'll take the best claims. There won't be enough."

"Not to wish them ill, but maybe those waiting in line to register will get discouraged and not stay to make the Run. Or if they do make the Run but fail to secure a claim, they will come back." She couldn't help feeling a slight surge of hope as she pictured the many folks who had left Paragon Springs. To her thinking, they should never have gone away in the first place.

"More likely they will go someplace else. Folks seem to think the grass is always greener wherever they are not at. They chase the rainbow. Some find it, I suppose. Most don't. They ought to stay put. Build their rainbow where they are, one little piece at a time. But try to tell them that." He grabbed the hem of his apron and wiped the sweat from his ruddy face.

"I agree with you one hundred per cent about staying put." She rewarded him with a smile. "Folks can always survive by sharing, and helping one another! We're going to be proof of that, Mr. Wurst. You and me and the others in this town who stayed."

He nodded and returned her smile, but shook his head as his eyes scanned his near empty shelves, his store vacant except for her.

On the way home she saw catty-corner across the way—in the gloomy depths of the livery—a small familiar figure shoveling manure from a stall. She was sure it was Knob, and yet Harlan had left for the Run days ago. She crossed to the livery in swift strides. Grocery basket in one hand, she used the other to lift her hems from the filth on the floor and strode to where Knob shoveled.

"That scoundrel, Harlan! He went off and left you, didn't he?" She dropped her skirt to swat a fly from her face.

He whipped around, surprised, then tipped his hat. "Mrs. Symington, mornin'." His moustache twitched. He couldn't seem to meet her eyes. His embarrassed expression revealed that she was right. His friend had skipped out, intentionally leaving him. Still, he defended Harlan, "I would have been just extry baggage, mebbe slowed him down. Man has got to be fast in that race. When he gets that land he'll let me know to come."

She wanted to tell him not to count on any such thing, but she held her tongue. She relaxed a little and said on an encouraging note, "I see you've found work."

"An hour or two here at the livery once in a while. Keeps me in grub, a place to sleep 'til I hear from Harlan. You hear of any more jobs, though, I'd appreciate knowin' of 'em, Mrs. Symington. I'm handy and I ain't afraid to work."

Any kind of paying work for anybody was scarce as hen's teeth, but she told him, "I certainly will let you know if I hear of anything. It is possible my husband, Owen, could use you. I'll ask. But don't stand on ceremony, Knob, you come to dinner anytime. As my brother-in-law's friend, you are always welcome." It wasn't easy to speak favorably of Harlan to any degree. But Knob was a good soul, and she hated what Harlan had done to him.

She just wished Harlan would fool her this time, and would come back for Knob. Although—she hesitated as a new thought struck and a smile played on her lips—if he didn't, there would be one more citizen in the town, one little Knob of a soul to help Paragon Springs thrive.

Her confidence grew. She and Owen would always be there, their children, too, and the others who chose to stay, just as she had promised Lucy Ann. The town was still county seat, and they still had their railroad.

Anyone who thought this town was done for, was simply wrong!

"Knob," she said, "there will be plenty of work for you, now that I think about it. We're going to keep this town sharp as a penny. Nothing is going to be allowed to go to seed or to dust around here!"

His shaggy brows lifted in question.

She explained, "The way I hear it, there won't be enough free land to go around down there in that foolish Oklahoma scramble. Likely many folks who left here for the Run will be back. Maybe they'll bring other failed folks with them. Lots of folks. It could happen. I mean to see that Paragon Springs will be here, as always as fine a place as any on God's green earth, for anyone who wants to make this town their home."

He was grinning widely at her enthusiasm. "Yes, indeed, ma'am." He tipped his hat to her.

"Yes indeed, absolutely." She smiled, eyes shining, then she turned smartly and left the livery. There were things to be done. Ideas must be exchanged, plans made on how *not* to let this recent loss, severe though it was, permanently ruin the town. They would be like people rallying around the sick-bed of a friend to make the friend well again. But her town would recover and survive!

A fine way to set off a fresh start would be to have a celebration. She would make the cakes, it was the least she could do. When all was said and done, this town—this dusty, hard-to-live-in yet somehow *magical* place—held her heart; she owed it so much. Paragon Springs had given her a life, had brought her deep abiding love, and joy. Paragon Springs was home. She raised her glance at the sound of a wagon coming

313

up the street. Recognizing the familiar vehicle, she smiled and waved and Owen waved back. *Owen.* He could stay out at the ranch only so long before coming to town to see her. She could hardly wait to tell him her plans.

# Irene Bennett Brown

Irene Bennett Brown has known she wanted to write books since age thirteen when she read *Little Women* and other historical novels.

Although she has lived most of her life in Oregon, she enjoys using Kansas, where she was born, as the background for most of her books. This interest in her native state stems from listening to many true stories elder members of her family told about early times there.

The significant role women and children played in developing the West against incredible hardship has long been neglected. It is their story she particularly wants to tell. She has authored several award-winning young adult novels, including *Before the Lark*, which won the 1984 Western Writers of America Spur Award nomination for the Mark Twain Award. In 1988 she was recognized by the Oregon Library Association with the Evelyn Sibley Lampman Award for significant contribution to the field of literature.

She turned to adult historical fiction in 1994 with *The Plainswoman* which was a finalist for a Western Writers of America Spur award in 1995. She continues her love of the historical novel with her Kansas-based series, "The Women of Paragon Springs" for Five Star. *Long Road Turning*, the first in the series, was published in October, 2000. *Blue Horizons* in September, 2001. *No Other Place* will be followed by *Reap the South Wind* in March, 2003.

Brown lives in Oregon with her husband, Bob, a retired

research chemist. Her favorite leisure pursuits are reading and exploring historic places. She is a founding member of Women Writing the West.